TO SNAP A SILVER STEM

BY SARAH A. PARKER

The Moonfall Trilogy
When the Moon Hatched
The Ballad of Falling Dragons

Crystal Bloom Series
To Bleed a Crystal Bloom
To Snap a Silver Stem
To Flame a Wild Flower

Sarah A. Parker

To Snap a Silver Stem

A Crystal Bloom Novel

AVON

An Imprint of HarperCollinsPublishers

Without limiting the exclusive rights of any author, contributor, or the publisher of this publication, any unauthorized use of this publication to train generative artificial intelligence (AI) technologies is expressly prohibited. HarperCollins also exercise their rights under Article 4(3) of the Digital Single Market Directive 2019/790 and expressly reserve this publication from the text and data mining exception.

This is a work of fiction. Names, characters, places, and incidents are products of the author's imagination or are used fictitiously and are not to be construed as real. Any resemblance to actual events, locales, organizations, or persons, living or dead, is entirely coincidental.

TO SNAP A SILVER STEM. Copyright © 2022 by Tree Sap Books Pty Ltd. ACN. All rights reserved. No part of this book may be used or reproduced in any manner whatsoever without written permission except in the case of brief quotations embodied in critical articles and reviews. For information, address HarperCollins Publishers, 195 Broadway, New York, NY 10007. In Europe, HarperCollins Publishers, Macken House, 39/40 Mayor Street Upper, Dublin 1, D01 C9W8, Ireland.

HarperCollins books may be purchased for educational, business, or sales promotional use. For information, please email the Special Markets Department at SPsales@harpercollins.com.

Avon, Avon & logo, and Avon Books & logo are registered trademarks of HarperCollins Publishers in the United States of America and other countries.

hc.com

Originally published as *To Snap a Silver Stem* in the USA in 2022 by Sarah A. Parker.

FIRST AVON PAPERBACK PUBLISHED IN 2026.

Character illustrations by Dmonyart

Interior design by Aubrey Troutman

Library of Congress Cataloging-in-Publication Data has been applied for.

ISBN 978-0-06-347654-7

Printed in the United States of America.

25 26 27 28 29 LBC 5 4 3 2 1

For those who hide the broken bits

GLOSSARY

Stony Stem — Orlaith's tower.

Bitten Bay — The bay at the bottom of the cliff below Castle Noir.

Safety Line — The line Orlaith hasn't stepped over since she came to Castle Noir when she was a child. It surrounds the estate—running the forest boundary and cutting through the bay.

The Tangle — The unutilized labyrinth of corridors in the center of the castle that Orlaith uses to travel around in a more efficient manner. These corridors are typically without windows.

Sprouts — The greenhouse.

Dark zones — Places Orlaith has yet to explore.

The Keep — The big polished doors guarded by Jasken. One of Orlaith's dark zones.

The Plank — The tree that has fallen across the selkie pond and is often used for Orlaith's training.

Spines — The giant library.

The Safe — The small door where Orlaith places her offering every night.

Whispers — The dark, abandoned passageway Orlaith has turned into a mural.

The Grave — The storage room where Orlaith discovered Te Bruk o' Avalanste.

Puddles — The communal bathing chambers/thermal springs.

Hell Hole — The room where Baze often trains Orlaith.

Caspun — A rare bulb Orlaith relies on to calm her attacks brought on by her nightmares and sharp sounds.

Exothryl/exo — The contraband drug Orlaith takes in the morning to counteract the effects of overdosing on caspun every night to ensure a good sleep.

Conclave — A meeting that consists of all the Masters and Mistresses from across the continent.

Tribunal — The monthly gathering where citizens get to voice their woes with their High/Low Master.

Fryst — Northern Territory.

Rouste — Eastern Territory.

Bahari — Southern Territory.

Ocruth — Western Territory.

Arrin — Central Territory that was destroyed during The Great Purge.

Lychnis — The crystal island.

Mount Ether — Home to the Prophet Maars.

Reidlyn Alps — The mountains that block the border between Fryst, Ocruth, and Rouste.

The Stretch — The band of barren land at the base of Reidlyn Alps that is riddled with Vruk traps.

Parith — The capital of Bahari.

River Norse — The river that flows through the continent. The main trade route.

Quoth Point — The only area on the western shore that is not a cliff. Territory battles have been fought here in the past.

The Great Purge — The event that wiped out the Unseelie.

The Blight — The spreading sickness.

Candescence/candy — Ground Aeshlian thorns.

Whelve — The obsidian stone rings scattered across the continent that offer refuge from the Vruk.

Te Bruk o' Avalanste — The Book of Making.

Valish — The ancient language.

Shulák — Faith dedicated to the words the Prophet carves into the stones at Mount Ether.

Moal — People who work the Vruk traps on The Stretch.

Forgery — The place where cuplas are forged.

Mala — The afterlife.

TO SNAP A SILVER STEM

18 years ago

PROLOGUE
Rhordyn

Arms crossed, I regard the locked door opposite the entrance to the northern tower, its stone face illuminated by a shard of silver light pierced through a window—a gift from the bitten moon sitting low in the sky. My pocket is heavy, the wall brisk against my back as I listen to Mersi descend the tower's coiled stairwell.

Her steps are slow, my patience thin. I can smell the contents of the goblet she's carrying from here.

Closing my eyes, I release a heavy sigh, balling my hands into fists. I swallow, drop my head forward, and slam it back against the wall.

Hard.

The bludgeon of pain ricochets through my skull, rattling my brain, and for a moment, I'm anywhere but here.

For just *one fucking moment*.

I drop my head and whip it back, repeating the process. Again.

Again.

"High Master?"

I look to the right. See Mersi emerge from the tower's entrance, breath labored, the apron tied around her waist still blotched with a mosaic of food stains. She steps into the shaft of light, igniting her rosy hair, freckles stark against her pale skin.

Clearing her throat, she extends the crystal goblet. "I'm guessing you can take this off my hands?"

I glance at its blushed contents, wanting to snatch the thing and dash the liquid across the floor.

My gaze flicks up, catching the condescending glint in hers.

"Of course." I relieve her of it—the stem fragile in my grip. One squeeze and it would snap. "Thank you."

Two full words have never sounded so hollow.

Mersi gives me a curt nod.

I reach into my pocket and withdraw the necklace Aravyn gave me moments before I took her life, the crystal, once clear and scintillating, now *black*. So black, it has a cosmic pull; as though you could look into it and see your own horizonless oblivion.

I defiled Aravyn's gift to her daughter—a shame I'll always bear. Even so, I hold it out, chain bunched in my fist, the jewel swaying back and forth like a morbid pendulum.

Mersi's gaze darts to the gem with wary curiosity. "For *her?*"

I nod.

"What does it do?"

Too much.

Too little.

"She'll look ... different than she does now. Very different.

But she'll be safe to live a normal life. She must never take it off. Do you understand?"

Her eyes widen. "Never?"

"Correct."

I'm not just hiding her from others, but also from herself.

"Do you intend on telling her about the proph—"

"No," I snap. "There will be no speak of *Gods* under this roof. Or anything that might lead her toward the truth."

No child should be forced to bear that weight.

Mersi's jaw moves as she appears to chew on her response, staring at the necklace still dangling from my outstretched hand. "With all due respect," she finally says, "you need to give that to her yourself."

Blood crackling, I step toward her, jerking my hand forward. "Take the fucking necklace, Mersi. That's an order."

Lips clamped into a thin line, she meets my stern gaze, releasing a sharp exhale. "Pushy bastard," she mutters, snatching the pendant.

I'm swift to pocket my clenched fist while she studies the debased jewel. The chain. Her attention seems to narrow on the clasp—perhaps noticing the color tone is lighter than all the other metal links. "*Iron ...*"

I nod. "You can remove the anklet I gave you when she arrived. I assume she's been wearing it day and night?"

"Of course." Her snippy response is quickly followed by a grave sigh. "I mean yes, *High Master.*" She dips into a half-hearted curtsey.

"Thank you."

Spinning, I charge down the hall, barging through silver slants of moonlight.

"You save her, then insist on having nothing to do with her ..."

I halt at the bitter bite to Mersi's words but keep my stare on the faraway end of the gloomy hall. Keep my hand firmly clasped around the fragile stem of the crystal goblet.

"Eight months since you brought her to the castle, and you've not seen her *once*. You can't just throw a fractured child at me and wipe your hands of all future obligations."

Slowly, I turn to meet her wary gaze.

For the first time, I notice the dark smudges beneath her eyes, the disheveled mess of her hair, the lack of color in her cheeks.

"You look tired," I say, voice lowered to soften its edge. "If you'd like to resume your full-time position in the kitchen, I can find a replacement to step in and tend to the child's needs."

Fists swinging at her sides, she stalks forward. "I'm not tired of tending to the *child's* needs. I love Orlaith like one of my own. It's my *heart* that's tired," she chokes out, dashing away a tear.

I clear my throat. "I'll find someone trustworthy enough to help. But if you're asking me to be involved, I will not."

"Stubborn man. She needs more." Mersi shakes her head, stare beseeching. "There's death in her eyes that doesn't blink away. She's *broken*, Rhordyn."

A vicious spark flares in my gut.

I stride forward so fast liquid sloshes over my hand. "*You think I don't know that?*" She recoils as I arch over her like a rioting storm cloud heavy with a deluge of self-hatred.

"I am her roof—the shadow that dims her light and keeps the world from seeing that mark on her fucking shoulder. *Nothing* more."

Mersi drops her stare to the floor. "The nightmares are getting worse."

I open my mouth; close it ...

When she looks at me again, there's fire in her eyes. "Sometimes I wish her screams weren't silent, then maybe you'd notice."

I notice. Feel her fear in the pit of my soul like a torched tree. It makes me want to rip the fucking world to shreds.

Makes me want to *kill*.

"I've taken to sharing the bed with her so I can hold her through the tremors," Mersi continues, tone matter of fact.

Sighing, I look at the tower's door.

I hate that fucking tower. This goblet.

Myself.

"She's suffering, High Master. And you're the only one who understands what she went through. What she lost."

"I want nothing to do with the child." I spear my gaze at the woman. "Nothing."

"And when she grows old enough to ask questions?" She waves the necklace at me. "If she realizes you've been hiding her from herself? What then?"

I shrug. "She'll hate me, no doubt."

At least she'll have lived.

"And you're okay with that ..." She speaks slowly, as though choosing her words with care.

"Her hate is the only thing I'll accept. That, and *this*," I hiss, waving the goblet through the air.

Mersi's gaze drops to her feet, a tension-filled silence strung between us.

"I'll protect her. Give her the tools to protect herself. I'll be her fucking storm if I have to. She'll want for nothing—always. I can do all that without being involved."

Mersi looks me right in the eye, fierce and brazen. "Everything is nothing if you're in pieces, High Master. I think that's something even you can understand."

She spins on her heel before I have a chance to reply, black skirt swaying as she stalks toward the tower's entrance, pausing a few steps from the door. Glancing back, her voice is fractured as she says, "She hides beneath furniture. Veers from the sun. Thrashes and digs her nails into my arms when I try to coax her out for a play in the grass." Her face twists, words sharpen. "She won't draw or smile or dance like a normal child her age."

"Mersi—"

"Her tears no longer sparkle like they used to."

I suck a breath and blow it out, feeling the blood drain from my face.

"I'm no medis, but she seems determined to follow the rest of her family to an early grave."

The words are a sword through my sternum, and it's an effort not to fold forward and vomit.

"You don't wrap a wound without treating it first. It'll do nothing but *fester*." She shakes the necklace at me, pendant swinging. "You can't protect her from herself."

With that, she disappears up the tower's stairwell, the echo of her footsteps attacking me as I chew on her words.

Choke on them.

Mersi's right, of course. I can't protect her from herself. But I can try.

Chapter 1

Orlaith

A domed shell of lucent crystal shields us from the haunting eddy that keeps slashing.

Slashing.

The beasts kick up dirt and pulsing red embers every time their powerful paws assault the frosty soil—leverage for their frenzied attack on the dome. As much as it's protecting us, I feel it *taking* from me. Little sips that turn my blood thick and cold.

My brother shivers in my lap, burrowing deeper with every ear-blasting blow.

They can't have him.

I tighten my arms around him, bury my nose into his whitewash hair, and close my eyes, savoring the smells of paint and spice and a hint of toffee apples. Smells that stuff my chest with warm love and conjure up visions of chiming giggles and half-moon smiles. Of familiar rooms decorated with a patchwork of vibrant pictures stuck to stone.

Home.

I want to stay with the image and never leave ...

A dense thud. A hiss of breath.

I open my eyes to see a fat, stubby nose slick with moisture pressed against the crystal, fogging it with a violent chuff.

Slowly, I reach out my trembling hand, brush the dome's smooth interior, and gasp at the sudden, gulping tug that comes from deep inside my chest. I flatten my palm, splay my fingers, and peer at the beast through the gullies between them.

You. Can't. Have. Him.

Its upper lip peels away from its teeth, and a violent roar blasts free of its boastful chest while the others alternate between slashing at the dome and trying to bore beneath it.

"W-what do they want?"

My brother's small, fractured voice has me snatching my hand back, gasping as I battle the shadowed haze threatening to overtake my vision. He's watching through wide eyes, his jagged limbs flinching at every blow—each quivered recoil an axe to my heart.

I cup the side of his face to shield him from that blood-lusting stare.

But I hold it. Threaten it.

What do they want?

Me.

You.

"Everything," I whisper, bringing my gaze back to his. "But they can't have you."

Because in this nightmare, I'm bigger. Stronger.

I'm going to be *his* hero this time—not the other way around.

He blinks at me with big eyes that lack their usual luster. "They already got me, Ser ..."

The words lock my spine.

"No. *I've* got you." Teeth chattering, I tighten my grip. "You're here with me. S-safe. *Forever.*" A snarled challenge to the circling beasts.

Another onslaught strikes the dome—the strident sound cutting through me like a blade. He doesn't flinch. Not even when a splintering crack attacks us from all angles.

A warm dampness blooms against my palm, and I look down, pulling my hand from his back. I blink away the frosty haze, trying to focus on the smear of wetness there. Like I've been finger painting with liquid starlight blushed with a kaleidoscope of muted colors.

It's ... it's *him*.

My heart splits like a seam, inch by painful inch, and I try to breathe past the pit in my throat as I bury my face in his hair.

Chase his fading scent.

I close my eyes but can no longer see the patchwork paintings. The colors. The half-moon smiles.

All I see is black.

My face crumbles, and I squeeze him tight while thorns attack the backs of my eyes. While the monsters continue to slash. Hack.

Roar.

"*Stop!*" I scream, voice cracking, heart shredding.

Please don't take him again.

Another screech splits the air.

I look up to see a fracture scribbling across the crystal like forked lightning, and I stamp my hand against it, letting it gulp.

My body grows colder. Slower.

Another savage swipe rattles my bones, and the cracks spread like a mosaic plague.

"We don't end here." My belted words somehow rival the clamorous wrath attacking us from every angle. "We've barely started."

My brother doesn't respond. Doesn't move. Doesn't flinch when another blow shrieks across the crystal dome.

I squeeze my eyes shut, warmth dashing down my cheeks, leaked from the part of me that's painfully aware.

He's gone.

"Don't leave m-me ..."

I wish he could hear. That I wasn't so alone. That I was bleeding out in his arms, and not the other way around.

"Don't leave me," I repeat—louder this time. A curse to myself because they took him. Not me.

They always do.

An unfurling knot of black, sizzling hurt stirs beneath my ribs, striking its own malicious heartbeat. Gnarled vines slither up the walls of that chasm inside my chest, feasting on my pain. Growing bigger.

Stronger.

"Don't leave me."

I didn't get to say goodbye.

Those vines writhe, whip, stab at the underside of my skin, digging for release.

They want freedom.

Revenge.

I just want my brother back.

Another jagged rupture rips across the surface. Rather than patch it up, I tear my hand away, sever myself from those greedy draws, and watch the entire thing bloom with a field of fissures. There's a keen popping sound, and shards of light splinter my skin. Slice it up.

Bleed me.

I bow forward and shield the limp body in my lap from the shattered assault, pulling him so close I can feel the lack of a beat in his chest. Everything stings, but it's nothing compared to the grief gnawing on my heart.

The terrible commotion stills.

Silence.

Something wet lands on me, and I dare a shielded glance at the thick rope of drool hanging off my arm. I tip my face to the sky, look into big, inky eyes that reflect my dazzling stare ...

The Vruk's ears are pinned back, his mammoth form eclipsing the stars. There's deadly intention in his narrowed eyes, thick on his fervid breath hitting me with every vile exhale.

I can't tell who's the bigger monster.

Him. Or me.

His barbed snarl digs beneath my skin, and that vicious jaw cranks wide, revealing a tomb of dripping ivory sabers.

I hold his savage stare and let him take his fill—let him see how unsatisfying his impending kill is going to be ... because I'm empty.

Bled dry.

I'm already dead.

The wind snatches my short-lived scream, the crunching, sloshy sounds of my own masticated flesh and bones haunting me to wakefulness.

I jerk upright, gulping briny air.

A nightmare.
Not real.

I become aware of the creak of swaying ropes, my world tipping back and forth in a deep, monotonous sway beneath a litter of midnight stars.

Clutching my swirling belly with one trembling hand, the other fists the jewel hanging around my neck, as if my subconscious was tempted to snap the chain and rip it free.

I release it, draw a deep breath, and *hold* until my lungs are about to burst, pulling my focus from that echo of raw hurt, from the feel of my brother's motionless body lumped in my lap. Swallowing hard, I knead my throbbing temples with a near-deadly force.

They already got me, Ser ...

I drop my hands, slam my spine against the thick, wooden mast at my back, and stretch my legs—bare feet pushing through the gaps between the wooden spindles and poking over the edge as I rub the sleep from my eyes. Lazy wind plays across my sweat-slicked skin, ruffling my loose hair and delivering gruff voices to my sensitive ears ...

"Does she always scream in her sleep?"

"Hard to tell when the wind's up, but she usually wakes in a fit like that." Vanth's apathetic voice is as hollow as this void in my chest.

"It's chilling. Makes me regret stepping in for Roal in exchange for his serve of salted pork. Why's she even up there? It's a lookout, not a loft."

"Who fucking knows."

"Cap's not pleased about it. Did you hear Brock's been ordered to lock her out of the nest if the wind passes eighteen knots? He's afraid to nap and risk a lashing."

I doubt my guard and the barrelman occupying the central mast a stone's throw away know I can hear them over the slapping of the sails, billowing and slack ... but I can.

"She still hasn't changed out of her black garb?"

"Not hard to guess where her loyalties lie," Vanth snipes.

He's taken a nightly shift on the central mast on the pretense that he's required to keep constant guard on the Western Territory of Bahari's future High Mistress.

Me.

Scratching the itchy scab from my fading bite mark, I scowl at the cupla caught around my wrist ...

His watchful chokehold on my actions is suffocating.

Edging around the mast until I'm partially hidden by the slab of shadow untouched by the moon's harsh glow, I reach for the stuffed sack tied to the rails and brimming with all my belongings—a grain sack I traded my basket for with the obliging cook. I loosen the drawstring, retrieve a small parcel, and peel back its layers of damp cheesecloth to reveal a bulb of caspun the same deep shade of indigo as the sky.

Stamping my nose against the sawn-off nub, I draw on the potent, earthy punch ...

The smell only adds to my pain—makes that swelling pressure thrash as though it's afraid to be silenced, taunted by the pacifier I refuse to indulge in.

A deep sigh is snatched from my lips by a whip of humid air.

I rewrap the bulb and tuck it amongst my belongings, rummaging past my wooden sword, fingers tangling with a slip of silky material my face and palms are achingly familiar with.

My heart flops.

Rhordyn's pillow slip.

A swallow. A short, shuddered breath as horses gallop through my chest.

Blood-boiling fury and finger-tingling desperation battle inside me, and I steal a moment to pretend I'm stronger than I really am before the desperate flood of *need* bursts through me like a gulp of icy water. I free the slip, burrow my face into its soft pleats, and draw my lungs full of *him*—spiked with equal doses of rapture and self-loathing.

I'm sailing toward my promised, still drugging myself with the fading dregs of another man. My final vice. The hardest anchor to cut loose.

The one I don't *want* to cut loose.

Unlike the caspun, I don't limit myself to just one breath. I inflate myself with gluttonous gulps until I'm light-headed and floating before I tuck it beneath my sword and retrieve a parcel that's long and heavy for its small size.

I unroll it—slow and cautious.

Nestled between the folds is a fork I stole from the galley, its pronged tips sharp enough to puncture flesh. I keep unrolling, and a spoon tumbles into my lap.

I stare at it, trying to ignore the two silhouettes leering down on me from their loftier perch—hard to do when their voices keep pecking at me.

"You know she asked the cook for some preserve jars and baking twine so she could 'tie 'em to the mast to root her clippings'? You should've seen the way he looked at her."

"Witch, I tell ya," Vanth bites out. "I've known from the moment I watched her pick mushrooms off a pile of shit. High Master's been beguiled by that round ass and fuckable face."

"Not me. Something about her eyes makes me want to shit my drawers." A small pause, then, "Gage seems to like her ..."

"Only because he no longer has to pull night shifts on the aftermast."

Snatching the utensils in white-knuckled fists, I suspend them before me, teeth gritted, stare stabbed through the spindles and out across the ocean that looks like crumbled moonlight. I fill my lungs with salted air and tune into the sound of water slapping against the side of the ship.

Muscles bunched, I tighten my sweaty palms around the tools and bring them together ...

Tink.

The sound chips at my bones. Releases a flood of pressure from somewhere deep inside my chest, racing to attack the confines of my skin until it feels like I'm about to split ten ways.

It takes me too many drawn-out breaths to shore up the courage to drag them down the length of each other—a sharp, screeching sound that snaps my eyes shut and has me clamping my lips against the urge to scream.

I fill my lungs, hold, release ...

Repeat.

"What's," footsteps shuffle, "what's she doing?"

"Some weird ritual. She's done it every night since we set sail."

I ease deeper into the shadow, thoughts thrown back

to the time I forgot one of Baze's vital rules and tucked my thumb before I threw a punch at his face.

We both heard the crunch seconds before the blow of pain crippled me.

For weeks, I couldn't braid my hair, shoot an arrow, swing a blade. Worst of all was not being able to wield my diamond pickaxe or even hold a paintbrush.

I never tucked my thumb again.

Pain taught me a lesson then; my penance for not listening was weeks of a dashed routine. Now, it's the only shield I have against *myself*. A reminder that, should I forget what I'm capable of—what I've done—I could lose control again.

"Told you," Vanth mutters. "She's fucking nuts."

I crack my neck. Feed on their words. Drag the utensils against each other—harder this time.

The sound can't break me if I'm already in pieces.

Beads of sweat dart down my temples while violent *things* erupt against my skin and skull, rooting around like an army of caustic, flesh-eating worms. Because that's what it is, I realize—the raging pressure that strikes every time I'm triggered.

Those sizzling roots seeking freedom. Seeking something to *saw*.

I look to the stars, doubting Rhordyn knows how ugly I am beneath the pretty skin he's forced me to hide all these years. Layers upon layers of *lies*. Either way, the dull metal clasp at the back of my neck now feels too flimsy.

The crescent moon taunts me with its smile. Tries to pull a different sort of hurt forth.

"You reckon watching her family get eaten alive messed with her head?"

Screech.

Blood dribbles from my nose to my chin, then drips.

Drips.

Drips.

"Perhaps. I don't know. Something about it doesn't add up."

"What do you mean?"

"I look in her fucking eyes and I don't see a survivor. I see guilt and ghosts and my own death flying at me. I think she's cursed. I think her family learned that the hard way and paid the ultimate price."

Guilt and ghosts ...

Swallowing, I close my eyes and pretend I'm drenched in sunlight, folded on a windowsill in Stony Stem—not tucked in the crow's nest halfway up the aftermast, shackled by a bold blue cupla and feasting on my pain. Molding it into a different sort of Safety Line.

A numb shield for my bruised and battered heart.

Chapter 2

Orlaith

Soft light spills through the wide gaps between the rails—a warm kiss to the cheek that seeps into my pores and kindles my blood. I squint across the sea that looks like a stretch of undulating rose petals.

Morning.

I've been scratching swirls and jagged bends into the wooden floorboards by lantern light, adding to my busy mural for so long I barely registered the darkness lifting.

I wrap my diamond pickaxe with a small piece of cloth and tuck it in my back pocket, turning the dial on my lantern hanging off the balustrade. Stretching my back and arms, I push my legs through the rails and reach my toes toward the sun—imagining them dug deep into grass or sand or soil while warmth paints the bare pads of my feet.

I miss plucking round stones off the beach while Kai frolics in the bay. I miss the steady ground and the morning breeze rich with the smell of dead leaves and dew-dappled moss.

Forcing my legs to recoil, I roll onto all fours.

Shuffling around the thick, wooden post pierced through the center of the nest, I crouch beside the bucket tied to a makeshift pulley and slosh a cloth through the water, wringing it out over the soil-stuffed jars tied to the mast, feeding my clippings a few drops of treasured water.

Thinking about my last-minute balcony dash around Stony Stem—wielding a tiny wooden dagger to cut small branches off my favorite plants—I almost smile. Wisteria, lemon tree, various roses ... they all found lodgings in my sack with a few jars of soil.

Small snippets of home.

Sponging my face and behind my neck, I steal peeks at the bleary-eyed sailor climbing the central mast to assume his daytime shift in the nest. Jerid, I think. The only one who makes a concerted effort to keep his back to me as much as possible.

I bag my blanket, noticing three dark shadows circling just below the surface of the ship's wake. At least until the cook tips a bucket of fish frames and sloppy innards overboard.

But it's not the bones and the guts they're after. It's the seagulls that swoop down from their midair coast, risking it all for a scrap of offal—some falling victim to the lunging sharks that erupt from the water with cranked maws and fierce, thrashing bodies. They chomp on their feathery prey so fast there's barely a fluttered wrestle.

Kai used to tell me sharks prefer warm water. Made me promise not to go swimming in Bitten Bay without him during the summer.

Now I understand.

The farther south we've sailed, the more turquoise the water's become, and the more skulking shadows drift through it at all hours of the day.

The bell attached to my bucket line jingles—loud and crisp.

Tucking a length of hair behind my ear, I lean forward and pry the metal loop from the divot in the floor, heaving the hatch open. I peer down the ladder at the peppering of sun-stained men slugging away at their chores, my stare drawn to the boy standing at the base of my mast over thirty feet down.

His head is tipped, heaped plate in one hand, the other shielding his eyes from the morning glare while he looks at me.

Zane.

I toss him a wave, then pull back, pinning my hair into a half-updo before I tighten the drawstring on my sack and check it's secured, lower myself through the hole, then start the tedious climb down the ninety-five wooden rungs—five to every deep sway of the ship.

No sooner do I stamp my foot on the smooth, wooden deck, do I hear, "I used the cook's morning shit break to snoop around the kitchen and forage for all the best bits he keeps hidden for himself."

My small, secret smile is a stolen treasure I don't deserve—gone by the time I spin and look into bright blue eyes framed by thick lashes and a shock of windswept, caramel hair. "Morning, Zane."

"Managed to get this, too," he continues, stabbing an eager hand into one of the many internal pockets of his well-worn, velvet cloak.

A gold token is waved in my face.

I grip his wrist, stilling the motion so I can study the token's filigree face. "You little pickpocket. Is that a—"

"Bahari token. You have favor tokens in Ocruth, yeah?" He tosses it in the air before snatching it up. "Mine now. Figure the High Master owes me a favor."

"That's ... I don't think that's how it works."

He shrugs, tucking it into the pocket of his rumpled pantaloons. "Worth a shot."

"Aren't you serving time on your uncle's ship because your mother's at her wit's end with your thieving antics?"

Bit of a botched remedy since barely a day goes by where he's not boasting his loot at me.

"Yeah, why?"

"Should you really be"—I drop my voice to a low whisper, using a hand to shield my words—"*stealing gold tokens?*"

He frowns. "You're not gonna tell, are you?"

"Course not. I just don't want to see you in trouble with the Captain." I steal a glance at the broad-shouldered man standing at the helm, hand on the wheel, eyes cast ahead, a gruff confidence spilling from his easy stillness. "He looks the type to dish out tough love like it's a privilege."

"Only if you're not his favorite nephew." Zane drops to the deck, legs crossed, and looks up at me with wide eyes, his round, freckle-dusted face dashed with a mischievous, lopsided grin.

My heart twists.

A dazzling stare belonging to a different boy blazes in the forefront of my mind, and I swiftly shove it into that deep place I try to ignore.

I sit and stab my focus on the stack of fried flatbread,

nuts, and dried fruits and meat, reaching for a strip of the latter.

Zane yanks the plate toward himself, eyes twinkling with a flash of mischief. I arch a brow and pull the small cheesecloth parcel from my back pocket. His eyes widen with his broad smile as I wave it at him and hand it over.

He unravels it with frenzied hands, plucks the pickaxe free, his hand engulfing the small handle as he holds it in a blade of sun—scattering colorful confetti all over the deck while I pick at the food, chewing without rapture.

Best cuts or not, our meal pales in comparison to the feast of his wide-eyed wonder.

"I just love it so much ..." he whispers.

I lean my head against the mast, watching him twirl the wooden handle so shards of color chase each other. "I know you do."

In the eye of a confetti storm, we sit in comfortable silence, sharing the plate of food while the busy crew keeps a wide berth, lumping crates together and securing them to the deck.

I'm aware of their glances, feel them bounce off my hardened regard without leaving a dent.

"Uncle said the storm's regathered," Zane mumbles around a dried fig. "That it's chasing our wake."

I look to the north. "I can't see anything ..."

"He can taste it on the air."

The side of my face prickles when Vanth emerges from the lower decks wearing fresh clothes and a complimentary scowl that only deepens when he catches me watching.

I refuse to look away. At least until the cook appears behind him—buckets swinging in his bloated hands, his rotund belly almost throwing him off balance with every step.

"Oh," I mumble, planting my left foot on the deck so my leg doubles as a shield for the plate of contraband when he passes. A putrid waft of aged fish guts nearly makes me gag.

Favored nephew or not, if Zane gets caught thieving by the wrong person, Cap would be forced to inflict some form of corporal punishment or risk his social standing.

The cook stomps up the stairs to the helm, works his way to the back of the ship, and heaves a lumpy slop of offal over the balustrade amid a frenzied swoop of seagulls.

An eruption of splashing ensues.

"If the storm hits, it'll be hell up there," Zane says around a bite of jerky, pointing the frayed strip at my nightly perch. Eyes still on my twirling pickaxe, he kicks up his left leg, foot planting on the deck, shielding the remaining food as the cook wobbles past again. "They sometimes use it as a form of punishment."

I don't tell him that's half the point.

"I'll be fine," I say, shuffling a little further from the ladder when Gage—the aftermast's main barrelman—emerges from below deck and strides toward us, spyglass in one hand, a leather satchel hanging off his shoulder.

"Cap will drag you below once the storm reaches us."

He can try.

I tuck my head and hone my focus on the food as heavy footsteps approach, a shadow falling over me before metal-capped boots settle in my peripheral.

Slowly, I roll my gaze up, straight into a pair of milky-blue eyes crinkled at the corners.

Unlike the rest of the crew, Gage's head is shaved,

showcasing his tattoo: a trail of inky buttons and stitches that spans across his skull, down the back of his neck, and weaves below his shirt—as though he's stitched together like a patchwork doll.

Tucking the spyglass into his leather satchel, he digs through his pocket, pulls out a sharpened piece of charcoal, and offers it to me. "In case you want to add some shading to your scratchings."

I look from the charcoal to his eyes and back again, reaching out to receive it. "Thank you ..."

He nods, grabs hold of the ladder, and starts to climb.

I flick the gift over my fingers a few times and tuck it in my pocket.

Zane finishes the last of our meal, wipes his hands on his pants, and flattens the cheesecloth between us. He sets my pickaxe at the edge, then rolls it up—slow and gentle and precise.

If he'd seen the way that thing slugs through stone, he wouldn't be so careful, but I love his delicate regard.

"He keeps looking at you," Zane mumbles, stealing a glance toward the helm.

I'm aware that he's not talking about his uncle, but my guard. The man who spends every spare hour of the day up there—five steps above me—boasting crossed arms, a puffed chest, and perfectly pressed pantaloons.

I take the pickaxe from Zane and stuff it back in my pocket, watching him set the tin plate on its side and flick it into a spin. "Vanth doesn't like me very much."

"I don't think his brother does either."

"I didn't know he had a brother?"

"Your other guard, Kavan."

Oh.

"I didn't realize …"

Zane nods, a divot of concentration etched between his eyes. "They say you're a witch. That you chew on acorn shells and pick mushrooms off piles of horse shit."

Right.

I won't be offering *them* any dogwarth tea if they end up with crippling flatulence or a blood infection.

He flicks me a glance, violet flecks bursting from the pupils of his powder blue eyes. "I tune them out. They're easy to steal from when their tongues are flapping."

"Makes perfect sense to me."

There's a thundering sound from above, and I look up to see Gage descending the ladder at a rapid pace. He leaps off it from ten rungs up, lands heavily beside us, then sprints up the stairs on a beeline for the helm.

Movement stills, a hush falling over the ship as men seem to watch and listen. Some even file up the same stairs toward the back of the ship to catch their own glimpse of whatever it was that ripped Gage from his perch.

"Weird," Zane mutters, standing. "I'll go check it out."

He trots off in a flutter of velvet.

I shove to a stand, reaching onto my tippy toes in an effort to see through the congregating crewmen, then stab my stare up the aftermast. I climb a few rungs, pausing to peer past the stern over a gathering of loose hair and tawny, low-hanging buns.

The sharks are gone. Even the gulls have scattered.

A ripple in the water draws my eye almost ten ship-lengths beyond us, and a shock of silver scales disrupts the surface before drifting out of sight.

The men mutter ... point ... *shout*. The Captain bellows something that cleaves a path for him to charge through—spyglass in hand.

Frowning, I continue to climb, settling high enough that I have a decent vantage point to cast my gaze back upon the water.

My heart lurches.

There's a long, slithering shadow double the length of the ship that's weaving just below the surface.

Closer than it was a few moments ago.

A massive, gossamer dorsal fin volleys out of the water, leaving a trail of misty spindrift.

A lump lands in my belly, thrashing like a creature swallowed alive ...

Something's following us.

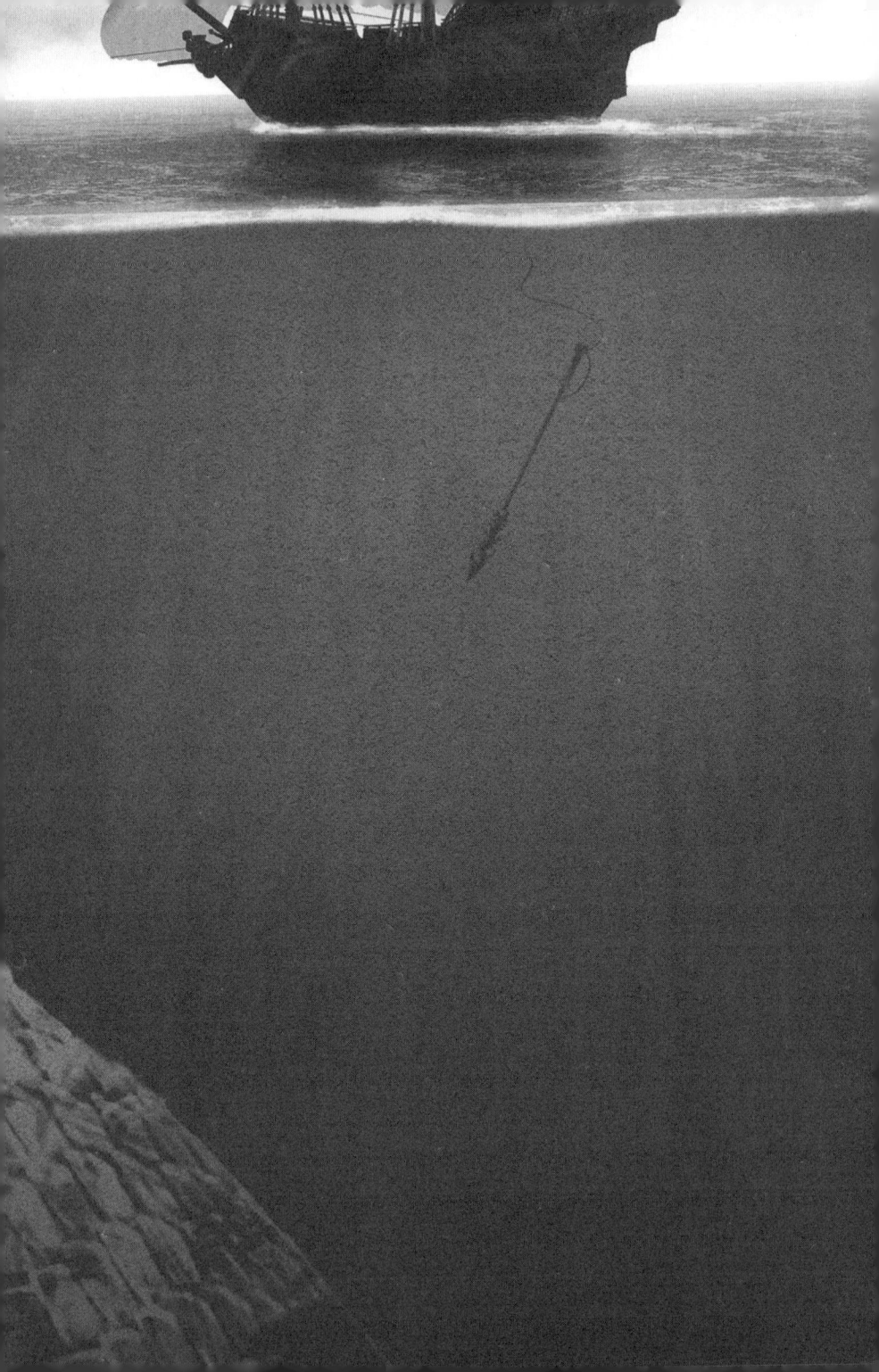

Chapter 3

Orlaith

"Batten down the hatches!"

Cap's order sledges the air, sending men tripping over their own feet in a rush to busy themselves. He catches Zane by the arm and marches him down the stairs, leaving only Vanth and the first mate at the helm, nose to nose, spitting words at each other.

Vanth rips away, stalks toward the back corner, and unlatches the scope on the huge, metal harpoon mounted on the deck.

My stomach knots, attention veering to the creature gliding through our wake. I mutter a curse and clamber down the ladder, skipping the last few rungs and landing in a crouch. Bare feet slapping against the deck, I run to the stairs, verging on the helm seconds after a shirtless, mussed-up Kavan, who looks like he just fell out of bed, snatched two spears, and charged onto the deck without his shoes.

"Did you see that thing, Vanth? It's fucking huge!" There's genuine fear in Kavan's rushed, high pitched words. "It's coming right for us—"

"Don't worry," Vanth says through a tight jaw, still locked in a stare-off with the first mate as he takes a spear. "I'm dealing with it."

"You're outta line," the first mate growls. "The captain has given no such orders."

I crouch into the shadow of a large water barrel—out of sight, but close enough to hear.

Observe.

"And by the time he does, it'll be too late," Vanth growls, fist crushing the edge of a nearby tarpaulin as his chest inflates. "You're forgetting that *I'm* charged with protecting the High Master's promised. I have direct orders to do whatever's necessary to keep her safe."

He snaps his arm down, ripping off the tarp in a ruffle of heavy leather, unveiling a pronged rack loaded with six claw-tipped metal bolts taller than me. Thicker than my arm.

My blood runs cold.

I look to the approaching creature again—closer now as it breaks the surface in a slither of frills and scales that reflect the sun. It frolics through our whitewash, stitching the sea in big, loping curls. Like it's ... it's *playing*.

My pulse pitches, the boisterous stomping and yelling and bustling about the ship's upper deck fading into oblivion ...

I've seen the vicious charge of impending death.

It looks *nothing* like this.

Stomach swirling with a thick oil of unease, I barge from

the shadow and move past the first mate, planting myself in the middle of it all.

Three pairs of wide eyes whip in my direction.

"I—I agree with the first mate." My fractured voice echoes through the sudden void of silence, and I've never felt so loud.

So bare and small and silly.

I clear my throat and shove my shoulders back.

"It's not showing signs of aggression, but *curiosity*. I'm guessing it'll veer off once it's had a sniff around."

Vanth throws me a dirty look, setting his spear aside and dragging a bolt from the rack with a sharp scrape that pumps my skull full of pressure. Teeth clenched, he heaves it up, slides it down the hatch, and cranks it into place, cheeks reddening from the strain. "And what do you know about the outside world, *Mistress?*"

His righteous tone lacks the force to overshadow the desperate boom in my chest, my frantic gaze nipping at the creature dancing toward a brutal, bloody end.

"Not a lot," I admit, trying to keep my voice steady. "But I do have experience with deadly, inquisitive creatures. It's acting much the same as the sharks, probably lured by the offal we've been dumping overboard. If it wanted to attack, it would've hit from *beneath* before we caught a sniff of danger."

There's a digestive pause, feeding my courage with scraps of hope.

I step closer, a flutter in my chest as I offer a small smile. A silent plea to bury our differences. "Please, Vanth. Nobody needs to die today ..."

He looks me up and down, gives me his back, then rotates the weapon until it's pointing toward the creature.

My stomach flips. Smile falls.

He peers down the scope. "If the High Master thought you were capable of guarding your own wellbeing, he wouldn't have assigned you babysitters," Vanth bites out. "Take her below deck."

A big hand grips my shoulder.

I whip my head around to a blur of sun-kissed brawn and scuffing boots as the Captain wrestles Kavan into an armlock so deep I'm surprised his shoulder is still notched in its socket.

His discarded spear clatters across the deck.

"Who the fuck do you think you are, boy?" Captain lowers Kavan to the deck with such commanding poise, my own knees threaten to buckle. "That's our future High Mistress you were about to manhandle like an *animal*."

Lumped on the ground in a wheezing, red-faced knot, Kavan suddenly looks so feeble.

"*Captain,*" Vanth bites out, and I spin, stare flying to his finger curled around the trigger of the brutal weapon he's wielding. I look at his target—a lengthy ruffle of corrugated silver, its movements fast and fluttery and so much closer now.

Happy.

Like it's stealing the space between us one treasured inch at a time.

My heart batters my ribs.

"Vanth," Captain grinds out, Kavan still pinned beneath his might, hissing spittle onto his polished black boot, "I see you're perfectly capable of arming a harpoon.

Well done. I hope you're not planning to shoot anything with it."

An easy *out* Vanth should absolutely tighten his fists around.

He clears his throat, tone defensive when he says, "Madame Strings tells stories about serpentine beasts launching from the water in rabid fits of rage, shredding vessels into splinters. I'm sure you've heard the same stor—"

Captain chuffs out a sound of disgust, strain etched around the edges of his pale blue eyes. "I don't trust the slimy words of that agitator, even if she does claim to know everything. You shouldn't either."

A deep red creeps up Vanth's neck and across his cheeks. His grip on the trigger tightens, blanching the tip of his finger and halting my heart.

My foot slides forward an inch.

Don't do it. Please.

"Well, I count at least ten of *your* men down there who were raised around her fire, feeding on her legends—"

"You shoot that thing," Captain growls with merciless candor, "and all you're going to achieve is to anger it, earn yourself ten lashes, and a court-martial once we dock. Finger off the trigger, before I snap it off your fucking hand and throw it to the gulls."

Vanth's eyes glaze with resolution, and he looks to the creature, strangles the trigger—

I leap, slamming into him as the *boom* of the discharged weapon knifes my gut.

The bolt plunges toward the snaking shadow at lightning speed, striking the water with a sickening *whump*.

A serrated moan rips from the ocean, a swirling symphony of pain that rips my heart in two.

Hands fisting Vanth's shirt, I release a sob as the creature writhes into a knot of soft and sharp frills. As it bulges above the surface like a glittering mountain birthed from the sea, spewing a river of red from the fleshy wound staked by that brutal bolt—straight through a fold of fins.

Silence sweeps across the ship as its tortured cries squeal through the still and ripple across the ocean, battering my skin like a tangible thing. Like the ocean's crying—its tears a pattering attack I can't wipe away.

I look at all that blood-tarnished beauty and fail to blink away the needling sting in my eyes.

The creature unspools in slow, spineless increments, slithering below the surface ...

Gone.

All that's left is a blossom of blood bigger than the ship; a temporary gravestone that fades a little with each of my hammering heartbeats.

"You *monster*," I rasp through the fire in my throat and whirl on Vanth, looking past a sheen of tears into merciless eyes. "What have you done?"

CHAPTER 4
Orlaith

"What have *I* done?" Vanth yanks me so hard our chests collide, his warm breath popping against my face with every blasted word. "I was aiming for the head, and I definitely missed the fucking head. You may have just killed us all, *Mist*—"

He's blasted from my grip by a shove that lashes him against the railing. Captain charges forward and clenches his collar, bending him backward over the handrail, hanging his life in the crush of a fist. "Damn fool."

The shrill jingle of a familiar bell has me searching the aftermast, finding Zane halfway up—clinging to the rungs and looking at me.

Pointing at the sea.

I frown, a deep sense of unease rooting through my chest.

"Cap ... the aftermast ... look."

Frowning, he does, face blanching when he spots Zane. "I locked that boy in my quarters. The hell is he doing up there?"

Zane continues to point portside, screaming one word over and over again.

"That blasted wind ... Can you tell what he's saying?"

"Bubbles," I murmur, stepping forward to look past the balustrade. Leaning over the rail, I catch sight of something shimmering beneath the froth floating on the restless waves, stomach dropping. "*Everyone, hold on—*"

The ocean erupts, and I'm ripped backward, gasping as the serpentine beast punches through with a torrent of water that pelts the ship like a storm. The world bucks beneath my feet and I lurch to the rail, squinting through the cold spray to make out the creature's head—boxy and barbed and dusted in jeweled scales, its piercing green eyes shaded by a mantle of shards.

It's beautiful. Statuesque.

Huge.

Towered above us, it sways, the sharp fins on one side of its body unfolding like a fan, revealing a stretch of webbed, triangular panels.

Water wings.

The other is pinned by the bolt staked through its front, blood spilling from the frayed wound.

My stomach tips.

Its maw cranks wide, and I take in the fatal set of canines that could crunch through this ship in a single bite, its cavernous throat reeking of dead fish and embers. It spews a violent roar that rattles my bones, its clamor beating against my skin, followed by a chilling squeal that rips a sob from my throat.

With another curdled wail, the creature lashes against the ocean, tossing the ship with such violent force my feet whip out from under me.

I slam against the deck.

Wood groans, and the ship begins to roll to a symphony of screams.

Anything not bolted down becomes a deadly missile, and we plane sideways, lashing against the spindles in a groaning tangle of limbs. I scramble to grip hold of the wooden rails only seconds before we slam into the ocean's livid face.

Water hammers me—a crushing attack that rips my fingers from the rail. I flit with the heavy current for a few harrowing seconds, then collide with one of the masts, the breath punched from my lungs from the violent assault.

I hold tight, a rinse of bubbles exploding against my face.

The mast vibrates when a strident *crack* ratchets through the water, like a tree splitting. *Snapping.*

This is how I'm going to die.

I lose track of which way is up, which way is down, the ship lurching side to side like a wild, bucking beast, scrambling my organs and making my head spin.

My hold begins to slip, gravity pulling me down.

Water drains with the easing motion, and I land in a lump, gasping a treasured breath. It hacks out of me in retching increments that almost split my chest.

I roll onto my back. Open my eyes.

Silence.

Blurry clouds swing side to side—something that strikes me as odd until I realize the boat is swaying.

The silence morphs into a blare of blood-curdling screams; the sort of loud that makes me want to squeeze my eyes shut and clap my hands over my ears.

But I've done that all my life. Blocked out the noise.
Enough.
I battle into a sitting position and survey my surroundings. My blood chills.

The floorboards are laden with puddles, some red and syrupy. People's clothes are slicked to their skin, torn in places, revealing fleshy wounds with shards of bone poking through. Some are groaning through twisted expressions, cradling limbs hanging at odd angles.

Some are deadly silent.

The few men who survived the roll unscathed cling to the splintered balustrades, searching the surface for any signs the wounded beast will return to serve more bloody vengeance.

"*That stupid bitch ...*"

The strangled condemnation comes from behind, and I peer back to see Vanth pushing to his feet, a deep slash in his forehead spitting a bloody ribbon down his face.

Caught in a daze, I watch it drip while he scans the commotion with keen, desperate eyes. I shore up the energy to crawl toward the Captain, who's motionless, wrapped around the base of the harpoon. Rolling him onto his back, I inspect the grisly gash on his head, then set my ear against his chest.

A choked sound erupts from Vanth, and I see him folded against the handrail, gaze pierced across the ocean. "*No ...*"

I haul myself up, tracing Vanth's line of sight to Kavan— slung over a bobbing barrel a ship-length away. Blood gushes from a gnarly wound in his arm that's torn through by a shard of bone, feeding the ocean and a circling shark three times his size.

My heart flops. Chest constricts.

"Help!" He chokes out a desperate cry. "Brother, *help me!*"

"The dinghy," I blurt, stare flying to the spot on the deck where the small vessel is usually stored.

All that's left is a tangle of snapped ropes.

"Gone," Vanth growls, striding toward a wooden box bolted to the deck. He unlatches the lid, tugs it open, and hauls out a small crossbow.

Bile sears my throat, and I cast my gaze on Kavan now trying to kick at the predator drawing closer with every turn. He scrabbles to fit his entire body on the barrel, only to roll forward headfirst and dunk beneath the waves. He resurfaces, gasping and splashing as he tries to stay afloat with one good arm.

The shark circles closer, *closer* ...

Kavan's scream shreds the air. "*Help me!*"

Vanth notches a bolt and cranks it back, face tight, lips shaping silent words. His lids sweep shut for a few drawn beats that hit me in the chest like a hammer.

He opens his eyes and pulls the trigger.

A bolt whistles through the air, grazes Kavan's tilted chin, and thuds deep into his chest at a skewed angle—straight through the heart.

I flinch, releasing a strangled sound as Kavan's eyes go wide and vacant. His limp body eases back into the water before he's snatched beneath the surface in a lather of blood and thrashing fins.

I rip my gaze from the sight, but Vanth watches, motionless, eyes flat and empty.

Captain croaks out a sound, still lying in a heap on the bloodstained deck, bleary eyes peeling open. "Z—Zane ..."

It lands a kick to the chest.

Heart thundering to the chorus of screams, I scan the crewmen littering the deck, chest tightening as I comb through until there are none left. Moving to the balustrade, I set my hands on the rail and find the courage to survey the ocean, flicking between bits of bobbing shrapnel, doing my best to avoid the thrashing shadow now feasting amongst a pool of red—all that's left of Kavan.

I dart to the other side of the boat, drawn to the blue swirl of our torn sail drifting on the surface, kept partially afloat by large pockets of air. Amongst it all, a bright blue pop of material wafts around a small form face down in one of the puddled divots.

Zane.

I charge down the stairs.

Someone bellows my name, tells me to stop, but the sound fades into oblivion when I reach the handrail, climb atop, and jump.

The wind whips at my hair and steals my breath, stomach rising in my chest.

I slam into the water's unforgiving face, all the air clapping from my lungs as I sink into the deep abyss, crushed by the sense of its infinite stretch.

When my body finally slows, my limbs power into action, and I push toward the surface with a litter of bubbles, breaking free with a heaving gasp. Ignoring the bellowed words coming from the ship, I throw my head around and gather my bearings, adjusting to the seascape—so different down here amongst the tattered remnants of the ship's lost bits.

Everything looks bigger. More *alive*.

Farther away.

Shoving down nudging thoughts of sharp, shredding teeth, I propel toward the bold blue sail bubbled above the surface, every kick lacking, every pull of my hands paltry and weak and—

Not fast enough.

With chapped lungs and a face full of sting, I finally reach the sail, getting tangled amongst the material in my frantic search as I gather and shove, gulping breath every chance I get, until I finally fist Zane's velvet cape and *pull*. Flipping him, I wrench his head above the water.

The sight of his still face and pale blue lips brands my soul.

"I've got you," I splutter, painfully aware of his motionless chest, of the endless ocean beneath us. "I'm so sorry." Choking back a sob, I unhook his cloak and free him from the anchor of his much-loved loot.

I drag him to the edge of the sail, tip onto my back, and rest him against my chest so his head stays above the water while I propel toward the ship—feet churning with the rush of my labored breaths.

Little waves fold over us, stinging my eyes and blurring my vision.

Every second that drips by is another breath lost. Every volley of water that batters his face is another dose of death up his nose. Down his throat.

Not fast enough.

My head bumps against something hard, and I jolt to a stop, feet sinking. I look up the steep edge of the ship to a handrail lined with bloody, frantic sailors. To the rope ladder hanging down the side.

"Grab hold!"

Our bobbing vulnerability makes my stomach turn.

I can feel the sharks lurking—watching. Any moment one could hit, snatch us under, tear and thrash and *chew*. Or perhaps the sea serpent will charge from the depths again and swallow us in a vengeful gulp.

My grip on Zane tightens as I flounder for the rope. Putting his limp body between myself and the ladder, I try to haul him free from the skulking threats.

"I can't pull him out on my own!"

My voice is foreign—sharp and desperate.

I shove hair off my face to see Cap scaling the ladder, blood dribbling from his chin.

"Can you climb?"

With my nod, he grips Zane by the back of his shirt and hauls him from my clutch, lumping him over his shoulder. A surge of relief shoots through me.

He's safe.

I follow them up the ladder, my hair a sodden anchor down my back. The flimsy rope blisters my fingers with every pull farther from the mauling threat below, and I tingle from the base of my spine to the soles of my feet.

Certain I'd see my own death rushing toward me with a wide-open jaw, I don't look down—not even when I realize we are well and truly in the clear.

Zane and the Captain disappear from sight, and I'm

gripped on the back of my shirt like a kitten, then lumped upon the deck.

I watch in muted horror as Captain pinches Zane's nose and breathes big bouts of air into his lungs, inflating his chest.

Breathe ...

Breathe, dammit!

He paws at Zane's face with calloused hands. "Wake up, my boy. Come on. Open your eyes and look at me." A harsh, desperate sound escapes him as he rolls Zane onto his side and batters his back. "*Wake up!*"

The seconds drip by like oil in water, refusing to blend, coasting across the surface of my soul. I feel like I'm falling through a hole in the ground with no air in my chest to scream.

Perhaps they're not seconds at all, but minutes, hours, *days*.

Perhaps this limbo lasts forever.

There's a hacking sound, a splutter and a spill that makes my heart and stomach lurch in tandem.

Zane's eyes blink open—so shot they're more red than white. They swivel, latching onto his uncle with a faraway stare, like he's trying to reconstruct some sort of puzzle.

Cap's face crumbles, a curdled sound rupturing from his lips ...

I fold forward and vomit across the floorboards.

Chapter 5
Orlaith

The sour reek of vomit clings to the tangle of salt-and-spew-crusted hair dangling in my face. I flick it over my shoulder with a blood-slathered hand and thread a band of torn sail beneath Gage's upper thigh. It must hurt when I twist the tails into a knot and pull them tight, but he doesn't flinch.

Doesn't make a sound.

He just silently watches me work, eyes as flat as the tattooed buttons on his shaved skull while the high-hanging sun beats us with its relentless heat—starving pockets of shade until they're nothing but frail slivers.

The air refuses to stir, leaving the sea unnaturally still, clogging our lungs with hot, dense breaths thick with the smell of baking death.

It happened moments after Zane was taken below deck to be checked over by the medis. The wind stopped snapping at the torn sails and nipping at our sodden skin. The ocean lost its lively beat and glossed over like a mirror.

Just ... *stopped.*

The men watched and murmured about an omen from the Gods—that perhaps the creature was important to them, and by slaying it, the rest of us are doomed to float until we die of thirst as punishment. But the moment the Captain charged back onto the main deck, they all snipped their words and got to work.

Now, people are barking orders, pushing things into place, littering the deck with bloody boot prints. There's a line of tattered men weaving up the stairs from below, passing full buckets of sea water from hand to hand and tipping them overboard.

Apparently, there's a hole in the side of the ship. Nothing major, but when you tally it with the snapped foremast and the lack of wind to fill it anyway, we won't be sailing free of this watery graveyard anytime soon.

I tighten the bind around Gage's thigh, the material squelching with my desperate attempt to stem the blood oozing from a gruesome, fleshy wound slashed to the bone. But the tourniquet isn't enough to keep him from slipping away.

I can see it in his eyes—the vacant look of a man waiting to die.

"Hey ..." I shove lumps of cheesecloth into the wound, his life puddling around my fingers. "You still with me?"

He heaves a low grunt, and I peer up to see him looking toward the sky. "I used to be a captain, you know. One of the other ships."

His voice sounds clogged.

"You did?"

He gives the slightest nod. "Gave it up so I could work the aftermast."

I pull out a wad of sodden cheesecloth from his wound and slop it on the deck, swiftly replacing it with a fresh bit. "Yeah? Why's that?"

"I prefer to look backward ... rather than forward."

My hands pause, gaze lifting to his face. I follow his stare up the aftermast, landing on the underside of the crow's nest.

"I liked your drawings," he croaks, and I take in his wrought features. "Searching for the new ones every morning gave me something to live for again."

I clear my throat, noting the pool of warm blood swelling beneath me, stretching further down the floorboards ...

I'm sitting in so much of him, I'm surprised there's anything left for his heart to pump.

A warm, swollen ache claws up my throat.

"Do you ... have family in the capital?"

"Dead. Blight took 'em four years ago. Parents, brother, my *woman*." He winces, eyes screwed shut as he chokes out, "Our daughter. She ... she used to draw for me." The last words come out cracked, and I feel the shards pierce my heart.

The backs of my eyes.

"I'm so sorry, Gage ..."

"Don't. Today, I meet them in Mala." A single tear escapes him, catching in the stubble dusting the tattoos stitched across his skull. "Long overdue."

I try to swallow the lump in my throat while I study his smooth face. It occurs to me that the wound through his heart is just as fresh as the one through his leg—and far more painful.

He opens his eyes, gaze cast up to the underside of our nest. "Do me a favor, would you?" His gruff voice wobbles with the question.

"Anything ..."

"Reach into my shirt pocket. There's something in there I'd like to hold ..."

With a nod, I wipe my hands on my pants, then wiggle my fingers into the pocket, pulling out a tattered patchwork doll with button eyes and soft pink stitching that's come loose in places. I set it in his palm, wrap his cold fingers around it, and hold it up so he can see.

His glassy gaze clings to the sight for a few stretched seconds before he nods, and I lower it over his heart. Another tear slides down his cheek as his knuckles whiten with strain, the doll swallowed within the clenched confines of his hand. "Now," he croaks, throat bobbing, "loosen the tourniquet."

My gaze drops to the bloody knot suspending the inevitable, but my hands suddenly feel like boulders.

I look at his eyes—watching me, more present than I've seen them since he handed me that piece of charcoal weighing down my pocket.

In case you want to add some shading to your scratchings.

"Please ..."

I nod.

With trembling fingers, I ease the material's hold on him, then slowly unpack the wound. Blood oozes—a silky river of red gushing to freedom.

Gage begins to sing, his deep, abrasive voice carving out

foreign words in such a way, I don't even want to know what they mean. What the song's about.

They bleed me anyway.

A man limping past stops, slowly looking at Gage from beneath a mess of flaxen curls, then swiftly at the ground. He sets his vial of water on the floor, bows his head, and salutes.

A *captain's* salute.

He harmonizes the chorus with his robust voice, joined by another. And another. Each saluting the man pooling around my legs.

My throat tightens as I watch Gage's blood flow free. Close my eyes as the song draws to a close without him, warm tears sliding down my cheeks. When I find the courage to open them again, I see his own are wide and lifeless.

I whip my stare across the ocean—so smooth it doesn't look real. So extraordinary.

The beauty is lost on me.

All I can see is the barrel Kavan tried to clamber on top of in a desperate bid to salvage his life; the too-pink tinge to the water that doesn't seem to fade.

Footsteps thud across the deck, heavier than the others. I let my gaze pan to the Captain, his brow stitched as he surveys the deck with grim eyes that eventually land on me.

His navy shirt is ripped in places and rolled to the elbows, revealing thick, weather-worn forearms splashed with blood.

He scans my face, my hands, the pool of blood I'm sitting in.

The man stretched out on the deck before me.

His chest inflates, lips part, breath spilling out in a rush.

Then he kneels beside me, hand coming up to brush down Gage's face, closing his eyes. "He was a good man."

I nod.

His gaze drops to the makeshift tourniquet, the edges still loose in my hands.

"I ... ah ..." My voice is not my own. It's cold and vacant as Vanth's words chant through my mind.

Killed us all.

Killed us all.

Killed us all.

"Orlaith?"

I blink away my sightless daze. "I did as he asked."

"I know." Though his voice is gruff, there's a softness to his words, his eyes, his posture. Gone the next second.

He grips my shoulders and hooks my full attention, searching my eyes. "You injured?"

I shake my head, whisper a no.

"Good," he mumbles, nodding slowly. "How familiar are you with a needle and thread?"

I taste bile, bunching my hands into fists, feeling that phantom prickle bite the tips of my fingers. Hating it.

Missing it more.

"Very."

His grip tightens, as though he's trying to anchor me. "Then I have a *very* important job for you."

Job ... I've never been given one of those before.

"You do?"

He nods. "If you think you're up to it, I need someone to help the medis stitch up the rest of the crew."

Chapter 6
Orlaith

I step down a dark, narrow staircase into the suffocating confines of the makeshift infirmary, so different from the above-deck racket stomping overhead. The low roof coupled with the lack of windows thickens the hot, potent residue of spew, pain, and body odor.

The floorboards are slathered in vomit and blood, sloshed through the remaining seawater. Someone dry heaves, and I clap my hand over my mouth as a lumpy splatter wrestles with the dull chorus of groans.

Swallowing bile, my attention jumps between packed-in wooden cots partitioned by sheer drapes. Between stricken sailors with powdery eyes—some present, some flat and vacant, as if the pain has ferried their minds somewhere that doesn't hurt so much.

One man looks straight at me and silently holds my stare. My gaze drops to his left leg that now ends in a bandaged nub, and something inside my chest pulls taut.

My fault.

"Mistress?"

I blink, stare sliding to a young man with tousled, bright blond hair and kind, tired eyes standing between two cots, shirt rolled to his elbows. He wipes his bloodied hands on a shredded piece of cloth, then whips it over his shoulder.

"Just Orlaith."

"I'm Alon," he says, and I stare at his hand for a bit before realizing he wants me to give him mine.

He shakes it like he's checking it's still attached, and I clear my throat, glancing around the room again once he lets it go. "Can I, ahh, help at all?"

Relief brightens his eyes.

"I won't look a gift horse in the mouth. Are you good with a needle?"

"I've had some experience, yes."

"Excellent."

He drops to a knee before a dented metal box set on the ground, gesturing for me to do the same as he cranks the lid. I knot my hair into a low bun, then roll my sleeves, listening to the crash course on the various jars of ointment and their uses—most of which I'm already familiar with. He points out the different tools I may require, shows me where to find rolls of dressing, and even gives me a demonstration on how to sanitize a needle.

Little does he know, I've sanitized a needle almost every day for as long as I can remember.

He hands me a corked bottle of rum. "Let them have a swig before tipping it on. Stitch them up, swipe some ointment, bind them in gauze, then move on to the next."

My chest tightens as he drops a pair of metal snips into my other hand. I clear my throat, wrapping my fingers around the sharp instrument. "Got it."

"It'll hold, if that's what you're worried about."

The man I just stitched together scowls at my handiwork, lets out a gruff sound, and pushes to his feet, making for the door without looking back.

I swipe the dappled sweat from my forehead, then move toward Jerid sprawled on the adjacent cot with a blood-soaked tourniquet bound around his arm.

His gaunt stare swivels to me.

"Last I saw, you were climbing the mainsail. What happened?" I ask.

"Was in the n-nest. Wrapped my hand in ... r-rope so I wouldn't float away," he stammers between short, sharp breaths. "Ship s-self-corrected ... turned my body ... into a wh-whip."

I wince, arching back so I can peek past the draped material for the medis. He's elbow deep in someone's abdomen three cots down the line.

Dammit.

"I've never set a bone before," I admit, stepping closer, meeting Jerid's wide-eyed stare. "But I can give it a shot?"

"Fuck me," he mumbles, then accepts my bottle of rum and takes a generous swig, hissing through clenched teeth as I unwrap the bandage and gently unpack the wound.

My stomach knots.

A jagged piece of bone has punched through his skin,

leaking blood like a faulty faucet. He's also sporting an angry rope burn around his wrist and hand.

Pressing the sodden lumps of gauze back into place to stem the flow of blood, I retrieve everything I need from the med box and set my supplies atop a small wooden crate beside his cot. I look between the different instruments and frown. "Wait here."

"Where else would I go?" he tremors, lips nudging into a wan smile.

I rush to the back of the room, though as I pass the end cot, I feel the probe of someone's gaze against the side of my face, down the lines of my body.

Pausing, I seek the source.

Vanth is seated on the edge of a bed—shirt undone to the sternum, hair askew, azure eyes snatching my breath like a phantom hand sliding around my throat.

Tightening.

There's blood dripping down his face from the meaty gash through his eyebrow and up into his hairline, a bottle of rum snagged in his grip and hanging between his wide-open thighs. He leans back, tips his head against the wall, and watches me from below heavy lids as he draws a deep glug.

There's something in his leer that's hard for me to rip away from, but I do, barreling down the steps toward the galley on the lowest deck. The last three are immersed, and I'm forced to slow as I wade into the murky water.

I pluck a path to the galley, the water peppered with rolled oats and bobbing apples that bump against my legs as I rifle through the drawers. Finding two wooden spoons,

I head back toward the stairs, footsteps hurried when my bare feet hit the deck of the infirmary.

Standing beside Jerid's cot again, I dig into my pocket and pull out a piece of damp night bark. "It'll help with the pain."

His eyes flash with relief before he opens his mouth and lets me place it on his tongue, which surprises me. He's not the first person I've offered this bit of bark to.

He *is* the first person not to screw up his face or tell me pain relief is for pussies.

While I wait for him to work through it, I pour alcohol on my hands, thread a needle, and fire the tip—ignoring the swarm of fluttering nerves in my belly.

"Now, bite down on this," I say, weaving the handle of a wooden spoon between his teeth while he flicks me an anxious look I try to ignore. The moment his jaw clamps down, I draw a deep glug of rum, wincing at the bulb of fire easing down my throat.

I pull the material from his wound and splash it with alcohol to the haunting tune of his muffled screams. I don't give him the chance to work through the pain before I grip his arm in two places and wrench the bone back into place.

His howl almost rips a hole in the atmosphere.

Face screwed up, I splint the break with the second spoon, using string to secure it, then stitch the raw edges of his wound together. I'm so busy concentrating I don't realize he's passed out until the other spoon clatters onto the floor.

I sponge away the rest of the blood, apply another tip of alcohol, slather the rope burn in a balm made from rendered pig fat, then wrap his arm.

A small, accomplished smile teases the corners of my mouth as I clean my hands and instruments in a bowl of cloudy water. Turning back to the room, I wander between the cots, searching for anyone else that needs attention. Finding nobody, I look in the direction of Vanth's cot tucked in the corner behind a curtain, then at Alon—still elbow deep in that man's innards.

"Crap," I mutter, drawing a shaky breath.

I gather my stuff in a basket, push my shoulders back, and approach, skin pricking the moment I cross into his line of sight.

"Is it just the head wound?" I ask, rifling through my med box.

He chugs a draw of rum, his eyes clinging to me as he drains half the bottle.

Right.

"It needs to be cleaned, then I'll stitch it up." I dampen some cheesecloth with a tip of alcohol and fish out the needle, threading the eye before sparking a match and firing the tip. "Do you want something to bite down on?" I ask, shaking out the flame.

He takes another swig.

His legs are spread so far apart, the only spot for me to stand is right between them. Trying not to show how uncomfortable I am with his power play, I clear my throat, step forward, and dab at his face, swiping away the blood.

He doesn't flinch—not even when I begin threading the fine needle through his flesh, tugging the torn edges together in tidy increments.

The wound is a long, messy gash, requiring every ounce

of my concentration. So when his rusty voice breaks the silence, I almost jump right out of my skin.

"Our High Master told us to protect your virtue," he slurs. "But I find it hard to believe you and Rhordyn weren't fucking."

The words pierce me, and I pause, looking into his vacant stare, watching his pupils tighten as he draws his focus to my face.

"I saw the way he looked at you." He gives me a thin-lipped smile laced with poison. "Like a man who's already staked his claim. Torn your seams wide open."

The only seams Rhordyn ever tore were the seams of my heart.

I shove the needle into Vanth's head, feeling it collide with bone. He jerks back, hissing through clenched teeth.

"Oops." I grab his head, pull him close again, and continue stitching. "Sorry. I'm new to this."

He lifts the bottle and drains it, blowing his breath all over my face when he says, "How did you not learn to stitch? Most women know, and I saw the way you spent your days. It's not like you lacked the time to learn."

"I was too busy fucking Rhordyn," I mutter dryly, tugging the next stitch so taught the skin puckers.

"Slut," he slurs, swaying to his own tide as I stitch and tug, stitch and tug. "I wonder ... do you fuck dirty?"

My heart lurches into my throat, and I still for a moment before regaining my composure. "You'll never know."

I continue to stitch—faster now—eager to tie him off and be done.

Vanth's energy seems to swell, like he can smell my vulnerability beneath my hardened exterior. I become painfully aware of my position between his legs—of his eyes leveled with my chest.

Of this space, so cut off from the rest of the crew.

"I saw him carry you away, you know. Saw you return wearing his shirt." His hands slither down the length of his thighs, settling on his knees, and something inside me pulls tight. "I've seen you sniffing that pillow slip."

I stop, needle half threaded through a messy lip of torn flesh.

Slowly—so fucking slowly—I let my gaze track down the crooked line of his cross-stitched wound to settle on his eyes.

In them, I see deep-seated pain, malicious intent, and a spark of fire I wish I was blind to.

The moment stretches, the smell of rum thick on his steady breath as I wait to see what else he has to throw at me.

"My High Master is not merciful," he whispers, though the words still gouge my skin. "Not when it comes to *traitors*."

"I'm no traitor."

"Perhaps not." He shrugs, lifting his left brow, making his stitches pull enough to dribble blood down the side of his face. "Perhaps I should present him with the evidence and see what he has to say."

His words land like boulders on my chest.

I open my mouth to speak, close it, stiffening when I feel something feather up the back of my thigh ... over the curve of my ass ...

"Or perhaps ..."

My spine stiffens, blood chilling.

"Perhaps what, Vanth?"

"We come to some sort of arrangement," he's quick to respond.

Heart in my throat, I repress the urge to shiver.

To *scream*.

Instead, I drop into a dark, dead place deep inside that's immune to the pain of my past, present, and future, feeling my face wipe clean of all emotion. Feeling my heart do just the same.

I break from his gaze, getting back to the task at hand—quick, efficient stitches. I tie off the thread, then use my snips to cut it free before I shove forward a step, pressing close enough to Vanth's crotch that I feel his raging manhood hard against my thigh.

His eyes widen with a flash of excitement.

I settle the sharp tip of my snips against his swollen cock, and he sucks a breath through bared teeth—a hiss of surprise that gives me too much satisfaction.

I put my lips to his ear, letting them coast his skin as I whisper, "How about this ..."

I push a little harder.

Dig a little *deeper*.

"You keep your slithering fingers to yourself and I won't snip your dick off."

His hand drops like a rock, and I shove back, pocketing the scissors and flexing my fingers. I hold his gaze like it's some sort of conquest, reveling in the bead of sweat that darts down his temple.

"You think you're *special*?" he sneers.

"I think you're grieving, and I think you're drunk."

He laughs low—a boiling sound that would scald if I could feel. "And whose fault is that?"

Mine.
All mine.
Fissures crackle across my shield.

I reach into my pocket, retrieve a piece of night bark, and hold it out.

His eyes flick down. "What's that?"

"You need to sleep off that bottle of rum."

He shoves up and smacks the bark from my hand, spitting at my feet as he elbows past and weaves a wobbled path toward the stairs, the back of his shirt stained with dark blotches of blood. It's only once he's out of eyesight that I pull from the inky depths of my emotionless sea—posture crumbling.

My hands shake, knees threaten to buckle. It suddenly feels like the ship's caught in a wild swell, though I know that's not the case.

It's just my world that's tipping.

Churning.

Using the wall as a crutch, I reach behind my arm and pinch the softest piece of skin I can find.

Hard.

The bite of pain distracts my mind, anchoring me in place while Baze's parting words echo in my ears ...

You don't know what it's like out there, Orlaith.

He's never been more right.

At Castle Noir, I spent *years* learning the erratic shape of the halls—tumbling, bruising my knees until I'd pinpointed each gouged divot and uneven slab that could trip me up.

That raw, burdened castle became my home. My sanctuary.

My safe space.

Now ... I'm back to being blind.

Chapter 7
Orlaith

I set aside the bottle of rum and plant my hands on my lower back as I scan the hot, stuffy infirmary. The few lanterns that survived the roll cast the morose scene in an amber glow, creating a wistful illusion only disturbed by the odd deep, nasally snore. No footsteps overhead. No creaking sounds.

No agonized moans.

The men wounded badly enough to require heavy intervention are passed out either from the rum or the pain or the night bark.

"Go to bed, Orlaith." I look at Alon draped in the wobbly chair at the end of the room. He rubs his eyes, mouth cranking wide, wrestling his next words through a yawn. "We've done what we can for now."

I thread my hand around the back of my neck to knead the stiff muscles there. "I doubt I'll be able to switch off while the ship's still taking on water."

"The hole's been fixed." The gruff words batter me from behind, and I spin to see Captain sponging his forehead with a cloth he then dunks in a pail of water. His chin is dusted in tawny stubble, the undersides of his eyes bruised from lack of sleep.

"We've also fixed the sails best we could, but we can't go anywhere until the wind gets up," he says, crouching by the med box and frowning at its contents. He splashes something on his bleeding knuckles, stabs the bottle back into place, slams down the lid, and pushes to a stand.

"That was hemorrhoid tonic," Alon calls helpfully from the back of the room.

Captain just grunts and continues to stare me down. "Alon's right. Get some rest. It's late."

My thoughts are lured to the crow's nest—to the way Gage's blood puddled around my fingers—my stare tugged to the floor by this anchor of guilt I can't seem to shake.

Rest ...

Chances of that are slim.

With a nod, I flip the blood-splotched cloth off my shoulder and onto the end of a nearby cot, then turn for the stairs.

A big hand wraps around my elbow, and I look back, straight into the Captain's unveiled eyes, the lines around them deeper than they were this morning. "You saved my nephew's life today."

I put it in danger first.

"I've been told you didn't hesitate to dive in."

Don't thank me.

Please.

"He would've done the same if roles were reversed," I rasp, filling the void with words so he can't bask me in pleasantries I don't want to hear.

Don't deserve.

"Is he, ah ..."

"He's well."

My chest loosens a little, my sigh of relief hewn from somewhere deep and dark and bruised.

The corner of his mouth twitches. "Though he keeps asking about his cape."

Shit.

"And you."

I look away, swallowing the ache that has risen in my throat.

He grips my shoulder, his hand warm and heavy. "You did the right thing today."

"People are dead." The words come out flat.

"And sea serpents have thick *plated* skulls."

I look at him, frowning.

"Vanth was aiming for the head," he grinds out, "but that *boy* hasn't traveled the Shoaling Seas and seen one of their skulls up close—prized for their impenetrability. If he'd struck between the eyes, that bolt would've bounced right off, riled the animal, and we'd all be dead. Instead, it struck close enough to the heart that it's fair to assume you saved most of our lives today, not just Zane's."

I clear my throat.

The reproving stares of the crew won't burn like they did, but there is no surge of relief. Just more death on my hands.

He pats me on the back and weaves between the beds, checking his injured men. Like a thief in the night, I head for the stairs, rising from the dense humidity of the infirmary, though the smell of sweat and blood still plagues every breath. I doubt any amount of swabbing will lift the morbid veil that now seems to haunt the ship.

I walk onto an eerily silent deck, the static night clinging to my tacky skin. The topside lanterns must have burst, leaving only the smile of the moon to guide my path across the warped floorboards.

There's a heavy splash not far from the ship, and moonlight bounces off the glassy wrinkles.

Seems the sharks are still hanging around.

I give the prickling backs of my arms a brisk rub as I make for the aftermast, ignoring the sound of my howling stomach. The thought of breaking my fast without Zane feels more hollow than this hungry ache. It'll be worth it tomorrow when we share a meal together—a thought I cling to with aching fists, trying to ignore the tremble.

Beginning the steady incline up my ladder, I pull myself above the noxious smell of sunbaked blood, absorbing the sip of familiarity like the lifeline it is. Perhaps if I manage to fall asleep, I'll wake tomorrow and realize this day was just a nightmare.

I wrap my hand around the next rung, lifting myself up, and the notched piece of wood comes away with a splintered *snap* that mimics my heartstrings.

Shock snatches my voice as gravity grips me, and I plunge, arms flailing, yielding to the punishing pull.

Time seems to slow. Stretches so thin I study my nest cast in the moon's silver glow, stark against the black velvet backdrop.

It looks like Stony Stem ...

Such a strange thing to notice while I'm plummeting to my death.

I almost laugh, wondering why my fear has tucked tail in the corner while mania rears her wild head and gnashes her teeth at the smiling moon. Something that should probably concern me, but I can feel the floorboards rushing at my back.

I'm all out of beats.

My fingers tangle in my bucket rope, and my survival instinct has me gripping.

Hard.

Palm burning with the fire of an angry ember, I feel a painful pop blaze through my shoulder an instant before I collide with the deck.

Thwack.

I can't feel a thing.

Not my toes, fingers, heart ...

It's a peace that seems to hold its breath, as though death is wielding a scythe to my throat, deciding whether to slash.

Live or die? Live or die? Live or—

Pain strikes like hands gouging through my ribs with the force of their violent punch. They snatch my organs and squeeze.

Hard.

Mouth agape, I try to suck air down my too-tight throat.

I can't move. Can't breathe.

Can't scream for help.

Wild panic finally erupts as a shadow shifts across the smiling moon, and I watch the silhouette tip a bottle. Hear a full swallow, then a hissed release.

"Are you afraid, *witch?*"

Vanth.

My heart takes short, sharp punches at my battered ribs.

"*He* was. He was fucking petrified. Do you know how I know?" He crouches, bringing his face so close to mine that I can feel his stale breath hitting my cheek. "He hated the water. Ma couldn't bathe him as a child without listening to him scream." He pushes a lock of hair off my face and cocks his head to the side, voice cracking as he says, "Kavan died screaming, and you will, too."

My stomach rocks.

I pull the smallest breath—fuel for a pitiful, half-croaked whisper. "*Va—*"

He tips the bottle, filling my mouth with a deluge of rum that sprays the back of my throat.

I choke and sputter and heave.

"Are you not going to scream?" he drawls, tipping ...

Tipping ...

I rock my head, but he grabs my jaw and locks me in place beneath the blazing waterfall.

"Try harder, witch. *Scream!*"

A gurgling sound bubbles up my throat. A drowning plea.

He stops the spill, snatches my ankle in a vice-like grip, and drags me along the deck, my head smashing against a barrel.

The stars and the moon blur and sharpen.

Blur and sharpen.

Pressure builds, surging through my veins, hunting for freedom. A vile voice slithers against the underside of my skin, singing to me from the ugly depths of my scorched soul ...

Break it ...

I'm dragged up the stairs, head bouncing against the sharp steps, but the strikes of pain have nothing on the bulging weight inside my skull as all my ugly tries to spill.

Vanth drops my foot and fists the front of my shirt, lugging me up until I'm seated on the railing—the vast ocean stretched behind me like a hollow throat waiting to gulp.

"*Scream,*" he snarls.

All I can smell is rum and wrath. All I can see is Vanth's hollow eyes, his moonlit features ripped with rage.

Warmth dribbles from my nose.

My ears.

I wrap my legs around his waist while gouging his shirt and skin with clawed fingers, clambering for traction with my one responsive arm. He flings the bottle overboard, then uses the same cold hand to grip my throat.

He pulls me so close our noses crush together. "It'll come in those final moments. You'll beg me to put an arrow through your heart, but I won't." He drags his lips along my cheek and plants them on my ear. "I'll just stand there and watch them *chew.*"

He shoves.

The fabric of his shirt slips through my fingers as I plunge, spinning, hand reaching. I snag the lower rung of the railing, and my body whips against the side of the ship, knocking a strangled scream from my lungs.

There's scuffing, yelling, fleshy thuds that sound too far away. My sweat-slicked fingers yield a little more with each tight breath.

There's a loud splash from somewhere beneath me, and panic fires up my throat.

"*H-Help ...*"

My desperate sounds are too soft.

Too brittle.

My fingers give up one by one until the entire weight of my body hangs off two remaining digits ...

I slip.

My wrist is snatched in a hold firm enough to snap bone, though my stomach continues to dive as I'm reeled skyward to the blare of frantic voices. I'm hauled over the balustrade, pulled against a warm chest, and cradled like a child.

"I've got you."

Captain's rusty voice offers me a sense of ease.

"You're safe."

Safe.

That word hurts more than everything else. Reminds me of home—a different sort of safe that felt impenetrable ...

Darkness tugs me under.

CHAPTER 8
18 years ago
Baze

Moaning, she whips her head to the side, dashing a burst of black hair across the equally inky sheets, exposing the side of her petite face—her skin so pale it's almost translucent. Eyes closed, her pretty pink lips spill sharp moans, filling the poky room that's dense with the smell of sex, sweat, and spirits.

Her gossamer shift is bunched around her waist, the globes of her thick ass spread in my kneading hands, her cunt so silky smooth my balls tighten with every deep thrust.

"You like that, pretty girl?" I grind between tight breaths. "You like the way I fuck you?"

"*Yes* …" The word rips free with a keening wail, and she wriggles—pulling at the binds keeping her wrists bound behind her back. A string of sweet, garbled pleas tumble out of her painted lips. "Please untie me. I want to come."

When I don't oblige, she arches her spine a little more, rolling back to meet every brutal thrust, making her ass slam against my thighs.

I groan, wet my thumb, and dance it around the taut, pink, puckered ring that's so beautifully exposed. She hisses, and the mewl she makes when I fill her with the thick digit spears straight to my cock.

Her pussy clamps down around me—a fluttered warning that makes me snarl.

"Ah ah—" I pull out and slap her flushed entrance. "Not yet."

She whimpers, rocking back, spreading herself so much more—red, swollen, and glistening.

A gaping invitation.

I fist my cock as the door shoves open, rusted hinges creaking. A broad-shouldered man draped in black fills the entry.

The woman squeals, and I still. Hear him sniff. Sense his stare grating across the cooped and craggy surrounds.

Inviting himself in, he shuts the door and leans against the wall near the bedside table that's sporting a small stack of silver coins and a blazing candelabra—the only source of light in this two-bit room.

He knocks back his hood and stark, silver eyes attack me.

"High M-Mas—"

Kicking my hips forward, I snip the woman's words as I punch my iron length back into her warm, silky depths, groaning with every sunken inch.

Her high-pitched gasp is a mix of delirium and mortification, and she tries to edge across the rumpled sheets.

She doesn't get far—tugged back so her ass is nice and snug against my thighs. I set my hand between her shoulder blades and push her deep into the straw-stuffed mattress, watching her cheeks flare as red as her ravaged pussy. "No need to get up and bow, beautiful. You're already on your knees."

Rhordyn crosses his arms, stare unwavering, even as the woman watches him with a hungry, wide-eyed wonder that seems to ignite her wet, fluttering cunt.

She likes being watched.

Guess we'll give him a show. Payback for stalking in here without a single fucking knock.

I smirk, pull back, and shove deep.

Hold his crucifying stare.

"I thought I cut you off." His deep voice batters the sultry atmosphere.

My thoughts sway to the buffet bench pushed against the wall behind me; to the bottle of whiskey that's almost empty, unlike the empty tumbler beside it.

I don't bother to look guilty as I say, "Stole a silver candlestick on my way out the back door. Fetched a pretty price."

"And you couldn't think of anything else to spend it on but whiskey and whores?"

I shrug, glancing down, seeing my sweat-slicked abs tense with every brutal shove. "I'm not particularly creative," I hiss through clenched teeth.

"Certainly not when you don't try."

"On the contrary. I think I'm trying." I lean forward, lips brushing the shell of the woman's ear as I murmur, "Wouldn't you say?"

She releases a strangled moan.

With a low chuff that tastes like whiskey and bad decisions, I fist the sheer, black fabric of her shift, pulling her up until she's flush against me, bared for Rhordyn with smudged rouge and smoky eyes that are heavy hooded, brazenly suggestive. She holds his gaze even as he holds mine with a detached apathy that only spurs me on.

I pinch the frilly neckline, pulling it down, spilling her full breasts that bounce every time I thrust into her. With a coarse moan, she tips her head back into the crook of my neck as I knead the heavy mounds until her nipples are pebbled.

I'm not much of a tit man, but perhaps Rhordyn is. Perhaps he likes seeing her bound and fucked and hopeless—though I doubt it.

Perhaps that sort of depravity is only preserved for my particular brand of fucked up.

I trail my hand between her legs, using my fingers to spread her further as I shove my cock deep. I don't so much as graze her clit for a few hard thrusts, swirling my middle digit around her slick, pouty nub before her body locks up. Cunt tightening like a clenched fist, she releases a melody of short, high-pitched wails every time I hammer into her.

It's those sounds that knock me over my own edge and send a vicious, ravenous zap straight down the length of me.

I pull out, push her onto the mattress, and pump my release all over her bare, flushed ass, painting it in ropes of white.

I'm still coming down as the shame hits like a punch to the gut. That deep, disgusted sort that always makes me want to hurl.

Every fucking time.

I snatch my pants off the chipped bedpost and step into them, whipping them up and fastening the buttons before I roll the woman—can't remember her name, though I doubt I bothered to ask—onto her side.

She's smiling at me, her dreamy stare betraying only small slits of her sea-green eyes. I unbind her wrists, toss the length of rope on the bed, then dash the hair out of my face and spin toward the buffet lining the back wall.

"Your coin is on the nightstand," I mutter, uncorking the bottle with a brutal pop.

Shuffling sounds ensue—her gathering herself and slipping off the bed. The soft pad of her bare feet against the rough, wooden floorboards before the *tink* of coins being slid off the nightstand.

More shuffling, then, "High Master."

Her voice is more demure now that I'm not balls deep inside her, perhaps because she's come down from her own high and is now painfully aware of our audience. I don't doubt she's curtseying, though it seems a bit odd after he just watched her come all over my cock.

More hurried footsteps, then the door snicks shut.

Silence.

The sort that grates against your bones and makes your heart race.

I fill my glass with a glug of whiskey that empties the bottle, then toss it back with a sharp hiss as it bites a blazing trail down my throat.

I slam the glass back on the buffet. "What do you want, Rhordyn?"

"You don't want to wash your hands before we chat?"

My smile is wolfish. "She was pretty clean, actually."

He releases a low grunt. "I need you to come home."

Wearing a tight frown, I turn a little, passing him a sideways glance.

"Castle Noir," he clarifies, stare unwavering.

"Hard pass. You know I hate that fucking place."

Gripping the empty bottle by the neck, I stride toward the door, grab the brass handle, and pull it open. I step out into the dingy hallway that's lit like the rooms in this shithole—with only a few candelabras bolted to the walls, each with short, stumpy candles spilling long tears of wax over the edge of the drip pans.

I'm three steps down the runner that smells too damp not to be a health risk before Rhordyn's voice batters me from behind.

"I have a ward. A child no older than three. The only survivor of a Vruk attack that took her entire family."

The words bolt me in place. Bolt my heart to the back of its cage.

Ahead, one of the doors creaks open, and a woman pops her head out, eyes widening as she takes in the presence that's now an electric force at my back.

Her face blanches, and she shuts the door so fast I can already picture the look on Rhordyn's face before I even turn.

Deadly.

Destructive.

Like something is rooting beneath the surface of his skin, keening for release. His eyes are polished obsidian, stare stuck to the woman's door like he's trying to see through the grain.

I regret leaving the room without my dagger strapped to my calf.

I lift my hands. "I don't know what's happening, Rhor, but the people here are *good*."

"Get back in the room," he barks, and I do, corralled by him as he slams the door shut behind us. Then he's searching the free-standing wardrobe, punching through my sparse belongings before he stalks toward the back wall and yanks the window wide, filling the space with an icy blow that ruffles the frayed curtains.

I toss the empty bottle on the bed and reach for my top, fumbling with the buttons, stare stuck to the back of his head. "How did a *child* survive a Vruk attack?"

He doesn't answer, head poked out the window as he scans the street below that's lit by tree-tall lanterns, bathing this village in an illuminated safety net.

"*Rhor.*"

He slams the window closed, but continues searching through the frosted panes. "She's Aeshlian. Aravyn's child. She's ... got a black mark on her shoulder that doesn't look natural."

Light will bloom from sky and soil,
Skin tarnished by the brand of death ...

My knees buckle, hand whipping out to grip the bed post that feels too brittle as all the blood drains from my face.

Rhordyn spins, spearing me with a stare that roots through my insides. He must see the turmoil I'm grappling with silently—the need for acknowledgement. Because it can't be true.

It can't.

His grim silence, his terse nod—they flay me down the middle.

I shuffle back a step and fall onto the bed, half sitting. "How did you stumble upon the frayed thread that unraveled my entire species?"

"Fate."

The single word coupled with the look in his eyes is bone crushing, like deep rendered agony that's trying to break past the silver bars of his composure.

My heart sinks.

"You mean—"

"Yes."

A beat passes before he clears his throat, moving toward the upholstered chair in the corner of the room that's smudged with an abstract collection of stains. He unbuckles the sheath around his chest, resting his sword against the wall before he sits heavily—like a man who's got the weight of the world lumped upon his shoulders.

"None of this is her fault." He's looking at the floor when he says it, though that somehow makes the hit land harder.

"I know." The acknowledgment is shoved past the pit in my throat that won't fuck off. A swell of hurt sown from a thousand lost lives.

Some I knew. Loved. Didn't get near enough time with.

An entire species already struggling to claw itself back from the brink of extinction, decimated by the blow of Maars's chisel when he carved those words to stone. When he singled us out as the bearer of a single shadow seed that would call upon the end of the world.

He's to blame.

The *Gods* are to blame.

I stand and cast my gaze out the window toward the flaming street lights, threading my fingers together behind my head. I draw a breath, hold it in my cheeks, and blow it out. "Who else knows?"

"About the mark?"

"Yes."

"Mersi. That's it."

I drop my hands and look at him. "The cook?"

His head is still hung between his shoulders, gaze punched at the floor. "Correct. She's caring for the child."

"Then why do you need me?"

"*I* don't." He spears me with a stare. "*She* does."

I frown. "I don't understand. You just said—"

"According to Mersi, the girl's not well. She refuses to step into the sun, even though I have her housed in the northern tower that gets the most of it. She hides. She won't leave the castle walls or even touch the grass." He pauses. "She's slowly destroying herself."

The words are all sharp edges honed enough to hack me open.

I release a shuddered breath as realization hits. "You want me to—"

"Lend her your light, yes. I refuse to be involved. At all. But *you* can be the family she lost and coax her back into the sun. Give her a chance at life. "

I look down at my feet and choke on the swell of self-disgust. That feeling that I am not worthy enough for anyone but my feasting demons. "I have very little to give, Rhordyn. You know that."

All too well.

He doesn't answer, but his silence roars.

I clear my throat, glance around the room. "Look at this," I say, dashing my hand at the bed. Myself. "Look at *me*."

"I am."

I sigh deep, pace ... stop. Peer out the window again, then squeeze my eyes shut. Finally, I nod—small and slow and so fucking self-serving it makes me sick. "Fine. I'll do it."

A beat of silence, as if he were expecting a different answer. "There will be rules. She won't be exposed to any of this shit," he says, gesturing around the space.

"Got it."

"Good." He shoves to his feet, snatches his sword, and straps the sheath across his chest. "Gather your stuff. I'll wait for you downstairs." Then he's stalking toward the door in a flutter of hardy black.

"What sort of life am I giving her, Rhordyn?" He pauses with his hand wrapped around the doorknob, swallowing it whole. "You and I both know where this ends."

The air stiffens so much it's hard to pull breath. When he looks at me over his shoulder, there's war in his eyes.

Cold, bloody, brutal war.

"Every year, every hour, every *breath* ... it's something."

He jerks the door open and stalks out, slamming it shut behind him.

Chapter 9
Orlaith

Another fetid roar shreds the air, and my brother jolts in my arms. Heavy footfalls rattle the ground, vibrating the lemon-yellow tablecloth we're shielded under in a knot of shivering limbs.

"They're getting closer ..." His fear-spiked whisper sends liquid fire searing through my veins.

"It's okay," I coast my fingers through his hair. "I'll look after you."

Always.

His grip around my middle tightens.

Another roar, and deep whuffing sounds grow louder ... *louder,* a different, more destructive force pumping through me.

I refuse to watch him die again.

"Stay right here," I murmur, planting a kiss on his forehead. I untangle from him, tuck him beside the rock wall the table is pushed against, offer a warm smile that brightens his tear-filled eyes, then turn and shove past the tablecloth.

Unfurling, I squint against the midday glare.

Lush trees cast a dappled shadow on the forest glade that's dusted with lemon-yellow flowers and fluffy fronds of grass swaying in the wind. But the seven slate gray Vruks prowling toward us muddies the view, their snarling maws dripping evidence of their hunger.

Astute, midnight eyes bounce between me and the table strewn with pots of paint.

We came here to paint in the sun.

They came here to kill.

No more.

Sizzling ire roots around the underside of my skin, searching for weak spots in my shell.

I stalk forward.

"You can't have him."

They snap at the air and prowl closer—spines arched and lips rolled back. Talons punch free from their paws.

Part of me wants to fold into a screaming ball at the sight, but that part is weak.

It dies a little every time I watch my brother die.

I grip the necklace caught around my throat like a noose. "You can't have him." I growl, voice laced with something dark and harrowing. A cruel smile kicks up the corner of my mouth.

My arm jerks down, snapping the chain.

The necklace falls from my fingers and thuds to the ground.

Chaos explodes, vile and merciless.

A burst of black vines lash from the cracks in my porcelain skin. The noxious scribble scalds and severs—wild and cutthroat.

Murderous.

Snarls turn to whines that are music to my ears.

The beasts tuck tail and run, but they don't get far.

They can't have him.

The words repeat until I'm cold and empty, and the ugly snips off, leaving tender skin and a charred heart devoid of regret as I scan the sea of fleshy bits that reek of scorched death. The grass is burnt back to smoking nubs, the lemon-yellow flowers ash on the wind.

It's all dead. Every last green bit as far as the eye can see ... gone.

There's a crackle of burning wood behind me, and I spin, breath catching when I see the table.

Afire.

The cloth is ash, the pictures gone, the paints sizzling puddles of color dripping off the sides.

I dash forward and grip a blazing wooden leg. The flesh on my palm melts as I flip the table, littering the air with a wake of fiery spindrift.

My knees hit the ground.

A choked sound rips from somewhere deep at the sight of my brother strewn across the dirt ...

Unmoving.

Skin bubbled and blistered.

His wide, unseeing eyes reflect the vast scope of my desolation. Reflect me—beautiful, dazzling death.

I drop my face into bloodied hands and scream.

My eyes spring wide, the howl from my dream alive in my sandpaper throat.

I focus on the low ceiling—on the lantern hung from it, drenching me in yellow light.

Lemon-yellow flowers.

Yellow tablecloth.

The air is thick and hot to match the sizzling pressure in my head, pecking at my temples like an angry, bone-stripping bird.

My frantic gaze bounces over four wooden walls, one pocked with a small window—a frame for the gloomy night outside that fails to make the room feel less cooped.

I realize my clenched fist is wrapped around my pendant, the chain so taut against the back of my neck I'm surprised the clasp hasn't popped. I drop it, wipe the wetness dripping from my nose, pulling my bandaged hand back to inspect it ...

Blood.

Fuck.

I push up from the cot—

Crushing pain explodes down my arm, hazing my vision and ripping a wail from my dried lips as it all comes crashing back.

The fall; Vanth emptying his bottle of rum into the back of my throat; the way his warm flesh gathered beneath my nails; his vacant, moonlit eyes the moment before he shoved me overboard.

I groan.

Breathing through the pain, I flip the blanket off my legs with my good arm, then cradle my other at the elbow—every inhale waging war against my unhinged shoulder.

I think it's dislocated. Guess Alon didn't realize.

Crap.

More blood dribbles from my nose as I hang my feet off the side of the cot.

I have to get out of this closed-in cabin.

I rock to my feet, wobble, vision splitting. Another wave of brain-bloating pressure threatens to bring me to my knees, and I stumble toward the door, grip the handle.

Twist.

It doesn't budge.

"Fuck!" Eyes squeezed shut, I rest my forehead against the grain. *"Fuck, fuck, fuck!"*

I can't kick and scream and demand to be released without causing a scene.

Drip.

Drip.

Drip.

My eyes pop open, and I take in the small puddle of red blossoming on the ground, reflecting the bold, yellow lantern light—

The vision of my brother's wide-open stare hacks at me, and a whimper bubbles up my raw throat.

I have to get out.

I pull my hairpin free from my hair, loosening my mane in a drop of matted tangles as I delve the long, sharp piece of metal into the lock, close my eyes, and rest my ear against the door.

Dig ... Flick ... Twist ...

There's a dull clunk, and I release a breath, pulling my ear from the wood now stamped in blood. With another low curse, I pocket my pin and yank the door wide, stumbling down the stuffy hall lit by a single lantern.

Despite the still, silent sea, my steps are slow and unsteady. I'm forced to use a closed door as a crutch to catch my breath, taking another swipe at the drip from my chin.

A few more paces, and my brain bloats so much I slam my hand against the wall and suck a sharp breath through my teeth, folding forward, eyes squeezed shut ...

I just have to get to the nest before I pass out.

The squeaking sound of a door opening echoes around me, and I look up to see a bleary-eyed sailor shove his head out from one of the dorms—hair mussed and chest bare.

He takes me in, eyes widening as he mutters a curse. "Someone fetch the Captain!"

I groan, kick myself forward again, and amble past, throwing him a side-eye.

Snitch.

By the time I'm hobbling across the upper deck, I'm sweating through my shirt, each humid breath more punishment than reprieve, reeling me toward the inky promise of unconsciousness.

Head resting against the cool grain of the aftermast, I struggle to gather the strength to move again.

Visions of Baze flash on the underside of my lids—of the

way he'd punish me whenever I got tired and lazy at the end of a sparring session and failed to protect my vulnerabilities.

Of course he'd haunt me now.

Snarling, I set my foot on the ladder, grip hold of the rung with my bandaged hand, and heave myself up. A fractured cry rips free, but I stamp my lips together and snip it off.

Always shield your weakness.

Bolts of pain ravage me as I battle the rungs, teeth gritted, stare stabbed through the velvet night. My bad arm is useless, so I keep it tucked close to my abdomen, using my chin as a hook whenever I need to alternate my grip.

I'm halfway up when heavy footsteps assault the deck, but I don't look down when the Captain bellows for me to stop.

I just have to make it to the nest.

The scuff of boots ascending the ladder trails me as another wave of pressure strikes.

My mouth pops open in a silent scream.

I quicken my pace, bruising the underside of my chin while hot tears dash down my cheeks. But I keep going. Keep pushing. Refuse to look down or up, knowing that if I do, my composure will shatter.

I stretch past the snapped rung, rasping a warning between gasping heaves, "Broken ... rung. Don't ... fall."

"Orlaith, *stop.*"

Captain's gruff voice chases me, strained with concern.

The backs of my eyes sting as I clench my teeth and climb faster.

Faster.

It's another ten rungs of gut-twisting nerves before I reach the hatch, already open, and haul myself onto the landing, catching a glimpse of Captain reaching past the broken rung, looking straight at me.

He mutters a curse.

I swing the lid shut and latch the lock, falling against my damp sack still tethered to the rails, heart beating me up from the inside.

Growling, Captain pummels the hatch. "Open the damn thing, Orlaith. Now!"

I stare at the loose loops of twine strung around the aftermast.

The jars—my clippings—they're gone.

My wisteria ...

Throat aching, I rub the twine between my fingers and fail to swallow the hurt. Another piece of home ripped from my grasp, like I'm deconstructing piece by piece. What's going to be left once I'm done falling apart?

More blows rattle the hatch.

"Leave me alone!"

Sliding atop the door, I loosen the knot on my bag, then retrieve my small pickaxe from down the back of my pants. I dig through my belongings one-handed, finding Rhordyn's pillow slip and the cheesecloth parcel containing my caspun.

Captain keeps hitting the door, bellowing gruff, leaden words overshadowed by the tumult beneath my skin.

Stuffing my face against the silk, I draw my lungs full of the muddied dregs of *him*.

But one breath isn't enough.

I pull deep, hungry breaths—the slip hugged close to my chest as I rock, white-knuckling my caspun in a fist that can't shake its tremble.

"I'm fine," I lie to myself, imagining I'm punched through the clouds, surrounded by plants and rocks and paints. Imagining Rhordyn's body wrapped around me, twisting me up in the ways I hate to love.

Such a poisonous thought.

I claw the material, tip to my side, and close my eyes, ignoring the pain in my shoulder and the hollow ache in my chest. Ignoring the fist pounding on the wood an inch from my head as I give myself to the hurt rioting beneath my mask and savor every scalding lash like the penance it is.

Drip.

Drip.

Drip.

"I'm fine ..."

Another lie to stitch my skin.

Chapter 10
Orlaith

My world is rocking back and forth with a creaky swing, a chill wind nipping at my cheek. I open my eyes, watching the patchwork sail whip against a background of fluffy, white clouds clotting the sky like a sponge painting. A string of salt-crusted hair blows across my face, tickling my nose, and I lift my hand to push it away—

Big mistake.

A wail rips free as a bolt of pain tears through my shoulder.

Eyes squeezed shut, I roll to the side, hissing through the echo of hurt that bites into me with every thud of my heart. I unfasten the top two buttons of my shirt and ease it down my arm, exposing a gnarly bulge now protruding from the round of my shoulder.

All the breath puffs out of me.

Definitely dislocated. Looks just like diagrams I've seen in medis books in Spines.

I let my hand fall, head tipping as I close my eyes, sweat

dappling my brow despite the cool stir of wind that seems to have woken the sea.

If I call for Alon, they'll drag me down to that small, poky room. Probably lock me out of the nest for good.

I have to pop it back in myself.
Somehow.

Reinspecting the disjointed protrusion, movement catches my eye, dragging it between the gaps in the railing and out across the rolling ocean.

My next breath is snipped mid pull, frantic gaze hopping from one navy sail to another …

"Fuck."

A hive of ships surrounds us—some closer, others so far away it's hard to make out the finer details.

I thought Cainon was being dramatic, but he brought an entire *fleet*. Too many ships to be considered a courtesy hand over as trade for my hand.

My heart sinks.

What the hell have I gotten myself into?

I drop my stare to the first of many rowboats shoving through the choppy ocean; to the statuesque man perched at the nose of it, wheaten hair pulled back, tan skin struck by the sun.

Sky-blue eyes pinned to me.

My breath hitches.

Something inside me squirms, the rest of me paralyzed by a suffocating string of tension coiling around my limbs and body.

Cainon, High Master of the Southern Territory of Bahari.
My promised.

His mouth cuts a hard line, stare unwavering as the two

men working the oars ferry him closer, every pull adding another horse to the galloping herd in my chest. They dock against the ship, rope ladders thrown overboard by grim-faced crewmen. Cainon finally breaks his stare to climb up the edge, and my posture crumbles.

I tip onto my back and stare at the sky, then down at the cupla shackling my wrist—gold accents catching the sun and tossing it back at me.

The fierce sledge of my heart accelerates.

Shit.

I edge up, hissing a pained breath as I cradle my arm, shuffle forward, and shove my head through a gap in the spindles, my hair falling heavy around my face.

Cainon eases over the handrail and steps aboard.

The crew are standing at attention in a long line, white bandages starkly contrasting their weather-beaten skin. Cainon stops before our stoic captain, and I watch them converse.

Crane to listen.

The thieving sea breeze pockets their words before they can make it to me.

Cainon looks up the mast, catching my eye and breath in the same motion. My stomach swirls as he breaks away, stalks toward my ladder, then grabs hold of the bottom rung and yells, "Open the hatch, Orlaith. I'm coming up."

I glance across his bobbing fleet, back to the top of his head. "The lock's rusted shut. Might take me a while to chip it open. I'll just meet you there."

He pauses, skewering me with a stern gaze. "Someone bring me an axe!"

The bellowed words slice. Hack.

Slay.

Blood drains from my face, leaving me dizzy and light-headed, and I shake my head as a memory burns to the forefront of my mind ...

A big man walks toward me and the boy. His head is shiny, and there's one of those wood-cutting things hanging from his hand. I think it's called an axe.

Why is there red stuff dripping from it?

My entire body locks, that *thing* inside me arching like a coil of snakes ready to strike.

"Not an axe ..." I shake my head, wide eyes screaming the words my mouth can only whisper.

Please.

"Open the hatch!"

I jolt back and heave a violent breath, battling the bolt with trembling hands. I swing it open and bunch myself into a pain-riddled ball for far too long before I register Rhordyn's pillow slip still crushed against my chest, my small parcel of caspun sitting beside me on floorboards blotted with my blood.

All my weaknesses aired for him to see like the open wounds they are.

I stuff *him* and the bulb in my sack for safekeeping, fingers brushing the pommel of a weapon I'd rather pretend wasn't there. My hand jerks back, but I don't have time to knot the drawstring before Cainon pushes halfway through the opening.

We both still, his scrutiny tracking over my face like a razor blade, and I swear his pupils swell.

"Orlaith—"

"Cainon."

"Why is there blood on your face?"

My bandaged hand whips up to the crust caked along my upper lip. "Just a nosebleed," I croak.

His shrewd gaze darts to my ear.

"The warm weather brings them on," I'm quick to add, and his eyebrows lift the slightest amount.

Rhordyn's right. I need to lie better.

Cainon clears his throat and climbs onto the landing, scanning the mural I carved into the floorboards.

The urge to stretch and smother it gnaws at me.

He reaches for my sack. "Do you have any fresh water in there?"

I push in front of his hand, making my shoulder blaze. "Yes." Chewing on a wince, I dig through my contents. "I'll find it."

His stare tracks my movements, leaving a prickly trail on my arm, up the side of my face. I pull the waterskin free and hand it over.

Taking it, his attention flicks to my injured hand. "What happened?"

"Captain didn't tell you?"

He pulls a square of blue cloth from his pocket and dampens it with a tip of water. "I want to hear it from your lips."

Of course.

"I fell. Got a bad case of rope burn."

"That's not the answer I'm looking for, Orlaith."

I bite my tongue so hard it bleeds. If he expects me to give him a step by step on just how twisted his guard became during the short time we spent together, he'll be sorely disappointed. He'll receive no ammunition from me.

I can't hold Vanth's actions against him—not when I've bathed in the same oily muck his sanity slipped on before he shoved me off the railing.

Heartbreak can cripple the body. The mind.

It has no mercy.

My own grief has punched its teeth into flesh and silenced heartbeats. And there's something slithering inside—a coy awareness that hisses its truth like a snake.

I'd do it again.

Cainon crouches, setting down the skin and the square of dampened material. With a deep sigh, his eyes flick up, watching me from beneath thick, golden lashes. "Your right shoulder is hanging lower than your left."

"It's fine—"

Before I have a chance to blink, he has me gripped by the bicep, his other hand firm against my injured shoulder. Then he's wrenching my arm in such a way I'm certain he's tearing it free.

An acute *pop* echoes through my bones, and I scream—howling through my ripped throat.

"I forgot ... how much of an ... asshole ... you are," I bite between sharp breaths, sinking into the flood of relief that swiftly follows.

He grabs my other hand and guides it around to support my elbow. "Would you have preferred I warn you, petal?"

I snarl as he begins unbuttoning his shirt, revealing well-defined muscles that look like chiseled sandstone, unmarred aside from a two-inch scar almost directly above his heart. Hard to appreciate the view through my red-veiled vision.

He didn't even give me something to bite down on, the ass.

He threads his shirt under my injured arm before I slap his hands away. "I've got it," I mutter, using my chin and some well-practiced finger work to forge the shirt into a makeshift sling. Perks of relying on one for the first few days after I snapped my thumb.

I look up to see Cainon perched on his heels like one of the Rouste Dune Cats I've seen in picture books—huge, regal, slick gold fur, and statue still.

There's a world of calculating astuteness behind those purple-flecked, cerulean orbs.

"I see you've grown some spine since I saw you last."

My head snaps back.

I've grown nothing. All I've done is lose.

"You can leave."

He pops a brow. "You're dismissing me? From my own ship?"

"Yes." I shuffle toward the mast, set my back against it, and tip my head, casting my gaze on the finger-painting sky riddled with circling gulls. "Close the hatch on your way out."

A long moment passes before he clears his throat, plucks the damp cloth from the floor, and moves so close I can feel his static. "Like it or not," he murmurs, breath hot on my face as he dabs my upper lip, "you can't stay here."

"Why not?"

"Because I'm going to sink this ship."

My heart flips, breath catching as I look straight into the merciless clutch of his sky-blue stare. "You're kidding."

"Dead serious. The injured crewmen are being hoisted down to the rowboats as we speak."

I bat his hand away and level my stare. "Can't you just ... fix it?"

He looks at the floorboards, then cracks off a loose splinter of wood, gouging a dent in one of my doodles. "Broken things can't always be fixed. Unfortunately."

Something inside me recoils.

"I'd rather spend my resources on more important things." He pockets the splintered token. "Chin up."

Right.

Tipping my head, I cast my gaze skyward again, until Cainon dabs at the bruised peak of my chin. I flinch, but he steadies my face and continues his ministrations—swiping the sharp line of my jaw to the lobe of my ear, down the length of my throat. "You have a very beautiful neck."

He's never seen my neck. My face.

The real me.

"Now you return with a compliment. That's how this courting thing goes."

"You're not courting me."

"I am."

"Then you're off to a shit start."

There's a brief stretch of silence while he swipes back up my throat, across to my other ear. "I take it you're not impressed by my fleet."

"Not unless it's going straight to Ocruth," I deadpan, and his hand pauses.

I drop my gaze, watching from beneath lowered lids as his face dawns with stark realization.

"You were listening ..."

To his and Rhordyn's very *private* conversation.

"Guilty," I admit, my voice entirely void of it.

"Interesting ..."

"So? Are they going straight to Ocruth?"

Wind whips my hair into a flaxen scribble between us while he watches me, eyes coasting back and forth in smooth, calculating paths. "There's a storm coming from the north—"

"And these ships were built to withstand rough weather. Firsthand witness," I say, raising my bandaged hand. "They self-correct."

"—What we call a *ship smasher*," he continues, ignoring my negation. "It's five days to a safe port southward. Weeks to Ocruth with kickback from the swell."

"So you're turning back around."

A long pause, then, "Correct. Straight back to the capital."

Something cold and acidic spills through me, settling deep.

I swallow, stab my stare skyward, and watch the gulls churn. "Then no," I mutter. "I'm not impressed by your fleet."

He grips my chin and tugs my face down with commanding poise, snatching my stare, scattering my heartbeats. "That's not very nice. It came all this way to see you."

"For being a *few days late*."

"You're a *week* late. And I did warn you, so no point being pissed about it."

My eyes widen. "I thought you were *joking*."

"Why would I joke about such a thing?"

I swear, he looks genuinely baffled.

Sighing, I rip my chin away and tip my head against the mast, suddenly more tired than I've been in days. "You're exhausting," I mutter, closing my eyes. "Just ... let me go down with the ship."

That sounds peaceful.

"Not an option, I'm afraid." I can tell by the strain in his voice that he's pushing to his feet. "Let me help you up."

Internally, I groan.

Prying my eyes open, I rock to the side, using my bandaged hand to push myself to a wobbly stand. Cainon's hand snakes around my side to steady me, but I shove away, grabbing hold of the handrail. Feeling his stare blaze across the side of my face, I watch a slew of rowboats pull away from the ship—piled full of injured crewmen.

"You're far more ... what's the word ... *hostile* than normal."

When I don't respond, he kneels and gets to work on the rope securing my sack to the mast.

A storm bulges in my chest as I anticipate him digging through its contents ...

Dreading what he'll find.

If I leap at it now, it'll only draw more attention.

I internally catalog its inventory while he battles the series of knots, preparing excuses to toss at him like boulders. Hard to come up with one for the talon. Or the pillow slip. Or the parcel of shit-shrooms I never got the chance to pottle.

Crap.

The sack falls from the mast, and he grips the ties, pulling them tight enough to strangle someone, then twists the tails into a tidy bow while I almost vomit with relief.

"Anything breakable in here?" he asks, waving it at me.

"Depends what you classify as—"

He tosses it over the balustrade, and I watch in stunned silence as it plunges to the deck below and lands with a heavy thud.

I feel that sound in my gut.

Staring down at it, I finally manage to sift some words from the coals of my fiery rage. "What the *hell* is wrong with you?"

"More than you could possibly imagine," he mutters.

A vast assumption. He has no idea how broad my scope is for the various levels of fucked up.

"Come here."

My gaze slides to his open arms and very bare, very smooth, sun-kissed chest.

"In your dreams."

He flashes me a wicked grin. "Oh, Orlaith. My dreams are far more devious than that, I assure you."

My cheeks flare with prickly heat, mind scrambling.

He pops a brow, giving me a come-hither gesture that sends my foot sliding back.

"No," I blurt. "Not happening."

"*No?*"

"I'm surprised you're not better acquainted with the word."

His eyes lose their spark of amusement. "You can climb down on your own, can you?"

Probably not.

I lift my chin. "Absolutely."

He sighs, ignoring my yowling protests as he scoops

me up with ease and tucks me against his muscular chest. "Stop wriggling and wrap your arms and legs around me."

Averse to the idea of making more of a scene, I clamp my legs around his trim waist, thread my arm around his neck, and stab my stare across the sea now littered with rowboats.

"Unless you want to fall again, I suggest you lean closer and tighten those pretty thighs."

"I'll tighten them around your neck," I mutter, and he chokes out a laugh.

"Once we're coupled," he says, maneuvering us through the hatch, "I'll hold you to that."

Realization strikes a match to my face, and I'm silently begging he drop me now so I can plummet to a swift death.

Instead, he confidently scales the ladder, my injured arm tucked between us the only barrier preventing our bodies from being flush—something that heats my skin but rattles my soul.

Cheeks burning, I watch the small boats drift and disperse amongst the rest of the fleet, the men stealing peeks over their shoulders at me clinging to their High Master, being pulled from the perch I stubbornly set myself in.

"This is humiliating."

"So is waiting *days* with bated breath for your promised to dock at her new home, to no avail."

Bated breath, my ass.

I don't know much about managing a fleet, but I doubt he could prepare one on such short notice. He probably put the order in the moment he returned. Hell, he probably sent a mail sprite before he even left Castle Noir.

I'm forced to admit there may be some weight to Rhordyn's condemning observations ...

Cainon has ambition.

"Tuck your head under my chin," he gripes. "I'm getting a kink and not the fun sort."

I do as he asks, refusing to take his verbal bait. Refusing to take *any* enjoyment from having my cheek pressed against his chest—no doubt his intention.

He reaches the bottom and steps off, one hand weaving around to support the underside of my thigh.

My breath hitches. "I can walk, Cainon."

"Clever girl," he muses, and bends to retrieve my sack before striding to the rail and tossing it.

I twist in time to watch it thunk into the hollow of one of the three remaining rowboats still tethered to the ship's side, right beside an austere sailor's booted foot.

"I wish you'd stop throwing my shit around," I mutter.

"*Out,*" Cainon bellows, and the two sailors clamber into another dinghy already stuffed with five other men. He turns as Captain approaches. "Is the ship clear?"

"He's the last," Captain says, gesturing toward an injured sailor being hoisted off the side.

"Good."

Captain turns to bellow down at the crew, not even glancing my way, and a splinter of guilt lodges itself deep in my chest.

I've disappointed him.

Cainon tosses his leg over the rail, maneuvering us down the long, wobbly rope ladder flush with the ship's side. I'm forced to tighten my grip around his neck, drenched in the scent of citrus and salt.

"Getting quite cozy there." He drops into the boat's hollow, somehow managing to maintain his balance as it bucks so furiously it scrapes against the ship. "Seems a shame to part ways now. Perhaps you can sit in my lap while I row?"

"I'd rather be tossed over the edge," I murmur, and he laughs, setting me on the back seat that's splashed with sea water.

He's still chuckling as he readjusts my makeshift sling while I scan the resting fleet blotting the horizon—loose blue sails flapping in the wind.

His laughter stops abruptly.

"Who gave you this?"

My gaze drops to Cainon's fingers pinched around the black jewel that must have slipped free from my shirt, Kai's conch resting beside it.

My heart stops.

I snatch it back and tuck the precious pendants under my collar.

His eyes narrow, darkening. "Who gave it to you, Orlaith?"

I look him square in the eye. "I've had it since I was small."

Not a lie. Not the truth he was looking for, either, but if I tell him it was a gift from Rhordyn, he'll justifiably insist I take it off.

Not an option.

"Since you were small," Cain mutters, stare dragging across my Ocruth garb as though he's counting each and every black fiber and stacking them against my character. "Hmm."

He reaches past, unties the rope tethering us to the ship, then takes his place in the seat before me. Strangling the oars, he digs the paddles deep, pulling us away from the ship now void of life.

His muscles bulge and strain, features impassive, stare stuck to my face.

Stab, pull.

Stab, pull.

Stab, pull.

Wind grapples my hair, twisting it into messier knots, the odd sprinkle of foam flicking up from the nose of the boat and hitting me in the face.

Cainon's gaze doesn't drift. He barely blinks. All the while, Rhordyn's pendant burns a phantom brand against my skin.

You can run off and tie yourself to your pretty High Master, but I'll hunt you to the four corners of the continent. Not because I want to, but because I can't fucking help myself.

A shiver rakes through me ...

Growing uncomfortable under the weight of Cainon's perusal, I drift my stare beyond him to a small rowboat, a mere speck compared to the giant ships swaying with the sea's beat. It appears to be bobbing toward us—boasting a single sailor with hair the color of corn.

When we finally cross paths, the man's appearance strikes me.

He has none of that Bahari glow I've become accustomed

to, his skin sallow, eyes sapped of life, expression void of emotion. There's a lesion on his hand that's weepy and red.

Frowning, I watch him over my shoulder, the distance between us expanding with every powerful pull of Cainon's oars, but the man just keeps rowing toward the ship we came from.

He docks against the side, then scales the ladder.

"Why is he—"

"You should have come with me when I left."

Cainon's words jar me, and I spin, looking into his bold blue eyes. He looks so much larger outside of Rhordyn's castle, like he's shed some sort of skin of his own. Or perhaps it was Rhordyn's dominating presence that cast Cainon in a crushing shadow.

"You said it was okay for me to come on a separate ship."

"A mistake that almost cost your life. I underestimated how little Rhordyn taught you about the outside world," he dredges out. "He may have saved your life when you were a child, but he's failed you every moment since."

I can't deny it, but I'm no damsel. Not anymore.

Never again.

"You're not giving me enough credit."

"You almost *died*. You might still, should your hand become infected."

I don't tell him I have enough herbs in my sack to disinfect an army's worth of wounds for fear of drawing attention to its illicit contents.

Straightening my spine, I watch a dinghy being hoisted onto the deck of a larger vessel. Silence stretches, dented by sloshing waves and the clunk of the oars rotating in their rungs every time Cainon stabs and pulls.

Stabs and pulls.

"Tell me, is there a reason you're still dressed in Ocruth garb?"

I catch his stare.

Hold it.

"I like black," I answer simply, because there's no easy way to say I'm all caustic blackness on the inside. That it feels fitting to wear it on the out.

I'm not here to fit in.

I don't.

I *am* here to make peace with the mountain of death lumped inside me; with all those condemning stares that watched me from the wall in Whispers.

I'm doing this for the ships. So Rhordyn and Zali have the vessels they require to sail the Shoaling Seas and work their way into Fryst through the Northern Territory's back door. So they can cork the spill of Vruks at the alleged core and put a stop to the devastating raids shredding through the continent.

I'm doing this so they can *save* lives.

His gaze flicks to my cupla, then over my garb again. "The crew don't see you as one of us. Which means they don't see you as *mine*."

"I don't belong to you," I snap so fast I barely register the words passing my lips. "I don't belong to anyone."

"Perhaps, but you *are* expected to play the part. You're a soon-to-be High Mistress. Like it or not, sacrifice comes with the title."

"What is that supposed to—"

An ear-splitting explosion rips across the ocean, and I whirl, seeing the ship we just came from riddled with writhing flames, vomiting a cloud of smoke and ash as the vessel is violently demolished.

"Who—" I swallow past the lump in my throat. "Who lit the fuse?"

A harsh blow of wind breathes boisterous life into the fire and batters me with the smell of burning flesh.

Something inside me withers.

I can't breathe. Can't speak.

All I can do is stare.

"The man you just saw traveled aboard one of the other ships." I spin, flayed by Cainon's cutthroat perusal. "He came down with the Blight two days ago. I couldn't risk the spread."

Another explosion erupts from the south, rippling across the waves, and I gape in wide-eyed horror as a second ship flares like a torch. Screams erupt, men caught in the clutches of billowing flames as they dive off the side—a charred feast for the waiting predators.

Couldn't risk the spread ...

A dense, gray cloud muddies the sky and blots out the sun, and I blink, feeling Cainon's perusal track the tear that darts down my cheek.

One by one, men fall to the flames or the sharks, their screams snipping out like blown candles. It's only once I've watched the bubbling water swallow the vessel that I look to my promised.

Stab, pull.

Stab, pull.

His eyes are vacant as he drops a word on my chest that somehow weighs more than my heavy, aching soul ...

"Sacrifices."

Chapter 11
Cainon

Fuck.

Pulling the door shut, I glance at Iven approaching down the hallway, hand dragging along the gold-brushed handrail to steady him against the swell, the other balancing a gilded tray topped with a large cloche.

He tips his head when he draws close. "The meal you requested, High Master."

I lift the lid, revealing a bowl of steamed trout in a milky broth, crusty bread, and a stumpy chalice of sea-greens. I break off a fleshy piece of citrus-and-salt-spiced fish that melts in my mouth, but it does nothing to make me feel even the least bit satisfied.

"Toss it to the gulls," I mutter, stamping the cloche on the immaculate feast.

"All of it?"

"I've lost my appetite."

Iven's round, ruddy cheeks lose their pallor, eyes darting to the door behind me and back again. "She's ... not hungry, sire?"

"Apparently not. She also said she'd rather eat with the rats than share a meal with me right now," I say through a stencil smile.

I stalk past, shoving through the door that leads to the upper deck.

The breeze attempts to corral me the moment I step outside—a sharp chill pushing from the North. It whines and whips at the loose sail as a heavy, gray cloud shoves in front of the sun, casting the scene in a solemn shroud to fit my fucking mood.

The air is charged, the swarming crew securing anything loose to the deck and preparing the ship for the worst. Something bumps against the side, and I scan the deluge of Bahari scraps littering the ocean.

I spot my quartermaster holding a spyglass to his eye as he inspects the roiling horizon.

"We need to leave," I yell, charging forward. "Now. I don't want to lose another ship to this shit show."

"Agreed." He slams the spyglass into its holster. "I'll signal the others to raise sail." Brow arched, he digs through his leather satchel and hands me a rusty key. "She settled in?"

Pocketing the key, I make for the bow, muttering a curt, "No."

I retrieve the splinter from my pocket—the remaining sliver of wood from Captain Gunthar's sunken ship—and pinch the sharp tip between my teeth. I blaze down three flights of stairs, then a glum, poky hallway that leads to the stowage. A kid no older than ten is crouched by the door at the end of the hall, peering through the keyhole.

"I'm *sure* this area's out of bounds ..."

He spins, cheeks reddening. "High Master. I'm sorry, I—I didn't mean to pry."

"Zane, is it?"

His eyes widen. "You know my name?"

"Of course. You're Gunthar's nephew, correct?"

"Yes, sire." He drops into a bow, then straightens, chest puffed. "I'm good friends with the future High Mistress."

Well.

I remove the splinter from my mouth and crouch, meeting his gaze at eye level before flashing him a half smile. "That makes us *instant* friends."

His freckle-dusted cheeks swell with a grin, and he nods. "I'd like that very much."

"Good. Now," I say, roughing up his hair, "close the door at the top of the stairs on your way out."

"Yes, sire."

He takes off toward the stairwell, footsteps so silent I barely hear a thing, reminding me of Orlaith.

"Zane," I call, before he disappears from sight.

He stops and turns, dashing hair from his eyes. "Yes, High Master?"

I point the splinter at him. "No more snooping through this keyhole, you hear?"

I've never seen a more enthusiastic nod.

"Good boy. Off you go." I dismiss him with a flick of my hand, chewing the splinter while waiting for the door to snick shut at the top of the stairs. I jam the key in the hole and twist just as the ship creaks and groans—kicking forward.

The stowage door swings wide, and I step into the murk,

screwing up my nose at the smell of piss, body odor, vomit, and hard liquor. There's a lantern hanging off a hook by the door, and I turn its dial, spilling light throughout the room that's half packed with barrels and crates and casks of spirits stacked against the walls.

And in the middle of it all is Vanth—on his knees, stretched arms bound around the wrists by separate ropes attached to opposite ends of the ceiling.

A soiled strip of rag gags him, head lolled to the side and resting on his shoulder, right eye swollen and framed with a gnarly punch of purple skin.

I clear my throat.

Groaning, he sluggishly seeks me through a squint, then jerks to full awareness.

"Well," I say, dragging a crate across the floor and sitting before him. I pull the splinter from between my pursed lips and point it directly at his face. "You, sir, look mighty uncomfortable."

He nods, trying to shape words around the material clogging his mouth.

All that comes out is a garbled mess.

Retrieving the small blade strapped to my calf, I slide it between his cheek and the gag, watching him flinch as I cut it free.

"Better?"

He stretches his jaw before he speaks, the words coarse through his cracked lips. "Much. Thank you, High Master."

"Of course. Thirsty?"

His gaze shifts to the bucket and ladle nearby. "It, ahh ... it *has* been a while since I've been offered a drink."

I set my blade on the crate and drag the bucket close, then place the brimming scoop against his mouth and tip.

He drains it, and I repeat the process twice more before he nods.

"How's that?"

"Much better," he says through a deep, satiated breath. "Thank you, High Master."

"Think nothing of it." I toss the ladle back in the bucket and give him my full attention. "So, did you have something you wanted to say?"

He chews the inside of his mouth, appearing to deliberate. "Permission to speak freely, sire?"

"I'm all ears. Fire away."

He nods, some of the tightness leaving his face, and even his strung-up posture seems to loosen. "I believe your promised has been deflowered by the High Master of Ocruth."

My head kicks back, as though he just punched me in the face. "What drew you to *that* conclusion?"

"He refused to let her go," he deadpans. "She had to fight her way free. Even so, I believe she carries a reminder of him with her ... a pillow slip I've caught her sniffing more than once."

Interesting.

"With all due respect, her loyalties are questionable." He lifts his chin, looking me dead in the eye. "She's a liability to our territory."

"*My* territory."

"*Your* territory," he blurts with a dip of his head, his deep, grated voice hitching. "Sorry, High Master."

"Forgiven. Slip of words." Rolling the splinter between

my fingers, I let the sharp end drag against my tongue. "So, let me get this straight. Your concern is that my judge of character is ... *lacking?*"

The pulse in his neck ratchets into a frenzy. "No, that's not what I sai—"

"It's what you implied, Vanth."

His mouth moves as though he's shaping words he doesn't have the balls to speak.

"And tell me," I continue, "did you or did you not shove *my* promised overboard?"

When words seem to evade him again, I say, "Nod for yes, shake for no."

Slowly, he nods.

Right.

"So, what happened, Vanth? There's a missing chapter in here"—I tap my temple—"and Orlaith is reluctant to give me ... well, anything. Be a good man and fill in the blanks, would you?"

A bead of sweat darts down his temple. "I—I don't remember much. I was blackout drunk, sire."

"Yes, I gathered that from the general aroma in here. Before that, though?"

He grimaces, spitting his response through clenched teeth. "She's the reason my brother is dead."

Ahh.

"I was forced to put—" his voice cracks, a coarse sob pushing through, "to put Kavan out of his misery. All because *she* ruined my perfect shot."

"I see," I mumble, flipping the splinter through my fingers. "Eye for an eye?"

"No ... I mean yes, my brother's gone—"

"See, *that* I understand."

Relief flashes across his face before he deflates like a spent lung and drops his stare to the floor.

I blow out a breath and recline. "There's a hiccup, though."

He frowns, glancing up. "Hiccup?"

"Yes. What's this I hear about *mutiny?*"

His mouth falls open.

"Captain Gunthar's a good fellow. A level-headed man. Certainly one of my best, which is why I trusted him to transport such precious cargo back to the capital. I can't for the life of me understand why you'd question his authority."

The stuffy air grows taut.

"I ... I believed killing the beast would be the best option to preserve the life of your promised, sire."

"Whom you later tried to murder."

Silence.

The reek of fear ratchets up, coating the back of my throat.

"Nod for yes. Shake for no."

It takes him a minute, but he finally nods. Once. A small, feeble thing.

"Right," I mutter.

"I assumed—"

"You assumed wrong."

He shuts his mouth so fast I hear his teeth clank together.

I grab my dagger, set the tip atop the crate, then flick it into a whirl and watch it spin. "Kavan was a great man. But Vanth ... you almost cost me *everything.*"

Snatching the blade in one hand, I drag the splinter's honed tip along a deep scratch ripped across his neck—like

Orlaith clawed at him, frantic and desperate—then use it to pierce the underside of his chin. He sucks a hiss through clenched teeth, eyes popping as I press firm enough to send blood shooting down the splinter's length and across the expanse of my fingers.

"Now, be a good lad and poke out your tongue for your High Master."

His mouth opens. Closes. Opens again. "High Master, please—"

"I won't ask twice."

A gasp inflates his chest. "I—I have a token! A favor passed down through generations since our ancestor's home was destroyed to make way for the wall!"

Well.

Leaning back, I look him up and down. "Where is it?"

"My pants pocket. The left one. I always keep it close."

"That's handy," I mutter, flicking the splinter on the floor. I weave my bloody hand in, drag my finger along the line of stitching, then pull it inside out. I lift a brow.

"The—the other one! I must have put it in the other one ..."

I dig into the other, pulling out a Bahari blue cupla with gold accents. "What's this?"

His chin wobbles, and he looks at me through a sheen of tears. "K-Kavan was tasked with returning that to the forgery. A task he took very seriously. I want to complete it for him," he says, voice cracking. "It's the last thing I can do."

"How sweet."

I tuck it in my back pocket, and his eyes widen as

I search his pocket again, flipping it inside out. "Nothing else there, Vanth."

He turns a sickly shade of gray, then his face twists into an angry knot. "The kid must have taken it. He's a little pickpocket!"

"Well, you should take better care of your things," I chide. "Tongue. Now."

His crotch blooms with wetness, the tang of piss ripening the air. He makes a wobbly, wailing sound that's caught behind his lips before he finally parts them, pushing his tongue out slower than a threatened snail.

"Good boy."

I pinch it between my thumb and forefinger, whipping the blade through so fast I doubt he realizes it's gone until the thick chunk of flesh thuds to the floor between us.

There's a flash of disbelief, and then he screams a wild, bubbling howl, blood painting his chin and chest.

I grip his chin—grip it *hard*—forcing him to hold my stare as he releases an anguished sob. "Now, tell me you're sorry."

He sucks a shuddered breath and, eyes desperate and pleading, releases a pathetic, garbled whine.

I click my tongue. "Not good enough, I'm afraid."

Swiping my bloody knife on his pants, I spin toward the exit. "Don't choke on the blood," I mutter, slamming the door behind me. "I'm not done with you yet."

Chapter 12
Baze

The amber contents of my half-filled mug spills over the side with every barefooted plod.

Step, *slosh*.

Step, *slosh*.

A whistle of wind nips at my face and fingers, stirring the thin layer of ankle-high mist that looks like cobwebs woven across the coarse coastal grass, giving me a brief reprieve from the stench.

I hate the smell of a war camp—a potent cocktail of piss, shit, smoke, mud, fear, poor man's porridge, and unwashed ball sacks. Its only saving grace is the slight tang of ale that always pinches the air.

Lantern in hand, I cut a wobbly path between lines of domed, black tents—silent sentries in the dark. Each entrance flap is marked by a silver lantern hanging from a pike, casting the sleeping quarters in a huddled halo of frosted light.

Step, *slosh*.

I almost trample a white flower poking above the haze, somehow surviving against the odds and wrenching my thoughts straight back to *her*.

Another numbing sip doesn't stop my mind from tumbling, pecking apart the past eighteen years. A vulture with a pile of sun-bleached bones.

The wind moans through the thick forest fringing the camp like a lofty wall, the wailing sound battling the crash of waves hammering the nearby shore. The same sound that battered me over and over while I sat clumped behind that rock—cold, alone, and crippled by my raw, exposed skin. Knowing she was leaving. Knowing there wasn't a damn thing I could do about it for risk of boasting my ugly shame to the world.

Always shield your weakness ...

I guffaw into my mug.

I'm such a fucking fraud.

Stumbling a step, I almost topple into a man shitting over a bucket. "Sorry," I mumble, receiving a low grunt in return.

Most of the men are asleep, but it'll be a far different story once the sun begins to rise in an hour or so—by which time I plan to be passed out in the cabin, cock in hand, with a belly full of so much ale my mind can't thread two thoughts together.

Blessed fucking numbness.

Approaching one of the many campfires, I toast the stars for being cunts, and drain my wooden mug before tossing it in the pit. Sparks erupt, little bits scattering on the dull wind as I set my lantern by my feet, cross my arms, and watch the glowing embers throb. With some hissing and spitting, the thing eventually catches light, warming the air the slightest amount.

Another burst of wind snatches that heat away, and I sigh, tightening the twist of my arms.

I should've been honest with her. Should've told her everything the moment she started to root around for answers. Fuck Rhordyn and his fucking secrets. He's happy to absorb her hate, but there's not one single part of me that's ever wanted that for myself.

Something thunks against my forearm, and I'm about to blindly swat at it when a sharp trill breaks my bitter silence.

I blink away the haze and hone my double vision on the round, black eyes that dominate the petite mail sprite standing on my arm, dressed in felted garb thicker than they usually wear and looking utterly vexed to be standing in my presence.

You and me both, pip-squeak.

"You're the one that bit my finger," I mutter, hiccupping. "I think. That hurt, by the way. Went all the way through my nail."

She crosses her arms, eyes narrowing.

"Wanna see?" I shove my finger in her face, but she bats it away with her tiny hand.

Guess that's a no. Hard to find good company at this hour.

I move my arm so I can scan her from all angles. "Where's your scroll? Did you lose it?"

She stamps her hands on her hips and hisses, baring a hoard of tiny pin-like teeth, forcing me to focus on her features. Her hair's so teased from the elements her head resembles dandelion going to seed, her lacy wings are lacking the usual layer of powder, and her cheeks are flushed from the cold.

I've never seen a mail sprite so worse for wear.

Spotting the black bead pierced through the tapered tip of her right ear, I slap myself on the forehead. "Fuck, I'm sorry. You're the little ocean scout we sent after Laith. No wonder you look so ... roughed up."

She stomps her foot. "*Geif han dak't le neivala va me! Shashkina me lashea af ten ah!*"

Wrong thing to say, apparently.

"Sorry, sorry. I'll pay closer"—*hiccup*—"attention."

Spitting a few more words too fast for me to decipher, she flutters up, drops onto my shoulder, and tilts toward my ear.

Her hushed words stack sobering stones upon my chest, one by fucking one, shattering my numbness and draining the blood from my face.

I plummet back to reality at a sickening speed that threatens to turn my stomach inside out ...

Fuck.

I shove a branch out of my face to see him looking out across the angry ocean as a mottled masterpiece of muted color drips upon the world.

Wind whips at his cape, the cliff a sheer drop at his booted feet, and I can tell he's heard my clumsy advance by the set of his pelt-shrouded shoulders. By the tension-riddled air—stiff enough to snap.

"They've turned around," I mutter, the coarse grass

crunching beneath my boots as I enter the cliffside clearing lantern-first, wrapped in my illuminated safety net. Precautions—the light a lethal weapon that strips the Irilak into a steaming heap of bones and not much else.

Though they mostly reside in the South, the light is a safety net I prefer not to part with.

"The entire fleet?"

"Every ship besides the two that ..." I clear my throat, "sank."

"*Which* ships?"

The deep thump of his question rattles my bones—a storm in his voice to match the one brewing on the horizon. I stuff my free hand in my pocket to stem the shake. Not from fear, but from an anger that's grown its own caustic heartbeat.

Orlaith's out there, vulnerable, underinformed, and brimming with justifiable rage. Blame is a hot coal in my hand ready to be tossed, because fuck me ... it *burns*.

"*Baze?*"

I bite my tongue, studying the sword sheathed down his spine.

Finally, he turns.

I open my mouth, but the words are clogged by the raw sight of him.

There's a violent unbalance in his cutthroat stare—a hollow darkness that's gobbled up his irises, leaving nothing but frail silver halos keeping the black contained. He hasn't shaved since she left, and his regular stubble has grown thick and dark, a wildness to match the untethered look in his eyes.

"According to the sprite, the, ah ... the ship Laith boarded at Castle Noir took extensive damage."

"What about *her*?"

I watch a bead of blood slip down the length of his thumb from up under his sleeve and drip ...

Drip ...

Shit.

"Answer me, Baze."

"Somebody had to carry her off the ship before it sank. That's all I know."

"*Somebody* ..."

"Mm-hmm." My gaze flicks down, up again. "You're bleeding," I mutter, and he wipes his hand on his pants without breaking eye contact. I gesture toward the cord caught around his neck, secured to the small bladder of Orlaith's blood tucked close to his heart. "Perhaps you should have a sip."

"You're offering self-medication advice?" He looks me over. "Right now?"

"Shocking, I know."

His stare holds for a few drawn beats before he grunts, gaze casting across the ocean.

We've been scanning the point for Cainon's fleet for days—since we received confirmation he deployed a boastful number of ships down the west coast. Being constantly prepared for an uncertain attack, we're wasting precious resources and getting restless in this horrid limbo.

Quoth Point is the only weakness along the western coast accessible by fleet. The only scrap of Ocruth that slopes into the ocean rather than chopped with a sheer, unscalable drop.

If an army were to attack from the sea, it'd be here— the small, craggy stretch of black sand littered with rusted arrowheads, teeth, and shards of bone. Testament to battles long past.

But I'm not concerned about an attack we're well prepared to beat back, and I know that's not *his* main concern.

It's her.

Over the past week, I've seen Rhordyn become progressively more abrasive, and I've become progressively more drunk.

Same problem, different coping mechanisms.

With a low growl, he spins and stalks toward the brush in long, determined strides. "Try to keep up without tripping over your feet."

Rolling my eyes, I trail him through the trees, stepping over rocks and fallen logs until we converge with the camp's silver glow.

He leads me between two rows of tents, a barrel of ale standing sentry at the last, topped with a number of brimming, frothless mugs. I snatch the fullest one as we pass, just tipping it to my lips when Rhordyn smacks it from my hand, painting the side of someone's tent with a frothy smear.

"So wasteful," I slur, flicking up my hood.

"You finally understand."

"Do you have to walk so fast? I'm seeing doubles."

Someone exits a tent with mussed up hair and bleary eyes, takes one look at our High Master, and loses all the color in his cheeks, bowing.

Rhordyn charges on without a pause in his step. "The next fleet of trade ships heading down the River Norse?"

"What about them?"

He grabs a full bladder of water off a table from the hydration tent pitched atop the well and continues, hooking it over his shoulder by the sling. "I need you to replace the traveling merchants with soldiers knowledgeable enough to captain their own vessels. We need to secure those ships before Cainon finds another meager excuse to use them against us."

"I thought you said he could go fuck his ships?"

Exactly that, actually. But I'm mid-swing in this *fuck you, fuck me, fuck everything* routine and it seems a shame to back down now.

"Only a fool would be too proud to demand what Orlaith *earned* Ocruth and Rouste by stepping on that ship."

"Silver lining," I mutter. "Should we talk about how this entire situation could have been avoided had you simply been honest with her?"

He growls, the sound so deep and wild even the wind stops whistling, and a deeper silence settles over the camp.

Time to stop nipping at the beast.

I rub at my scratchy, sleep-deprived eyes as we round the large, black barn at the edge of camp that's seen better days—the sharp smell of manure souring the air.

"I already put the word out about the ships, just in case Cainon decided to pull back. We leaving, then? I'll need to grab some shit. My sword's in the cabin."

Rhordyn tugs the wooden door open, releasing a warm glow, the stablemen already feeding horses and mucking pens. They bow as we pass, though Rhordyn only stops once we reach Eyzar's stall at the end.

He spins, digs through his pocket, and hands me a small, flattened scroll—black seal intact.

"What's this?"

"One of my sprites returned with this uncracked. Seems Zali's gone rogue."

My spine stiffens.

I set the lantern on a table and hold his shadowed stare, knowing full well the sprites refuse to fly too close to the Alps these days.

"The Stretch?"

Rhordyn nods.

A snarl rips free.

She needed to see for herself. She could've fucking told us first.

"You want me to take it to her?"

Silence stews between us while he watches me, jaw set, as though he's biting into the throat of his own deliberation. "I don't trust anyone else."

I stuff the scroll in my pocket.

Rhordyn nods, then gets to work tacking the massive black stallion that looks as restless as his master. Every now and then, the beast paws the straw, puffing plumes of steam from flared nostrils.

Like Rhor, his eyes are black and astute.

Unnerving.

I can tell Rhordyn's mind is far from here as he buckles the saddle. It's not until he's led the beast into the crisp morning air and is climbing atop its back that I let my musings spill.

"I did warn you this would happen."

He snarls, and Eyzar paws his agitation deep into the mud. He does a tight spin, ready to run.

"The wheels are in motion, Rhor. We both know where this ends. It was over before it started."

More blood drips from his hand. "What if it's changed?"

I frown. "What?"

"The *prophecy*," he growls, and my mind whirs, stare stabbing to the forest path Eyzar's facing.

He's going to see Maars ...

If his indifference was the answer, it would have been scratched off by now. We would've heard about it.

"And if it hasn't?"

He doesn't look at me; instead yanking the reins and screaming, "*Yah!*" Eyzar rears, then takes off at a sickening pace, whisking the fog into a stir as he gallops down a forest path.

Gone.

Orlaith has no idea what's about to hit her—a man who knows the sour taste of loss hell bent on twisting fate to his own fucking will.

I seek the fading stars through watercolor clouds ...

"Sadistic fucks."

Shoulders bunched around my ears, I take off toward the camp to gather some shit.

No sleep for me. Not today.

I'm headed for the Alps.

Chapter 13
Kai

I'm reeled through inky layers of muted reality by a brutal pain—deep and throbbing.

Deadly.

Like I've been gaffed in the chest.

I drag a gurgling breath through my gills, then another, still parched and left with the desperate desire for *more*. Growing frantic, I open my mouth, gulping crisp air down my throat as a bolt of pain strikes my inflating chest, like a fist punched through my ribs and tore out something vital.

Head spinning from the drugging rush of air, a face flashes through my mind: lilac eyes, hair the color of sunken treasure, a crescent moon smile.

Orlaith.

A gouge of pain rips me back as I heave a strangled gasp. I peel my eyes open, pulling gentle half breaths, heart stilling as I take in the size and shape of my surroundings through blurry, sleep-stung eyes.

A small room, one corner stacked high with a collection

of unfamiliar bounty—little boxes, rusted toys, a leaning stack of mugs. Most of the bits are made from stone or metal or wood, missing chips and pieces.

Not my trove.

The walls and roof are made from a familiar treasured stone packed with a kaleidoscope of muted colors that ricochet off every chipped facet. A stone born from one place and one place only ...

Lychnis.

Must be a dream.

Nobody makes it onto that lonely relic anymore—not since the water around it became still and haunted.

I draw another breath that impales me with a gnawing blow.

Not a dream, then.

The magnitude of that realization, of where I am, is overshadowed by the cold silence within my ribcage ...

Too silent.

Panic flays me.

Zykanth isn't boiling in my chest, slithering, alert, and tapping at my ribs. Not even at the sight of four walls carved from the stuff he's feeble for, roughly hewn in a way that makes my aching heart flutter. That would usually have him losing his fucking *mind*. What's more, I'm laid out on a soft nest in the corner with thick, white pelts covering my *legs*.

My weakness.

Wild fear coils up my spine, frighteningly aware that every moment I'm severed from Zyke weakens our connection.

Weakens *him*—something too many of us learned the hard way.

'Where are you?'

Nothing. Like he's burrowed so deep inside my chest I can't catch even a glimpse of his silver scales.

But he's there. I can feel his dull and distant beat.

Faint ...

Why is it so faint?

A memory strikes, and I'm sucked into its churning fury.

Zykanth growing sick of following the ship from a safe, comfortable distance. His desperation to take over the reins. He just wanted to catch a glimpse, see her for himself. Confirm she was okay.

And then he wasn't.

I remember the deadly thud of pain—too close to Zyke's heart. Remember his savage surge of pulverizing violence.

The boat tipped. Screams silenced in increments as sharks tore and thrashed and chewed.

Drifting into the deep, dark hollows, leaving a plume of blood in our wake. I shoved him inside my chest *so I could cradle him close. Protect him. Heal him.*

He didn't even fight.

The sight of the bolt straight through my chest.

The encompassing blackness a never-ending unknown as pain overrode my ability to function.

Giving myself to the sea's pull.

A guttural sound rips up my throat, and I grip a fistful of furs, tugging them down.

My breath catches.

There's a large scale stamped over my pectoral, concealing the wound I can feel gored right through me.

It's bronze and shimmery.

Not mine.

I pick at the edge. Try to peel it up—

There's a sharp hiss, some hasty shuffling, and then my hand is slapped.

A dainty, ethereal face eclipses my view of ... *everything*. Long, wayward hair littered with twigs floats around a fresh, unfamiliar face like a scribble of whitewash. I look into wide, sunshine-yellow eyes framed by alabaster lashes that brush snowy brows as she scans me up and down.

She's half my size but assessing me like it's the other way around. A brown shirt almost swallows her whole, hanging to her knees and rolled to her elbows, concealing most of her shape bar spots where the material's torn or frayed— small windows that reveal hints of filthy, sun-brushed skin.

"Who are *you*?"

I don't recognize the croak of my voice.

Her brows knit together, and she tilts her head to the side. She wraps the furs up around my chin, as though she's tucking me in for a nap.

"*No.*" I pull my arm free and bat her hands away, shoving the pelt down so I can pick at the massive scale fused with my skin. "I need to see how bad it is."

How close they got to killing *him*. Killing us both, had I not been fast enough to preserve myself.

Another sharp hiss has me looking up to see her lips peeled, revealing bright white teeth and canines much sharper than mine.

"You win." I whip my hand away. "Just ... put your teeth away. I'm in no state to tussle."

She makes a clicking sound with her tongue, pats the tapered edges back into place, and brushes her fingers over the seam between scale and skin, making a chill crawl from my tailbone to the base of my skull. She tucks the furs over my chest, hiding the burst of gooseflesh that broke out across my body, and scurries toward a workbench that takes up the length of one wall, pitted with a basin.

Bare legs; long, slender, golden-brown ... *dirty*.

Bare feet that remind me of Orlaith.

My heart dives.

She grabs a bowl hewn from the same sparkly stuff that makes up the walls, stuffs some kelp in the hollow with a few other things I don't recognize, and sits cross-legged on the ground. Setting the bowl before her, she hunches over and begins grinding down the contents with the blunt end of a thick stick.

Odd.

"Did you ... bring me here?"

She continues to pulverize the mixture, putting her entire body into it.

I sigh and try to look around—hard to do while I'm horizontal. "I'm sitting up," I warn, and she flicks her hair off her face, watching me through shrewd eyes.

Grind.

Grind.

"Right. Here we go." I use my elbows as leverage to crank my upper body off the nest of furs, but the motion casts an agonizing bolt through my chest.

I groan, face twisting as I reach for the wound.

There's a flurry of movement, then her warm hands are on me—poking and prodding. She pushes close to my sternum, striking me like there's a knife on the end of her finger, piercing through flesh and muscle and—

A scream saws out of me, wild and unleashed.

Head cocked to the side, she watches ... listens? Then she pinches the edge of the scale.

"What are you—"

She pulls.

I roar.

She absolutely used some sort of adhesive to stick that thing down, because there goes a layer of skin.

Panting through the red haze of throat-cinching pain, I look down, eyes bulging as I take in the gruesome wound in my chest ...

My pulse pitches.

It's a big, fleshy crater unlike *anything* we've ever sustained.

Even so, Zykanth should've healed us by now.

Unless ...

The bolt must've nicked our heart.

The female drops her head close to the wound and sniffs, long and deep, then prods at its edge from a different angle. Another barreling wave of pain curls through my chest, forcing my body to buck as a hoarse cough hacks free.

Something warm splatters down my chin.

The female snarls and darts to her heaped treasures, pausing with her hand outstretched, like she's reluctant to disturb their ramshackle order. She delicately shifts tarnished trinkets and gnarly bits of driftwood, easing a coil of rope from where it's looped around the hook of a rusted anchor.

I'm still gasping through the pounding echo of pain when she straddles my crotch, manhandles my arms, and binds my wrists together with hands so fast they blur.

"Woah, hang on—"

She struggles to knot the thing, hissing at it.

"Look," I spout as she gives up and tucks the tail between my wrists instead. "I like where this is going, and I'll absolutely regret saying this, but I really don't think this is the right time."

She lifts her bum, sets my bound hands atop my crotch, and sits on them, pitching my pulse for an entirely different reason.

I realize just how bare she is beneath that oversized shirt. Just how soft and warm and—

My brain empties. Even the pain seems to dull.

Her hand plunges into me in a searing punch of pain straight through my fucking *core*. Brows knotted and eyes closed, she roots through my torn and bloody flesh.

I scream so loud my voice cracks as I jerk my arms and buck my hips.

Try to toss her off.

She tightens her thighs around me and continues to rearrange my insides. My body begins to shut down from the overwhelming surge of pain. A dark haze swells at the edge of my vision, sweeping me under, and my head lolls to the side ...

Darkness.

I drift through a void of muddy delusion, ripped back to consciousness by another savage surge of pain. A violent roar claws from my throat as the female whips her hand free from my gaping wound, bloody fingers pinching something short and pointy, eyes glazed like she just won the fucking treasure hunt.

Sharp, shuddered breaths cut through my clenched teeth while she inspects the piece from all angles, her hand slathered in glossy blood drawing wiggly lines down her arm before dripping off her elbow.

She hisses at it—this vicious, wild sound.

I really hope she got it all. I'm not doing that shit again.

She dashes to the wooden door, rips it open, and darts out, leaving me smothered in blood and battling every painful gasp. The room floods with brisk air and a blinding wash of prism light, and I'm just squinting around, trying to find a piece of cloth to pack inside my wound when she returns—*loudly*—dragging something long and hard along the floor. It's only once she slams the door and snips off the glow that I realize what it is.

The bolt that tore through my fucking body.

What a morbid keepsake.

"How did a ... little thing like you manage to ... lug that all the way ... here?" I force out between labored breaths, watching her scan the barbed head.

No answer.

Piecing it in place, she clicks her tongue and tosses the intact bolt against the wall in a surprising show of strength. It clatters against the ground, the sharp sound echoing off the walls.

My cheeks fill with the remnants of my tortured breath before I slowly blow it out.

Guess she's stronger than she looks.

The rope around my wrist unravels on its own, and I'm just slipping my hands free when a bowl of teal coagulated goo is shoved under my chin.

I blink up into wide, expectant eyes.

Tempted to scrunch my nose, I look at the putrid contents ... back again. "Eat? Really? Right now?"

The pain in my chest makes me more inclined to gag than swallow, and the thought of trying to stuff that crap down my gullet does nothing to quell my queasiness.

Her head tilts to the side.

I sigh, rubbing the ache from my wrists while easing up to the challenge, then dig two trembling fingers through the muck.

Hissing, she slaps my hand.

Got that wrong.

She pretends to spit in the bowl, then shoves it under my chin again.

"You want me to *spit* in it?" I say, brows raised.

She blinks.

I pretend to spit, pointing at the bowl and nodding. "Yes?"

Another blink, followed by a slow nod, quickening until her hair is a blur of motion around her pretty face.

Progress. Kind of.

I move my tongue around my mouth. Dry as a bone. "I have none ..."

She frowns.

"Mouth. Dry." I point to my lips. Poke out my tongue.

Her eyes widen, and she leaps off the bed, dashing to the corner of the room where a large bucket resides. She gets behind the thing and shoves it along the ground, sending water sloshing over the edge, until she stops right next to the nest and collects an armful of furs. I'm lugged forward, groaning as she stuffs them behind my back, then scoops water within her cupped hands and awkwardly brings it to my mouth.

Some dribbles free, paving clean paths through the blood painting my chest.

I peek up, catching her stern stare and my breath.

Right.

Tentatively, I open my mouth. Her silky fingers graze across my sensitive bottom lip, wetting my tongue with a small tip of icy water—barely enough to swallow since I'm wearing most of it.

Even so, I moan at the crispness that lacks a salty pinch. Realize just how thirsty I am.

She scoops more, and I line her cupped hands with my much larger ones and guide them to my mouth, gulping whatever makes the journey past my dried, cracked lips. Before I even have a chance to ask, she repeats the process, brow pinched as she watches me gulp. And gulp.

And gulp.

How long have I been out?

"Thank you," I gasp, curling her fingers up to signal that I'm done.

She grabs the bowl of muck and she shoves it in my face again, nodding vigorously.

The corner of my mouth kicks up, but she snarls and shoves the bowl closer.

Not a smiling matter, then.

I spit, and she's swift to plow her fingers through the muck, mushing it all together before scooping up a healthy handful and stuffing it in my wound.

Motherf—

I scream through bared teeth.

Damn her to the depths of The Shoaling Seas—I'm certain it hurts more than the fucking bolt did when it punched through Zyke's chest.

She continues to ram the wound full while I growl, huffing, puffing, unable to flip her off without drowning myself in guilt.

Just as I'm wishing for a swift and brutal death to end my suffering, the pain begins to ebb.

I tip my head, staring at the roof. "This is a tiny house of pain."

She wipes me down, cleaning up the bloody mess, then sets the scale back on my pectoral like a bandage, patting the edges into place with a surprisingly gentle touch for someone who just rooted around inside me like a vulture.

"I really hope this isn't an every-hour-on-the-hour ... *thing*."

Seemingly satisfied, the female darts to the trough that's brimming with water on the end of her workbench. There, she stands transfixed, eyes tracing something I'm unable to see from this angle.

If she pulls out an ocean leech, I'm gone.

In a blur of motion, her hand jolts into the water, hauls out a sleek, red fish by the tail, then bashes it against the sharp edge of the bench.

My mouth dries.

"You're a vicious little thing ..."

Her attention sways back to the water as she repeats the process, this time slaughtering a fat, glossy black fish double the size of the other.

She sits cross-legged on the floor with her bounty and scales both fish with a sharp stone—scattering little round disks all over her bare legs and feet.

Clever. Maybe she hates scales getting stuck in her teeth, too.

She uses the same tool to hack off the heads, then plonks the bodies in a large bowl before padding toward me. She climbs atop my legs and sets the bowl in my lap, grabs the smaller fish, bends it backward, then takes a hearty bite from the bulging underside.

Frowning, I watch her chew—transfixed on this strange female with cheeks jammed full of fish.

Her gaze flicks up, two bolts of blazing yellow striking me like a shaft of sunlight.

She grabs the other fish and shoves it at me, nodding enthusiastically.

I take the thing, pointing at it with my free hand. "Eat?"

She swallows, looks from me to the fish, and shapes the word with her plump lips.

I find myself struck with a slap of disappointment.

"Well, thank you," I say, taking a large bite from the plump underbelly. The tough, sable skin bursts beneath the force of my sharp teeth, giving way to fluffy wet flesh that tastes like the sea smells on a winter's morning.

My stomach grumbles the moment I swallow, and I take a deeper bite, watching the strange female feast. There's nothing tidy or quiet about the way she strips the bones and sucks them clean, a few rogue scales dusting her cheeks and arms and *me*.

She works her way down the fish's body—devouring every scrap of flesh, including the organs and entrails.

I find myself wondering who she is. If she has a name. How she ended up on this precious, untouchable island, surrounded by a small trove's worth of questionable keepsakes.

Her lashes sweep up. She stops chewing, head tilting again.

"Malakai. My name." I set my hand upon my chest. "Mine."

She swallows, eyes wide as her gaze bounces from my face to my hand and back again.

"Mal-ah-kai. Can you say that? *Gleish taj nah mi-nam, Malakai?*"

Holding my stare, she takes another bite and chews, clear fish juice dribbling down her sharp chin.

"Vicious? Should I call you that?"

Blink. Swallow. Another bite. She grabs the hand that's holding my fish and pushes it toward my face.

Sigh.

Under her intense scrutiny, I get stuck into my meal, mind churning ...

If we are where I think we are, how did she end up all alone on this island? How did she manage to get me here?

Why won't she speak?

And *Zyke* ... I wish he'd give me something.

Anything.

But he's so deep, I can't summon a single scale, and without a tail, I have no chance of outrunning the beast that haunts these waters. Which means I'm stuck here, on this island, with this strange and silent female—more weak and vulnerable than I've ever been before.

Oceans apart from Orlaith. From where I last saw her looking up at Zykanth with flat, fearless eyes I barely recognized moments before he buckled beside the ship ...

That, above all else, frightens me the most.

Chapter 14
Orlaith

Raging fire engulfs the house, devouring it until nothing is left but a black shell. It crumbles, feeding the swirl of ash and sparks skating on the wind with the cloying smell of baked flesh.

My knees buckle, a scream caught behind chattering teeth as I slam my hand against the sturdy trunk of a tree.

A hungry gravity makes the hairs on the back of my neck stand on end.

"*Found you.*"

Those deep, frosty words flog my heart into a wild gallop, and I spin, gasping at the sight of Rhordyn standing over me—masculine granite features lit by angry orange light.

His eyes are pewter spades unearthing me in heaped scoops.

His brow buckles, gaze spearing over my shoulder.

Frantic fear wrestles inside my chest.

Don't look.

Please.

I start to back away—

He grips my chin so hard it hurts, forcing me to turn, to stare at the flaming carnage reflected in his eyes.

"Milaje, what did you do?"

I snatch his wrist in an attempt to free myself, see that my hand is smothered in bold red blood.

Drip ...

Drip ...

Drip ...

I close my eyes. Squeeze them tight. Try to sever myself from the reality I can't escape.

What did I do?

"Everything," I whisper.

Killed him. Killed her.

Killed them all.

The air chills.

Rhordyn's hand slides around the back of my head, fingers threading through my hair and corralling me against his cold chest.

My shocked stiffness drains away, and I melt against him, choking on a relieved sob.

Something sharp kisses me between the shoulder blades, and my eyes pop open, head kicking back. My gaze collides with his stare that's all toiling anguish and lightning strikes of regret.

Frightening.

Beautiful.

"What are you—"

"I'm sorry," he bites out, and a cool slice of sharp pierces through me like I'm made of butter.

My mouth drops in a silent scream.

I feel my fragile heart split. Feel something warm spill through me in pulsing increments. Horrified, I look down to see the curved tip of a talon emerge between my breasts with a bloom of blood ...

A shuddered breath tumbles out of me with a bubble of warmth that sluices down my chin.

Drip.

Drip.

My knees give way. Rhordyn takes my weight, his face burrowed in the crook of my neck as he holds me close. "*I'm sorry ... I'm sorry ... I'm sorry—*" The words are ground out like he's carving them into stone with the tips of his fingers.

I feel a sharp tug, feel the talon slip free, and then he lowers me to the dirt, my eyes rolling back to take in the spindly stretch of the naked willow tree waving above.

I try to breathe but my chest won't inflate.

My heart won't thud.

I tumble into an eclipse, fall into the dark rather than the light, a speck of dust floating through an icy void.

Nothing. Nobody.

Gone.

I jerk upright with a gasp, hands patting between my breasts, blinking at the harsh bursts of silver light that seem to whip against the windowpanes, igniting the night in bursts.

No blade.

Not real.

Drawing gulps of air, I fold forward and cradle my hot,

sticky face as bolts of pressure explode against my temples. The tempest howls outside, churning the ocean into a bucking beast. The ship creaks and groans and shudders and sways and makes my stomach swirl.

Blood dribbles from my nose, onto the sheets bunched around me.

Drip.

Drip.

I growl, swipe it with my bandaged hand, then flop back onto the pillow—ignoring the strike of pain that rips through my shoulder as that *thing* inside me twists and toils and roots at the undersides of my skin.

Another flash of light illuminates the room—the Captain's quarters, all to myself, guarded at all hours of the day and night to preserve my *virtue*.

I close my eyes. Work through my shoulder stretches to distract myself from the phantom sting between my breasts ...

Found you.

I whip the blankets over my head and cut myself off from those silver strikes of light.

... Not real.

Chapter 15
Orlaith

Every pull of Cainon's arms powers us through the turquoise water slapping at the hull, bringing our rowboat closer to the monolith of navy marble dominating the bay like a thick, sturdy tower forged by nature. A large hole is bored through its base, creating a window to the other side, a clutch of empty rowboats bobbing in its protective embrace.

My gaze travels up the jagged staircase chipped into the edge of the gigantic structure, to a platform sitting atop it. From there, a rope bridge sways in the wind, stretching across the water to the top of the cliff that curls around the sheltered cove like a giant hook.

Protected in the cove, we don't feel the blast of wind that whips the bridge into a crawl, making Cap, Zane, and the seven unfamiliar men currently scaling it stop and cling to the rope rails. A vision that sparks trepidation in my chest.

"We should've gone first. That thing looks frail …"

Cainon steals a glance at the bridge over his brawny shoulder.

Hair tied in a loose knot at his nape, he's wearing a deep blue, tailored jacket with gold buttons that aren't done up, offering ample view of his muscled chest.

Of that scar just above his heart.

His oversized shirt is huge on me, rolled to the elbows and tucked into a large pair of navy pants cinched around my waist by a length of rope—all left outside my door this morning. A subtle order for me to change out of my Ocruth garb before we docked. It was the first interaction we've had since the violent storm struck after I boarded his ship a week ago, forcing the fleet to sit offshore and wait for the worst of it to pass.

"It *is* frail," he says, working the oars harder, shoving us through the silky stretch of water. Such a contrast to the riled ocean beyond the cove where I can see the fleet's bulk receding through the haze of rain as it sails away.

Somewhere.

"They're checking it for faulty planks."

My eyes spring wide. "You sent a *child* to check the bridge for faults? Are you mad?"

He shrugs, giving me a half smile that makes his eyes glint. "The kid begged me. He said you're his favorite person, and he wants to make sure you're safe."

My heart bobs, stunting all the words sitting heavy on my tongue.

Cainon spears his gaze at the sack between my feet and lifts a brow. "That's going to be a pain in my ass to carry up those stairs. They're steeper than they look. Sure there's nothing in there you can leave behind?"

I tighten my knees around my belongings and stab my stare at the heavily vegetated cliff face, watching Zane and Cap finally step off the other side and onto sturdy ground.

Relief cools my veins, and I skate my attention further around the harsh cliff—hands twisting, knee bouncing, toes curling as I picture them digging into soil for the first time in weeks.

A shadow cast by a tree weeping off the cliff's edge snags my stare.

Not a shadow.

Something ... *more.*

The huge, black blur steals my breath, like I've just been shoved beneath the water by a hand caught around my throat.

My heart thumps, skin flushing with a burst of goosebumps.

"What's that?"

Cainon twists to look in the direction I'm pointing, hand slipping off the oar. There's a grinding sound as it begins to slide free from the metal thole, and we both launch for it at the same time—my teeth gritted as we drag it back into place.

"What's what?" he asks, tone short as he spins again. But when I look at that tree, there is no dark smudge.

Nothing.

I frown, desperately scanning the cliff's edge.

Perhaps I'm going mad. Perhaps my nightmares are leaking from the shadows of my mind just to fuck with me.

"Never mind," I murmur, but the hairs on the back of my neck don't smooth, the air still tinged with a lingering charge that tries to shake me up.

Screams at me to *flee*.

"Where are we exactly?" I rip my gaze from the cliff.

"A back entrance." Cainon throws the oars forward, digging deep. "The palace is on the northern tip of this small island, two days' walk from here, with a bridge connecting it to Bahari's capital."

"The capital is Parith, yes?"

"Correct," he confirms. "The southernmost point of the main continent before it crumbles off into a litter of islands. Docking in the city harbor is too risky during rough weather. The chain goes up whenever the swell tops five feet."

"Why?"

"Too many rock shelves. I don't relish the idea of sinking another ship."

Blazing screams echo in my mind, and I'm ripped back to the ire I felt watching sailors dive off the engulfed deck, lathered in flames.

"Could've fooled me."

He shoots me a sharp look, and I close my fist around its cutting edge.

Refuse to look away.

He tsks. "Such pretty lips spitting such bitter words when there's much better things you could be doing with them."

"You have an overactive imagination," I mutter, and he flashes me a smile I don't reciprocate, shoulders bulging as he plows those oars through the water.

"Oh, petal. You have *no* idea."

My cheeks blaze, his words a lick of warmth to the area defenseless to the fact that I'm in a confined space with a powerful High Master twice my size, looking at me like he wants to drown me in a sea of pleasure.

I skim my stare across the water to escape in whatever meager way I can.

His responding chuckle only riles me more.

"As I was saying before you led my mind into such *delightful* territory, we've already taken severe damage from the storm. Much of my fleet will require extensive repairs before they're fit to sail again."

The blow to my chest leaves a dull ache.

So *my* hard-earned fleet won't be setting sail toward Ocruth anytime soon.

Wild panic worms up my throat.

"No welcome parade, then." The words are cold and crisp—something to fill in the silence while I try to tame this jittery beast swelling inside my chest. Because every day that slips by without Rhordyn and Zali's proposed intervention is another Vruk attack. Another slaughtered family.

Another child without a mother, or a father, or a brother ...

Every day, I fail a bit more.

"Not when we arrive, no. We'll save the official celebrations for when we're coupled."

He's watching me. Regarding me. Like he's waiting to see if my curiosity will snatch his dangling bait.

"And when might that be?"

His eyes gleam with a hint of satisfaction. "We only have to wait until the next full moon. Our ceremonies are unique and take time to prepare, so it's good we have a few weeks to get things in order. I'll settle for nothing but the best, since I only intend on doing this once."

Only intend on doing this once ...

Those words rummage through me.

"And the ships? When do you expect they'll be fit to sail?"

Another powerful pull strains the tendons in his arms, up the length of his neck. "By the time we're officially coupled," he puffs out, and my heart drops.

In other words: just accepting his cupla doesn't count for shit.

No coupling, no ships.

I have to open my legs for the man before he'll do his part to preserve innocent lives, and something about that grates me the wrong way, mining a humorless laugh from somewhere deep down in my ashy depths. It spills out while I hold his crushing cobalt stare like he's my captive and not the other way around.

He frowns. "Something funny, Orlaith?"

We drift into the hollow belly of the cave as my laughter tapers off.

He's forced to break my stare in order to maneuver our small boat right beside an empty one. Deep, amplified thuds bounce off the curved wall like an attack as he secures us to the edge of a smooth stone platform, and my feet burst with a tingling sensation that makes my toes curl.

I swallow, overwhelmed by the ravenous surge of yearning to plant my feet on that stone.

Cainon reaches for my sack—

I snatch it closer.

He stares down at me through blown pupils. "You're going to carry it up those stairs yourself, are you?"

I nod. "I'm sick of watching you throw it around like it's a sack of trash."

"And what about your hand? Your shoulder?"

I toss my belongings over my healing side, not even wincing from the dull twinge of ache. "Your medis's near-constant care over the past week has done them both wonders. My shoulder feels much better, and my hand has scabbed over," I say, waving it at him.

"The stone is slimy in places. With all the extra weight, you'll likely slip. Especially without any boots on your feet."

My heart drops, and a surge of desperation claws up my throat.

Softens my voice.

"I'm not used to shoes. I'm more likely to trip with them on than with them off ..."

Silence boils between us.

"I'll put them on when we get to the top," I add, peeking at the stone, resisting the urge to leap past him before he can object.

Please don't make me put them on yet.

Please.

"Very well," he finally says, indicating the platform that meets the nose of the boat. "Ladies first. Watch your step."

I scramble forward, ignoring his outstretched hand as I clamber off the wobbly boat and onto Bahari land. The blue marble is smooth and steady, packed with a warmth that soothes my soles.

Goosebumps sprout across my skin, and I close my eyes and pretend the stone is rough and black—that the slapping sea echoing through the cave is an ocean of silent clouds that stretches as far as the eye can see. That I'm on the balcony of Stony Stem, face tipped to the sky, bathed in warm beams of sunlight that rarely touched the rest of the castle.

For a moment, I'm *home*.

"Everything alright?"

"Fine," I croak, eyes snapping open.

I swallow the unwanted bulb planted in my throat and push forward.

Trailed by Cainon's heavy presence, I follow the platform that leads out the mouth of the tunnel, curls to the right, and meets the base of the stairs, cushioned in places by clumps of spongy moss. We begin the arduous climb, edging up the side in jagged increments, each stair a different height than the last and puddled in places, water splashing up my straining calves.

Though my legs are conditioned to this sort of labor, a few weeks stuffed in a boat has taken its toll, and my thighs are burning as much as my lungs by the time we near the top.

Trying to hide my labored breaths, I step onto the wooden platform saddling the monolith, head swiveling, hair torn about by the wind as I take in the vast expanse of the bay stretched beneath us in all directions—Cainon's anchored ship looking dwarfed from all the way up here.

Another blast of wind makes my feet tingle.

I shift further from the stairs, giving Cainon room, and trace the bucking swing bridge to where it's tethered to the top of the cliff.

The bridge is long.

Frail.

Cainon eases past, stepping out. "A few of the planks need replacing. Watch your step."

Adjusting my hold on the sack, I grip the rope rail with one hand and mimic his footfalls, heart dropping as I step over a gap where a plank is missing, the world falling away beneath my feet.

A giddy swirl in my gut electrifies me, a smile dragging up the corners of my mouth ...

One wrong step, and I could *plunge*.

A brutal burst of wind shakes the bridge, and I pause, hair churning into a tumbleweed of knots. A bubble of laughter pops from my lips.

Cainon looks back at me, frowning, but I can't seem to wipe the smile off my face as we bounce and sway to an erratic, exhilarating beat that makes me feel alive for the first time in days.

For some reason, balancing on this precipice between life and possible death makes my steps feel lighter, not the other way around, and I'm suddenly in no rush to reach the other end. Instead, I take my time, absorbing each bouncing blow, letting the wind have its way with me.

Closing in on the cliff, I can smell the soil, and desperation surges through me again, that vicious hunger intensifying. It shoves me forward so I'm just a few planks behind Cainon as he steps off the bridge.

There's a splintering sound, and I gasp when the wood gives way beneath me.

I drop—just a short, sharp moment that rips my heart up my throat before Cainon spins, snatches me by the front of my shirt, and hauls me forward.

A roll of laughter shakes my chest, and I'm set on solid

ground in a heap. My sack lands heavily beside me, my shoulder spasming from the strain as my laughter tapers off. I fold my knees up under myself and spread my hands forward across the damp ground, fingers stretching ...

Heart slowing ...

I press my forehead against the dirt and *breathe*.

"Do you need a hand up?"

"Just give me a minute," I murmur, clawing my fingers down past the grass, forcing dirt beneath my fingernails. I heap myself full of the raw, near-carnal smell with every intoxicating inhale.

The pain in my shoulder eases, the muscles in my back relax and loosen, and something inside me warms. Settles.

"It's too quiet," one of the men whispers, his gruff voice tight with concern—a thorn in my moment of peaceful reprieve. "Something feels ... *off*."

I think back to that dark shape I saw from the boat, chest tightening.

I peel up, like gently easing my roots from soil, and study the huddle of men clinging to metal-tipped spears, stealing nervous peeks at the trees.

Looking past them, I still.

From the cove, the land above looked like a lush, fertile oasis. But from up here on the edge of it all, I can see that the wild, overgrown foliage is hiding the remnants of a scorched town reduced to nothing but scattered blue rocks and half-standing walls.

Some of the larger trees are charred skeletons, hosts for loose vines that boast big, blue flowers spewing a burst of red anthers that look like flaming pupils.

There's a cleft in the jungle roof allowing dull, late-afternoon light to etch a path through the gloom—a path that's well worn compared to the rest of the underbrush.

Cainon offers a hand.

I ignore it and shove to a stand. "What happened here?"

He looks around as though he only just noticed the carnage, then rips a flower off one of the vines. "Blight got in."

The torn stem weeps a red tear that *drips*.

Drips.

Drips.

"So ... the entire community was torched?"

"Had no choice," he mutters, and I see that burning ship. See the way the rioting flames committed it to a watery grave.

I hear those distant screams—wild and hopeless.

The haunting silence that followed.

"Such a shame. A lot of our fresh produce came from here." He motions toward a half-standing pulley system protruding off the edge of the cliff. "Not to mention the acres of palm sugar crops that fell to the fire." He looks at the flower in his hand for a long, hard moment. "This is the reality of being confined to a small canvas of livable land."

I frown, thinking of the maps my curious eyes have traveled over time and time again. "But you *have* land. Not to mention hundreds of islands scattered across the ocean."

"*Infertile* land." He tosses the flower at the dirt, and it takes all my willpower not to pick it up and stash it away for safekeeping. The thought of all that color leaching away until it's nothing but a brown smear in the soil hurts.

He jerks his chin at my sack. "Boots, Orlaith. Before we go any further. We have snakes—poisonous ones."

Zane offers me a pout from his spot cross-legged on a stone, obviously listening in.

I return the gesture, digging into my sack and stuffing my feet into the claustrophobic hollows that cling too close to the backs of my heels, instantly mourning the soil's warm comfort.

"Let's get moving," Cainon says, voice raised enough for everyone to hear. "There's a brash pack of Irilak that have taken up residence in these ruins, but if we're quick, we can make it to Blue Hollow before the light fades."

The men murmur between themselves, lumping bags on their backs before they begin filing after Cainon.

It's hard to force my feet to move.

Pack.

Hauling the sack over my good shoulder, I follow him, scouring the deep pockets of shade for any sign of life.

I should be afraid, knowing what they're capable of—having seen the leeching doom firsthand the many times I dropped mice over my Safety Line.

Shay's special, our relationship cultivated over years of gathered trust and understanding, and I have no doubt he's the exception to the rule. I have no doubt that the Irilak in these parts are just as deadly as Kai insinuated when we flicked through *Te Bruk o' Avalanste* together what feels like a lifetime ago.

But there's no room for fear beside this overflow of *regret*.

Shay didn't have a pack. He was always on his own, except for when he was with me.

... *Me.*

I was his pack.

The realization chokes me, even more so when I recall the way he spoke to me right before I left. One soul-shattering word that echoed a million more ...

No.

Chapter 16
Orlaith

The nervous energy popping off almost every man in our party is palpable, tightening the air around us—a feeling that's only amplified since the thread of light falling upon the wiggly path has withered with the setting sun.

Sparked lanterns now provide a plump, protective shield that does nothing to alleviate the sense of being caged.

Watched.

Like the jungle itself is taking note of every crunching footfall. Every nervous glance into shadowed gulfs between trees. Every tightening fist clutching spears.

I've spent the otherwise silent journey scanning the jungle, hunting for signs of life and finding nothing.

Not a bird or a moth, or even one of the snakes that apparently likes to nest in pockets of dappled sunlight. But I can *feel* something out there just as surely as I can the thud in my chest, the peeling flesh on the backs of my heels, and the beads of sweat trailing down my spine.

Once we left the charred footprint of the desolated cliffside town, the jungle thickened, and the air became hot, sticky, and still. Even with the setting sun draining some of the heat, the humidity's still trapped below the tropical canopy.

My gaze hungers over big, waxy leaves that could double as shade sails, indigo flowers larger than a dinner plate, and vines strangling weepy, downtrodden trees. So used to ancient oaks clothed in lichen and roots that twist up from the soil, every step feels like I'm walking through the pages of a picture book.

The foliage is the color of the sea on an angry, weather-bent day—steel-blue with only the odd pop of green to lighten the mood. Remind me of home.

"You know what I'm looking forward to the most?" Zane asks, trudging along with a spring in his step, a lantern swinging from his lax hand. He seems to be the only one completely oblivious to this tense, suffocating feeling that won't seem to shake.

Flipping the piece of coal Gage gave me between my sooty fingers, I look down at the back of Zane's head boasting a rebellious dash of caramel hair he hasn't bothered to smooth all day. "What's that?"

"Momma's fish pie," he says, and I can hear the smile skating his voice. "It's the best."

"Kid's not lying," Captain rumbles from behind, his steady footsteps chasing mine. "It's his grandma's recipe. His mother and I grew up on that pie. Poor man's food that somehow made us feel like nobles."

A scorching trail blazes across my cheek, lifting the hairs on the back of my neck and making me gasp.

I snap my stare to the left.

Nothing.

Just the moody guts of the jungle, lifeless as ever, without even the chirp of an evening cricket to set the scene apart from a complex oil painting.

Even so, my steps slow, hand threading forward, fingers tangling with the back of Zane's shirt.

He stops, head tipping up to look back at me. "What is it?"

"Not sure," I murmur, searching every darkened gulley between the trees. "Something ..."

"Best we keep it moving," Captain rumbles from behind me, setting his hand between my shoulder blades and giving me a gentle boost. "All the lanterns are low on oil after the extra week at sea, and the sun's setting fast."

I nod slowly, loosening my hold on Zane. "Yes, Captain."

"Just Gun," he grunts out. "My ship's at the bottom of The Andler."

There's a restless rustle in the trees, followed by a heavy thud that ratchets through my chest and flames my blood.

I rip Zane back against me as everyone pushes close—heads swiveling, spears at the ready, the air thick with a chaotic energy that prickles my skin. There's the soft hiss of a blade loosening at my back, and it occurs to me how bitterly disappointed Baze would be that I'm not readily armed after all the work he's put into me over the years.

Silence prevails for a long, tense moment while I scour the jungle, my heart a wild thing beating me up from the inside. Violent fear has my scrunched hand shaking around Zane's crumpled shirt ...

You can't have him.

"Just a fallen branch," Cainon bellows from the front. "Let's push on. I can see the village's lights through the trees ahead."

Low murmurs rumble through the group, and everyone starts moving again, Zane easing from my grip with a lopsided smile tossed over his shoulder. I ruffle his hair, face hardening the moment he turns again, and I continue to scan the trees, heart lurching when I spot a stooped clutch of bluebells nesting at the base of a palm a dozen or so feet off the trail.

The tip of my boot hooks on something, and I whip off the track.

My sack goes flying, the piece of coal slipping from my grip when I hit the ground with a hard thud that rattles my teeth, my healing shoulder hunched beneath me.

But I feel no pain, barely hear the chorus of alarmed shouts as I stare at those bluebells with a stone-sized lump in my throat. Because that color right there—that *exact* tone—was the last puzzle piece that made up my brother on the wall in Whispers.

This feeling surges deep inside my gut that tingles all the way to the tips of my fingers. This need to have them. Hold them. Cradle them.

I ease up onto my knees, fingers stretched—

Firm hands land upon me, and I'm lugged back, brushed down, hair swiped from my face—breaking my sight of those bluebells.

"*I'm fine,*" I snap, batting Cainon's hand away.

His eyes flare, tension crackling, and from the corner of my eye I see the men stare at their boots, pretending they didn't just watch me chastise their High Master.

Perhaps they wouldn't be so confused if they knew he was inserting last-minute caveats that prevent my people from receiving promised, life-saving aid at the earliest possible convenience. That he holds all the power to change the savage tide of death spilling across the continent in the palm of his hand, and that he's dangling it over my head, just out of reach, until I *dance*.

All that proves is he doesn't trust me. Which makes it damn hard for me to trust him.

Cainon shifts forward, smothering me in the smell of citrus and salt as he crushes the space between us. I keep my chin high, even as a burst of goosebumps sprouts down the side of my neck. "We need to talk," he mutters against my ear.

"Then let's talk."

"Later." He picks up my sack, spins, and continues down the path with it lumped over his shoulder like a trophy.

I glance at the bluebells, heart heavy as I search the undergrowth for my lost piece of coal ...

Gone.

Hands bunching so tight I feel the scabs on my right palm crinkle and split, I look to my sack, foot swinging forward—

"Orlaith." Gun's blunt warning has my attention snapping back. He shakes his head, wearing a guillotine stare that suggests I'm trudging a line thinner than the pinch of his lips. "It's not the right time, luv."

Perhaps not. But it's not *his* body that's being sold for a promise that keeps slipping further between his fingers.

The sweet smell of sugar makes my tongue tingle as the trees thin, giving way to a hedge of tall buildings pressed against each other like a fortress. They're plagued by a constellation of blazing lanterns bolted to the cobbled walls blotched with fluffy moss.

The majority of our convoy falls back, ordered to follow a stable sign that appears to direct them around the edge of the village.

Cainon spears down a slender path cleaved between the otherwise impenetrable wall.

I charge after him, trailed by Gun and Zane, shooting out in the settlement's courtyard that's barricaded on all four sides by tightly packed buildings.

Everything's cobbled: the buildings, the ground, the water fountain in the center of it all—held in the bright embrace of tree-tall lanterns arching over buildings like bowing stick figures, their flaming heads caught in glass globes.

I shield my eyes from the glare as I stalk Cainon in long, determined strides, stare narrowed on my sack slung over his shoulder.

A sprinkle of wide-eyed people bow at the waist as he passes, their gazes strictly averted.

Cainon makes for a large building packed between two much smaller ones, a wooden sign hanging from its thatched awning:

"Keep her out while I secure our rooms. This is no place for a lady," he bellows over my head, glancing at me before swinging the door wide, spilling the smell of sweat and smoke and the lilting tune of a lone fiddle that's snipped off the moment he slams the door shut behind him.

Rage boils my blood.

I charge forward, clutch the doorknob, twist, pull—

A large, weather-beaten hand slams against the wood.

Frowning, I whip around, but Gun just holds my fervid stare with a narrowed look that hits like a sledgehammer.

"He's got my sack."

"It'll be safe with our High Master."

I huff out a joyless laugh and slide down the wall until I'm crouched. Head tipped back, I stare across the courtyard. "I don't believe in that word," I mutter, watching people go about their evening business.

None of them seem to notice they're in the presence of the child-survivor—an invisibility I've chased my whole life. Hard to appreciate with my mind so tangled up in the fact that Cainon has all my vulnerabilities lumped over his shoulder.

"If I move off this door and sit on that bench right there so I can smoke my pipe," Gun drones, pointing to the bench bolted to the wall beside me, "are you going to shove your way in the door like a bull and announce yourself to a group of drunken cane growers?"

"I can't move that fast."

"Don't believe you."

Chuffing, I drop the rest of the way to the ground, landing hard on my ass, and stretch my legs in front of me as a show of good faith.

Wind stirs, filling the busy courtyard with a swirl of the sweet steam pouring from a giant chimney across the way. It sticks to my skin and sugarcoats my lips as I watch a circle of kids play knucklebones—their eyes carefree and chests full of laughter.

Gun pushes off the door and strides past, lumps himself on the bench, and pulls a leather pouch from his side satchel. "Anything special in that sack?" he asks, tamping something sage green into his pipe. He sparks a match, ignites the contents, and puffs on the end while I think of my diamond pickaxe, the talon, Rhordyn's pillow slip ...

Special—noxious—inflammatory.

Mine.

"You could say that."

He grunts, takes another puff, and blows out a thick cloud of white.

Again, the bones scatter, followed by hoots and howls as one of the kids beats at his chest with victorious fists.

Gun sits forward, elbows on his knees. "What's that boy munching on?"

"Which one?"

"*Our* one."

I follow his gaze, finding Zane crouched in the shadowed awning of a house on the opposite side of the courtyard—cheeks full, fist clenched around a stick staked through the middle of a big, red apple.

My lips almost curl into a smile. "Toffee apple."

"I didn't give him any coin ..."

Shit. "I did."

"No, you didn't."

I wince, watching Zane take another oblivious bite. "Are you ... going to do anything about it?"

Smoke billows out of Gun's mouth as he watches his nephew enjoy his no-doubt stolen sweet. Probably nicked off somebody's windowsill.

Gun reclines against the wall and draws another long puff, making the contents of his pipe fizzle red. "Figure I'm off duty," he says, releasing a plume of white.

This time, my smile breaks free.

The door beside me swings open, and a petite woman pours out wearing a spill of blue fabric. She peers left and right, gaze touching me before she looks at Gun and says, "Where's the Mistress? I've been sent out to escort her to the maiden suite."

His brow bumps up, and he jerks his thumb in my direction.

Her attention flicks to me at the base of the wall, and her cheeks redden, offsetting bright blue eyes and all that golden hair piled on the top of her head.

She bobs a swift curtsey that makes her skirt puff full of air. "Mistress, I'm so sorry. I didn't realize—"

"No, it's fine, honestly." *It's more a compliment than*

anything. "Have you seen my sack? The High Master carried it inside. Did he set it down anywhere?"

She blinks, paling as she closes the door behind her and looks to Gun like she's a little afraid for her wellbeing. "I—ah—I'm just one of the barmaids ..."

"Don't harass the messenger, Orlaith. She's just trying to take you to your room."

I fill my cheeks, blow them out, and shove to a stand, then follow her past Gun and down a path cleaved between the buildings. Slowing before an inconspicuous door pressed into the stone, she pulls a key from her skirt pocket and battles the stubborn lock while I lean against the opposite wall and wait.

The hair on my left arm prickles, and I frown, breath snatching as a warm blow of air batters my side, teasing a raw, musky smell past my nose that pulls straight from my nightmares.

That deep-down voice screams for me to *run.*

Instead, I turn my head slower than a setting sun and stare along the tight alley that feeds into the unlit jungle beyond ...

There's something there.

My lungs compress, every hair on the back of my neck standing on end. My entire world—my entire *being*—seems to tunnel down to that slab of darkness at the end of the alley. Like I'm bobbing atop an inky ocean, feeling something brush against my wading feet.

Waiting to see if it'll strike.

Suddenly, I can't blink. Can't swallow. Can't so much as breathe. Crushed against the wall by the formidable form of this unseen force.

"Mistress?"

My plummet back to reality knocks my lungs into action, and I turn to the woman standing inside the open doorway that leads to a lit stairwell.

Clearing my throat, I shut myself off from the seeing shadows, and step over the threshold, a shiver scuttling up my spine as the door slams shut behind me.

Chapter 17

Baze

The Reidlyn Alps rise before me like wicked waves, crusted with pockets of permafrost that glaze bits of them in an eerie shine. The peaks are hidden by dollops of white clouds that stand out against the bruised evening sky.

I turn my lantern's dial, inhaling the smell of scorched flint as it flares to life, holding it before me, scanning the imposing shadow of the Alps.

Heart in my throat, I nudge Ale into the swallow of darkness, snow crunching underfoot, the lantern casting us in a protective, flaming aura. The temperature drops so fast my lungs cease for a beat—like leaping into an icy lake.

No wonder the sprites refuse to come out here anymore. The ones that risk it probably freeze up and drop dead the moment they flutter past this very line.

It's rare for even regular folk to step into the shadow of the Alps these days—the temperature too extreme, the risk of crossing a Vruk increasing by the year. A lot of the villages nearby have been decimated by them. Even the cashmere goat herders that dominated this terrain for centuries have been forced to shift their dwindling flocks to warmer, safer pastures.

Ale's ivory coat is stark against the black, matching the naked trees that reach from the ground like bleached claws. Ears straining, I listen for anything other than the sluggish crush of every hooved footfall and the hollow wails of the wind.

Ale pauses, tossing his head, flared nostrils steaming as he snorts his protest before attempting to prance backward.

"Come on, boy. Stop drawing attention to yourself." I nudge his sides, and he bucks, almost tossing me off the saddle. Tightening my legs and my one-handed hold on the reins, I growl, steadying the horse and nudging him deeper into the chill, past lines and lines of huge, sharpened rib bones staked in the snow.

Some are pointing toward the Alps, ready to impale anything that's not paying attention as it charges into the feast of Ocruth. Some are pointing the other way, protecting Fryst from our own spill of ruthless mutts.

The latter are spotless—untarnished by the dried smears of black blood that paint some of the former.

A shiver crawls up my spine.

Hours pass of trudging through powdered eddies, blowing big puffs of white onto my stiffening fingers and wishing I'd dressed warmer, before I spot the first marker: a large, pronged tooth stabbed into a gnarled tree rising from the snow like a haggard limb.

I guide Ale through the otherwise invisible trail, counting down from thirty-five before a round stone much taller than me comes into view. Next to it sits a windowless, wooden stable, its roof heavy with snow.

I leap off Ale and lure him into the musty building despite his backward pull, trying not to think about the ingrained stench of death that haunts its innards. About the fact that it's utterly void of life. I wrestle his reins around the worn post inside, dodging his prancing hooves.

"You'll be fine," I mutter, side-eyeing the blood splattered walls. "So long as you *settle down*."

I stuff a slab of hay in the half-barrel used as a feeder, then dip a few strands into my lantern's flame, using them to spark the others hanging about the space.

Ale pulls back, eyes rolling, and I brush a hand down his trembling withers in a failed attempt to soothe him. Can't blame the poor fuck, but he's not doing himself any favors. With all the snorting and squealing, he might as well be tolling a dinner bell loud enough to spill across The Stretch.

Sighing, I close the door on my way out, entombing him in its warm glow, hoping he'll calm and bed down for some much-needed rest.

Trudging through knee-deep snow, I edge around the rock some believe was placed by the hands of giants. It's so round and smooth and out of place amongst the otherwise level stretch of land only littered with the odd tree barely clinging to life.

I feel around its surface until I find the groove that runs down the side like a split seam. I kneel, checking over my shoulder every few seconds as I dig through a foot of snow by lantern light.

The tips of my fingers are numb, despite my thick gloves, by the time they scrape against the trapdoor embedded in the ground. I lug it open, peering into the throat of darkness. I give another quick scan of my bleak surroundings, then edge down onto the ladder in the hole, lantern in hand.

The rungs creak in protest with every booted step.

I leap onto the packed earth, the smell of beer and freshly fired meat smacking me in the back of the throat and making the muscles under my tongue tingle.

Or perhaps that's—

Pausing, I draw deep, looking up the ladder I descended. Studying each rung.

I sniff again, untangling the butter-spice residue of Zali's scent.

With a low growl, I charge down the tunnel until I reach another ladder, which I descend, then follow the narrowing corridor, its walls stabilized with inlaid bones. A crossbar supports the ceiling every few steps, but I still shiver at the thought of being buried alive.

The way finally opens to a large, smoky room with a pitched roof reinforced with pale wood beams, the space packed full of hollering, howling, yodeling men with filthy faces, chapped lips, and beards almost thick enough to hide them. Reeking of ale and wobbling on their feet, none of them seem to notice my presence.

Setting my lantern by the door, I swallow the smear of jealousy at their mindless states and study the throng.

The men are clothed in leather and fur in various shades of gray, boasting twine necklaces threaded with large Vruk teeth—mostly one or two, signifying a couple of years' service. Only a handful of men flaunt more than that. Hardly surprising.

These men are paid in Ocruth and Rouste coin to

maintain the traps that litter The Stretch and buffer the spill of Vruk back and forth across the Alps—a responsibility High Master Vadon doesn't appear to be holding up on *his* side anymore.

It takes a certain savagery to survive here, doing what they do. Living the precarious life of a *Moal*.

You come, make your coin, and try to get the fuck out before the Alps chomp down on you.

I scan the crowd again ...

She's not here.

A haunch of hog spins over a nest of hot coals in the center of the room.

My stomach rumbles.

Walking forward, I remove my gloves and pause by the blistered feast, prying off a shard of crackle with my still-numb fingers, scanning the display of bestial skulls lining two entire walls. I pocket my gloves, still crunching through the well-seasoned treat and reveling in my first hot bite in days, when the sound of merriment lulls.

The messy crowd's attention bores into me.

There's the *wisp* of loosening blades, too soft to be heard by the average ears. If I were to scope the crowd now, they'd all be wielding weapons black and curved at the tips.

Talons.

"And who the fuck are *you?*"

I wipe my hands on my cloak, warming them by the flames as I look up through the wet, stringy hair hanging over my eyes. "I'm looking for a woman. Likely dressed in Rouste garb."

"The 'igh Mistress?"

The question comes from a stocky, weathered brute

standing on the opposite side of the spit—red hair wild, hand lost beneath a thick, gray pelt broadening his shoulders.

I note the dark pall of his eyes. The vast collection of Vruk teeth hanging around his neck.

Hoarth.

I've heard of him—a Moal legend. No female or children to send coin home to. From what I hear, he does this shit for fun.

"That who ya lookin' for?" Bushy brows bunched, he grates out, "That's the only female in this shit 'ole."

Something inside me settles, releasing the line of tension that's been strung across my shoulders since I left the camp days ago.

"That's the one." I reach for a mug on a table beside the spit, collecting sharp stares as I turn the barrel tap and help myself to a pour of frothy ale. "Where is she?"

I hear the sound of Hoarth resheathing his weapon and turn to see him looking down his nose at me. "Out *there.*"

My movements still, mug halfway to quelling this deep, rooted thirst I've been cradling for days. "On the fucking *Stretch?*"

Hoarth gives a terse nod. "Tried telling 'er the first night she came, we don't stay out fixing the traps after sundown. She told me to mind me own business or else she'd lob off me cock with that pretty blade of 'ers."

I clear my throat, throw my drink back in three deep gulps that extinguish fucking nothing, then thud the empty mug on the ale-stained table. "Where is she? Exactly?"

"Skewers," a man behind me bellows, and I look over my shoulder, marking his bleak, ruddy eyes and the scar slashed from ear to mouth.

Upper lip peeling back, I whip my head around. "The main thoroughfare?"

Hoarth shrugs. "She had that look in 'er eye, lad." He toasts the air with a hollowed-out Vruk tooth large enough to be used as a mug. "*Bloodlust.*"

I spin on my heel, heading back the way I came, snatching my lantern off the ground.

"Oi!"

Snagged to a halt, I turn in time to catch an airborne vial before it pegs me in the face.

I tip it from side to side, watching the thin, black brine slosh around.

Liquid bane.

I catch Hoarth's eye.

"Just in case," he says with a wink.

"Thanks," I mutter, then continue on my way—that tension restringing across my shoulders, but so much fucking worse.

Skewers after dark …

She should know better.

Chapter 18
Orlaith

The room is modest, the simple wooden bed made up with crisp, white sheets that smell like starch.

"White?" I rasp, staring at them. "But Bahari's color is blue …"

Finished turning them down, the barmaid smooths the new folds into place, averting my gaze. "Tradition, Mistress. They're meant to showcase the evidence of a maiden's broken virtue should somebody break in and try to …" she clears her throat, a deep blush pinching the apples of her cheeks.

Force their way between my legs.

A blunt reminder that I've sold my body to a complete stranger.

"Right," I mutter bitterly. "Of course. What a silly question."

"Is there anything else you need at the moment?" She fluffs the quilt draped over the end of the bed before sparking another lantern. "Can I draw you a bath?"

"I'll sort myself out." I offer her a small smile, suffocating under this thick oil of unease lining my chest cavity. "Thank you."

She bobs a curtsey and turns to leave. The moment the door snicks shut, my attention drags around the room again.

I don't dash to the latrine to ease my overburdened bladder or begin running the bath, despite being covered in dirt, sweat, spume, and a mix of unfamiliar scents. Instead, I slide under the bed, running the tips of my fingers around the edges of all the floorboards until a splinter pierces me. I pare it back, snap it free, then wiggle out and tuck it beneath my pillow, sucking the swell of blood from my pinky.

Vanth caught me off guard. I refuse to let that happen again.

Inspecting the windows, I find them all sealed shut, bar the one in my washroom—high up and too small for most people to fit through. I leap off the latrine and take care of my business.

Twisting the tap, I fill the big brass tub, standing beside it as I watch the water tumble. I release a heavy sigh, my scratchy eyes, achy feet, and the twinge of pain in my lower back nothing compared to the bone-dead weight of my exhaustion.

Stripping down until my bare skin is exposed to the kissing steam, I move to the stone sink and grab a bar of soap, looking up at the small mirror hanging on the wall.

Frosted with fog, it reflects a blur of tan skin.

I lift my hand, swiping it across the glass, gasping at the reflection staring back at me—

Opaline skin ...

Iridescent hair ...
Glimmering freckles ...
Crystal eyes that break my heart.

Cracks weave across my skin, peeling off to reveal the caustic blackness nesting below the surface.

A figure steps up behind me. Robust. Statuesque.

Beautiful.

Him.

The soap falls from my hand as I stare into lifeless eyes I don't recognize.

"*Rhor—*"

He moves closer, and I swear I can feel his mighty presence pressed against my naked back. Can feel his powerful arm weave around my waist, hand threading between my thighs as he grips my throbbing heat.

I shudder, the sound snipped as a silver blade is whipped around and set upon my throat, dragged sideways in a brutal slice that cuts my voice and breath.

Blood gushes free, painting my bare breasts in a spill of red ribbons ...

I blink, shattering the illusion, heaving.

It's just me. Just *his* lie reflecting back at me—hair a wild mess, tanned from all the sun, more freckles dashed across my nose than normal.

I'm going mad.

I sob, insides lurching as I fold to the side and grip the latrine. My stomach convulses, vomit bursting from my trembling lips. My tongue aches by the time I'm done, stomach muscles spasming. I use some tissue to wipe acidic residue from my mouth, then toss it down the hole, pawing at the onyx jewel clipped around my neck.

Snarling.

I grip the latch with both fingers, tugging, making sure it's tightly fastened.

"Fuck you, Rhordyn." I shove to my feet and stare at his lie in the mirror again, pinching my face as though I'm pinching *him*. "You got what you wanted—me out of your way. You don't get to haunt me, too."

I spin, lift my leg over the edge of the bath, and dip my toes into the scalding water. A shiver travels all the way to the back of my neck.

Too hot.

I close my eyes, focus on the unwanted hug of my tight skin, and press the sole of my foot flush against the brass, sucking a sharp breath as the heat nips at the sore on the back of my heel—like rubbing salt in the peeled wound. Hissing tight breaths, I thread my other foot beneath the water and lower myself.

Every scrape riddled across my skin flares with a blaze of sting, but I force myself to endure the pain—the *heat*—until everything from my clavicle down is raw and straddling that fine line between hot chafe and blistering burn.

Easing back, I lean my head against the brass as the scald loses its edge. A droopy comfort takes over my limbs and mind, turning my thoughts sludgy and slow, my blinks getting heavier, longer ...

I see *them*—broken, bloody, in pieces.

Staring.

I feel warm blood tacky on my hands. See its polychrome

shine, born from the swing of an axe while my mother watched on and screamed.

My brother's.

Gasping, I jerk my head off the side of the bath, eyes popping open.

The bath, now warm like my brother's blood, makes my entire body shiver.

Fuck.

Groggily, limbs heavy, I clamber out, almost tripping over my own feet before I wrap myself in a towel and wring out my sodden hair. Pulling the door open, I step into the bedroom.

Breath catching, I still.

Cainon stands before the fireplace, hand perched on the mantle, staring into dancing flames.

My heart lodges in my throat as I spot my sack sitting on the end of the bed ... *open*.

"Vanth told me that Rhordyn refused to let you go." My gaze darts to the back of his head—the sketched undercut grown out so much I can no longer make out a pattern. "I'm wondering if it works both ways."

"What do you mean?"

Cainon turns, eyes chips of ice, and my gaze drags to the bunch of black fabric held in his white-knuckled fist.

Nostrils flaring, I take in the faintest hint of Rhordyn's scent that still hits like a punch to the chest, knocking my heart into a spin.

I bolt my feet to the floor and resist the urge to leap forward.

Snatch it.

He tosses the slip through the air, and it lands in a flutter on the floorboards between us.

Silence.

I hold his stare for a few thundering heartbeats before calmly taking a step. I pick up the slip, fingers clawing into the precious silk as I peel my eyes off him and inch toward my sack—as if these slow, soft movements will take the edge off this moment's sharp significance.

Cainon sighs, and I look up to see his eyes darken. "I told you to tug out those roots, Orlaith. But you're so determined to cower in his shade."

I pause, hand tightening around the silk. "*Cower?*"

He prowls toward me. "Yes."

I spin—calves flush against the wooden bed frame, the slip held against my chest like a shield.

"You have everything right here, staring at you," he says, arching over me until I'm forced to fall back against the mattress as his eyes dip to the pillow slip. "But your hands are too full to accept it."

Heart in my throat, I scramble up the crisp, white sheets, but he cages me in with strong arms planted either side of my head, knee notching between my spread thighs, making my skin burn.

I gasp ...

He looks so big and powerful above me like this, and the towel separating him from my nakedness suddenly feels so thin.

He leans close, lips skimming my ear. "What did he do to get so far inside your head, huh?"

I open my mouth, close it ... Realize there's no way to

explain without airing out my weakness like a still-stained shirt fresh from the wash.

Since I began seeing Rhordyn around the castle a few years back, he's been a punishing presence trying to push me out the door. Telling me to get out and *live,* like he was furious with me for not spending my heartbeats the way he deemed appropriate.

But with all that pushing, all I felt was a *pull.*

He'd drift into the room and I'd fall into his gravity. He'd glance in my direction and every cell would feel pinched by his perusal.

When he touched me on that balcony beneath a fall of rain, it felt real, but *not.* Like there was some sort of veil separating us that held a deadly significance.

Truth is, I fell in love with a ghost. Now I'm gone and still ... *haunted.*

Cainon's hand threads through my hair, gripping, gently tugging until my head is tipped, the residue of my thoughts thumping through my body.

Making me *ache.*

Face hovered above mine, Cainon looks down from beneath the lusty crush of heavy lids. "Did he fuck you, petal?"

The crass words are a purred attack, reeling my mind back to the feel of Rhordyn's fingers skirting around my entrance ...

Pushing into me ...

I throb, hips threatening to grind against the memory, choking on the fragrant scent of my arousal.

My cheeks heat.

Cainon's brow shoots up.

"No," I rasp. "He did not *fuck* me."

"So, if I took you right here, right now ..." He eases his other leg between my thighs and forces them wide. A gasp slips free as my bare core is exposed to the fire's licking warmth. "You'd bleed for me?"

Bleed for me ...

The words slap me.

My face hardens, and for one thrilling moment, I picture myself pulling that talon free from my open sack, pressing its lethal length against his throat, and asking him the very same question.

Part of me wants to, just to see the look in his eyes.

I set my hand against his chest and *shove*, snatching his wide-eyed stare as he rears back, frowning. "Yes, Cainon. I would."

The words are absorbed by the sudden hollow between us. A chasm of his own creation.

I'm here, keeping *my* promise, while he's dangling *his* over my head like a line of bait.

Perhaps he's under the illusion that simply being his High Mistress is enough to satisfy me. That he's giving me *everything* Rhordyn didn't and therefore, I should be grateful.

Truth be told, I couldn't give two shits about the title. About the pleasure his lusty eyes promise me in spades.

I want those ships.

All the heat snips from his stare, and he eases off the bed. "Fuck, sorry ..." He grips the bridge of his nose and digs through his pocket, flipping a tiny, weatherworn scroll through his fingers. "Not that it's any excuse, but I'm on edge," he says with a burst of nervous laughter. "If you can't already tell."

My curiosity cranes her neck.

"What's that?"

He looks between me and the scroll, then holds it out. "Rhordyn's headed to Bahari to retrieve his ships. Payment for his prized mare."

He ... *what?*

I leap off the bed and snatch the scroll, scanning the tiny scripture, then once more—slow, hungering over the slanted curves and delicate flicks in a way I know I shouldn't.

His writing.

A dainty scrawl so at odds with the man it spilled from. I'm not sure why that makes the organ thumping in my chest ache, but it does.

I stop myself just shy of running my thumb across the parchment, feeling the dent of each syllable scratched into the surface.

He's coming for the ships.

Unease wrestles with my insides as I realize there's a high chance I'll be forced into his proximity at least once before he leaves ...

Shit.

"While he's here, he'll be searching for weaknesses."

I look up, frowning. "What do you mean?"

"I can't remember the last time he bothered to visit my territory," Cainon continues, stuffing his hands deep into the pockets of his gray leather pants. "He could've sent someone else. The only reason he didn't is because he's seeking signs that you're not here of your own accord so he can use the law that protects people against extortion to his advantage."

"I don't follow ..."

Cainon snags the parchment and rolls it into a perfect little scroll. "Since Zali and Rhordyn publicly announced their allegiance at the ball, I've been outnumbered. The Eastern Territory of Rouste is almost the size of Ocruth, and Zali's army is savage, forged from blistering dunes that are near inhabitable. Together, they're a formidable match I have no hope of standing up against, and I don't know what their plan is. I just know it's *something*." He pauses, pocketing the scroll. "I'm a bug beneath his boot, Orlaith. You give him a reason to believe you're not here because you *want* to be, and he'll put his foot down—use his pretty new alliance to destroy me and my people."

I shake my head, thinking back to the most recent Tribunal—to the people who went to Rhordyn with cupped hands and ache in their eyes. "He has no need for extra land to manage. He's having enough problems as it is."

"But that's just it. The jungle that separates us from both Rhordyn's and Zali's territories is thick and dark and riddled with Irilak—a natural Vruk deterrent. It's *safe* here, and people are starting to notice. I'm packed full of refugees arriving on trade ships daily while the people that choose to stay behind are being slaughtered."

I chew on his words, trying to find a comfortable space for them to settle inside me.

Rhordyn thinks Cainon is seeking to shift the borders through a territory war, and vice versa. There's so much finger pointing that it's literally costing lives.

Cainon's palm grazes my elbow as he steps close.

"He's always been bigger, stronger, *better* than the rest of us. The fact that I'm his people's salvation is twisting him up. I can see it."

I look from his hand, now wrapped around my arm, to his eyes—wide and beseeching.

"You give him the faintest reason to believe I'm holding you here against your will before you're officially released from his guardianship and he'll exploit it. He'll use my own ships against me and that war neither of us wants will fall upon our doorstep. *That,* Orlaith, is why he can't have the ships until after we're coupled."

I see the sense. His words are easy enough to follow.

But it doesn't stop a frown from buckling my brow.

"Then why take such a risk on me?"

A broad smile makes it all the way to his eyes. "I saw something I wanted, and I had to have it. Damn the consequences."

"Seems a bit shortsighted."

"Quite the opposite," he murmurs, grabbing my face with both hands, warm and all-encompassing as he looks right into me. "Let me *save* you ..."

There's nothing left to save.

I almost say the words aloud. Probably would if it weren't for his hand now trailing down my neck, my arm, all the way to my bunched fist. One by one, he pries my fingers free, until Rhordyn's pillow slip is tugged away. Then he's stalking toward the fire.

"*Wait.*"

He stops and looks at me over his shoulder.

I approach, throat cinched as I take the slip, hand

tightening to the point of pain. Like that same hand just bored through my ribs and grabbed hold of my heart.

Don't think.

Just do.

I force my fingers to ease their desperate clutch ... and toss it at the flames, gaze fixed on the wild blue flare in Cainon's eyes, like he's desperate to watch that little piece of Rhordyn burn.

I turn from the scene, knowing that if I don't, I'll drop to my knees, screaming and digging through the embers until the flesh melts off my hands and my skin finally reflects that of my unsuspecting victims.

Cainon wants me to be his perfect High Mistress? Fine. I'll play the part. I'll earn those fucking ships. But if either he or Rhordyn use me to spark this political tiff, they'll find themselves at war with *me*.

And unlike them, I've got nothing to lose ...

Not anymore.

Chapter 19
Orlaith

Towel bunched around me, I sit on the bed, stomach in knots as I work through my shoulder stretches. The contents of my sack are spewed across the sheets, the hilt of my wooden sword poking out, its leather binding peeled back an inch—likely from being dunked in saltwater and left to steep.

I reach for it, wrapping my fingers around the pommel. It's cold in my hand, like it harbors the chill of Ocruth on a brisk spring morning when daisies are barely peeking above a veil of mist and frosted grass crunches beneath my feet.

A strange tightness bands around my chest.

Pulling the sword close, my eyes narrow on a scrawled flick of moss green—the tapered tip of a painted vine swirled around the pommel's tip, leading beneath the leather weave.

Frowning, I touch it, trace it, then pinch the binding's edge and begin peeling it away from the tacky bonding substance.

With every unwinding twist, more of the etched vine unveils.

Splits off. Sprouts leaves.

Blooms little pops of purple that dangle down the hilt and make the backs of my eyes sting.

My wisteria vine.

It's here. It's been here this entire time.

I fall back into the sheets, sword tucked to my chest as I stare up at the rafters ...

A *little bit of home.*

I'm not sure where it came from. Who painted it.

I just know it's my new favorite thing.

Rhordyn's coming to Bahari to retrieve his ships.

I reposition the pillow and toss sideways—a failed attempt to disband my rampant thoughts in hopes they find somewhere to settle. It's like I'm pumped full of Exothryl, but this is a natural charge that's not burning off.

I press the flat of my palm against my rioting chest and sigh, staring at the dying embers in the hearth, thinking back to that clutch of bluebells I spotted earlier today.

My throat tightens.

The thought of leaving them there, alone in the dark, fills me with heavy dread.

I sit up so fast all the blood drains from my head, kicking it into a spin. Once upon a time, those bluebells would've felt so far away. *Untouchable.*

But now ...

I can get them *myself.*

I leap out of bed and clamber into fresh, comfortable, better-fitting clothes the barmaid brought in with a supper tray. Digging my knapsack from the bottom of my sack,

I knot my hair into a high bun, then scour my room for something small, hollow, able to stand upright—

The clay mug on my tray catches my eye.

Perfect.

I stash it in my knapsack, along with one of the lanterns plucked off a wall hook, before looking at the door.

Can't take the obvious way out—who knows who I might run into on my way down the hall. I doubt Cainon would be very pleased to catch me sneaking out of my *maiden* suite in the middle of the night, especially given the conversation we just had.

Grabbing my wooden sword, I head for the washroom, step onto the latrine directly below the window, and unlock the latch. I swing the pane wide, set my sword and knapsack on the sill, then climb through—slow and tentative to avoid agitating my shoulder.

I maneuver onto the window trim until I'm chest first against the cool rock, and excitement crackles through my veins, igniting me from the inside.

This is risky. Dangerous. *Wrong.*

So wrong.

But it feels so fucking good.

I look down on the empty alleyway sandwiched between this building and the one beside it, then edge along the window trim—peeking out over the courtyard alive with a lazy, midnight beat. The crowd's changed, thinned out to clusters of pipe smokers, ambling men who can't seem to see straight, and scantily clad women who hang off them like lusty shadows.

A slow drizzle lit from above lifts sweet, botanical smells off the stone, and I draw deep before I turn the other way, spotting a trellis bolted to the side of the building that supports a trailing vine.

That'll do.

I stuff my sword in my knapsack and ease it over my shoulder, then edge down the wooden grid.

The cobbles are smooth against the bare soles of my feet as I dart toward the courtyard, nudging into the shadow of a tall, potted shrub. I use my hands to delve a peephole through the branches, checking the inn's bench is no longer burdened by an eagle-eyed Captain before picking a quiet path around the courtyard's perimeter.

I pass sleepy households, sweet shops shuttered up for the night, and a large building that boasts a Sugar Mill sign.

Here, everything smells sweeter—like the stone beneath my feet is cast from blocks of sugar and the sprinkle of rain is treacle tears. A few wooden carts laden with empty sap chutes are parked at the front, and I weave between them, passing two more shops before finding the tight alley we entered the village through earlier this evening.

Wedging between the tall buildings, I dig the lantern from my knapsack and turn the dial, hands shaking with a surge of excitement. I'm about to step out of the illuminated safety net when gooseflesh bursts across the back of my neck.

I spin, shuffle back a step, and slam against the wall.

From here, I have a clear view of the Blue Hollow Inn on the opposite side of the courtyard and the neck of the alleyway just below my room.

And a man—broad and hooded and caped in black—standing in the shadowed midst of the potted shrub I stood beside only moments ago.

My heart races, a cold sweat prickling my skin as I study him.

He fills the space so effortlessly, like he was hewn for the darkness. Forged beneath its arcane pressure. For some strange reason, I picture him wrapping that same darkness over my face and using it to suffocate me.

I blink, and he's gone.

Gasping, I flick my gaze over the surrounding space, kicking off the wall to garner a broader view of the courtyard.

Nothing.

Either my swelling insanity is carving specters from the shadows *or*—

A low laugh crawls up my throat, morphing into a growl.

I pull out my sword, punch my lantern over the threshold, and charge into the night.

Damp earth clots between my toes with every haloed step. The lantern flame is my shield; the heady chorus of crickets my companion; the soft, barely there rain a refreshing spritz to my face and hands as I backtrack our earlier trail, glancing over my shoulder every few steps.

Packed full of restless energy, I scan the ground for whatever it was that tripped me earlier. I spot a root poking free from the earth like an upturned worm, and excitement bursts in my belly.

Waving my lantern off the track, I illuminate a sea of wet, bobbing shrubs attacked by the odd heavy drip of rain breaking through the canopy.

I think this is right. It looks so much different under the full cover of night ...

I check the path both ways before tiptoeing off the tailored soil, my bare foot breaking through the carpet of loose twigs and rotting leaves ...

Too loud.

Wincing, I check over my shoulder and rock into another crunching step, then another. The sleepy bundle of blue dawns into view, taming my galloping heart and easing my lips into a stolen smile.

Found you.

A shiver scuttles up my spine as I kneel in the damp earth, lay my sword in the soil, and pull the mug from my knapsack, tamping it full of soil that sticks to my hands. I use my finger to dig a trench around the bluebell's base—

The crickets stop chirping.

Just ... *stop*. Like they all dropped dead.

The hairs on my arms lift, and a chill shrouds the back of my neck as the air around me hollows, like it's suddenly *starving*.

My next breath out is an alarming blow of white.

I freeze, pulse pounding in my ears, gaze fixed on the bluebells as a familiar perusal scribes across my skin like a cold flick of oil ...

My heart stops, dug from my flesh and lumped in the soil as I let my eyes flutter closed.

Squeeze them tight.

Not him.

It's not him, Orlaith.

I force them open and continue digging up the root ball as though the cold, prickly presence is nothing but another specter of my insanity, swiftly tucking the bluebells in their little mug-home. I pack some extra soil around the edges so they're nice and snug, then pull it close to my chest and breathe.

Breathe ...

Purposely leaving my sword in the soil, I slowly rise to my feet, swallow thickly, and spin.

Still.

I loosen a shallow breath—a meager sacrifice to the creatures pinning me in with their combined presence.

Three Irilak hover around me, the biggest over twice the size of Shay, looking down on me through black, beady eyes set in the twin hollows of a bleached skull. An infinite stare that etches over my skin, making my eyes mist ...

There's a comfort in it—one I miss.

Mourn.

So many regrets.

A low, grating sound rattles in the back of its throat, lifting the hairs on my arms as my eyes sway to the smaller creature on the right. Then to the tiny one notched close—no taller than my kneecap.

My heart lurches.

They're ... a *family*.

A sharp symphony of clicking specks at me from the baby one. A familiar sound.

Hunger.

A mouse in a jar would be mighty helpful right about now.

Part of me wants to flee—the part that's keenly aware of their predatory disposition and the frail flicker keeping me safe. But that part is small, overridden by a deep, instinctual urge to make myself as tiny as possible.

To show *respect*.

Slower than a setting sun, I drop to my knees and dip my chin.

There's a creaking sound from above; a rustle and a swish before an almighty crack ratchets through me.

The Irilak scatter.

I shove back, bunched in a protective ball around my precious potted cargo as something long and heavy thuds against the ground.

Silence prevails.

I lift my head and peer past the fine-tipped fronds of a fallen palm branch ...

Air shreds out of me in a milky haze.

My lantern's been knocked across the ground. Light cast upon the track, I'm bare and vulnerable as the Irilak surge forward so fast a blow of brisk air batters my face. They stop just shy of folding over me in a shadowed gulp, caging me in, and I look up into the reflective stare of the largest one, hovering like an ebbing wave of ink about to drain me. Or perhaps it'll strike the killing blow, then drift back and let the others feast.

I expect the thought to stake through me with a spike of fear, but it never comes.

The seconds stretch.

And stretch.

The rain grows heavy, spilling through the canopy and pinging against the lantern's panes, weaving between a crack in the glass and snipping out the flame.

Still, we watch each other—water seeping through my

clothes and weighing down my hair, dripping off the end of my nose while I wait for them to pounce.

To *feed*.

To pour over me and suckle the life from my body until I'm nobody.

Nothing.

Seconds seep into minutes that feel like a small eternity, and I cock my head to the side, curiosity peeking from my shadows. Slowly, tentatively, I thread my hand into the space between us—*reaching*. Threatening to tangle my fingers with its smoggy murk.

It makes a sharp sound that flips my heart as it darts back, pausing.

The corner of my mouth kicks up ...

It's not going to eat me.

Chapter 20
Orlaith

I jog down the trail, mud splattering up my calves, knapsack smacking my hip in rhythm with my thundering heart. The three hollow presences flit around me like a churn of restless spirits.

Almost as if they're *playing*.

Swiping sodden hair from my eyes, I give in to the reckless laugh popping up my throat, setting free a raw, *happy* sound that feels foreign on my tongue.

Though the rain has stopped, my clothes still cling to me like a second skin by the time the floodlit village comes into view between the trees. My feet slow with the Irilak's easing spin as I edge toward the light, grip tightening on the mug-o'-bells held close to my chest.

I pause.

A deluge of men have spilled out into the mud and collected around a large circle of lanterns—a fighting ring for the two shirtless brutes that are bouncing on their toes, shooting little jabs while the raucous crowd chants, slurs, and hollers from just outside the staked line.

"Crap," I mutter.

I could pick a path around the village perimeter and sneak in through a different access point. Or I guess I could ... *blend in* and walk straight past them all, pretending I didn't just emerge from the jungle with no lantern to protect me from the supposedly vicious creatures chasing my every step.

The thought spikes my blood with adrenaline, making my heart hammer as another chorus of slurred shouts echo through the night ...

They're all too drunk to notice me, anyway.

Dropping to a kneel, I lower my bun so it's sitting at my nape, similar to how the men wear theirs. I scoop some mud and smear it across my cheeks, then look over my shoulder at my small adoptive pack hovering uncertainly at the fringe of light.

I give them an awkward wave.

The baby flicks forward—like it got jolted with a spark of curiosity—swiftly corralled by the largest one, who rushes it into the thick pall of shadow.

Gone.

Slouching a little, digging one hand deep into my pocket while practicing my man-walk, I step into the light, the mug tucked close to my side as I trudge around the fractious throng, keeping my eyes down.

A meaty thud makes me wince, and I slip between the shelter of the two tall buildings.

The rain appears to have emptied the courtyard entirely, allowing me to cut a swift, silent path toward Blue Hollow Inn. I'm nearing the alleyway that leads to my lodgings when a roll of rusty laughter has me backing up against the wall.

Listening.

A giggle chimes in, and I curse, peeking around the corner.

A woman clothed in scraps of blue, back cushioned by fluffy greenery that's twisted through the trellis I climbed down earlier, throws her head back as the man holding her in place drags the front of her bodice down, spilling her plump breasts.

I whip my gaze away and climb it up said trellis to my washroom window on the second floor ...

What unfortunate timing.

Her giggle melts into a moan, snapping my attention to the man's hand roaming up the bare length of her leg that's hooked around his waist. He grabs a healthy handful of her equally bare ass, and something deep inside me clenches.

Aches.

She undoes the front of his trousers, fingers nimble, frantic as she drives them down the front of him. Her shoulder drops, elbow finding a deep beat, and then it's *he* who has his head thrown back while she pumps—again, and again, and again.

My cheeks burn, eyes widening.

He shoves down his pants, revealing an ass that's a lot less tanned than the rest of him, then hooks her other leg back, punching his hips forward—

She moans, burying her face into his neck.

I swallow, unable to rip my gaze away from the wanton scene as he pumps up into her at a heart-thumping rate, her small body somehow absorbing every thrust.

That ... that *right there* is what's expected of me at our coupling ceremony.

That. Right. There.

Will I want it like she does? Will the moment take me over and spike me with thrill?

How will I feel after the comedown, having given all *that* to someone I quite possibly wouldn't have chosen for myself had the circumstances differed?

My chest tightens.

Ducking behind the wall, I look to the sky. Another threadbare moan rings through the balmy air, curling my fingers and my guts.

I hold a breath in my cheeks, blow it out, and swing my stare toward the Inn's main entrance. Edging closer to the window so I can look inside, I see a lazy churn of movement amongst the smoky atmosphere.

A bard on a corner platform carves a tune, tapping his foot to the lively beat while barmaids balance overburdened trays on their heads and weave between the crowd. Stumbling men clunk tankards, sloshing amber liquid on both themselves and the scantily clad women perched on their laps.

My gaze is drawn to a flight of stairs and the sign on the wall beside it that reads *Overnight Guests Only*.

Relief washes over me like a cool bath on a hot night.

Fingers crossed I'm wearing enough mud to pass as a scrappy teenager out past his curfew, I reinitiate my man-walk, wobbling a little for good measure as I stomp toward the door. I wrap my hand around the handle, draw a deep breath, and pull.

Stepping into the stuffy rabble, I resist the urge to bat away the sweet-smelling smoke swirling at my eye level.

A firm hand grasps my shoulders, slamming me against the wall, a big body blocking me from the room, and I look up the line of Gun's broad back to a swathe of salt-and-pepper hair.

"Gods give me strength," Gun growls, a low chastisement that saws at my bones. "What in Kvath's name were you doing out there? Do I even want to know?"

"I went to get a plant," I whisper-yell, and he looks over his shoulder, eyes lowering. I raise my hand so he can see my little mug-o'-bells in their full, drooping glory.

His thick brows smack together. "Are you mad?"

Yes.

"You're sodden. And where are your boots?"

"Forgot them. Why am I backed against the wall?"

"*Forgo*—" He bites off the word, shaking his head. "Because there's a guard on your door."

I roll my eyes, tapping my bare, very muddy foot against the wooden floorboards.

"When you do that, you remind me of my partner," he mutters. "And not in a good way."

"I think I'd like them."

"You would. He's also a pain in my ass."

I smile, cracking the mud on my cheek.

"So ... what now?"

"First, I'm going to buy you a mead," he says, thieving one off the tray of a passing barmaid when she has her back turned.

I raise a brow.

He gives me a do-as-I-say-not-as-I-do look and ushers

me toward a sheltered corner table with two leather seats, pinching a cap off one and slapping it atop my head. He nudges it low, casting half my face in shadow and concealing my mess of wet hair that's dripping all over my shoulders. "*Then,* you're going to sit right here until the shift swap in an hour and hope like hell the High Master doesn't come back and recognize you through all that mud."

I take the corner seat and tuck myself out of view. "He's out?"

Gun shifts his own chair, shielding me from all angles. "Yes," he says, tipping his mug and drawing a hearty gulp, frosting his mustache. "Why the plant?"

I twirl my mug-o'-bells round and round. "They remind me of someone ..."

"They're also one of the thirty-four ingredients required to make a certain outlawed drug."

My stare whips up, mouth dropping open. "How do you—"

"My Enry. He's a botanist with a big mouth. We have a plant shop in the city beneath my parents' old house."

"Your partner?"

"The one and only."

I lift my drink, sipping the sweet liquid that's crisp and cool and tastes a bit like honey. "Then I *definitely* like him."

He grunts.

I pick at the dried mud on my arms, and it falls to the tabletop riddled with discolored rings and burn marks.

"What do you know about this *Madame Strings* Vanth mentioned on the ship?"

Gun's hand pauses mid-lift, and he takes a stretched moment to set the mug back on the table.

Quietly.

"You have something you want to know?"

Lots of things.

I rest my cheek against my bunched fist and shrug, looking up at him from beneath the rim of my cap.

He clears his throat and checks the window nearby that reflects the rowdy crowd. "She's a nomadic merchant who claims no color and never seems to age. Comes and goes as she pleases," he finally grinds out. "Sells her *wares* in the city square. She can sometimes be found around a campfire surrounded by *impressionable* children who gobble up her stories like they're spiked sweets."

"And you don't believe them?"

"I don't *trust* her," he growls, the words grating across my skin as he drains his mug.

I frown into mine, like all the answers I seek are swirling at the bottom ...

Hate to admit it, but Vanth was right. Though provoked, that creature *did* end up almost sinking our ship in a wild lash of fury—just like in the stories he claimed to have heard from this *Madame Strings*.

I know it's a long shot, but perhaps ...

Perhaps she knows something about *me.*

The real me.

Chapter 21
Baze

The closer I creep to the mountains, the colder it gets. Like one of the Gods drained all the warmth from the world. The biting wind tills up flurried curls or snow, the half-moon throwing patches of light disrupted by racing clouds.

I can't see the Alps through the lantern's flaming aura, even as the trees thin along The Stretch—the band of barren land at the mountains' feet. But I *feel* their nearness like a waiting giant; can hear it in the way the icy snow cracks beneath my boots.

"*Shh.*"

My heart rate spikes.

Head whipping sideways, I squint into the darkness, making out the slight silhouette stooped behind a large pile of snow just beyond the reach of my lantern light.

I draw deep, almost groaning when I catch a hint of Zali's buttery scent on an eddy of frosty air.

Relief floods my chest.

Thank fuck.

Darting closer, I crouch beside her, dousing her in my protective light. "What are you doing all the way out here?" I whisper-hiss.

She squints up at me, grabs my lantern, and opens it, stuffing it full of snow and snipping out the light.

Panic fires up my throat.

"What the hell are you doing?" Heart galloping, I scour our chilled surroundings, certain every pocket of shadow is about to flit forward and smother us in suckling doom. "There could be Irilak!"

"I haven't seen any. Even if there were, they certainly wouldn't be interested in *us*," Zali purrs against my ear, the lilt prickling my skin—at least until she shoves the snow-stuffed lantern at my chest so hard I grunt. "They'd be too heartily fed."

Zero percent reassuring.

"Look."

I rip my gaze from her and follow the direction her finger is pointing. It takes a moment for my vision to adjust to the dim, the scenery coming to life.

The Stretch is just beyond, wide and vast and dusted in a fresh layer of powder. Far off in the distance, it meets the foot of the Alps' sharp rocks—a barricade of stony claws gouged in the snow.

Slate gray fur pops against the sea of white, slinking down a snowy chute that spits out on The Stretch ...

Vruks.

I count two ... three ... *five*—

My heart leaps into my throat. "Fuck."

"Exactly," Zali mumbles, watching them descend,

her expression harboring a savage sort of severity. "I'm sure you noticed all the gore covering the north-facing stakes on your way in?"

"I did ..." A tense pause, then, "You were right."

"Unfortunately." The word is whispered, stained with sadness.

I level her with a look that coasts across her elegant features lit by a shard of sterling moonlight. "Did you have to come all this way on your own to confirm it?" I don't bother to hide the bite from my voice.

Her actions were thoughtless. Reckless.

So unlike Zali.

Otherwise still as stone, her sharp eyes cut to me. A flurry swarms her face, collecting in her lashes. "I needed to see for myself. Validate our need for the ships. I have a hunch it's the reason Orlaith accepted Cainon's cupla."

The hairs on the back of my neck lift. "I need you to clarify ..."

She pulls that plump bottom lip between her teeth.

My eyes narrow. "Zali?"

"She was listening that day in Rhordyn's office." The words blast out of her as a blow of icy wind strikes, tossing back our hoods. "From behind one of the curtains."

My blood thins.

Of course she was.

"Shit," I mutter, filling in the gaps myself. "*Shit*."

I should have pieced it together. Laith mentioned she was securing the ships the day she left me broken and bare on a beach that's never felt so cold.

A whip of wind stirs Zali's hair, teasing the frosty

ends past my face. "I'm sorry, Baze ... I should've said something—"

"Why *didn't* you?" I growl, and she breaks my stare, like ripping a scab from a wound.

"She had enough reasons to hate me."

The words are detached, uttered in an empty, foreign tone I don't recognize. Not from her.

"Why do you care so much?"

Pushing flat against the rise of packed snow, her hand drifts to the bronze sword resting against it. "I like her." She taps a finger against the topaz-encrusted pommel, brow pinched. "She reminds me of someone."

I study her as she studies the Vruks, this scroll burning a hole in my pocket. "Coming out here on your own, risking your life—it's not the antidote to your guilty conscience."

"I needed proof," she murmurs flatly, flicking me a sideways stare that shines in the moonlight. "I'm now *certain* this is the loose spigot to explain our overflow of fluffy mutts. But"—her upper lip peels back—"I've also learned why so many Fryst-born Vruks are making it past our defenses."

"Which is?"

"The packs are much larger than they've ever been, with well-developed hierarchy systems. They're growing *tactful*," she sneers. "Watch."

By the light of the moon, the pack slowly pools at the mountain's base until they're all safely down. One of the mid-sized Vruks nuzzles the snow and begins the volatile trek over what appears to be a smooth, unthreatening stretch of land.

The beast tests the ground with a fraction of its weight

before committing to each prowling step—making for a slow, tentative journey. All the while, the others crouch and watch rather than burst across The Stretch the way the traps intend.

The approaching beast is halfway to us when the ground gives way beneath it, swallowing it in a large, snowy gulp. A shrill, bloodcurdling yelp echoes across the plains as it's skewered on the hidden cavalry of spikes below.

Silence.

I swallow thickly, then watch in wonder as a smaller Vruk confidently prowls the same path the previous took, its steps growing more cautious once it rounds the spent trap and continues on across new, untested territory.

"They're—"

"Growing smarter," she whispers as the lone Vruk heels, tips its stubby muzzle to the sky, and releases a howl that shatters the crisp silence. "Unfortunately."

The rest of the pack follows the track and spills across The Stretch in a single file gallop, kicking up a spray of snow from their thundering paws. I watch them draw closer, *closer* ... sticking to their trodden trail, not setting a single paw out of line despite their fierce pace.

"They're getting quite close, Zali."

A brief pause, then, "The traps usually thin out the pack a little more ..."

Aghast, I cut her a look.

She shrugs, standing, her withdrawing sword hissing its wake-up call as she pulls it free. "Your presence is timely, I'll admit. How drunk are you?"

"Sober," I mutter, the ground beginning to jolt beneath us. "Regretfully."

"Well, sorry to pry you from your padded nest," she says with a smirk, winking before she leaps out from behind the mound, making my heart lurch. Swift and sure, she whips her sword in a practiced arc that hacks through the thick, meaty neck of the first Vruk to bound across her path. Its front legs buckle, body collapsing against the ground in a jerking pile of matted fluff. Blood spills as it gurgles its dying breath, pumping in steaming spurts that ink the snow and the flutter of Zali's cloak.

My feet are already moving when another lunges at her, talons punched free from its reaching paws—

I leap, ripping my sword free from its sheath and slam it through the beast's ribs, feeling muscle, bone, and organs give way to the pierce of it. We crunch against the ground in a burst of snow and blood and fur, making my teeth rattle. I'm still straddling it when we come to a stop—warm blood swelling up to meet my hands clenched around the hilt of my sword.

I whip my head around, peering into the dark at two more snarling beasts charging toward us. "And you're usually out here on your own?" I growl, pulling my sword free with a wet grind.

"Yes," Zali pants, striding forward until we're hip to hip. "Nobody else is willing. The mutts have somehow realized."

We leap as one, colliding with the onslaught of feral, brute force, dodging whistling swipes of deadly talons like a collaborative symphony.

I slash my blade through a dense neck, crumbling the mighty Vruk to my left. Feeling the air shift behind me, I spin—slicing my sword around, blowing out a hiss as the honed edge kisses Zali's throat. Hers, too, is poised against my carotid, so sharp that if I leaned a little to the right, I'd slice myself. Bleed out in seconds.

Our eyes lock.

Despite the deep breaths heaving in and out of our lungs, there's a moment of utter stillness between us—both splattered in the blood of our kills. I take in the black glaze of her eyes. The rise and fall of her breasts.

A striking vision of fierce, feral beauty that's hard to look away from.

We pull our blades back, swiping them on our coats in the same brusque manner. She turns first, trudging away. "Quick, before the Irilak set in."

I almost leap out of my skin, dashing after her to the tune of her chiming giggle, my heart hacking at my ribs even after I realize she's joking.

"Not funny," I mutter, biting down on a full-body shiver that rattles me to the core. Shakes up memories I don't want to think about.

Her laughter tapers off.

Once we're sitting beside each other, backs to the packed snow mound and breathing hard, I dig through my cloak for the emergency flask I'd tucked away.

Feels fitting, seeing as we barely escaped with our limbs intact.

I unstopper the cork and take a swig, then offer Zali the flask. She accepts it, drawing deep and releasing a sharp hiss before she whips her arm back and lobs it into the darkness.

My heart leaps into my throat as I watch it disappear. "What th—That was vanilla brandy! Cost me a fucking pocket diamond to a traveling merchant!"

"Then you got ripped off. Only someone truly desperate would trade a *pocket diamond* for a flask of brandy. Meaning it's better off out there."

I snarl, leaning against the snow again. "You're just like your promised."

"But far more attractive," she purrs, rolling her sleeves, pulling her long tangle of wavy hair to the side, and parting it three ways.

"And with an ego twice the size," I mutter, watching her weave her locks into a messy braid. "I see you're not wearing your cupla."

She glances at her bare wrist, then back into the night. "We're lying to the people, not ourselves. Besides, I have little regard for the tradition."

I grunt, trying to pretend her words don't affect me like they do, arms perched on my bent knees.

"So," Zali murmurs. "How is Orlaith?"

"Gone."

Her head whips around, hands stilling. "What do you mean, *gone?*"

"Got on a ship to Bahari weeks ago." I reach into my pocket and pull out the tiny, flattened scroll.

"Why didn't you *lead* with that?"

I spread my hands, look around at the corpses, down at the gore covering my clothes, then back at her with a raised brow.

She rolls her eyes and pinches the scroll from my grip, unraveling it. "I had it under control."

"Didn't look like it," I state, tempted to hunt down my flask in the hope there's something left. "You should have sent a sprite to inform us of your location before you entered The Stretch. You're not indestructible."

"More than most," she says, reaching past. "Hand me that lantern."

I grab it, pulling it back. "This one?"

She snarls, reaching past me—our bodies brushing.

Scents *tangling*.

I hear her breath hitch, wish I had a little more light so I could see if her cheeks are flushed.

Pulling the lantern further away, I keep it *just* out of reach ...

She loses her balance, falling against me with an *oomph*, and I absorb every soft curve of her body.

It doesn't matter that we're both fully clothed and covered in gore—the smell of her, the mere proximity of her, the thrill of *danger* ... it has me stretching out, baring my throat the slightest amount.

"You're an ass," she snips, snatching the lantern.

"Not all the time." The words spill out raspier than I'd intended.

She glances up and stills, eyes glazing as they skim across my throat.

The bared length of fragile flesh.

The invitation.

A *plea*—pathetic and desperate and so fucking *shameful*.

She snarls, shoving off, like a slap back to reality.

I clear my throat, straighten my clothes, and hope it's too dark for her to see the bulge in my pants.

In a dash of snow and stolen breath she's straddling me, weight pressed on my aching length, blade kissing my throat, teeth bared and eyes flashing.

My breath snags at the feral look in her eyes.

She leans so close I can feel her warm breath against my ear before she whispers, "Don't ever play that game with me again. Do you understand?"

I swallow, rolling the ball in my throat, forcing my skin to nick against her blade. A dribble of warmth spills down my neck, and the air around us flushes with the scent of my blood.

She snarls, whipping back, her features so sharp every cell in my body is poised for that tangible zap of pleasure it's *starving* for.

"You know better," she growls, then shoves to a stand, gathering her supplies and stalking off into the night. I bask in my shame for a few deep breaths before I follow like the hopeless mutt I am. Because I do know better ...

I do.

But I also don't.

CHAPTER 22

Orlaith

My horse likes to bite.

She's black and white, and since we entered the stable at dawn, the only living being she hasn't taken a lunge at is *me*.

The stableman at the village told me her name is Rosie—right before she nicked the back of his arm and made him bleed, reminding me of Rhordyn's big, black stallion, Eyzar. Baze never let me ride him, insisting I use the hacks instead. Said the horse was too savage and unpredictable and that Rhordyn would castrate him if I got trampled to death.

Since we emptied Blue Hollow of its meager stable stock, and since Rosie took to nuzzling me for ear scratches rather than snapping at me, Cainon allowed me to ride her on the condition that I stay right behind him. Naturally, Rosie almost took a chunk out of his horse's ass, so now I'm leading our small convoy, pretending I'm by myself, going someplace where there are no expectations stacked upon my shoulders.

A pretty ruse.

And still ...

Everywhere I look I see *him:* in the stormy clouds that won't stop dumping on us; in the chill wind nipping at my blanched knuckles; in the waiting darkness between the trees.

I'm *haunted*.

That well of anger churns.

More rain filters down, pattering off the cloak draped around my shoulders as Rosie trots up a small hill. Cresting the peak, I catch sight of a blue-stone structure through the thinning foliage ahead and draw a deep, shuddering breath. With the end in sight, I've become painfully aware of my inner-thigh chafe and my back muscles pinched from sitting upright for over eight hours straight.

As we tread closer, the jungle gives way to a much wider path, and the palace comes into full, breathtaking view. The windows are trimmed with gold filigree, a stark contrast to the swirling blue of the walls, blocks of lapis lazuli stacked upon each other—all straight lines and square tops.

I gaze in awe at the sight.

It doesn't look as big as Castle Noir from this angle, and seeing a structure that's anything other than coal black is hard to wrap my head around.

Am I dreaming? Will I gasp awake in my bed at Stony Stem, breathless and sweating, fingers stretched toward a bottle of caspun?

Hooves clop against the hard-packed soil as Cainon's regal, white stallion canters past, narrowly missing another launching nip from Rosie.

"That horse really wants a piece of my ass," he says, winking. "She's got good taste, you know."

I offer him an overly sweet smile. "You have a rather high opinion of yourself."

"Hoping it'll catch on," he belts back, racing ahead, and someone behind me tries to cover up a laugh with a forced cough.

I peek over my shoulder at our plodding entourage, catching Zane's eye—sitting on the ass of a fluffy, brown horse, hands wrapped around the waist of a stony-faced Gun.

Wet hair pasted to his forehead, he gives me a lopsided smile that warms my chest.

A bell tolls, ripping my gaze forward, and the clank of shifting chains prefaces a mammoth crosshatch gate lifting from the soil like a square mouth preparing to scream at me.

A nervous breath stretches my too-tight lungs.

We filter through, filing into a courtyard three times larger than Rhordyn's ballroom and protected from the elements by a lofty stone roof.

The stark space fills with the echoing clop of hooves that litter mud all over the polished stone ground. The walls are tall and bare, buffed to a gleaming shine, the gold veins marbled throughout the stone standing out in stark contrast. A gold gate at the far end is twice the size of the one we just rode through—perhaps leading to the city Cainon told me about.

Aside from the stretch of stoic-faced servants, maids, and soldiers lined up by a large set of gold-brushed doors, there is no welcome party. The tight band of tension strung around my chest loosens a little as I breathe a sigh of relief.

Perks of being ushered in through the back door like some dirty little secret.

A man steps forward, boasting pressed blue threads and golden epaulets that make his shoulders proud and serious to match the look in his eyes. He bows, then reaches for Rosie's halter, almost losing his outstretched fingers to the snap of her teeth.

I steady her dancing feet, throw my leg across her back, and leap down, giving her sodden flank a rub while she paws at the stone. "Thanks, but it's okay. I've got her."

His eyes widen, and he swiftly lowers his gaze to the ground and concedes to his spot in the line while the rest of our convoy dismounts. I get to work unknotting my sack, watching from the corner of my eye as a footman carrying a golden plate laden with scrolls dashes toward Cainon, who pinches one off the top and breaks the seal. Brow buckling as he skims the script, he mutters a curse.

"Kolden."

A soldier with bright blue eyes that crinkle at the corners breaks from the quiet line, his hair only half pinned up, the rest hanging around his broad shoulders. "Yes, High Master?"

"Offer the future High Mistress some refreshments, then take her to meet Elder Creed. It's important we introduce her to The Bowl right away so she can start wrapping her head around the trial," Cainon says, splitting the seal on a second scroll.

"Wh—" I move to step forward but remember my horse hates everybody and think better of it, securing her reins around one of the holding posts. "What *trial?*"

"The one you must pass to prove the Gods find you worthy of being Bahari's High Mistress," Cainon murmurs, concentration split as his eyes chase the scrawl of another opened letter. "You'll begin practicing for it first thing in the morning."

I'll begin— *What?*

"Nobody told me this ..."

Cainon glances up. "Tradition, petal. Our coupling ceremony will be on the next full moon, and the trial takes place earlier that day. Unfortunately, there can be no ceremony unless you complete the task. You weren't aware?"

My heart plummets.

No.

I breathe deep, blow it out, then grab my sack off the ground. "Well, is there somewhere safe where I can set my things? I'd like to get started right away, if it's all the same to you."

He frowns. "You're tired, Orlaith. It's been a big day."

"I've been *sitting* all day. I'm fine," I bite out, ignoring the twinges in my lower back and between my shoulder blades.

He's happy to torch two ships and a crew of people to fit his philanthropic narrative. This is a far less destructive path to the same destination.

"*Sacrifices,* right?"

The words come out a little bitter, and both his brows lift.

Studying me for a long moment, he finally says, "Very well. Izel, take Orlaith's things to her suite."

A pretty, blue-eyed handmaiden dressed in a simple

cobalt shift breezes forward, hands outstretched. She's tall and austere, her skin lightly tanned, clothes so perfectly pressed she makes me feel like a scrunched-up piece of parchment.

Something I can't quite put my finger on has me eyeing her warily.

"I'll take it to your suite, Mistress."

"I'd rather do it myself. It needs to be kept upri—"

Cainon grabs my sack and hands it to the woman, and I'm forced to bite my tongue as I watch her step back in line.

I nail him with a hard stare, which he holds, his steeped in subtle chastisement.

Right.

Clearing my throat, I offer him a faux smile, drop into a tight curtsey, then look at Izel clinging to my worldly possessions. "Please keep that upright. There's a cup of soil in there, and I'll be devastated if it spills."

A brief frown buckles her brow before she nods, and I force myself to spin—trailing Kolden across the courtyard while reminding myself there's only one way to earn those fucking ships ...

Play along.

Chapter 23
Orlaith

I'm led to the western wing of the palace, then down a cavernous hall that echoes our steps and seems to go on forever, finally ending at an enormous pair of rough stone doors. Just before we reach them, Kolden ushers me through a side door and down a thin coil of stairs that spit us out into a long, dusty room that's doused in powdery light and the musty scent of old things.

Floor to ceiling windows line one entire wall, perfect frames for the world outside that showcases a blue stone bridge stretching across the angry bay, rising from the base of Cainon's palace. The bridge feeds into the city; a cluster of irregular-sized buildings that are big and small, tall and short, all hewn from the same Bahari blue stone. All kept in the tight embrace of a lofty wall sketched around the edge of it, keeping it herded against the rocky shore.

"Is that Parith?" I ask, as I gobble up the details through wide eyes.

"It is. This way, Mistress."

I rip my gaze from the view and follow Kolden through the room, weaving between stacks of books and tables overburdened with clear jars—each packed with different ... *things*.

Ears ... fingers ... teeth ... fluffy little paws. There's even a small sprite suspended in rosy liquid, wings frayed and black hair a motionless swirl around her face.

I look away and realize with a start I'm walking across a shaggy animal pelt twice the size of my bed in Stony Stem and an alarming shade of gray.

I quicken my pace, suddenly thankful for the boots I'm wearing.

We come to a wall at the end of the room that's littered with so many mismatched clocks it's hard to see the stone beneath, all *tick-tick-ticking* away as Kolden raps his knuckles against a smooth wooden door.

We wait in silence, his sturdy stare pinned forward.

He's short, built like a brick, and there's a casual confidence in the way he holds himself that suggests he knows precisely how to wield that half-spear strapped to his back.

"Any advice?"

He doesn't even look at me as he says, "None that I can give."

"Worth a shot," I mutter, and I swear the corner of his mouth kicks up before the door creaks inward and he steps inside the room, shutting me out.

Well.

I frown, looking around, turning my attention to a large sketchbook laying open on a table. I flip through its moth-eaten pages, unable to decipher the scrawled notes written along the edges in a different language, but it doesn't stop me from enjoying the illustrations of various animals and creatures scratched across the parchment.

The door creaks again, and I drop the page, spinning. Gasping.

My chest thumps so hard every beat feels like another stone lumped upon it, threatening to collapse my ribs from the crushing weight.

The figure standing in the open doorway looks to have just stepped off the wall in Whispers. I see no skin. No features. No feet.

All I see is the *robe*—the same gray robe I've seen so many times.

Too many times.

A meek sound boils in the back of my throat.

Get out of the way, kid. Mercy is not preserved for those who stand against the stones.

The memory strikes like a blade to the back of my knees, hand shooting out to steady myself against the table in a feeble attempt to quell this deep-seated swirl whisking me up inside.

"The future High Mistress, I presume?"

His abrasive voice only strengthens my belief that this man spawned straight from my nightmares. I almost expect him to push his hood back and reveal a bald, shiny head; for me to look down and see a blood-stained axe hanging from his hand.

Drip.

Drip.

The insides of my cheeks tingle, the space under my tongue pooling with the evidence of my cramping guts.

My foot begins to slide back—

Kolden steps past the man, wearing a frown that bolts me in place, looking between us both. "Orlaith, this is Elder Creed." A pause, then, "He's going to lead you to The Bowl so you can begin practice for the trial."

Though the Elder's face is hidden within the shadow of his hood, I can feel the reckoning sweep of his eyes up and down my body.

Is he seeing the slithering sizzle tucked beneath my skin?

Is he seeing just how *unworthy* I am?

Elder Creed connects his hands, scooped sleeves overlapping as his head tilts to the side. "Is she ... *mute?*"

His voice is a thorn in my chest. Like he's blistered and boiled beneath that hood, speaking to me from beyond the grave I put him in.

Murderer.

"Orlaith? Are you okay?"

I can't bring myself to answer Kolden. Can't bring myself to breathe or even blink. All I want to do is stand right here until Elder Creed disappears back through that door.

Kolden's frown deepens, and he steps closer, his hand brushing against my elbow as concern shadows his eyes.

A sharp breath cuts into me at the touch, and I rip my stare away, looking to the floor.

Pull it together, Orlaith. He's not the same man.

"I'm fine," I rasp, clearing my throat. "Apologies. Please, lead the way."

The stone doors look big enough to take a chunk from the moon, bracketed by sconces that cast gold light and airy shadows across their rough surface. Armored guards flanking either side crank twin levers in perfect synchrony, making deep clunks vibrate through the floor and up my legs as the doors begin to shift—spewing a stormy tumult from between the widening crack like the howls of a caged tempest.

Frowning, I peek back at Kolden.

"Just the ocean," he says. "The arena's partially underground. The sound beats down from above."

Oh.

I follow Elder Creed through the doorway, taking in the sphere-shaped amphitheater, so huge I could imagine a sun rising and setting across its vast ceiling. A crown of holes are punched through the lofty roof, stamping the moon's full cycle around the arena like an illuminated halo—the main source of light meant to drag the eye to one place only: a central stage with a pool scooped into the floor, round and wide as Stony Stem.

The Bowl.

My heart sits in my throat as Elder Creed guides us down the wide stairway lit by flaming bowls of oil, feeling my body grow heavier with each step.

There is nothing I like about this place.

Nothing.

I'm following a living relic of the night I lost everything, descending hundreds of steps past rows of empty seats waiting to be filled, heading for a stage girdling a basin of water that glistens just like the one I almost drowned in.

A handful of my nightmares, starring the worst of them all.

Me.

I shake off the noxious thoughts, tightening my fists and hardening my heart.

Get the job done.

Get the ships.

We step onto the arena floor etched with a sea of scripture, the words small and packed together.

I look down the steep blue sides of The Bowl half-filled with eerily still water, inky and foreboding in the confines of its dark surrounds. An arched beam saddles the pool, and hung from the highest point is a rope with a small, golden bell attached to the end, almost brushing the water's surface.

Illuminated by the dull beams of light reflecting the day outside, my gaze is drawn to the tall, clear, cylindrical tanks sitting on stone plinths around the rim of The Bowl. Each contains a different sort of living creature, swirling, crawling, flitting ...

Inspecting each, I move from one to the next while Elder Creed watches me from The Bowl's edge.

"Jellyfish," he says as I pass a creature pulsing through its watery cage like a pellucid heart. "Electric eels ... piranha ... turtle ..."

I pause by one, mesmerized by its writhing inhabitant.

Eight slithering tentacles paw at the glass while a big, eclipsed eye stares at me.

Into me.

The creature suckers onto the side like a splat of white paint.

"Octopus," I whisper, flattening my hand on the cool glass in the center of its star-like shape.

Flinching, it shifts from sea-foam white to jet black in the blink of an eye, as though my hand dropped paint upon the thirsty canvas of its skin. It shoves off the glass, spitting vines of ink that muddy the water, contorting into a tangle of texture amongst the murk.

"Which are you most drawn to?" Elder Creed asks, his voice a scathing drawl.

I whip my hand back. "None of them."

"You have to pick one."

I don't like this game. It feels like a trap.

I point to a lichen-covered stone. "That."

"The rockfish?" He tilts his head. "Clothed in constant camouflage?"

Shit me.

Exasperated, I sigh, pinching the bridge of my nose. "Can we get started? It's been a long day. I want to get this over with."

A pause, then he waves a clothed arm toward The Bowl. "Get in, then."

"I'm sorry, you want me to *climb in?*"

"Yes," he states. "The trial imitates the swell of beings that spilled from Mount Ether at the dawn of time. Only once you manage to climb back *out* on your own have the Gods found you worthy of this coupling. A task you must complete before the people of Parith on the morning of your ceremony."

I look at the water, remembering the last time I was submerged in a pool such as this—choking on life-altering memories I'll never be able to scrape away. "This is—"

"What?"

Ridiculous.

"Nothing," I mutter, kicking off my boots and unpinning the heavy cloak from around my throat, lumping it on the ground. I look down at myself, indicating my attire with a sweep of my hand. "What about ...?"

"The tailor will come by your room and take your measurements for the proper apparel. If you'd like to wait until—"

"No," I snip. "It's fine. So I just ... climb in and climb back out again?"

"Correct. On your own."

I work my healing shoulder into a deep stretch. "That's it?"

"Yes. Should you fail, bat the bell, and I'll throw a rope ladder into The Bowl which you can use to climb back out. You can practice all you want, but if you cannot complete the task on the morning of your coupling, you are not worthy of this great privilege that has been bestowed upon you."

Seems a bit harsh. Perhaps I should shove him in there and see how he fares. Or Cainon.

I'd like to see that.

I edge close, sit my ass on the side, and study the water that looks like a pool of ink, heart kicking against my ribs ...

Not Puddles.

A different pool.

Swallowing the lump rising in my throat, I drag a shuddering breath and shove off, sliding down the glassy slope. I plunge into the warm water, engulfed in a body-temperature gulp.

The deeper I sink, the more it feels like my ribs are caving in ...

Is this my last breath?

Is something about to snag me from below—refuse to let me go until I relive that night again? Until I hear my mother's bloodcurdling scream? See my brother's blank eyes staring at the wall? Feel my skin split to make way for ropes of wrath spilling from that place of hurt deep inside my chest?

White-hot dread severs my internal reins ...

I flail.

Panic.

Bubbles pour from my mouth, released with a squeal muffled by water that feels too thick. Too hot. Punching above the surface, I gulp sweet breath, heart hammering as I wade in place, frantically scanning my surroundings.

Not Puddles. It's not Puddles.

The edges are too high. Too smooth and polished and blue.

It doesn't smell the same.

Not Puddles.

"Is everything alright?"

My gaze catches on Elder Creed looking down on me from the edge of The Bowl.

"Perfectly fine," I sputter, choosing a target to focus on—

the glass aquariums looking like crowning spires from down here in the center of it all. Eyes fixed on the slithering eels, I kick like mad, propelling myself forward and up, flinging my arm skyward, fingers stretched toward The Bowl's rim.

I slam against the buffed side, clawing, feet scrambling for purchase.

I slide, swallowing water as I dunk below the surface.

Kicking hard, I rise back up, choking and spluttering, spearing my gaze on those eels again.

Growling through gritted teeth, I wade further back, giving myself a decent runup before I rock my body forward, dig my head into the water, and swim like I've never swum before—frantically kicking my legs and churning my arms. I propel up the wall, flick my arm up, slap it against the smooth side, and slide straight back into the warm pit of failure.

Over and over I lunge and fall, lunge and fall, until I'm gasping, head thrown back, treading water that feels like it's boiling me alive. Picturing the Gods dangling those ships above my head, watching me leap and leap and *leap*—

Laughing at me.

The waning light from above barely illuminates the pool's lip anymore—so, so far away.

Unreachable.

I look at the bell dangling on the end of the rope, a sob bubbling up as I wade toward it, heave my arm up, and bat it with my hand, then stop kicking altogether and just ...

Sink.

Entomb myself in the still like that little sunken sprite.

It's almost peaceful.

I'm pulled from my stupor by a splashing disturbance above, and I use my remaining scrap of energy to kick up and snatch the rope ladder floating on the surface—the pads of my fingers withered like dried flower buds.

The bell continues to sway back and forth, tolling my defeat.

Another sob, and I lug my heavy body through the water, reaching the side of the pool before climbing the ladder with quaking hands and legs that barely hold my leaden weight. Pulling myself over the rim, I crawl forward, drop my head, and vomit across the stone.

Boots thud into my line of view, pausing just before my swelling puddle of spew.

Lips trembling, I look up the line of gray pants to a broad figure I recognize, gaze shifting to Cainon's outstretched hand.

"You gave it your best shot," he says, and there's a softness to his words. "Nobody's ever gotten it on their first try. Time to eat and rest. You can practice more tomorrow."

I take his hand, but don't look into his eyes. I'm too afraid I'll see a nod to the thoughts plaguing my own mind ...

Not worthy.

Chapter 24
Orlaith

I trail Cainon past wall sconce after wall sconce—nothing but a blazing blur as I struggle to put one foot before the other. I glance back, catching sight of two stoic-faced maids mopping my wet footprints, like I'm nothing but a ghost gliding across the polished, gold-veined floor, before losing sight of them as we turn a corner.

We're moving through a grand atrium, its hard edges softened by sweeps of blueberry velvet hung from the window rails, when my gaze snags on an open doorway tucked beside a pillar—the gloomy innards unlike the rest of the palace from what I've seen so far.

Steps slowing, I place my hand on the doorframe and peer into the dim interior ...

My breath catches at the sight of a woman clothed in lantern light, facing away from me, her silver hair a trickle of thin waves down her back and piled on the floor. She's hunched on a stool before a large loom, manipulating threads with practiced dexterity.

I realize with a start that she's missing a thumb and forefinger, the sheer beauty of her work suggesting it's of no hindrance. The piece she's working on is magnificent: a blossoming tree in full bloom, the odd petal floating down into the unfinished nether.

Something about it casts little prickles on the backs of my eyes—makes me feel like someone just scooped out all my insides, leaving me empty.

A cognitive shell.

Her hands still.

"I see you've found Old Hattie," Cainon whispers too close to my ear, then relieves me of my boots hanging from my hand. "She likes her privacy. Especially when she's weaving. Come."

I snag one more glance of her still paused mid-motion, then follow Cainon, waiting until we're a respectable distance from the room before I ask, "Who is she? To you?"

"My old governess." He clears his throat, rolling his sleeves. "She no longer speaks. She was involved in a tragic accident that took her son and coupled."

His words strike like nails to the chest.

For the first time, I picture him as anything other than the suave, sarcastic male. Picture him too young to do things for himself. Things *she* would have helped him with.

Being so close, her heartbreak probably felt like his own.

"I'm sorry, Cainon ..."

No answer.

I'm led up a sweeping staircase that skirts past multiple stories, the silence pecked at by his heavy-booted steps. "I gave her a permanent residence here after the accident," he finally says. "She now spends her days nurturing her woven art."

"That's kind of you."

He shrugs. "So long as her hands are busy, she seems content, so I keep throwing yarn at her. Everyone in the palace knows to respect her privacy and leave her be."

At the top of the staircase, we enter a grand hallway—globed chandeliers that look like sitting suns hanging from the ceiling every few steps.

"High Master. Mistress." The monotone greeting snaps my attention.

Kolden swings a gold-brushed door wide, his stare stabbed at the wall. Walking past, I wonder if he knows how spectacularly I just failed.

We step into a lobby that boasts two other doorways, one on each side, and I glance back at Kolden—standing at attention in the hallway, wearing a blank expression.

I frown. "Is my room to be guarded ... *always?*"

"Of course," Cainon chuffs, stepping toward the door on the left while digging through his pocket. "Safety precaution."

"An *unnecessary* one."

I fail to point out the fact that the first round of guards didn't work out very well.

Quite the opposite.

"A *non-negotiable* one," he volleys back, brow arched as he looks at me from beneath a sweep of golden lashes. "Between my extended absence and compromised fleet from our little detour, I'm time-poor. I'll be spending a lot of the upcoming weeks offshore, overseeing repairs rather than being right here where I'd like to be. I need to know you're protected."

An idea hits, widening my eyes and soothing the restless beast in my chest. "I'll come with you! I'd *love* to see the islands ..."

See where the ships are stored.

"What? No, Orlaith." A deep roll of laughter tumbles with the words. "Island days are too taxing. I need you to spend every spare moment right here, practicing for the trial."

"You'd rather have me spend my days scrambling up the slippery side of an oversized bowl? Really?"

"Of course! You're going to need all the practice you can get. When you conquer it, we're one step closer to being coupled, and Rhordyn's one step closer to getting his fleet and sailing back to his world of problems. Isn't that what we both want?"

"Yes ..."

But the thought of floundering in that bowl for the next two weeks while Elder Creed watches on makes my chest cramp. Makes the ache in my shoulder throb with newfound gusto.

"As the High Master, can't you just ... *absolve* the tradition?"

His face pales, expression hardening, and I realize I've said something wrong. "I'm going to pretend I didn't hear that," he mutters, giving me his back. "And pray the Gods weren't listening."

Doubt it'll make a difference if they were. I'll probably never climb out of that fucking bowl because no God in their right mind would let *me* sit on a seat of power.

Not willingly.

I button my lips, watching him shove a long key into the lock. He swings the door open, revealing a large space and opulent furnishings bathed in rich, golden light from the abundance of chandeliers. It all passes by in a blur as I dash straight to the balcony's double doors, pulling them wide, inviting a blow of brisk wind that ruffles the sheer curtains and makes my damp skin prickle.

I swear it howls at me.

I draw a deep breath, savoring the smell of freshly fallen rain as I step out onto the stone balcony, eyes widening, struck by the brightness of the city beneath the sheet of night—such a blazing contrast.

Cainon lifts my heavy, sodden hair off my back, startling me.

"Sorry." He drapes a plush robe around my shoulders. "You looked cold. And it's unseasonably chilly at the moment."

I stuff my arms into the holes, then cross them over my chest, offering him a small smile. "Thank you ..."

"No problem." He runs his fingers through the tangled length of my hair, partitioning it off into three long sections he then begins to braid. "You have the best view in the palace," he murmurs. "You can see the entire city from here."

Huge, fire-filled bowls dot the bridge that spills from the palace grounds far below, stretching toward the mainland and the illuminated metropolis. Separating the city from the dark jungle beyond is the wall, its abundance of turrets blazing, creating a stark shield around the compact civilization.

It's breathtaking. Unlike anything I could have imagined. Little pops of excitement explode in my chest.

I wonder if the city is busy or quiet. What it smells like. Sounds like. What plants and wares and food it harbors. Whether *Madame Strings* is just beyond that bridge with all the answers I can swallow, my questions stacking up like a crooked pile of stones wobbling around inside of me.

What am I ... exactly? Are there more of us around? Do all of my kind have this noxious *thing* living inside of them? Is there a way to control it?

Destroy it?

Perhaps she even knows why the Irilak don't seem to be interested in suckling me to death.

Another blow of wind batters my face, and I shiver despite the robe.

He ties off my braid, then steps up beside me. "I trust the rooms are adequate?"

I spin, looking through the balcony doors, giving the vast space my full attention: lapis lazuli walls; gold trimmings; a plump, velvet floor pillow set before an open-mouthed, blazing fireplace. There's a four-poster bed that's low to the floor, the gold-brushed structure softened by blue chiffon curtains that flutter in the wind.

Again, my mattress is dressed in stark white sheets. Even the comforter folded at the end is white.

A blank canvas for me to bleed on.

I look away, toward a frosted glass door that likely leads to my own personal washroom, then to the dressing table overlooked by an ornate mirror hanging on the wall. Beside it, a dressing room packed with rows of gowns in the richest shades of blue—beaded with gold, threaded with gold, dusted with gold.

There's an entire wall of shoes, and my feet ache just looking at them.

I scan the bare walls of the suite, so straight and square ... no long benches for me to display my treasures. Drawing a breath, I fill my lungs with the sterile smell of eucalyptus and vinegar ... not the gentle, sweet aroma of flowering wisteria.

Another blunt reminder of just how far I am from home.

"The rooms are *more* than adequate," I say on a blown-out breath, forcing a smile. "Thank you."

"Of course."

Izel paces through the room, carrying a tray capped with a large cloche. She sets it on my bedside table, curtseys, and leaves without once meeting my eye.

"I'm having dinner with a Regional Master," Cainon says, pocketing his hands and heading for the door. "I'll leave you to eat and get settled in."

Tapping my finger on the handrail, I chew my bottom lip and stare at the glittering cityscape. Perhaps I've swum past the point of exhaustion and delved into energy reserves I didn't know I had, but I'm suddenly *charged*—my mind jumping from one thought to another like a skipping stone.

"Cainon?"

He looks at me over his shoulder from halfway across the room. "Yes?"

"May I have some coin?"

His brow buckles. "*Coin?*"

"Money? Drabs?" A blazing warmth spreads across my cheeks. "I, ahh—I only packed the basics. The storm was setting in, so we were in a bit of a rush when we left Castle Noir ..."

He frowns, and I shake my head, clearing my throat.

"It'll just be nice to have my own little purse for when we visit town, you know? So I don't have to ask in front of people ..."

"That won't be necessary." He strides outside, takes my hand, and pares back my sleeve to reveal the cupla caught around my wrist—gold veins threaded through the blue glinting in the firelight. "You just wave this. We share the only lapis lazuli cupla the forgery has crafted, so anybody who sees it will know exactly who you are."

I look into his cerulean stare. "But how do I *pay?*"

"You don't."

"I don't follow ..."

"Parith is the most decorated capital on the continent. Its future High Mistress can't be seen trading *coin* for goods and services, Orlaith. You can have whatever you please, whenever you please. My people respect that and are repaid tenfold by my constant protection."

"Oh," I mutter, trying to pull my hand back. "Sorry, this is all very new to me."

His grip on my wrist is unfaltering, tethering me by more than just his physical touch. "You're going to be happy here. *We're* going to be happy."

I look from my hand to his face. "Are we?"

"Yes." He tucks a sodden strand of hair behind my ear, the touch so tender I almost lean into it. "You belong here, in the sun. I'm going to give you everything you ever dreamed of. Everything *he* didn't."

He ...

My heart leaps. Skin pebbles. Even the buds on my tongue tingle, as if anticipating the taste of Rhordyn's presence on the air.

Craving it.

"And what's that?" I rasp, voice grated for all the wrong reasons. Shameful ones that burn in my heart.

He steps forward, a bold half smile crinkling his eyes. "*Me*."

I swallow, sliding back a step so that I'm pressed against the stone railing as another blow of chill cloaks me from behind.

"I smelled something while I was in your room at Castle Noir," Cainon says, voice dropped so low it's like he's passing me a secret he fears the wind will snatch. "Your last heat. Your desire to be *fucked*."

Every muscle in my body locks, and a burn floods from my chest to my cheeks, blazing with a shameful wrath that leaves me wide-eyed and voiceless.

He could smell that?

Looking him in the eye is torture, but looking away feels like some sort of defeat, so I force myself to hold his stare.

Force myself to breathe.

"I saw your *want* to be treasured in the tears you cried," he continues, pushing closer. "Felt it in the way you kissed me."

It was all a lie.

I want to scream it at him. Bunch the words, then bash them against his chest.

The woman he thinks he has—the woman he *wants*—she doesn't exist. Not anymore. Her flame was extinguished the moment she saw the monster she really is.

He steps so close his warm breath falls upon my face, eyes blazing. "I'm going to give you it *all*, Orlaith." He leans in, pauses, plants a swift kiss on my temple before he turns and strides back through the room. Out the door.

My lungs empty with a shuddered exhale.

I crumble against the balustrade, sliding down the smooth stone bars until I'm sitting cross-legged on the floor. Head tilted back, a spritz of rain peppers my face, just enough to give the wind something to catch on when the next blow hits, hard and heavy.

Almost a shove.

I spin, knees against my chest as I wrap my hands around the bars and peer out across the bridge to the illuminated city beyond.

Something twists inside my chest.

Being this high up, looking down upon the world, used to make me feel untouchable.

Safe.

Now?

All I can think about—*obsess* about—is the thrill of the fall.

Chapter 25
Kai

Even in the dead of night, this place shines with a haunted glow—colorful light spilling from the aurora strung across the sky outside. It filters through the crystal walls and the tiny, high-up window chipped through the side.

I look to the mound at my feet where Vicious is twisted in a ball, tucked under the heavy furs, her breath a summer breeze against my shin ...

Her spot.

Every evening without fail, once we've finished feasting on the fish she's bashed to death, she burrows beneath, ruts the furs into a mound, curls up, and promptly falls asleep, her shallow breathing making me picture her with one eye open.

I usually use the soft beat of it against my skin to lull me under. A warm comfort I've grown too fond of. One I look forward to.

Ache for.

But tonight, it's not working.

I can't switch off, my heart hammering so fast it feels like something's thrashing around in there. But it's not *him*.

Zykanth.

Still silent. Still so deep I can't feel a flutter or a coil of motion. I don't want much—just a single scale. A frill. The smallest *something* to resecure our connection and prevent his essence from shriveling up inside me.

The thought of a life without him makes my chest and torso feel crushed by a boulder.

Two icebergs clank against each other somewhere in the distance, screaming their own language in cracking tones and eerie echoes.

Vicious scurries out from under the furs and bolts upright, on the tips of her toes as she grips the windowsill and looks out across the sea. Ribbons of colorful light stain the smooth angles of her elegant face, her hair a dashed cloud, tanned legs exposed from the stretch of her.

Her lips pull back, flashing those sharp teeth as a soft snarl saws free.

"Hey, it's okay." I tangle my fingers through the hem of her shirt and give it a tug.

It slips down, revealing the fine slant of a sun-kissed shoulder and the full, healthy swell of her right breast.

Fuck.

"*Sorry.*"

She doesn't waver—that snarl growing louder.

Deeper.

I swallow, wrapping my hand around her slight ankle, teeth chattering. "V-Vicious ..."

Her bold, yellow stare stabs at me, and for a moment

it's hard to think under the force of her full attention while blinded by the wild, erotic elegance of her bared breast and pinched, pink nipple.

My heart trips over one of its hurried beats.

The colors of the aurora blend through her hair as she tilts her head, the motion almost predatory. For whatever fucking reason, I'm blindsided by a jolt of thrill.

She drops to a crouch and slaps her hand upon my clammy forehead, rinsing me in her sea-spray scent.

I groan for all the wrong reasons.

She inspects my perspiration now smeared across her palm, sniffing it.

I frown.

Why am I *sweating?* People only do that when they're overheating—something I'm absolutely not doing. In fact, I've never been so cold in my very long life.

She nuzzles into my neck, draws deep ...

I still.

Fucking *still.*

Her exhale rattles against me, and for a moment I think she's going to open that pretty little mouth and sink her teeth into my flesh.

"I'm fine." I coax the shirt over her shoulder again, then grip her by the upper arm. "Just tuck d-down and go back to sle—"

She whips the furs away, baring my body to the crisp air.

"Sweet seas," I mutter, reaching down to protect myself. "Avert your eyes. It's cold."

She settles her ear against my chest, eyes sweeping shut, snatching my breath as her hand flattens over my heart.

She *taps-taps-taps* her middle finger, and I drop my chin, watching her with baited intrigue.

On she goes—speeding up, slowing down. She even drums little patterns that have me frowning.

Perhaps she's timing those knocks to the beat of my heart? Maybe her concern is justified. That rhythm doesn't sound healthy.

"It's working, Vicious. I w-wouldn't be breathing otherwise."

Her other hand stamps over my mouth—a not-so-subtle way of telling me to shut it.

I groan, afraid of nipping her salt-stained palm with my chattering teeth.

A knock on the door has her head whipping up. Every bone in my body locks as I watch her leap off the bed with a burst of excited energy that sets me on edge.

I thought this island was abandoned. Has been for *decades*.

Maybe ... maybe she has a *mate*. Maybe that's *his* shirt she's practically swimming in.

Maybe this is their nest.

I try to cover myself with the furs, the movement stabbing me with a strike of pain.

"Who is that?"

I'm not sure why the words come out thick. Even a little ... growled. I wish Zyke would slither up and offer me a spike or two. Maybe a spine fin. I'd settle for a fucking scale at this point.

Vicious rips open the door, and relief swirls in my gut when I see nobody's there.

She bends, straightens, then comes back inside holding

a weather-worn basket. She dashes toward me, ripping off the cloth covering the mound of contents: a stack of dried fish and a tiny jar that reminds me of Orlaith. I catch sight of the lucent powder inside, and a bitterly cold chill strikes my heart, pausing its frantic beat.

"*Candescence* ..."

She snatches the jar so fast her movements blur, and then she's scooping a shell full of water.

"Who gave you that?" My voice is fractured with hesitancy. "Vicious? *Please* ..."

No response as she sprinkles the powder on the water's top and stirs it through with her finger, concentration dug deep into the iridescent swirl I can see from here.

Fear pulses to life—wild and unblinking.

If she drinks that ... she's not the person I thought she was.

Far from it.

"*Vicious*," I growl, then curse this communication barrier staked between us as I try to sit up. Not sure why. Perhaps to bat it from her hand before it makes it to her lips.

I kick my leg off the edge of the nest—

She snarls, head snapping in my direction.

"I'm fine!" The words belt free, even as that ache inside my chest spears deeper.

Clambering onto the furs, she straddles my chest and brings the shell to my lips, her eyes wide.

Like a tail slap to the face, I realize what this is.

She wants me to drink it because she thinks it'll heal me.

I squeeze my lips shut, hardening my stare.

Fuck. No.

Her eyes flash, then narrow as she tries to bore her finger between my lips, grunting at me.

Actually *grunting* at me.

I don't care how sick she thinks I am, there is not one single part of me that will *ever* be coaxed into drinking the ground thorns of an Aeshlian ear.

When she manages to get the tip of her finger past my lips, I nip at it, almost hard enough to draw blood. She whips her hand away and stuffs the tip into her mouth while she studies me.

"No d-drink," I berate, shaking my head. "No."

She nods—a lot.

And fast.

I shake my head with the same vigor. "*No.*"

Her gaze shifts from my eyes to my mouth, then to my gills, brow buckling when it settles on my nose. She pinches it hard enough to stop any air from flowing in or out, and my eyes widen.

With a surge of adrenaline, I snatch her wrist, flip us both, and pin her beneath me, dashing liquid candescence over the furs as I bear my weight down upon her and grunt in her face—deep and fucking rough.

Her eyelids flutter.

She stills, hair a tousled halo, looking up at me with full-moon eyes. There's something in their sunstruck depths, a shimmering lure I want to *chase.* Catch. Cradle.

Curl around.

Something in the way she's spread beneath me, pressed against my nakedness—soft and supple and savage to the core.

Beautifully feral.

An unbuffed treasure.

The hot surge of throbbing pressure between my legs crumbles my resolve.

Fuck.

I tip sideways into a heap to shield her from the prodding intrusion, and a slash of pain strikes me like another bolt to the chest. Biting down the urge to scream or vomit or maybe both, I hear a slosh of water. A gentle tap of glass to shell.

Vicious straddles my waist, and my spine bucks as she rips the scale off my chest so fast another wave of vomit threatens, then she's tipping the liquid onto my wound like a pour of fire.

She's going to kill me. Then probably eat me.

At this point, that seems peaceful.

I grind out big, aching breaths while she smooths the scale and pats down the edges before battling with the buttons on her shirt. One by one they give way until all her curves are bared to me.

My heart skips a beat.

Several.

I take in her tiny waist, full breasts and hips that could make the sea scream. Her smooth stomach leading to a dainty, white tuft at the apex of her spread thighs that are wrapped around me …

I feel my hard, naked length pulse.

Look away, you fucking brute.

She peels the shirt off, dashes it over me, eyeing my ready shaft as she does so. A pink blush spreads across her cheeks, and I shift my stare to the far side of the room.

Don't think. Or smell.

Don't fucking move.

A long silence drifts by, and I dissect each of her short, sharp breaths like I'm going mad—trying to twist them into words. Trying to convince myself her silence means something it likely doesn't.

She climbs over me, and I continue to stare at the wall, listening to her paw the furs, mounding the spot right beside me into a cushioned pile. She shifts my arm and balls up against my side, her breaths a warm patter on my ribs.

Slowly, her hand threads across my chest, settling on a spot near my hurt, and she *taps, taps ... taps ...*

They taper off with her deepening breaths, and I finally allow myself to observe her—balled up, naked, and untamed, hair cast to the side like a spill of bubbly water.

I pluck a twig from the tangles, gaze catching on something just behind her ear. The faint tip of three fine lines.

My heart splats against my insides.

I push aside her hair and swallow. Trace those lines with the tip of my finger, feeling her tremble against me with each tender stroke ...

She has gills.

I stopped hunting years ago. Thought I was the only one left—that Zyke and I were all alone.

I was wrong.

CHAPTER 26
Orlaith

One leg hangs over the edge of the railing, the other tucked beneath me as I drag my utensils against each other. Hard.

Squee.

I'm not even tempted to root through my pocket for the lump of caspun I keep close—just in case. The sound no longer makes me want to twist into a knot and scream, but rather pecks at my hardened shell. Like knuckles rapping against a door, checking if anyone's home.

I'm not.

The sentries make their evening rounds, pacing the front gardens lit by flaming bowls of oil and lofty lamps that tower above the trees and shrubs. They're easy to see from up here, balancing on the balustrade with my back against the wall, tucked amongst a fall of shadow on the edge of a sheer, unsurvivable drop.

My favorite spot.

It makes my blood rush. Makes me feel *alive*.

I've spent the past five nights sitting right here, studying the sentries' mannerisms, their routines—their exorbitant smoking habits where big puffs of white twist with the wind.

I've spent the past five nights growing more and more restless, watching the moon bloat in teensy increments that count down the days I have to figure out how to climb out of that bowl.

My days have fallen into a too-familiar pattern: mealtimes, trial practice, sitting tucked in my guarded room with too much time to stew, watching Cainon come and go from my spot so-high above the rest.

All the makings of a cog I don't want to oil and tend ... but *shatter*.

I have no guilt for what I'm about to do.

Cainon will get what he's promised—a woman by his side saying all the right things, smiling, waving, nodding ...

Lying.

But I tucked myself away for years, and I'm done living that life. There's too much I need to see.

To ask.

Perhaps Madame Strings is across that bridge, sitting around a campfire like Vanth and Gun described—

There's a subtle knock at my door.

I crane my neck to watch through the window as the door clicks open. Izel peeks through, looks left and right, then blows into the room like she's made of air. "Mistress?"

I doubt she knows I'm watching as she checks my washroom, my dressing room, before finally collecting my tray, her humble expression folding when she lifts the cloche to see my uneaten meal lumped on the plate.

Was hard to muster much of an appetite after I cut

through a piece of honey-glazed prawn and brought it to my lips only to find it sprinkled with the tiny black berries of a bane bush—enough to make me choke to death from a swollen airway.

It really put a damper on my evening.

After spending all afternoon at The Bowl, then spewing my guts all over the floor there, I was really looking forward to a nice, hot meal. Now I'm committed to sifting through *every* meal, avoiding soups and teas, watching the people who handle my food like a hawk until I find the culprit and understand the motive.

As Izel leaves, I catch a glimpse of Kolden through the open doorway, still standing in the same spot.

As usual, no chance of getting past him.

I look back down at the sentries, watching them traipse back and forth, back and forth ...

Castle Noir was my city. It held my sanity in its cold, black-stone fist.

That city over there—glittering against the bruised evening sky—it's a brand-new canvas with real shops. Real houses. Real streets to explore.

A new Tangle to lose myself in.

There are no *safety lines*.

Movement drags my gaze down the line of the bridge to a horse and cart clopping forth at the far end, and my heart skips a beat. The evening produce delivery—the cart heaped with so much fruit and vegetables, it draws the attention of *every* sentry.

I've been timing the nightly ritual, breaking it down into segments and factoring each into my burgeoning plan.

It takes around thirteen minutes for that horse to clop

across the bridge, giving me thirteen minutes to climb seven stories to the grounds below. I'll then have the *six* minutes it takes them to check through the cart's produce to sprint past the sentries unseen and make it to the midway rise in the bridge.

My blood races.

I leap off the railing, dash inside, tuck the utensils beneath my pillow, then knot my hair and tug on the cap Gun stole for me at the Inn. Snatching my prepacked knapsack from where I'd stashed it in a dresser drawer, I slam to a stop inches from the balcony.

My gaze drops to my cupla ...

If I get caught without it, I could get in a lot of trouble. But if anyone catches sight of it, my cover will be blown.

You can have whatever you please, whenever you please. My people respect that ...

I undo the latch, remove the cupla, and stuff it in the back of a drawer in my bedside table before heading to the far corner of the balcony outside. Stretching my shoulder, I do another quick scan, recounting the route I've been mapping out over the past five nights while practicing my scrapes.

To make it to the bottom, I'll have to climb from balcony to balcony, across a thin window ledge. There's a section where I'll need to rely entirely on the little grooves between the buffered bricks before the final descent down a drainpipe.

I search my insides for a spike of fear, apprehension, anything ...

Nothing.

Just that noxious, exhilarating excitement.

I leap onto the rail and crouch, cold air brushing against the back of my neck as I spin and lower off the edge. A frosty trail drags down my spine, up again, then hovers upon my nape, turning my blood icy.

Heart in my throat, I pause, waiting for the feeling to pass, but it just sits there like a soft *"Hello. Yes, you're fucking crazy."*

I grit my teeth so hard they ache, glancing over my shoulder toward the illuminated city ... down to the approaching cart ...

I'm running out of time.

Doing my best to ignore the intrusion, I shift my grip to the bottom edge and let my weight hang, toes pointed toward the balustrade below.

The wind goes eerily still.

I wait until I stop swinging, then drop, landing in a crouch on the rail and wearing a smile that's almost feline.

I repeat the motion until there are no more balconies—just a four-story climb to the ground below. My landing spot is only a few conveniently placed shrubs away from where two sentries are taking a smoking break while waiting for the cart to reach the gate.

Thankfully, they don't usually look up.

Usually.

I edge across the thin lip of a window ledge and turn to face the wall, pressing my body flat against stone, tongue between my teeth as I reach out and feel around for the first divot. Easing my weight to the side, I stretch my foot toward another deep dent, feeling around for a second handhold—my entire weight now hanging on the sheer stone face.

I like this.

Concentration honed, I maneuver down the wall, listening to my body's natural instincts, growing faster with every stealthy shift.

My confidence swells when I see the drainpipe almost within reach.

I stretch toward the next divot—

A bit of rock crumbles beneath my fingers, and I slip to the sound of cracking thunder, stomach tumbling, forced to use my foothold as a kick board to propel me sideways prematurely.

I fly, bag swinging, then smashing against my side as I collide with the drainpipe, latch onto it with both hands, and grip tight. Sliding three feet down the dewy surface, I notice the sentries don't even glance up, and I smile despite my smarting shoulder, breathing hard, thanking the timely bout of thunder for its rowdy cover.

I look back, spotting the cart pulling onto the grounds, guided by a red-robed merchant sitting atop the box seat ...

Didn't consider him.

"Shit," I mutter, scaling the drainpipe in slow, shuffling motions, hoping he doesn't think to look at the palace wall where he'll *absolutely* see me undulating down the edge of it like a caterpillar.

Watching the sentries douse their pipes and move away from my landing spot, excitement bursts in my belly.

I jump the final few feet and land in the grass, drawing a deep, intoxicating breath, digging my toes into the soil. There's only a brief moment of reprieve before I dart into the shadow of a bush, catching my breath as the cart rolls to a stop several paces ahead.

"Perfect timing," I whisper, watching the sentries

swarm it like flies, questioning the merchant, rioting through his produce.

I wait until their backs are turned before dashing across the cobbled courtyard, heart thumping, legs churning. Leaping into the thin line of shadow falling off the bridge's ornate entry column, I slam my spine against the stone.

Relief empties my lungs.

Nobody saw me.

I look at the blocks of shadow cast across the bridge, holding my bag close to my body as I dart to the next, the next, the next—my heart thrashing with each catapulting sprint until I finally rise over the midway point.

The bright city dawns before me like a sun punching above the gloomy horizon.

I spin, looking back at the palace poised on the island's tip like a square set of teeth. "Wow!" I trace the path I just descended, landing on my lit suite. A smile ghosts my lips. "I just did that ..."

A single taste of freedom has given me an insatiable hunger.

Not wanting the city folk to see me wandering down the bridge, I leap up onto the thick railing and swing over the side, dropping onto the massive pipe that threads beneath the structure.

Far beneath me, the ocean churns as I navigate the sloped path—heart in my throat, hands outstretched to keep my balance.

Waves smash against the bouldered shore. Fishermen perch in sheltered nooks with their lines cast, blazing lanterns and buckets with fish tails poking out by their feet.

None of them look up while I traverse the pipe above their heads.

The slope threads through the stones, forcing me to clamber up and over the smooth, slippery rocks. I edge onto a footpath fringing the esplanade, standing in the block of shadow falling off the bridge's imposing entrance.

Cap pulled down low enough to conceal half my face, I study the tall, compact buildings lit from above by an abundance of lofty streetlamps, drawing my lungs full of mosaic scents.

Carts loaded with fish are pulled through the street by restless horses, perhaps eager for their stalls. A group of bronzed sailors wobble on unsteady feet, chortling out an off-key tune. A scantily clad woman prances through the crowd, twirling two short, flaming sticks while a man trails behind, cap in hand, collecting a clink of coins from applauding onlookers. Golden-haired couples wander through the throng, arm in arm, as if nothing can penetrate the bubble they've built around themselves.

The city ... it's a special sort of monster, alive with a beat of its own. Never the same from one second to the next.

My gaze lands on a store that appears to be closed for the night, and my breath catches as I take in the sign hanging above the door:

Bulbs and Botany

Excitement flutters in my chest like a flight of butterflies.

I notice the garden box out the front of it, positively *spilling* a waxy-looking plant that bares thick, soft, pink leaves. "*No way* ..."

Vasil Alione—I've only ever seen it in botany books. I can't believe it's just roosting out in the open!

Digging through my bag, I snatch the tiny pair of gold nail snips I found in my washroom earlier and inject myself into the crowd's messy current. I zigzag around carts and sticky-faced children, stopping right before the planter box, eyeing up a healthy-looking tendril.

I quickly scan my surroundings, then snip at its thick, wood-like stem, fold the clipping in a handkerchief, and tuck it in my bag.

Victory tingles at the tips of my fingers.

I shuffle from the scene of the crime and closer to the window, a smile splitting my face as I place my hands against the glass and peer into the darkness. Squinting through the gloom, I can tell just from the shadowy shapes that the shop is packed full of plants in various forms and sizes. Erupting with elation, I spin, leaning back, caught in a world of wonder.

An entire shop dedicated to plants.

Wait ...

Gun mentioned something about a plant shop he and his partner owned while we were talking at the Inn.

I look over my shoulder, through the window ...

Maybe *this* is it?

Guilt plummets into my gut like a dropped stone.

And I just snipped their Vasil Alione.

Oops.

Something cold sweeps across my face—a slow, tender traverse that almost knocks my knees out from under me.

My heart riots. Breath hitches.

I scan the crowd, gaze landing in the pocket of black by the edge of the bridge. The same place I was standing only moments ago—now heavy with something other than shadow.

A man.

Big, broad, hooded—

Watching me.

That brush of chill is unrelenting, *unearthing* me, eating me up in a way that's impossible to shake. In a way that makes me feel raw, vulnerable, and exposed.

Something wild shudders and swells inside my chest, wrapping around my ribs ...

Run—it screams.

Run!

CHAPTER 27
Orlaith

My back is glued to the glass—a butterfly mounted on a corkboard with a pin straight through her insides as I hold that shadowed stare—chest heaving. Mind spinning.

Run!

A horse and carriage trundle past, snipping the view and the gravity of his crushing perusal. I burst onto the esplanade—dodging people, carts, fish stalls. Darting down side alleys riddled with wooden crates and barrels and puddles of filthy water that slop up my legs.

A scuffing sound scrapes across the ground behind me—*too close*—and a shiver attacks my nape, like someone's breathing down it. A chill nips at my skin, stealing bites of my warmth.

Devouring me one small mouthful at a time.

Heart pumping a violent, thrilling beat, some unhinged part of me flares to life knowing danger's snapping at my heels. I change direction again and again until my lungs are burning just as much as this toxic fire in my lower belly. Until I've twisted my lines into so many knots, I'll no doubt struggle to find the palace again before dawn.

The hairs on the back of my neck settle; the air goes hot and sticky.

Breathing hard, I risk a glance behind. Seeing nothing but an empty alleyway, I fall in a heap within a shadow against a wall and whip off my cap, wiping the sweat from my face. I shiver, despite the heat and my fervid skin, reliving the feel of that stare carving over me ...

Into me.

My heart leaps.

"Fuck," I mutter, tucking damp tendrils behind my ears, spiked with a wild restlessness I can't shake—that makes me feel more alive than I did sitting on the balustrade, or free-climbing down that wall.

My breath shudders as I try to ignore the shameful, incinerating ache between my legs.

Just my imagination. He's not here.

I replace my cap, close my eyes, then tip my head against the stone.

City sounds battle around me while I devour thick, exotic smells: spices, fried fish, the pinched musk of wine. A fiddle carves out soft, lilting notes, brought to me on a remedial breeze.

Leaning forward, I peer down the alley to the opening at the far end.

It's busy. Alive.

I push up, weaving around a puddle toward the merriment ahead, though my heart leaps into my throat when the smell of smoke coasts past me.

Madame Strings.

Lured further down the alley, I see a cramped courtyard off to the side, stuffed full of people surrounding a blazing firepit. I backstep behind the corner and watch—gaze bouncing from person to person, all boasting golden hair and bronze skin.

One of them laughs so hard he falls off the square stone he's using as a seat. Another stands, throws her hands in the air, and twirls until there's an amber shower flying from the mug she's wielding.

"Excuse me," I croak, stepping into the smoky orange atmosphere.

One of the boys twists in place, squinting. "You lost?"

Probably.

"Do you know where I might find Madame Strings?"

He laughs, eyes glittering with a sprinkle of mania. "If only I knew. Come see me if you find her. I'm almost out of candy, and her shit's the best."

Candy?

I'm about to ask what the hell he's talking about, but he drums up conversation with a girl who drapes herself across his lap, effectively dismissing me.

Right.

"Thanks," I mutter, continuing down the alley, toward the fiddle player and the source of the rich smells that make my empty stomach gurgle.

The alley spills out into a large, crowded courtyard—what I suppose is a town square alive with some sort of night market.

I stare in wide-eyed wonder at the huge, ancient tree that spawns from the center of it all. Riddled with small, open-mouthed hollows, its wide-reaching branches are dotted with lanterns and sitting sprites kicking their legs back and forth.

Mail tree.

It's so much bigger than the one at Castle Noir, circled by a stone fence that's a backdrop for a loop of carts selling drinks, wares, and tasty-looking treats that make my mouth water. Even the shops on the outer rim of the square are open, unlike the others I came across during my mad dash through the streets.

People are milling around, some wobbly on their feet with their heads tipped back in laughter. Some with children on their shoulders or big baskets hanging from their crooked arms, heaped with food and trinkets.

I step out amongst it all, keeping my hat pulled down to hide my face, the cold cobbles nursing the tender soles of my feet.

"*Found you.*"

I gasp, whipping around—

Nothing.

That deep, velvety voice echoes in my head, its blunt, frosty blow against my ear leaving a cool shiver that stretches all the way to my pinched nipple.

Further.

Heart rioting, hand coming up to brush the pebbled skin on the side of my neck, I scan the churning crowd, searching for a shock of black hair and silver eyes.

I swallow, shake my head, and shove the echo of rich baritone somewhere so deep it can't play with my strings and muddy my mind.

Not real.

Spotting a stall selling dusted dough balls akin to Cook's honey buns, my heart aches.

I approach, drawing a hungry inhale.

The smell is similar—creamy and rich with the scent of honey, but sweeter.

I look at the price boldly displayed on a plank of wood hanging from the bottom of the cart:

Chip. I wonder what that looks like. And where I can get five of them without having to beg at Cainon's feet again.

I push on, passing stalls selling toffee apples, impeccably carved glass flower figurines, meat sticks glazed in something dark and dripping, mulled wine that smells like cinnamon and cloves and is stirred in a cauldron big enough for me to crawl inside. There's another stall spilling a small forest of simple wooden racks across the cobbled ground, each packed with handmade cloaks that look like they would've taken *weeks* to sew.

I pull one free, folding back the front panels.

Fully lined, a deep hood, lots of little pockets to keep things in …

Zane.

It's the perfect replacement for the one I lost. And a perfect excuse to find out where he lives and pay him a visit.

A warm feeling floods my chest as I imagine him

unwrapping it, boasting that lopsided smile when he tallies up the pockets.

Gliding the hangers across the rail, I carefully sort through the stock, finding one—only *one* that's the perfect size for him.

I have to have it. Need to have it.

The store owner sweeps past while I count the pockets, his attention poking at me like the pointed tip of a sword. "You have any coin, boy?"

I turn, catching his shrewd stare.

Shit.

My mind whirrs, fingers curling around the cloak's hem.

I'm worried that if I'm forced to come back for it later, it'll be gone.

An idea explodes, bursting my chest full of warmth.

"I have something *much* better," I beam, digging through my knapsack. I withdraw a small parcel and peel back the layers, holding it out.

The shopkeeper looks down. "A *stick?*"

"Cutting," I clarify. "It's called Vasil Alione. It's very rare. If you dry it, then steep it in hot water, it forms a paste that can be used like a waterproof bandage, but it has many … other … uses …"

I trail off when a deep dent forms between his bushy brows, like he's disgusted at the very sight of my offering. He looks me square in the eye, and I've never felt so small.

"Are you *daft?*" he belts out, and the commotion surrounding us stills.

"I— I …"

Looking around, I notice some people have stopped in their tracks, watching on with wide eyes that take greedy gulps of my shame.

My cheeks heat.

"No, I'm—"

"You want to trade a stick for one of my fine, tailored garments?" He chuffs a laugh, and I close my hand around the precious cutting, pulling it close to my chest. "You must be out of your fuckin' mind."

All I can do is blink, staked to the stone like a statue.

I just want this moment to end.

He snatches a broom from where it's leaning against a rack and stalks toward me.

I bolt past nosy onlookers, feeling their sharp stares prick at me like tacks as I slink into the crowd, shoving past a hoard of drunken sailors. I weave past a dancing flutist, dodge a man on a unicycle, and get lost amongst the churning people—chest pounding, eyes stinging.

Pausing, I tuck the precious stem inside my bag, drop my chin to my chest, and breathe through the extra surge of shame flaring up my neck ...

Are you daft?

Hands scrunching into fists so tight my nails punch through the skin on my palms, I close my eyes, wanting nothing more than to blink out of existence. Disappear. To dash up Stony Stem and crawl beneath my bed.

How could I be so *stupid?*

My heart stops as something hard and formidable steps up against my back like a shield—a sturdy, too familiar presence that seems to say *I'm here. It's okay.*

You're not alone.

A weight settles on the crown of my head and an icy breath blows through my hair, casting prickles on the backs of my eyes ...

I almost believe it's real.

Almost.

Part of me even wishes it was. That *he* was. That I could lean back and crumble into him—tip my head and feel that same chilled breath thread across my face.

Ease my flaming cheeks.

The rest of me is so horrified my imagination would bring him here to taunt me in my most embarrassing moment that I want to scream and shout and spin and bash my fists against his make-believe chest.

A sob threatens to burst from between my clenched teeth.

"Go away," I whisper.

Plead.

A pair of strong hands settle on my waist, tightening—halting my breath.

My heart leaps so high in my throat I almost choke.

Not real.

All in my head.

I dig into my bag, trembling fingers snatching the snips. "*Go away!*" I scream, spinning, slashing the empty air, my words belting out across the quelling crowd of blanched faces. Countless pairs of eyes watch me punch and hack and stab at nothing.

Nothing.

All in my head.

My arm falls, chest heaving from the thrash of my unfiltered rage. Or perhaps madness is a better word. More accurate.

I look at the pathetic, tiny weapon hanging from my limp hand, then back to the silent crowd.

Definitely a better word.

Slowly, cautiously, they begin to shift into murmuring motion.

I squeeze my eyes shut and drop my chin to my chest, pulling deep, controlled breaths ...

Not real.

Chapter 28
Orlaith

The world around me regains its natural beat—scuffing steps, bursts of laughter, whistling. I open my eyes, seeing a small, silver disk notched in a nook between two cobblestones.

My pulse pitches.

Coin.

I pick it up, flip it, feel the heavy weight of it in the palm of my hand. It must be worth a bit. Perhaps enough to buy Zane's cloak? Though the thought of facing that shopkeeper again fills me with face-blazing dread.

Perhaps I can find one somewhere else?

My gaze drifts to the line of permanent storefronts bordering the courtyard. All well-kept, squished against each other, draped in the golden glow of a vibrant streetlamp. The largest shop takes up the same amount of space as three smaller ones, over three stories of massive, glazed windows staring down on the square. Its large sign squeaks in the wind:

TO SNAP A SILVER STEM

I move through the swirl of people, drawn to the window on the ground floor where a mishmash of things are haphazardly displayed—including a cabinet that seems to boast things of a much higher caliber than everything else.

A silver blade with an opaline hilt steals my breath and, bagging my snips, I press my nose against the glass to study its finer details.

It's a similar size to the wooden daggers Baze sometimes had us practice with—longer than my hand but small enough to tuck down the back of my pants or strap against my thigh without getting in the way. It even has a delicate vine and tiny buds engraved in the hilt, akin to the hidden illustration I found on my sword.

It's a *real* weapon. One I could wear at all times, train with in my suite without drawing attention.

Protect myself with.

I've never chosen a weapon for myself. They've always been given to me. And I think … I think Baze would approve. I think if he were here with me right now, he'd give me one of those lopsided grins that break across his face whenever he's proud of me, then he'd tell me to go in there and get it.

The thought makes my throat feel tight and achy.

Unraveling my fingers, I look at the coin, back again, then step toward the door and shove it open, tolling an overhead bell. Hot, musty air and the smell of old things smacks me in the face.

I cast my gaze around the cluttered room, past roof-high shelves stacked with an array of wares—old teapots, candelabras in need of a good polish, pretty glass tumblers in haphazard towers.

"Hello?"

No answer.

I move deeper into the room, weaving between the shelves, the floor creaking beneath my feet.

The bell jingles again, a chill crawling up my spine that I adamantly ignore, refusing to give my imagination the stage it's screaming for as I step into an open area that displays large bits of furniture. A big, stone counter dominates the far wall, doused in light from a collection of mismatched lanterns hanging from the ceiling.

I tap my fingers on the smooth stone top, looking around. "Excuse me?"

A man hobbles through a doorway in the back corner, belly so round he could probably set a plate on it and use it as a table. His gray hair is slicked with something shiny, his gold-buttoned garb so finely tailored he looks out of place standing amongst the drift of dust particles.

He squints at me through half-moon specs while wiping crumbs from the corner of his mouth with a dark blue napkin. "Yes?"

"I was hoping to take a closer look at the dagger in the cabinet in the front window display. The one with the opaline hilt."

"Of course." He wanders past, disappearing between the shelves while I drum my fingers against my thigh. He returns a moment later, moves behind the counter, and sets the blade in my open palm.

My eyes widen, chest tight and tingly.

It's even more beautiful up close—the little embossed buds catching on the spill of light. I wrap my fingers around the hilt, surprised to find it perfectly balanced in my hand.

Drawing a deep breath, I let it out slow and steady before I smile up at the man. "I'll have it."

"Superb." He takes it from me and spins, practiced hands folding it amongst some creamy tissue paper. "That'll be one drab."

Warm relief rushes up my throat with a shuddered sigh. Thankfully, I have one of those.

Just one.

There's a creak in the floorboards somewhere behind me as I slide my single coin across the counter with the tip of my finger.

Turning, his beady gaze drops to the bench. "That's a *chip*." He looks at me over the rim of his glasses, reaching out his hand. "The other nine hundred and ninety-nine?"

My blood chills, heart drops, sweaty palms wrap around my knapsack.

No.

His eyes narrow. "Is that all you have, boy?"

Please no.

He sighs, setting my precious parcel on the bench before

he stalks around the counter. "On your way, you little street rat. This is not a charity house!"

"Wait!" I squeal, scrambling back a step when he's so close the reek of his body odor overpowers the smell of dust. "I ... I have something else."

I hate how my voice breaks at the end. How my hands tighten around my knapsack now flattened to my chest, as if every cell in my body knows what I'm about to do.

Is fighting against it.

He stops, eyes cutting over me, like he's considering the many ways he could slice me up and profit from my flesh. "Something else?"

A milky breath blows out of me.

"Yes. Something"—*precious; irreplaceable; something not one single piece of me wants to part with*—"of worth. At least ... I think."

He sets his hand between us, palm up.

Swallowing the lump in my throat, I give him my back and dig into my knapsack, pulling open the side pocket to reveal my diamond pickaxe—pristine, despite the thousands of times I've used it to chip blank whispers from the wall.

This tool ... this beautiful, mighty, delicate tool ... it's felt the wear of my sorrow. My shame. My anger and my heartache.

It's seen my greatest fears come to life.

I grip its small, smooth handle and pull it free from the darkness. Light catches on its many facets, reminding me of my brother's eyes. I hesitate, glancing over my shoulder to the blade ... back again.

It feels like my heart's being ripped in two.

One half is more than happy to drown in the murky

waters of my past so long as it's curled around that one luminous seed—the sparse remnants of the boy who saved my life, only for me to turn around and do terrible, *horrific* things I'll never be able to take back.

The other half is swimming frantically toward the airy surface, lungs burning for a gulp of air.

I can't keep living in the past.

With him.

I have to find a way to move forward, one fallen whisper at a time, until the wall is deconstructed in my mind. Until it's no longer weighing me down like stones stacked in my belly.

Feeling a little piece of me crumble away, I turn and place the pickaxe in the man's awaiting palm, glancing up to see his eyes ignite.

"Hmm." Weighing it in his hand, he wanders behind the counter, stamping my sudden urge to snatch it back and dash out the door. He drags it against the glass countertop, and I feel the shrill scratch on my heart, making my bones hurt just as much as my aching soul. A long gouge is left behind, and he clears his throat, looking at me over the rim of his spectacles. "Is there any way you can authenticate it?"

Another creak in the floor.

"It's diamond, I assure you."

He shrugs. "With no paperwork to confirm its validity, it's as good as garbage."

I open my mouth, about to plead with him when he stabs a finger at the ceiling. "But! I'm in a philanthropic mood." He spins, grabs the freshly wrapped parcel, and sets it on the bench between us. "Just don't speak of my generosity to anyone. I can't afford to give charity to every barefooted urchin boy that wanders through my door."

I reach for both my parcel and my coin, but he pinches the latter before jerking his chin toward the door.

"Off you go. Try not to murder anybody with that thing. The outer rim is no place for a boy like you." He chuckles, snatching a looking glass off the table and giving me his back. "They'd eat you alive."

I want to cry. Scream.

Take it all back.

I force myself to edge back a step, another, feeling my little brother slip from my stretched fingertips ...

I jerk the door open and run from the store so fast I swear I leave my bleeding heart on the floor beside the counter.

CHAPTER 29
Rhordyn

Wild, restless rage swipes at my ribs.

The bell is still jingling from *her* dashed departure as I step into the aisle and stalk toward the store's rear, cloak fluttering in my wake. Cracking my neck from side to side, I pass the empty counter doused in lantern light.

They love their lanterns here. Think the bright can protect them from everything. Most of them are too young or uneducated to know that worse monsters used to *thrive* in the light.

Some of them still do.

I follow a whistling tune and the distinct aroma of roasted duck—a delicacy sourced from Ocruth. All I can smell is *greed* as I step through the open doorway at the far corner of the room.

The office is such a contrast to the rest of the shop, padded with expensive furnishings from all over the continent: a chandelier dripping beads of amber; plush, velvet chairs studded with sterling; an almond-shaped shield hanging on the wall, carved from the impenetrable skull of an Ocean Drake; the tan pelt of a Rouste Dune Cat stretched across the ground, so big it leaves only glimpses of the blue stone beneath.

There's even a Vruk talon mounted on his wall, long and curved and black.

The shopkeeper whistles away with his back to me, turning the dial on the tall, freestanding safe in the corner of the room.

My gaze is drawn to the glass statue of a broad male I recognize, his dreaded hair a transparent churn around his face, wrathful hunger consuming his lucid eyes, fangs bared as he hisses at nothing, *lunges* at nothing—the transparent Vruk talon he's wielding paused mid-strike.

Must have cost him a lot of coin to procure that statue. To have it carved from the inhospitable heart of Arrin, dragged for days across the stark, windswept plains, then hauled on a barge down the River Norse without even a hairline fracture.

Nobody would go to such effort unless they were bribed or paid a handsome sum. Unless, of course, he did it himself.

But I somehow doubt that.

The safe clicks open.

"You know ..." My words crack through the whistling tune, and the man whirls around so fast his spectacles slip off his face and clatter to the floor, Orlaith's pickaxe clutched close to his chest. "The Shulák say the battlefield at Arastile is sacred. That mining from it will bring you eternal bad luck."

"Wh-who are you?" he blurts, bending to retrieve his spectacles and thread them onto his scrunched face.

I turn to look straight at him from beneath my hood.

His mouth falls open, gaze flicking to the hilt of my sword that's visible over my shoulder, then to the brooch at my nape—the Ocruth sigil. He drops into a low, sweeping bow. "*High Master ...*"

Not tonight.

I gesture to the pickaxe. "That diamond right there? I mined it *myself.*" Body straightening, the man lifts his head, slowly glancing down his nose at the dainty tool in his white-knuckled fist. "A lump of it as big as your head," I say, pretending to weigh it in the palm of my hand. "Carved it into three small tools and gifted them to someone special."

Someone who needed to see that beautiful things don't have to be breakable.

He looks up, frowning. "You must be mistaken. I purchased this tool off an urchin boy—"

"Tell me. Do you make a habit out of taking advantage of naïve people to satiate your greed?"

"No," he blurts, puffing his chest, angling his body in such a way he shields the half-open safe at his back. "I'm an honest, hard-working man. I pay a yearly tithe and contribute to my territory in more ways than most."

I wrap my hand around the door. "Step aside."

The sharp, intoxicating scent of his fear slathers the back of my throat, all the color draining from his face. "H-High Master, I—"

"*Step. Aside.*"

His posture crumbles, and my gaze stalks him as he

edges away, breaking his frantic stare to look into the gloomy guts of the safe.

My heart drops. Stomach twists.

Lining two of the three metal shelves are numerous jars packed full of Aeshlian ears steeped in brine, some no bigger than the pad of my thumb. All still wielding their delicate, crystal thorns, not yet ripped from the flesh and ground into the fine dust these fuckers have discovered feeds them long life if they drink it. Inhale it. Smoke it. The withering race is free rein to some sick, twisted individuals who hang too much weight on the prophet's chisel.

The blood in my veins crackles and sparks, the silver script on my skin sinking its sharp teeth deeper into my flesh, wrapping me in a barbed-wire band.

I slowly turn, watch him stumble backward so fast he thuds against his desk, scattering his half-eaten meal and stacks of gold drabs I want to nail through his skull.

His large shop, his expensive taste in antiquities—it all makes so much horrible fucking sense. "You're a dealer."

"It's not what it looks like—"

"You're padding the streets with candescence. With the hacked off ears of men, women, *children*."

"I'm holding it for someone else! I swear! I'm just the middleman!"

"You're a *greedy* man," I thunder, and he almost jumps out of his skin.

Orlaith's pickaxe clatters across the floor.

I stalk forward, heavy boots thumping as I flip my hood and let him see my ravenous wrath in its full, unguarded glory—bled to the surface like a swelling sickness.

Squealing like a stuck pig, he scurries away, tripping

over his chair and landing on the floor with a hefty thud. He crawls, spins, spine pressed flat against the richly colored tapestry lining the wall.

"I'm from a time when greed got your throat torn open, jaw ripped from your face." I point at the Vruk talon mounted on the wall. "One of *those* punched through your chest."

Heaving breath, his beady eyes bounce from the glass statue to me and back again, no doubt drawing the parallels.

Little does he know, I'm much worse than the monster he glorifies.

"Do you know who dished out those deadly sentences?"

A sob bursts from his trembling lips as he folds into a pathetic, snotty knot at the wall's base.

I rip my dagger from the sheath at my hip.

Smell him piss himself.

"*Me*."

Chapter 30
Rhordyn

I flip the sign to *Closed* and shut the front door behind me, pulling my hood up as I ease into the crowd like a shadow ripped free of its maker.

Drawing deep, I catch a hint of *her*.

A breath shudders free, as though some great beast inside my chest just settled into a satiated coil, and I follow the trail, expecting her to lure me on another hunt through the city. I frown when I round a cart selling frosted dough balls to find her bunched on shallow steps that lead to the mail tree, seemingly watching a one-legged busker carve a tune from his fiddle.

Her arms are wrapped around her knees, cap pitched so low all I can see is the tip of her freckle-dusted nose, the slant of her rose-petal lips ... the slightest tremble to her chin that makes the binds on my skin gnaw.

I brush my hand against the cart, then circle, lurking from shadow to shadow, stalking every breath, every bump of her knee or tap of her foot, every pulsing flutter down the side of her neck—devouring her like the monster I am.

So fucking selfish.

I move up the stairs, drag my fingers across the stone gate behind her, then step so close I could crouch down, weave my arm around her waist, and crush her against my chest. I could dip my head into her neck and fill my aching lungs ...

No.

I wrestle the pouncing urge and force myself back—down a step, another—until I'm easing between two lofty buildings a few long paces from where she's sitting. An alleyway so tall and long, barely any light from the overhead streetlamps makes it down into its damp clutches.

Leaning against the cobbled wall, I survey the crowd bustling beneath the clawed reach of the mail tree. Watch them veer around Orlaith as though they're afraid they'll fall into her—whether they realize it or not.

A tear slides down her cheek, drips off the edge of her jaw.

I trace its trail ...

Can she feel it? Does it cut like a blade? Caress like the breeze? Does she feel haunted, like she's haunting me?

Another tear.

Don't cry.

A fish-laden cart ambles between us, and I arch to the left—carving into the time she's cut from my sight—only to see the step empty. Like she just evaporated into thin air.

"Fuck," I mutter, about to shove forward when the stamp of a cool blade settles upon my throat.

A small warmth presses against my back and tames my rioting heart.

There she is.

The smell of amber and wildflowers wraps around me in the way her body does not, and I smile despite myself. "Hello, Milaje."

Silence. Not even a breath.

She steps closer, pushes that blade *deeper.*

"Careful. The sword you're flattened against is sharp."

"So is mine," is her rasped response—three words that temper my wild and narrow my attention on the weapon poised at my throat.

I reach up, thread my fingers around her wrist, thumb brushing the spot where I've seen the bitten scar that I'm almost certain she made herself. "I can see that."

Gentle.

Don't scare her off.

"How did you make so much progress?"

"I did all the breaking at once," she snaps, the words pattered blows between my shoulder blades. "You're in the wrong place."

Wasting precious time.

Her thought comes to me like smoke on the wind.

"I'm *exactly* where I need to be."

"Then I need you to leave me alone."

My upper lip peels back. "Can't do that, Milaje."

In one swift motion, she's drawn the blade I had strapped to my thigh. Has that, too, set upon my throat. "How about *now?*"

"No," I growl, pushing against the sting, hand tightening around her wrist to keep it there. "You'll have to dig a little deeper." The smell of my blood muddies the air, and her hand starts to shake—the slightest tremble that carves the edge from my voice. I loosen my grip on her wrist. "Drop the blade, Orlaith. Let me see your eyes."

"Why?" She laughs—a cold, hollow sound that blunts my next breath. "So you can check your lie for cracks?"

I snarl, shoving back a step and forcing her to shuffle again and again until I have her pinned against the wall. I spin, fully prepared for those two blades to slash my throat clean open in the effort to see her face.

My forehead collides with cobbled stone as she seems to dissolve into thin air.

I spin again to see her leaning against the opposite wall, a blade hung loosely in each hand dangling at her sides. Head swung to the left, she looks out the alleyway to the swirling crowd ...

It's like all her fight has bled free, leaving a hollow aura that guts me.

I wipe the trickle of blood from my throat and open my mouth to speak.

She gets there first.

"I keep having dreams."

Nightmares.

There's no heartbeat in the words that pass her lips, but her thought is a storm rioting through me. Catastrophic.

"About?" It's an effort to keep the word steady.

"They change." She looks down at the two daggers—hers smeared with the slick of blood she drew and mine, a simple iron blade with a wooden hilt. "The theme is the same every time."

I watch her swallow.

"And that is?"

"Death." The word lands harder than if she'd flung that iron dagger at my chest. "Every time. No matter how hard I try to stop it."

The sky crackles like the blood in my veins.

"You killed me in one of them." Her lashes sweep up, and I can't tell if it's her words or that empty stare that guts me, but they both attack nonetheless. "Put something sharp through my back. I felt my heart split. Felt the life drain from me."

"Then what?" I regret the words the moment I set them free.

"Nothing." Bile blazes a trail up my throat. "Darkness. A colder darkness than I've ever felt before."

She drops her chin so the hat hides her eyes. Perhaps I should welcome the reprieve from her crucifying eyes, but I'm too fucked up to feel that way.

"I don't know why I'm telling you this," she whispers, the words snatched by a gust of humid air that teases fallen leaves down the alleyway's gloomy throat.

She doesn't think I care.

It's almost enough to bring me to my knees.

I did that to her.

I fucking did that to her.

Turning her head, she tracks the people milling about beneath the mail tree.

The cleft between us seems insurmountable. Regardless, I try. "I watched you climb down that building like you had nothing to lose ..."

No answer, but there's acknowledgement in her silence.

She finally blinks, breathing deep before she meets my

eyes and tosses my blade to the ground. It clatters into the space between us, and there's a challenge in her stare. For some reason, it thrills me to the core—the way she looks at me like she's unbreakable. But it also frightens me because she's not.

Far from it.

I bend a knee, pick up my blade, and stab it in my sheath.

She doesn't drop her chin—just watches me down the line of her nose, lashes dipped so low her eyes are nothing but lilac slits.

"How long are you here for, Rhordyn?"

"Until I get what I came for."

"The ships."

I don't bother correcting her.

"Well, I need you to stay out of my way."

I push up, towering over her as violence surges inside me.

Can't. Won't.

She glances at her bag, releasing a deep sigh before she bends and picks it up, tucking her blade inside. Turning, she moves toward the churning crowd on bare, silent steps.

"Orlaith."

She pauses. "What?"

I reach into the pocket of my cloak, retrieving a heavy pouch I toss in her direction. Her hand whips up, and she snatches it without breaking her stare on the crowd, keeping her back to me. I hear the drawstring loosen, see her head drop the slightest bit. She half turns, looking at me over her shoulder, her eyes like purple gemstones starved of light as she cradles the yawning pouch in her palm. "What's this?"

"Enough coin to buy every shop in the square and still leave you with plenty left over."

Her face twists with a fury so potent I taste it on my next breath. "I'm not your problem anymore. I don't want your charity."

Never my problem.

Always my tragic ever after.

"It's not charity, Milaje." I step forward. "That shopkeeper short-handed you. I simply remedied the situation."

"Remedied the—" Her eyes widen, and her sun-soaked skin seems to lose its healthy pallor.

I can see the question in her eyes.

What did you do?

Little does she know, there's nothing I wouldn't do for her.

Except let her go.

She clears her throat, gaze dropping to the small sack of gold. "I remember finding that pickaxe on the end of my bed, along with the matching hammer and chisel. At the time, I thought it came from Baze. Now, I'm not so sure."

"Is there something you want to ask me, Milaje?"

She opens her mouth, pulls a breath. A long moment passes before she blows it out empty.

Disappointment lands in my gut like a rock as she turns to walk away.

"Don't climb the wall that borders the city. It's dangerous."

Pausing, she scoffs. "What happened to '*get out and live*'?"

I arch a brow at the deep voice she puts on, swiftly lowering it when she steps so close we're only separated by a charged slice of space I want to cut through. Leave in ribbons on the ground at our feet.

"What?" she purrs, the word scraping over my skin like a blade. "The rules suddenly change now that you've gotten me out the door?" Tilting her head, she looks up at me with that ice-pick stare. "Am I a bit hard for you to keep up with, Rhordyn? Now that I'm *free?*"

"Is that what you really think?"

She frowns, taking another step so that our bodies are flush. I look down into her. Relish her sharp breaths that batter us closer as I reach into my pocket, pull out her piece of coal, and hold it up.

Her eyes flare, and I hear her heart skip a beat.

Another.

"The *entire time?*"

"From the moment you stepped off that ship," I growl, and she snarls, snatching the coal.

"Anything else you'd like to add?"

"Yes. Stay away from the town square over the next week."

She looks over her shoulder at the bustling crowd. "Isn't *this* the town square?"

"Market square. The other is bigger and on the eastern side. You somehow managed to avoid it during your sprint through the streets."

She sighs, cleaving me with her full attention. "Why?"

"Because I noticed them cutting a tree down on the edge of the jungle."

"*And?*"

"And things are done differently here. That boundary is only ever cut into when they're preparing to burn someone at the stake." Something flickers in her flat gaze, but quickly returns to the cold, apathetic mask that hurts to look at. "Cainon's way of keeping the order—hacking into his peoples' safety net then forcing them to watch somebody burn. You don't need to see that."

Her upper lip trembles, like she's about to bare her teeth. Instead, she spits words at me like I'm nothing but a squelch of shit between her toes. "You don't know me."

Spinning, she stalks off, spearing a path through the crowd as though they share a hive mind, and I have to bite into my urge to follow.

"But I do," I mutter, stepping back into the shadows.

Chapter 31
Orlaith

I finish tallying the remaining coins spread across my crisp, white sheets, scoop them into a pile, then snatch my dagger and flip it from hand to hand, my resecured cupla swaying with the motion. I drag my finger along the blade's smooth face, dangerously close to the sharp edge that slid through Rhordyn's flesh ...

It brought me a twisted sense of satisfaction to watch him bleed for me.

I wanted more.

I wanted to rip into his throat with my teeth. Taste him as he dribbled from my lips.

The thought shocked me.

Frightened me.

I got out of there before I did one of the many stupid things barreling through my head and went to buy some of that mulled wine I'd seen earlier.

There was blood on the coins.

Not all of them, but enough for me to know it likely

came from the shopkeeper at Thrift while he piled gold into that little leather pouch.

I simply remedied the situation.

Flipping the blade high, I snatch it by the pointy end, eyes narrowed on the shard of my reflection displayed on the buffed silver ...

I don't know who I am anymore, and I barely recognized *him*. It wasn't just the extra facial hair roughing up his appearance, or the way he looked at me like he was some ravenous beast chowing down on every second. It was something deeper. Something that made me feel seen in a way that coaxed my cowering fear.

Why is he looking now, when I've got *everything* to hide?

With a snarl, I flick the blade with such gusto, it whistles through the air and sinks into my corner post, pinning the gossamer curtain in place like the lucid wings of a butterfly.

A door clicks open in the lobby, and my head swivels at the sound of footsteps echoing off the walls. There's a light knock, then the rusty voice of the guard who stands in for Kolden sometimes. "Are you okay, Mistress?"

"I'm fine."

Fuck off.

I pull the dagger free, then slip off the bed and walk to the balcony door, spinning when I reach the opening. I lift my arm and aim for the same damaged divot—

A cool rush swirls across the back of my neck, pulling my eyes shut, and I shiver all over, heart lurching so hard I'm struck with a sense of vertigo. I grasp the doorframe for support, slowly opening my eyes, and look to the stone bench on the balcony to my right, just below my window.

A small, leather sheath sits upon it.

My breath shudders free.

I stalk to each corner, looking down at the palace grounds, then up toward the roof before snatching the sheath by the strap. Prying the small scroll from where it's nesting in the hollow, I unroll it, study *his* slanted script—three small words that plant sizzling embers in my chest.

I'd completely forgotten about that. Guess it was spent on a ship, wrapped in a storm, suffocating on nightmares of Rhordyn putting a talon through my chest.

I pocket the note and shove the blade straight in.

Perfect fit.

Shaking my head, I grind my molars, hand crushing the leather strap. I'm certain he gave me the pickaxe, the bluebells, *this*. Perhaps he was even the one to paint the wisteria on my wooden sword. But it doesn't change the fact that he hid me from myself.

Lied to me for *years*.

Doesn't change the fact that he locked me in his fucking den after kissing me like there was no beginning, no middle, no end. Just that one catastrophic moment blazing like a single star in an otherwise empty sky.

I wrestle down the thought and cast another look around the balcony, then lug the doors shut, slamming the lock into place before backing toward the bed one slow step at a time.

The big, heavy glass doors ... they suddenly look so fragile. A pathetic, frail barrier he could shatter in a heartbeat.

Ripping my hair out of its low bun, I breathe deep, trying to tamp the shameful surge of thrill I'm struck with at the thought.

Sitting on the bed with my back to the balcony, I toss the dagger aside and reach for the large woven satchel I purchased to pile all my stuff into, pulling out two thick, velvet cloaks and spreading them across the sheets—the larger for me, smaller for Zane. Smiling when I think about the lovely merchant I found tucked in the corner of the market square. How she helped me choose the perfect sizes and explained the Bahari coin system when it became obvious I had no idea what I was doing.

I paid her double for her kindness.

I neatly fold Zane's cloak, then wrap it in some cloth, smiling as I imagine his face lighting up when he opens it. Legs crossed beneath me, I drape mine across my shoulders and flick up the hood.

Reaching back into the woven satchel, I retrieve a paper bag filled with the honey-bun knockoffs and dust my lap and fingers in powdered sugar as I take a bite so large my cheeks bulge, a glob of pure honey oozing from the center.

I close my eyes, savoring the way the fluffy dough and honeyed cream harmonize together, more flavor bursting with each slow chew.

Not as good as Cook's, but delicious nonetheless.

I stuff the rest in my mouth that's still half full and reach into my satchel again, retrieving a blue shirt, brown pants, a terracotta mug with a hardy handle, and a wooden box filled with paints. Then I grab a leather pouch of paintbrushes and a small, homespun bag I filled with clippings as I made my way back to the palace.

I bite into another bun, staring at my collection of wares as I chew, brow pinched, mind churning, gaze darting between the mug, the paints, the clippings ...

Something plops onto my chest, and I glance down to see a drizzle of honey smeared all over my necklace, through the links, glazing Kai's conch.

"Crap," I mutter, dashing my hood back and setting the bun aside as I swipe at the stickiness oozing down my chin and chest. I undo my shirt buttons and ease my cloak off my shoulder a little so I have better access. The last thing I want to do right now is bathe, but I can't leave myself and my necklace smothered in honey ...

A rebellious thought strikes, and I stand slow, something restless planting in my chest as I glance at those fragile doors again, remembering the last time I unsullied myself from *his* lie.

He knew. Somehow.

I will not beg you to protect yourself, Milaje. Put the fucking necklace on. Now.

The words were spoken like the very thought of me not wearing it *tortured* him. Well. I'm not opposed to the thought of him suffering a little. A silent *fuck you* for stalking me for the past week.

I double-check the lock, draw the curtains, and make for the bathing chambers to the beat of my thundering heart.

The large, blue-stone room is lit by decorative lanterns hanging from gold wall hooks, their tall glass panels casting the space in an underwater tone.

Reaching behind my neck, I pause, touching the clasp with trembling fingers, trying to calm my staggered breaths.

I swallow, grit my teeth, and release the clasp.

My necklace falls heavily into the palm of my hand, the sound of the tinkling chain seeming to echo through the room.

I shudder.

The tightness peels down, freeing me from its snug embrace in skin-tingling increments that make my chest swell and my lids flutter closed—a deep breath pouring into me like it's my first in weeks.

I clench my hand around the jewel, squeezing.

I know I'm a monster—that this pretty skin has split to release something truly horrific. I just hate that something so wrong feels so good. So natural and free and *me*.

Opening my eyes, I avoid looking in the mirror as I run the necklace under the tap, massaging the links with a lather of soap; avoid paying attention to my hands—to my skin that feels silky smooth and petal thin. Just like ... my brother's.

My throat aches with an unwanted swell of emotions.

This was a bad idea.

Heart racing, I scrub harder, faster, rinsing off the suds. The lantern light catches on something scrawled across the latch, and I pause, pulling it close, squinting at the line of script so dainty it's impossible to make out. "Weird," I mutter, holding it closer to the lantern hanging beside the vanity.

Movement catches my eye, and my gaze shoots to the mirror, a gasp escaping when I see Old Hattie with her papery skin and tumble of silver hair standing right behind me.

Stomach dropping so fast I almost vomit, I whirl,

necklace clasped in one hand, the other whipping up to shield my thrashing heart.

She watches me. *Studies* me—her frantic gaze scouring every inch of my exposed skin.

Though I can see my radiant reflection bouncing off her insipid eyes, she appears unruffled by my river of pearlescent hair; by my ears that taper and the crystal thorns that line their shells.

Her attention homes on my bare shoulder partially covered by my hair, and she steps close. Panic fires up my throat as her withered hand rises, a blue cupla dangling from her frail wrist, bony fingers unfurling in a way that reminds me of Shay. She eases the tendrils back, exposing my bare shoulder and heaving chest.

She swallows, eyes rising to meet my own.

There's something unsaid wedged there like a quiet barb ...

Something I don't understand.

Gripping my chain, she tugs hard, urging me to release it from my white-knuckled grip.

"No." I tug back. "I *need* this ..."

She grunts, an ember igniting in her otherwise flat gaze that rocks me to the core—that grips me by the spine and shakes me until every one of my muscles loosen.

Urgency.

My fingers go slack.

She takes the jewel from my hand and twirls her wrist, indicating for me to turn. I swallow and spin, catching a swift strike of my crystalized stare.

Murderer.

A stinging sensation flares across the backs of my eyes, and I squeeze them shut, tears tracking down my cheeks as

Old Hattie lifts the weight of my hair, threads the necklace around my neck, and sullies me in the suffocating grip of Rhordyn's lie.

My next breath is tight.

Constricted.

I hate it.

"Please don't tell anyone ..."

Hattie gathers my hair, tucks it down the back of my cloak, then turns me to face her, cupping my cheek with her warm, calloused palm. A wonky smile stretches her lips.

"You won't, will you?"

She shakes her head, and a calm settles inside me. I offer her a wan smile in return—until a clunk at my wrist lures my gaze to my cupla now falling away with her nimble fingers.

My smile falls.

I stare wide-eyed as she scurries back a step and waves it at me, eyes bright with mischief.

"What are you—"

She turns and dashes through the door into my suite with impressive haste.

My heart flips.

I dart after her, watching her scamper around my bed, trailed by her silver braid that drags along the floor. "*What are you doing?*" I whisper-hiss, glancing at the closed door that leads to the lobby. And then it hits me like a sledgehammer to the chest.

She *is* going to tell Cainon.

"Please don't," I plead, realizing there's a very high chance I'm going to have to wrestle this old woman for my cupla before she reaches the front door, then lock her in my dressing room until I work out how to keep her from spilling my secret.

Oh, Gods. This is bad.

Really bad.

All I wanted was to stick it to Rhordyn a little. Now I'm contemplating abduction.

She veers toward my dressing room and disappears into the depth of it.

I stop, frowning.

She walked herself right into that one.

Snatching my blade off the bed but leaving the stupid sheath behind, I follow, glancing over my shoulder before drawing the door shut behind me. She hobbles toward the long mirror mounted to the end wall, pries her fingers around the edge, and tugs it open on silent hinges. Mouth falling open, my curious heart ignites into a flaming ember as I look down the semi-lit tunnel beyond.

Wasn't expecting that.

"Guess that's how you got past my guard," I muse while she reaches in and around the corner, pulls out two blazing lanterns, and thrusts one in my direction.

My gaze bounces between it and the heavy intention in her powder blue eyes, realization slamming into me. "No. *Hell* no. I am not going down there," I whisper-yell.

Even if I kind of want to.

She gives me a wide, toothless grin, then tosses my cupla down the tunnel. I gasp, lunging forward, listening to it tink, wincing a little with every shrill bounce. "I can't believe you just did that." She waves her hand at the darkness, and I chew my bottom lip, looking between her, the lantern, the shadowed hollow. "Fine," I snip, tucking my blade into the back of my pants. "But only if you go first."

She flashes me another wide, toothless grin before stepping into the gloom.

Checking over my shoulder, I flip my hood and follow.

I locate my cupla partway down the coiled stairwell, brushing it off and checking it for damage before clipping it around my wrist. Hattie continues, and I waver, glancing back up the stairs ...

Fuck it. Might as well keep going.

I charge after Hattie.

The stairwell smoothes into a tunnel that seems to go on and on, finally ending at a wooden door Hattie pushes open. A burst of fresh air batters my face, and I pull a deep breath, struck with a cacophony of sounds within the midnight jungle: chirping crickets, the whisper of leaves brushing against each other, the distant boom of thunder. I step out, drawing on the rich smell of damp underbrush, digging my toes into the soil as a cool wash of calm bathes my insides.

Hattie's hair trails her like braided moonlight, and I dash forward to catch up, following her down a shadowed track littered with fallen branches and shards of blue stone. Inquisitive stares nip at my skin, casting it in prickly paths that make my heart race.

Irilak.

Three lithe shadows stalk the edge of our glow, and a clicking presence darts behind me. I whip my head around in time to see a baby one flicker close to my lantern light, then burst back, like it's playing some sort of game.

I smile, wondering ... *hoping* it's the pack from the village we passed through.

Their presence falls away as we push free of the jungle onto a wide, flat clifftop that drops into the ocean.

Soft grass cradles my bare feet, the wind punching my hood back, and a beam of moonlight pours through the split clouds, highlighting the lone tree perched on the cliff's edge—an aged knot of gnarled wood with a spindly reach.

A lone sentry to the view far below.

Thousands of glowing jellyfish litter the heaving ocean—a living, breathing night sky turned upside-down, smudged only by the mound of a small island in the distance.

"It's beautiful," I whisper, stepping toward the tree, my words snatched by the wind like a stolen secret. Peering over my shoulder, I see Hattie watching me from her flickering web of light. "Do you come here often?"

Her soft smile doesn't match the teary glaze of her eyes when she offers me a nod, her disfigured hand pressing against her chest.

"It ... helps your heart?"

Another nod, and my throat aches, eyes sweeping shut as I breathe deep ...

She's sharing her special place with me.

Perhaps she can see I'm hurting, too.

I open my eyes, about to thank her for her gift, but she's already edging back up the trail.

Instead, I whisper it to the wind.

Placing my lantern on the ground, I study the tree, then grip a sturdy branch and pull myself up. Settling on it, I lean against the trunk, taking in the ever-moving constellation of life below.

They look so free down there, floating around without a care in the world.

Jealousy bursts in my chest.

I want to float. To be lulled by the ebb and flow of the ocean's quiet dance. Instead, the ever-swelling moon tides me toward that piercing moment when my body will no longer belong to me, but to my promised—a man who has no idea that I'm very different beneath the skin he thinks he knows.

All the while, I'm locked in the orbit of a man who sees too much, and I can't escape. Can't pull myself free.

Tonight, it became abundantly clear that the distance I shoved between us did nothing to pry Rhordyn from my soul ... but something's changed.

Shifted.

I felt it in the charged space between us. In the way he knelt before me, holding my stare with such dominating confidence, chest bared like he *welcomed* my barbs. I felt it in the way I salivated at the sight of his blood dribbling from the cut I made ...

I swallow thickly, drawing a shuddered breath I blow back out in a rush.

With that blade to his throat, I felt more alive than I have in weeks.

I want him to hurt.

To *bleed*.

I want him to snap, just like he snapped me.

He's the ailment, yes ... but also the remedy I wasn't expecting. A punching bag that absorbs my blows with unflinching stoicism.

How much will he take before he bursts at the seams?

I lift the conch to my lips and brush a kiss across its knobbed surface, tempted to whisper my ugly truths into its hollow in an effort to purge them from my soul.

I squeeze my eyes shut, press my lips together ...

Tuck the shell beneath my collar.

Kai deserves better.

Chapter 32
Cainon

Rhordyn's standing at the end of my private pier, black cloak snapping in the wind like an Ocruth war flag. My ship's moored before him—the restless, turquoise sea clawing at its sleek hull, my bustling crew stealing glances at him while they prepare for our morning sail.

I stalk the length of the pier, steps thumping in rhythm with my surging heart rate. Whoever let him across the bridge and onto the palace grounds without notifying me has some explaining to do.

"It's been a while since you last graced Bahari with your presence," I call ahead. "Much has changed, has it not?"

Turning slowly, Rhordyn looks upon me with savage regard. Like I'm fucking prey. "Where's the rest of your fleet?"

I laugh to myself, stopping before him. "Straight to business?"

He stands like a statue, arms crossed, masticating me with a single look.

Right.

"They're getting repaired. There's been some rough weather." I loosen the tie around the pouch sitting heavy in my hand. "They'll be ready around the same time my coupling is sealed. With Orlaith," I clarify, garnishing the blow with a smirk, holding out the bag filled with recently dried fruit. "Fig?"

He continues to stare at me while wind snaps at the loose sails.

"Well, this is frosty." I pluck out a sugared slice and toss it in my mouth. My face twists when the sickly sweetness explodes across my tongue and slurs down the back of my throat. "Hmm, actually, good choice. They've been oversteeped." I toss the rest off the side of the pier, pouch and all, and reach for the waterskin slung around his neck. "Water?"

He glares down at my hand as though he'd rather see it hacked from my wrist.

I lift a brow. "Not the sharing type?"

Not even a fucking blink.

"How rude." I shove past and scale the gangway, accepting a canteen from one of my sailors eagerly holding it out as I step down upon the deck. "Especially since we're practically family, now that I'm fucking your ward."

I uncork the bottle and tip it to my mouth, drawing deep, the electrified air lifting the hairs on the back of my neck.

Silence.

Even the scuffing, creaking sounds of my readying crew seem to soften.

Lowering the canteen, I see his back is turned to me. "Did I say something wrong?"

"There are signs of the Blight in the outer rim of your city," he grinds out, cracking his neck.

I slam the canteen against the chest of someone passing by. "*And?*"

"Your people are too packed in. It would be more manageable if you cut into the jungle. Expand your livable land." He spins, and there's a darkness in his eyes that might chill me if I didn't hold all the power in the palm of my hand.

"Land that is inhabited by a thriving nest of Irilak that make it near impossible for a Vruk attack on my borders. Among other things," I tack on, throwing him a wink.

That darkness deepens. "You think I have anything to gain from sending my army through that jungle into this Blight-infested pit?"

I shrug. "Last I checked, it was *me* taking refugees from *you*."

"*Exactly*," he snarls. "I'd be hurting my *own* people. People who are here not because they want to be, but because they have no choice."

"Though I hardly blame them, if Castle Noir is anything to go by," I continue, ignoring his outburst, kneeling to snag the tail end of a rope from a pile lumped at my feet and looping it around my arm. "Seriously, have you not changed a thing in all these years? It's a fucking crypt."

He stares at me; I stare at him—winding the rope in long, controlled pulls.

He folds his arms across his chest again as a burst of wind assaults us, ferried all the way across the crumbled bay and punched with the smell of the city's fish market. "There are more important things to spend your tithes on than golden doorknobs, Cainon."

"Like cutting into my land to make more space for *your* people?"

Another bout of frosty silence. My arm strains with the weight of the rope.

"Forgive me for being a little self-indulgent, but I won't risk the capital if I can help it. It's the trading hub of Bahari. Parith falls and my entire territory suffers. Besides, statistically speaking, Vruks kill more people than the Blight, and I have it well managed."

His brow lifts. "You're talking about the wall that splits your poor from your rich and condemns the former to an early grave?"

"Those who are contributing to my territory keep well away from the outer rim. Seems to be a good incentive." I jerk my chin toward the city glistening in a rogue shard of light breaking through lumpy, gray clouds. "Sometimes a High Master has to make sacrifices. Something I learned from *you*."

Tension claps between us, and he kicks his foot forward, boot kissing the edge of the gangplank.

I snatch a look at the hilt of his sword over his shoulder. Reassure myself that there's a blade shoved down my boot as I lump the nest of rope at my feet. "Does it hurt? Knowing your actions led to your parent's suicide?"

Another long, admonishing stare.

This one, I enjoy.

"And now your little toy favors *me*. She caught sight of the sun and realized what a monster you are." I slip the lid off a barrel and snatch a bright green pear, biting deep, talking through my mouthful. "Seems to me like you have trouble keeping people around."

He regards me through unblinking eyes, watching me chew.

Why does he never fucking talk?

I shrug. "Hardly surprised the only way you could secure a fuck was to coerce your oldest friend into a political pairing."

"Spoken from the man who offered to purchase Orlaith's virtue after formally meeting her *once*."

I raise a brow, the gangway dragged onto the deck beside me, severing the ship from the end of the pier. "Keeping tabs, were you? On her virginity, I mean."

His knuckles pop, chest seems to swell, and there's the slightest tremble to his upper lip that spikes me full of satisfaction.

He *does* have a weakness for her.

I take another bite, chewing through my words. "She loves me. I'll prove it to you at dinner tonight. You can see just how happy she is, then you can fuck off back to Ocruth. I'll send the ships once our coupling is sealed."

The sailors ready the sail. Rhordyn's words spear out the moment we jerk forward and crack away from the pier. "Feels like you're in a rush to get rid of me."

"Or ..." I toss the core, and it clatters across the pier as wind drums at the bulging sails, "perhaps you're just looking for an excuse to start a war and snatch my land for yourself. You do, after all, seem oh so invested in how it should be run."

He continues to hunt me with those unnerving eyes as we drift further apart, making for the mouth of the scalloped bay. Perhaps he realizes I have him by the throat. Perhaps not. Either way, I have no intention of rushing this process.

I've been looking forward to watching him *squirm*.

Chapter 33
Orlaith

With wet, straggly hair hanging heavily down my back, I slam another door closed and stalk the lofty corridor, wearing tender bruises on my hips and elbows like the war wounds they are. I thrashed myself against the edge of The Bowl for hours, earning nothing but a few scathing remarks from Elder Creed that planted bitter seeds in my chest.

I shake my head, teeth gritted as I round a corner, walking into a pretty maid carrying a stack of folded towels that tumble to the polished, blue-stone floor with a soft *whump*.

"Oh my! I'm so sorry, Mistress." She bobs a curtsey, cheeks pinked as she bends to gather them up with hurried hands. "I'll be more careful from now on."

"No, it's fine. It was my fault." I fold a towel, stacking it on top of her re-forming pile. "You don't know where I might find the library, do you?"

I can't sneak to the city during the daytime to hunt for

Madame Strings, but I refuse to sit idle. I need to find a book that can tell me something—*anything*—about myself.

Preferably in a language I understand.

She shakes her head, dashing tawny hair off her face as she looks at me. "I'm new, Mistress. I haven't come across one ..."

Damn.

"Thank you, anyway."

Another tight curtsey, and she continues on her way.

Bag tucked close to my side, I open a gold-brushed door to another bright, breezy, spotless guest bedroom, disappointment dropping into my belly like a stone. "This is ridiculous," I mutter, charging toward a door on the opposite side of the hallway and opening it, slamming it shut when I see a perfectly made bed. "I just want a damn *library*."

Turning a corner, my gaze grabs a much larger door on the right, cast ajar, bracketed by blazing wall sconces. My heart lurches, a tug in my chest luring me forward, and I check over my shoulder before placing my hand on the door and pushing it open further.

More sconces give flickering, golden life to a flight of stairs that digs downward, and I cradle the spark in my chest that ignites whenever I've stumbled upon something interesting.

The hem of my skirt hampers my descent, and I curse the ridiculous thing. Hoisting it to mid-calf, I hasten my pace, and follow the spiral, spitting out in a long, narrow, dusty corridor sparsely lit by a sprinkle of wall torches—so different from the rest of the palace. Even the ground is different, the stone aged and scuffed and chipped in places.

My eyes widen, stare panning right, hungering over the countless tapestries lining the walls, leaving only slivers of stone between the vibrant masterpieces.

Excitement bubbles in my chest.

There are big ones, small ones. Some that make me want to tilt my head to fully grasp their concept, while others look so real, I want to dive into their woven depths. Enter another realm.

Become somebody else.

I swing my gaze to the left—

Shit.

Heart rioting like a caged beast, I flatten against the wall.

He didn't sense me.

Didn't sense me.

Didn't—

"Hello, Milaje."

The words are gravel, punching into my soles and buckling my composure.

Dammit.

Head tipped, I wait until my full-body shiver has run its course before I slam down my walls and shore up enough courage to shove into the light.

"What are you doing here?" I ask, tone firm.

He turns and walks backward—a flaming torch in one hand, his other shoved deep in the pocket of his black leather pants. "Your *promised* invited me for dinner."

That's a terrible idea.

"Well," I say, studying his neck in the dim light, seeing no clear scar slashed across it. Nothing to pay homage to my almost slitting his throat last night. "Feel free to leave and come back precisely when the meal starts."

"Getting quite bossy, aren't you?" Brow arched, he holds my narrowed stare for a few triggering moments before he turns and continues down the way he was going. "I like it."

Grinding my back teeth, I lift the hem of my skirt, rip my blade free, and advance, dagger wielded, intent on escorting him from the palace by the point of it. I'm about to reach up and whip it around his throat when he whirls—catching my wrist, my gaze, my *breath* in one smooth motion.

That silver stare roots through my insides, his rolled sleeves giving way to thick, tattooed forearms corded with unyielding strength.

My heart pounds.

One squeeze and my wrist would snap. A thought that shouldn't thrill me like it does.

"I also like *this*," he says, gaze flicking to my blade suspended between us. "Just so we're clear."

"You're not going to like it when it's hilt-deep in your flesh."

"I wasn't talking about the *dagger,* Orlaith. I'm talking about your living, breathing fire."

An oily blackness spilling out in vicious, torrential spears.
Burning.
Silencing.

My stomach drops, arm muscles soften.

His brow buckles, and I whip my hand away from his loosening grip, shoving past.

"Milaje ..."

I gather up the front of my skirt, weaving the dagger back into the thigh sheath I fashioned from a torn strip of sheet, because fuck him and his fucking gift. "Cainon's having his ships repaired on one of the outer islands. It would be in everyone's best interest for you to find them and focus your attention *there*," I say as I continue down the dusty hallway.

"That's exactly what I'm doing."

I spin so fast my sodden hair slices through the air.

Brows raised, I scan the lengthy hallway that harbors *zero* ships and cast an icy glare his way. "Try harder."

The challenge is tossed at him like it's made of fire.

He watches me with a honed regard, his torch casting harsh shadows across his sculpted face that's painful to look at. The very reason I don't blink. Don't break away.

Drug myself on the hurt.

He storms forward, holding my stare and lungs in his stony grip. "I intend to." The words are pledged on a low growl as he charges past, his torch gasping for breath.

I grit my teeth and turn, watching him light a wall torch, illuminating more of the tomb of endless tapestries. He lifts one off the wall like a curtain, setting his torch on the floor before he raps his knuckles against the stone. "Interesting." Another few knocks, and then he's tracing the vein-like divots. "There used to be a hallway somewhere here," he mumbles, and my curiosity rears her unwanted head.

Groaning internally, I dash forward, shoving into his frosty aura, ignoring my prickling skin as I run a hand over the stone and inspect the wall for any hidden seams. "Where did it lead?"

"Everywhere." His hand runs the same path as mine, as though he's chasing the trail of warmth. "An underground tunnel that wove beneath the city and stretched to some of the islands."

Ahh.

He sets his ear to the wall, eyes closed. "It's been barred up in other parts of the city, too."

Internal walls rising swifter than my dropped hand, I narrow my stare. "Are you trying to poison me against my promised by insinuating he's hiding something?"

"No," he murmurs, knocking on the stone again, shifting a little. "You have big, wide eyes. You can see perfectly fine without my help."

"What's that supposed to mean?"

Pushing back, he lets the tapestry drop with a thump that scatters a riot of dust. "I won't determine your steps, Milaje. I'll even let you trip. But I *refuse* to let you fall."

My hands bunch into fists. "I don't need you watching over my shoulder."

"Not an option, I'm afraid." His gaze hardens as he prowls forward, swallowing my space until I'm backed against the wall, smothered in the rich scent of leather and a crisp winter's day. "I told you. I'll hunt you to the four corners of the continent."

The words wrap around my heart like a noose, all the blood draining from my face ...

He's not just here for the ships.

"I thought you were being—"

Another step reduces the space between us to a fragile sliver. "What?"

Goosebumps explode across my skin as that final inch is crushed, his body fitting against mine as though we were cast from the same mold, then split two ways.

His exhale falls upon my upturned face like a midwinter breeze, and I draw deep, barely managing to stifle a moan.

I don't need this.

I need it to *hurt*.

"Dramatic," I rasp, feeling each of his breaths crush me further into the stone, grinding me down.

His gaze drops to my lips, up again. "It's not in my nature to spit words without purpose."

"Well," I scoff. "I wouldn't know."

I don't know you.

"Then I'll repeat." The words blast me like a blow of frost. "So it's *perfectly* clear."

I lift my chin. Hone my stare.

Challenge him to make it *sting*.

"There is nowhere you can hide. Nowhere you can go. Even if *this* were to stop beating," he says, threading his hand over my rioting heart, "I'd follow."

The final two words carve under my skin like a sawtooth blade, and I see something very different staring back at me from behind those blackening eyes. Something savage and deadly.

I should be frightened ...

"But I'll let you trip, Milaje. Because it's those trips that spark your flame—something you're going to need in this cruel, *greedy* world that has no fucking mercy, because it doesn't think before it *chews*."

Neither do I.

I roll my head to the left—veer the final blow and escape his scouring stare. My gaze lands on an open archway between two tapestries, a sliver of bright shafting through a dull skylight, illuminating—

Books.

Stacks of stored *books.*

Finally.

"Great chat. Super uplifting. Now, if you could step out of my way ..." I try to wriggle free, but all that really does is familiarize me with the stony slants of his powerful body. "I've found what I was looking for."

He glances over his shoulder to the opposite wall, and though he doesn't move an inch, I somehow feel less stuck to the stone.

Jerking free, I snatch his sputtering torch off the ground and dash toward the room, stepping within the eerily silent space, breathing thick, musty air as I scan the uneven piles of books—some almost twice my height, others no higher than my knee. *So* many books, I'm certain I could spend the rest of my life pawing over the words and never make it through them all.

I think.

I have no idea what my life expectancy is. Perhaps I'm eternal. A simmering stain that doesn't rub out.

That's one of the things I'm here to find out.

I weave down a wiggly path between the stacks, settle near a navel-high pile, and blow the thick icing of dust from the top, batting the swirling particles that rush up to meet me.

It's no Spines, that's for sure.

"These symbols on the front ..." Rhordyn's deep, echoing voice rattles me as he reaches past, casting shivers up my arm.

Across my chest.

I feel my nipples pinch into tight little peaks when he traces the gold-brushed stamp pressed into the leather.

A shifting mountain would feel less significant.

"It's ancient Valish for mathematics," he says, the words a cold blow against my ear. "In case you were wondering."

"You ruined the surprise," I croak.

"Apologies."

"Not forgiven."

Jaw set, he makes this low, rumbling sound that almost buckles my knees, then paces between the stacks, inspecting the scene as though he's studying a field for the most advantageous way to battle amongst it. "It appears Cain shifted his entire library down here."

Probably thought they looked messy stacked in his pristine, blue-stone shrine.

"Better than using the books for firewood," I mumble flatly, receiving a grunt in return.

I pry my gaze away from the brutish anomaly tucked between the fragile stacks, leaving little room for me to breathe.

Or think.

No.

Frowning, I force my lungs full and snatch the book from the top of the pile, flick through the pages, and confirm that it is, in fact, entirely dedicated to mathematical equations.

Snapping it shut, I set it aside and scan the stacks ...

It's going to take forever to find what I'm looking for.

Shit.

To be fair, I could just ... ask Rhordyn for all the answers I'm seeking. He seems to be in a talkative mood.

I risk a peep, watching him skim through a book that looks so frail in his large hand, brow pinched.

No. I'd rather eat my own liver than send my curiosity marching to his slaughterhouse.

Again.

Worse—what if he *indulges* it?

I'm not sure how I'd handle that.

Not anymore.

It'd be more a curse than a gift. Would make it a little harder to hate him.

Resigned to my fate, I get back to the small pile before me, cut the stack in two, sit cross-legged on the floor, then snatch one to flick through. Mercifully, it's written in the common tongue.

A tense silence stretches between us.

It's full of thieved glances past my hair; of nipping flutters of chill that hit me in the side of the face when I least expect it—his scent packing the room full, drugging me a little with every contraband breath.

My body reacts to his nearness, *desperate* to fall into his orbit.

Subtly, I reach around and pinch the back of my arm, the action hidden by my veil of hair ...

No.

I massage the back of my neck, a thick, leather-bound volume on the art of war bared across my stretched legs; my brimming knapsack lumped on the floor beside me.

My stare runs off the page to where Rhordyn's crouched like some perched beast, blowing off the spine of a small, red-bound book. He begins flicking through the pages with a voracious sort of hunger, pausing before snapping it shut like a monster's maw.

I flinch.

He pushes up and turns, striking me with his full attention for the first time in hours as he stalks forward, strong thighs tensing with every powerful step, making me feel *miniature*—tucked on the ground in a dusty fold.

He stops before me and extends the book.

Frowning, I look between the blank spine and his condemning stare. "What's that?"

"A somewhat accurate translation of Valish." My heart thuds to a stop, and I swear he sees straight through my skin and flesh and muscle and bone to the startled organ. "Thought you might find it useful."

His stare dares me to look.

To *see*.

To pour over the pages and assuage my hungry curiosity.

I glance at the book again, regarding it in a whole new light—a single word hacking at me like the honed tip of a diamond pickaxe.

Milaje.

Milaje.

Milaje.

"I'm not sure I have any use for it," I rasp, buttering my features with bland detachment.

"You can't think of a single one?"

"Nope."

He dashes a smear of dust on his pants like a slap of paint, drops to a crouch, and stuffs the book inside my knapsack. "Just in case."

I snatch the crochet straps from his outstretched hand, the bag heavy with every book that looked even slightly promising. "You're different."

The words blurt out of their own, like they're desperate to bridge some sort of gap between us.

I'm poisoned by instant regret.

"So are you."

The words hit.

Disable.

Almost make my throat close up.

A challenge and a question disguised as a statement, like he's asking me to spew my ugly at his booted feet.

I remember how that felt—to look at him and wish he'd give me something.

Anything.

I remember the cold snap of disappointment that swiftly followed, time and time again.

"That's because I'm done," I mutter, giving him my back as I shove to a stand and stalk toward the exit. "Don't follow or I'll make you bleed again."

Chapter 34
Kai

The clear sky bears down on us, light bouncing off every angle of this island of clustered crystals, casting prisms of color across my sallow, sweat-dappled skin and striking me in the eyes.

The crisp sea air nips at me, and I hiss through chattering teeth, squinting down the narrow path chipped into the rock—kicking forward another wobbly step that threatens to tip me over the slope to my left. A slope that falls directly into a long, jagged ravine alive with the sound of gushing water.

This is a bad idea.

I've known it from the moment Vicious thrust this old, knotted stick at me—long and bleached, as though it weathered the ocean's current for decades before it washed up on this shore only to bear the brunt of my torture. But saying no to her determined eyes and fierce, over-enthusiastic nod felt more catastrophic than using the last drips of my fading life force to please her bizarre whim.

But with every shiver that rattles me to the core and every labored step that threatens to buckle my knees, I question that logic a little bit more.

Vicious shuffles behind me, setting her hot hand between my aching shoulder blades, making me shiver for entirely different reasons—the contact sending a zap all the way down my spine.

"I'm tired, Vicious ..."

She gives me a gentle shove.

I think she wants me to exercise. Perhaps she thinks it'll make a difference.

I know better.

I'm fading. Day by day, hour by hour, a little more of my fight drips away. Candescence didn't help. This arduous morning stroll certainly won't.

I want to go back to our nest, curl around her little warm body, and fall back into the deep sleep she dragged me from. Nothing like a nip to the ear to rip you free from a cozy state of numbness that feels beautifully eternal.

Though to be fair, it would be nice to see the sea again ... to taste it ... feel it swirl against my skin ...

One last time.

Perhaps that's where she's taking me.

Sliding my foot along the stone, I tighten my grip on the cloth wrapped around my waist, protecting what modesty I have left but doing nothing to alleviate this bone-deep chill rattling through me. "Is that it, Vicious? Are you taking me to the sea?"

Every word feels thick and syrupy; every step heavy

and forced. My lids droop, neck struggles to hold my head straight.

I look back, right into her all-consuming stare.

She doesn't nod. Doesn't blink. Certainly doesn't speak. Simply stares at me with an intensity that makes me feel seen in a way that rips my heart in two and fills my chest with a desperate, possessive warmth that almost knocks my feet out from under me.

On an island of the most precious stone in all five seas, I'd leave with empty hands if I could have her.

I would have kept her. Brought her back to my trove and shown her my treasures. The melancholy thought wrestles inside me, frantically snatching my heartstrings, tugging them so taut it feels like I might spew.

Another gentle shove, and my head lolls forward again, making something twang inside my chest. Like I just stretched the threads of something lethal. Blood breaks the seal of the scale stuck over my wound, and I feel it weave a warm, wet path down my middle, the smell too sour to be healthy.

I'm urged around a sharp bend one gentle shove at a time, and the ocean dawns before me.

Almost breaks me.

It's so beautiful and smooth and *so far down*.

'Zykanth, look at that ...'

No answer.

Heaving shuddered breaths, I drop the cloth, reaching up to pat my fist against my chest in an effort to wake him up.

'Wake up!'

Eyes cast on the glassy ocean, my steps become faster. More determined.

Vicious threads her arm around my middle, halting me.

I cast a wobbly stare to the left, down a set of stairs that look steep and unforgiving. They lead to the shallow mouth of a ravine and a rippled pool of red water that feeds into a tiny waterfall tumbling off the sheer cliff.

It all clicks into place, and I crumble, caught under the arms by a small pair of hands that help lower me to the ground until I'm sat on the top stair.

It's the same soothing liquid that pours into the ocean. The same soothing liquid I've bathed in many times.

Years ago.

So far away.

I lose grip on the walking stick. Watch it clatter down the steps.

Vicious hisses, darting after it, her oversized shirt swimming around her scrambling form, her hair a trail of spindrift that leaves me breathless.

"Beautiful," I whisper, my heavy lids easing down, the racket of my tumbling stick becoming a muffled, distant sound ...

My vision of Vicious splits.

Another deep blink, and then the world is tipping sideways—toward the steep slope that falls into a clifftop overlooking the ocean I yearn to pull through my gills ...

My shoulder smacks against the stone, punching a gnarled sound from my blazing lungs as I slide, plummeting toward the cliff so fast the world blurs.

My mind gives out.
Shuts off.
Darkness.

A blast of pain tearing through my chest rips me back to consciousness, and an agonized groan rends from my parted lips, legs swaying ...

Body *hanging.*

I look up the sheer cliff face, see a halo of wild, white tendrils brushing my stretched arm. See a hand wrapped around my wrist—fingers straining.

She caught me.

A red waterfall gushes beside me, spraying my face and the side of my body as it plummets off the edge of the island. My gaze drops to the thousands of crystal shards below, jutting from beneath the silky water.

I look back up to the straining tendons in her arm ...

My feet tingle, stomach lurches.

I'm going to pull her over, too.

"You have to let me go!"

She snarls, as though she understands me for once.

Her grip tightens.

"*Vicious!*"

I kick my feet, trying to wiggle free from her iron-clad clutch.

Her eyes widen, and she shakes her head.

"*Let me go!*"

She closes her eyes and yanks so hard her face reddens from the strain.

I'm lifted, little by little, until I'm high enough to punch my arm up while screaming through the hack of pain plowing through my chest. More warm wetness dribbles down my front as I grab hold of the cliff's sharp edge.

Vicious reaches with her other hand and grips a fistful of hair at the back of my head, using it to haul me up—ripping a roar from my throat as she hoists me until I can shift my weight forward and scramble over the lip. I fall in a heap on the smooth stone, chest heaving.

I look up at the pale blue sky, stomach churning, mouth gaping, breath sawing in and out. Heart hammering so hard it's crippling.

In a scurry of white hair and golden limbs, Vicious straddles me, planting her forehead against mine.

We absorb each other's labored breaths as her soft hands come up to cup my cheeks, and I thread my arms around her back. Tangle my fingers with her fluffy hair.

She goes stone still, breath halting.

I open my eyes to see hers wide and staring right into me, and the world seems to stand still.

Though she has no words on her lips, I *feel* the weight of her thoughts pour upon me, a crush that shoves the air from my lungs. Her lashes flutter closed as she melts against me, my pain paling in significance to *this*.

She's so warm and smooth and soft ... then taut and tight as her back arches.

She growls, sharp and fierce.

Frowning, I open my mouth, but before I manage to say a word, she dips her face and snatches my bottom lip between her teeth, biting down.

Hard.

Her hold on my face tightens, stare digging, and I feel her teeth pierce my flesh. Feel the growling sound she's making rattle through her chest to mine.

Warm blood dribbles down my chin, and every cell in my body locks.

"Phishious—"

She bites harder.

"That hurts."

Keeps snarling.

Her eyes are wide and fearful, ferocious and accusing all at once. She blinks, snarls, and a tear escapes.

My heart flips, almost choking me.

Holding her stare, I trail up the line of her spine, feeling her smooth skin burst with goosebumps as my fingers glaze the side of her neck. I thread them through her soft tendrils, skimming her skull. Once my entire hand cradles the back of her head, I clench a fistful of hair, tugging gently.

Her lids flutter.

"It's okay," I battle out. "I'ng orite."

Her sound softens.

"You can let go."

So fucking slowly, she eases her jaw open, though I keep pulling her head back—seeing my blood coating her teeth and chin and throat.

Fuck.

I suck my bottom lip into my mouth, tasting me. Tasting her—smooth like the ocean and just as crisp and clear.

From somewhere deep inside me, Zykanth stirs. One small slither of movement that has my heart leaping high into my throat.

'Zyke?'

Silence.

But that tiny slithering motion ... it's *everything*.

Vicious rips away, leaving me bereft, cold, and drained. *Empty*.

She scurries down to my feet, wraps her hands halfway around my ankles, and begins lugging me along the clifftop, toward the red pool gurgling near the edge.

"You're very ... emasculating ... sometimes," I battle out, feeling the stone grate at my skin. Watching the sky slip by between heavy-lidded blinks, not even bothering to fight. Not even sure I could.

She hooks her hands under my arms and tugs me forward until I'm folded with my face in her neck, groaning from the strike of pain that stabs through me.

I blow a shuddered breath. "I want to sleep," I murmur. "*Please.*"

Her hands slide around my waist and, taking my weight, she pulls me into the swirling warmth, a sigh easing out of me that morphs into a whimper as she lowers us onto a smooth stone ledge—submerged until the bold, red water laps at my clavicle.

Her hands weave between us, fiddling with something. I don't realize what until the material swirling against my skin is suddenly yanked away, leaving no buffer between our bare flesh.

I don't pull from her neck, even as her bareness straddles me. Presses against me. Does things to me that I can't bring myself to be ashamed of.

There's a wet plop behind me, and she eases me back until my head is resting on the pile of her sodden shirt.

My eyes drift shut, lacking the energy to voice my protest as the scale is peeled from my wound in slow increments.

Water seeps in, its soothing warmth a pleasant balm.

I reach for her blindly, but she beats me to it, leaning forward, sealing her body to mine. Her heavy heartbeat thuds wildly against my chest as she nuzzles my neck, her breath a soothing patter on my prickling skin.

"Don't leave me," I whisper.

Please ...

I don't like being by myself.

I don't want to die alone.

Her hand weaves around the back of me, settling on the left side of my body where she *taps*.

Tap.

Tap.

... Tap ...

I drag my fingers up and down her ribs, her silky skin a dream I want to fall into ...

Oblivion sucks me under.

Chapter 35
Orlaith

"Are we almost done?"

My pretty, austere handmaiden steps between me and the ornate vanity, yanking a piece of hair like a leash, twisting it around a metal rod that's been dipped in the flaming fireplace. "You have a lot of hair, Mistress."

Izel releases the coil, separates out another lank tendril, then back-combs it at the base of my skull until it resembles a hen's feather—her delicate, Bahari blue stone cupla dangling with every sharp jerk of her brushing hand.

I peer at her through fluffy, gold tresses. "I like your"—*yank*—"cupla. It's very pretty."

She glances at it, speaking through tight lips as she offers a curt "Thank you."

I bite down on my desire to release a hiss of pain as she combs with a little extra gusto. "Are you coupled? Promised?"

She looks into the mirror, nailing me with an icy stare.

"Widowed. My promised was on the boat you sailed here on. He didn't return."

My heart drops so fast I almost vomit. "I-I'm so sorry, I had no idea …"

She throws me a tight-lipped smile, eyes void as she says, "Your words won't bring him back."

Any response clogs in my throat.

She continues to fluff and smooth and twist and tame, coiling tendrils around the iron like she didn't just drop a boulder on my chest. I lower my gaze, watching my fingers twirl around the ribbon of blue silk knotted around my waist rather than my coiffed reflection as she finishes taming my heavy, corkscrew mane, then brushes out the curls. She glides toward the mannequin to retrieve my gown—similar in style to the one Cainon had fashioned for me while I was still at Castle Noir.

The one Rhordyn shredded right before tossing me his oversized shirt that swallowed me stupid.

"I can dress myself."

She catches my stare in the mirror's reflection, then steps toward a bucket of water beside the fire that's stuffing the room with unnecessary heat.

"I'll do that, too."

A small, tight-lipped moment passes, then she curtseys and exits without another word.

The door closes, my shoulders folding forward as I exercise my lungs in a way I barely managed while she was finishing my hair.

If she's the one who planted the poisonous berries in my meal, I don't blame her.

She probably didn't step into her coupling the same way

I did—with a stranger, on a single-minded mission to rescue lives and absolve her guilty conscience. Her story was likely a *true* fairy tale filled with all the lovely things I've read about in fantasy stories.

I took that from her.

Me.

The thought sits in my heart as I stand, swathed in a yard of blue silk that clings to every curve. I make for my knapsack perched on the floor pillow beside the fire and retrieve the books I found earlier, singling out the little one with the plain red cover.

It feels heavy despite its size, and I stare at it while the flames from the fireplace lash warmth upon my face and hands. Pressing my nose against the leather, I draw my lungs full of *his* barely there scent, remembering the way he handled this book—hand wrapped around the spine like he was clutching the throat of his enemy.

Mining the courage to open it, I flick through the delicate pages until I land upon the *M* section and slow my pace, letting my gaze drag up and down the columns as though I'm digging my own grave. Shoveling a little dirt with every tentative flick.

"Ma ... Ma ... Me ..."

My chest is tight, hands shaking.

Flick.

Flick.

"Mg ..."

Flick—*I can't breathe.*

"Mh ..."

Flick.

"*Mi*—"

I slam it shut and toss it in the fire so fast I shock myself—gasping, shuffling back a step when sparks explode and fire engulfs the leather in a blazing swallow.

The corners curl, red charring black as the pages singe and scold. I peel off my dressing gown and let it fall to the floor in a puddle of silk, standing naked before the bold flames.

Empty.

Emotionless.

Vigorous heat paints my body, and I feel it *everywhere*, feeding on it as if it's the scalding lashes of *his* disappointment when he realizes my disregard for everything he's tried to gift me.

I don't want to know.

Prying my stare from the sizzling sight long enough to collect my Bahari blue gown off the mannequin, I continue to watch the book burn, dressing myself one gauzy strap at a time.

There's a thick band around my middle that ties at the back, and I pull it tight ... tighter ... so tight my breath is just as cinched as my waist, the band imitating the support I'm used to around my chest.

I reach for the back of my arm and pinch so hard I'm watching the fire burn through a haze of unshed tears.

There's a knock on the door, and I blink out of my reverie.

The book is ash; the fire reduced to nothing but embers pulsing with their waning life force.

"Coming," I call, voice as dead as I feel inside. I spin, putting my back to the drowsy hearth, grabbing the shoes and reticule that match my dress. I hitch the silky drawstring over my shoulder and make for the door in a tinkling, skin-baring charge—the beaded tendrils of my gown slithering behind me like slack corpses of gold-encrusted snakes.

My hand hits the handle just in time for it to swing out of my reach, snatching my breath.

Cainon fills the doorway with more than just his physical self, smelling like spume and sunshine. The vision of careless candor wearing a deep blue shirt that looks butter soft, a few buttons popped at the top, revealing a peek of his tawny chest. His sleeves are rolled, hair pulled back and knotted low, half concealing his undercut.

"I see you got my sprite." He devours me with an appraising look that coats my skin like a drizzle of honey. "Now I'm wondering if we should call it off. Keep this sight all to myself rather than waste it on *him* ..."

The silken compliment splats against my icy armor.

"I have a condition. For joining you at this ... *political* dinner I have no interest in attending."

He lifts a brow. "You're holding me ransom?"

"Yes."

He looks me over again, the corner of his mouth kicking up. "Smart girl. Have at it."

I sweep my foot back and slip it into the strappy blue shoe with a *very* high heel—a shoe I want to toss in the fire with what's left of that book. "I want to go to town. Tomorrow. I want to explore."

In the daylight.

A frown chases away Cainon's carefree demeanor. "That's a tall order, petal. I'm needed on one of the islands again tomorrow." He crosses his arms and leans against the doorframe. "Call me a blushing romantic, but I wanted to be the one to show you around the first time you visit the city."

That ship's already scorched.

I set my foot on the ground, kicking the other back and working the heel straps into place. "You're not going to leave me locked in this palace the same way you accused Rhordyn of doing, are you?"

He watches me for a long, tense moment.

I set my other foot down and hold his eye contact, chin raised.

"Chaperoned," he finally says. "You can see a lot from the safety of a carriage."

"That's not what I'm asking for."

His eyes harden as he steps forward until all that's separating us is a hair's breadth of space. Until I'm marinating in citrus and salt and the prickling wrath of his brewing frustration. "And *I* certainly didn't ask to have Rhordyn roaming around Parith like some rogue mutt pining after his lost bone."

My breath snags.

That's what this is about …

Him.

Seems ironic that Rhordyn spent so many breaths trying to coax me past my Safety Line, and now he's *here*, keeping me trapped without even realizing it.

Or perhaps he does.

"Fine," I blurt before Cainon uses his freshly flung weapon to slaughter the idea altogether.

"It's settled, then?"

"A *female* escort," I tack on, carving around him and shoving through the door into the lobby, smoothing the strands of my dress as he follows me out. He snatches my free hand and threads it into the crook of his arm before Kolden opens the door for us both, and we make our way down the hall and then the sweeping staircase.

"You're extra sharp tonight." There's a long pause, then his arm muscles clench under my hand when he says, "You've seen him already."

Him.

"Yes." I keep my chin high. Keep my steps steady. "An uneventful reunion."

Silence ensues, only dented by the tapping of my heels. "Well, I need you to be on your best behavior."

"I'll try to oblige."

He shifts, latching onto my upper arm and spinning me to a stop, walking me back. I thud against the cold stone wall, his body hot against mine, his strong scent *everywhere*.

Heart thumping in my ears, I look into his hardened stare. "I mean it, Orlaith. He's a dangerous enemy to have. A dangerous man."

"I can handle Rhordyn."

His low, husky laugh ripples across my flushed skin. "Not alone, you can't. But we're in this together now." His fingers thread around my cupla and my wrist. "*I've got you.*"

Not alone ...

We're in this together ...

I've got you ...

He tweets such perfect tunes.

This should be right. An easy love come to me on a gilded platter. One that doesn't dig down enough to breach the vault of my deepest, darkest flaws. That doesn't stare me down like he wants to disassemble me, then assess my broken bits.

This should be right.

I draw a breath to speak—

His lips slam against mine in a crushing kiss, deep and sensual and thought muddling, his hands painting the bare strips of my body with a blazing trail of attention—grabbing and kneading and tracing the lines of my ribs. It's only when he pulls back and swipes the smudged lip lacquer from below my bottom lip that I realize I'm panting, chest heaving.

Drenched in affection, yet somehow *parched.*

"Come," he purrs, brushing his knuckles along my jaw. He studies my face with a pleased glint in his eye that ignites the violet flecks. "I want him to see this blush in your cheeks before it wears off."

Him ...

I swallow the anxious pit in my throat as Cainon threads my arm through his and leads me down the stairs.

Chapter 36
Orlaith

Late afternoon sun bathes the large, lavish room in golden light, spilling through an entire wall of tinted glass windows and warming the backs of my arms. The high ceiling is crowned with a gilded chandelier that's dripping beads toward a lapis lazuli table twice the size of the one I used to eat at daily.

Stoic-faced servants file through the room, dressing the table in an array of heaped platters, among them seafood cooked in their shells and slathered in butter, deep bowls of spiced vegetables topped with crumbled nuts and herbs, and sweating urns of mint water.

Besides them and the finely dressed bard perched on a stool in the far corner of the room, it's just us.

Me and Cainon.

He's seated at the head, I'm along the side—the first seat in—and there's a place setting opposite me that's yet to be filled.

A male server with heavy steps walks into the room with

a bottle of wine, making my heart leap into my throat—thoughts going to the bag stored beneath my chair.

To its contents ...

My wine flute is filled, and I tip it to my lips, taking a large, bubbly gulp, welcoming the buzz that settles in my gut.

Not that it really helps.

The hairs on my arms lift, and the next set of steps are unmistakably *his*—each foot landing with that resounding thud I know so well.

I keep my attention cast on a stack of glazed shanks, feeling his gaze upon me; tracking across my lips, the cut of my dress, the bare windows of skin it reveals.

All the places Cainon touched me.

Perhaps he doesn't realize his walls are down. That I can feel how much it rankles him just by the string of tension stretched between us.

A shiver pebbles my skin. Makes my nipples squeeze into points, obvious through the thin strips of material barely keeping them covered. I feel him absorb the crude evidence of his effect on me—*hating* myself.

Hating the hot throb between my legs.

Lashes sweeping up, I catch his silver regard, breath hitching as his nostrils flare. I lift the flute, holding his eyes over the foot of my glass as I gulp.

And gulp.

And gulp.

He's beautiful, dressed in the same black clothes he wore today, sans cloak—the same shirt that hugs his barreling chest, compliments his deep skin tone, and makes his eyes stand out in stark contrast; the same form-fitting pants that cling to his muscled thighs too well, still streaked with dust, like he's boasting the evidence of our unsolicited rendezvous.

"Rhordyn. Right on time."

Stalking into the room like some great, prowling beast with his hackles up, Rhordyn looks to my promised, then stops, looks down the table, up again, frowning. "No advisors? Masters or Mistresses? I thought we'd be using this time productively to discuss some pressing matters."

Cainon reclines in his seat, leg cast over the arm as he assesses his nails. "Hard on such late notice. I figured you wouldn't be opposed to an intimate setting *unperturbed* by political banter. Given we're practically family now."

I'm going to need more wine.

"Come," he says, waving Rhordyn forward. "Take a seat. Let us share a meal together."

Tense moments tick by while I grip the stem of my flute, willing it to magically refill.

Rhordyn finally steps up to the table. He lifts his seat, silently sets it down, then sits, watching me while my heart thumps harder than it ever has.

Cainon kicks his leg off the arm of his chair, leans forward, and plucks up a big, bloody strip of meat, slapping it straight on his polished gold plate. "Well, this is delightful."

Someone's overly optimistic.

A servant sweeps close and blessedly fills my glass almost to the rim while I drop my gaze to the spot where my own plate should be, noticing for the first time that there is none. All I have is a knife, a fork, and a tiny spoon I can't imagine a use for.

"Am I to eat off the table?" I mutter beneath my breath, looking to Cainon who is filling a second plate.

Ahh.

Still feeling the cold brand of Rhordyn's stare, I clear my throat, cross my hands over my lap like a good little girl, and wait patiently for my meal.

Ladling some green paste upon a pile of flaked fish, Cainon says, "She looks good in blue, does she not?"

I choke out a cough, hand flying to my mouth.

"Orlaith would look good in any color."

My gaze darts to Rhordyn, who's watching Cainon with a warpath stare.

"Except black," Cainon volleys, dropping the ladle back into the bowl of slop, scrunching his nose when he sucks a bit off his thumb. "Drowns her out."

That's the fucking point.

I bat my lashes at my promised. "My love, must you talk about me as if I'm not here?"

Cainon flashes the slightest raise of a tawny brow, a wicked half smile. "Apologies, *my love*."

I don't dare look at Rhordyn as Cainon makes his way around the table one slow step at a time, then sets the laden plate before me.

I stare at the oversized stack of food, heart sinking. No lamb shanks for me. Instead, I've got fish, green slop, fried bone marrow, a pile of steamed spinach bigger than my fist, and a few other things I can't identify. Nothing I would have picked for myself, but my stomach still grumbles at the prospect of a feast I can enjoy without first sieving for life-threatening berries.

Though the tips of my fingers itch with anticipation to dig in—to feel my food yield and slip and *burn* as I work through it—I look at the golden fork next to my plate.

Picking it up, I feel Rhordyn's stare track my hand when I prod the fish, breaking off a piece that managed to avoid the slather of green goo. I bring it to my lips, eyes flicking up, watching him watch me with a force greater than the sun—unblinking as I drag the metal prongs against my teeth and start to chew.

His chest expands, deflating slowly.

Cainon sits before his meal, drapes a napkin across his knees, and glances at Rhordyn's empty plate. "Is our food not to your liking?"

Rhordyn doesn't bat a lid. "I'm not hungry."

"Ahh." Cainon shoves a piece of meat in his mouth, chewing. "How's the fish, Orlaith?"

I swallow, washing down the mouthful with a numbing swig of wine before letting a smile touch my lips. "Delicious. Caught locally?"

"Correct. Tropical perch. One of our more perishable delicacies we're unable to ship down the river to Ocruth. It's a shame you've never traveled far enough to taste it."

His words are flaming arrows aimed to maim the stoic man sitting across from me, but I doubt he realizes they thud into *my* chest instead.

I had plenty of opportunities to leave the castle grounds before my mind was plagued by the carnage of my past. Opportunities I didn't take.

And now this *delicacy* tastes like ash, much like the air I pull into my lungs.

"Well. Now I can have it often. Along with ..." I skim my fork through the green slosh he slopped all over my meal, "*this*. It smells"—*like spew*—"delicious."

"Malaweed. Nutrient rich. Important if we're to produce an heir."

My insides clench.

Silence.

Bone-chilling *silence*.

My breath comes out like a blow of smoke, and I stuff my lungs full in an effort to kick-start my heart again, letting my gaze drag halfway to Rhordyn before I think better of it, not wanting to feed the beast.

Cainon shoves another bloody strip of meat into his mouth. "What about you, Rhordyn? Are you and Zali planning to conceive?"

The words peck at old wounds I've tried to convince myself were healed, and my throat constricts, threatening to return the fish and wine to the table.

Rhordyn leans back, fingers steepled. "I'm seeing a lot of your father in you lately."

Cainon stops chewing, eyes glazing over. "Is that a threat?"

"An observation," Rhordyn answers, thumping the word down like a meat cleaver.

Suddenly, the room feels too small, the table between these men too fragile.

That war I've been trying so hard to avoid? It's waging right before my eyes. The chilling prologue to a mass demise. If I don't intervene, I'm not entirely sure they won't launch across the table and feast on each other.

Perhaps I should let them have at it. Sit back and watch them bleed each other—like they each want to bleed *me* in their own twisted ways.

Maybe that's taking it too far.

Clearing my throat, and with the chilled brand of Rhordyn's stare attacking my hand, I shovel the fork into the lump of fish most drenched in sauce, encouraging the sharp metal tips to drag across the plate.

I don't even flinch.

"Orlaith." Pounded by the full force of his attention, I look him in the eye. "You don't have to eat that."

He's not talking about the food. Precisely why I shove the mouthful past my lips and chew, cheeks bulging, nose blocked, and breath held as I masticate the metallic-tasting crap like I'm *fanging* for it. Like I'm desperate for Cainon to give me everything he wants to give. For him to drive past that chaste barrier Rhordyn so bluntly shied away from when I begged him to take me on my balcony in Stony Stem.

He swallows—a crack in his armor.

Cainon chuckles. "Looks like she doesn't care what you think, Rhordyn. She's too smart these days."

"She's always been smart," Rhordyn mutters, holding my stare, a spark in his darkening eyes like a single surviving star.

A squire jogs through the door, breathless, bowing at the waist before he speaks. "High Master, forgive the intrusion—"

"Not now," Cainon snaps, but the man steps further into the room.

"With all due respect, it can't wait. There's"—his shrewd gaze nips at Rhordyn for a beat—"a *messenger* in your office. He insists on seeing you right away."

Cainon groans, shoves to a stand, chair scraping across the floor before he storms toward the door.

I shovel another mouthful past my lips, the underside of

my tongue tingling, stomach cramping as I chew—gaze cast on the mound of food Cainon served me.

Fuck me. Getting through all this is going to take some gall, but I'm too committed now. In over my head in more ways than one.

"Milaje."

Tucking a loose tendril of hair behind my ear, I look up. "You're still here?"

There's a long, frosty pause, and I swear that flare in his eyes intensifies, even as his irises deepen into a darker, stormier gray that pinches my defiant nipples and sparks my blood with a strike of thrill.

Some small, fucked-up part of me—a part I *loathe*—is feeding off this toxic game of chase.

"Did you read the book?"

"No." I set my fork beside the plate and dab at my lips with a napkin. "But it made *fantastic* kindling."

His eyes widen.

The blow of satisfaction it punches me with is intoxicating.

I reach toward a plate of sweet-looking sticky treats dripping with a sunshine glaze, shoving one in my mouth and licking the residue off my fingers. Slowly. Precisely. Cleaning all five before I say, "There was something so satisfying about watching it burn."

His chair groans as his knuckles whiten, scouring the musician with a threatening perusal the poor man must surely feel.

"Something you want to say, Rhordyn? Or do?" His stare hits me like a stone, and I lift my chin, pushing the cascade of curls over my shoulder. "Choke me, perhaps?"

His heaving chest stills.

I look down my nose at him as I trace a trail with the tips of my fingers from my bottom lip down, *down* ... over my throat, all the way to the chain encircling it.

The obscure curse he *shackled* me with.

"Burst my flesh with your teeth?" I purr, and a low, primal growl vibrates from his chest to mine, making my skin prickle.

It stirs me up and untangles me in the very same beat. Makes me want to dash out of this chair just to see if he'll chase.

No.

I punch the underside of my fist onto the table hard enough to clatter the cutlery. "Lock me in your fucking *den?*"

There's a challenge in my voice because I want him to yield. I want him to bend so much he fucking *snaps.*

He exhales, swallows, then, "There is something I want to do, yes."

"By all means."

I tip the flute to my lips, his punishing stare skimming my throat as I swallow.

His eyes lift, striking mine, baring a brash confidence that's utterly charged. "I don't think Cainon would be particularly pleased to walk back through those doors and see his *promised* spread across the table while I feast between her thighs."

I choke, sputtering wine down my chin.

Between my breasts.

An ember throbs to life deep inside my core as I fight to erase the mental image of him charging around the table, taking chase.

Catching me.

Clearing the food with a swift swipe of his arm and dashing me across the marble. Gripping me by the thighs—brutal, yet tender as he splits my legs apart and bares my flushed, naked core, humming at the evidence of my twisted arousal before he laves at it like he's fucking *starved*.

I swallow.

Try not to squirm.

His gaze continues to punish me—hurting in a way that feels good.

Too fucking good.

"But by all means, Milaje. You wave that white flag, and I'll choke the life out of the consequences in the blink of an eye."

His savage words rip a hole through my composure, dousing the heat between my thighs.

War.

Cainon was right ... Rhordyn *wants his land.*

I stand fast.

He stands slow.

Our stares clash while I breathe hard and shallow, half tempted to flee. Half tempted to fight.

He garnishes me with a look that suggests he'd relish both options and plants his fists on the table, leaning forward, watching me from beneath that flop of sable hair as he cocks his head to the side. "So, what's it to be?"

Cainon stalks into the room, pausing for a moment when he notices us both standing, then moves to his chair and flops down. "Apologies. Why don't you fill me in on whatever riveting conversation you were having?"

Rhordyn opens his mouth and my heart riots, words

erupting from my own lips. "I was just telling Rhordyn that I can't *wait* to seal our coupling."

His eyes flare like twin moons cast in a pall of black. *Eclipsed.*

I almost feel bad for what I'm about to do.

"Is that so?" Cainon asks, and I look at him, heart beating so hard I swear it's about to thump a hole in my ribs and thud onto my plate in a bloody, sloppy mess.

"Yes. And on *that* note—" I drop low, retrieving my reticule from beneath the chair and loosening the drawstring. "I have a gift for you, my promised."

The air stiffens. The light pouring through the window dims, as if a cloud just blew over the sun.

Cainon lifts a brow, flashing Rhordyn a swift, gloating look. "Really?"

I nod, wrapping my hands around the small mug stashed inside, questioning myself for a split second before revealing the nest of thriving bluebells.

Drawing a deep, steadying breath, I extend the gift toward Cainon, feeling the pulse of Rhordyn's attention like a pickaxe knocking around the edges of my fortified shield. As though he's *desperate* to pry me from this picture so I can thump into the palm of his hand like one of my blank whispers.

I've realized he likes gifting me precious, well-thought-out things. It's his own illusive way of showing he cares.

So does he see the symbolism I'm shoving in his face?

This is a personalized attack meant to hurt us *both*. Meant to bleed this twisted thing that is *us*.

I look at Cainon with love-glazed eyes and bare him

a honeysuckle smile while I let the hurt douse me. Let my message blare loud and clear.

I don't need my crutch anymore.

Don't need *him*.

I'm fine.

If I repeat it enough, I'll eventually believe it.

Cainon takes the weight of the gift, flashing me a full smile. "Wow, for me?"

It takes all my will not to snatch it back and cradle it close to my chest. "Yes. I collected these *myself*."

Rhordyn steps away from his seat, lifting it, setting it down close to the table before he spins and stalks toward the door.

"Where are you going?" Cainon's belted words echo through the space, and Rhordyn stops, casting a glance at me over his shoulder. There's ... *something* in his eyes I've never seen before.

Something that looks a lot like hurt.

"I've seen enough." He goes, leaving a hole in the room's atmosphere that makes me picture a hollowed-out chest cavity.

I tune into the music. Realize how loud it's blaring in the back corner, the sharp notes slashing against my skin like the swipes of a talon.

I lift my chin, plant my ass on the chair—keeping my spine straight as I pick up my fork—and continue to eat, refusing to look at the bells, convinced they'll no longer appear naturally droopy ... but *sad*.

"Orlaith?"

I glance at Cainon, watching me with a regard warm enough to thaw even the iciest heart.

Unfortunately for him, mine's not ice.

It's ash.

"You did good, *my love*."

"I know." I shovel my mouth full, avoiding the empty chair opposite me.

Too good.

Chapter 37
Orlaith

I'm fine.
I'm fine.
I'm fine.

I repeat the internal mantra as I'm escorted back to my room. As Cainon bids me goodnight with a kiss to the knuckles I want to punch through the wall. I watch his back until he disappears around the corner, a pit of dread sitting in the well of my stomach.

Releasing a shuddered breath, I turn toward Kolden. I'm not sure what he sees in my eyes, but he mutters something about guarding from further down the hall. Only once he, too, is almost out of sight, do I move into the lobby, taking a few moments to stack myself with bricks of courage.

I open the second door and step into my suite, moonlight casting shadows around the room, making every inch of gold appear sterling. Every inch of blue stone appear black.

Castle-Noir black.

His scent hits. A blow to my brain, my heart.

My fucking soul.

I spin, closing the door with a gentle thud, settling my forehead against the cool grain. "I thought you said you'd seen enough?"

The air shifts, and I feel him everywhere.

His icy breath hits the side of my neck, his hands landing on the door either side of my head, casting me in a cold cage that should make me feel trapped.

But doesn't.

I'm not sure why my eyes sting at the realization, but they do.

I'm fine.

"I know what you're doing, Milaje."

The words are uncharacteristically soft, unlike my answer—hewn from that hard and scarred space within.

"No. You don't."

I feel him shift closer. Feel his body align with my spine—a balm to the scalding slither I can't expel. That disgusting, vile thing inside me.

The truth.

His lips skate the shell of my ear, his whisper a hushed attack. "You want me to hurt?"

Yes.

I want to lash myself against him until I'm bruised and bent and broken. Until I can no longer hear their burning screams.

I want to hurt him so much I don't even recognize myself.

Perhaps he'll finally rip me to fleshy shreds in a way that serves my due. After all, he's the only one who's ever been able to leave a lasting scar to rival this hurt I feel inside.

The only one who truly has the power to ruin me.

"No," he growls. A command and a pledge and so much more, as though he's studying the fabric of my thoughts.

A flash of anger sparks in my chest, my upper lip curls, and that frosty hardness returns with a vengeance.

"Get out." Of my head. My heart. "I have everything I ever wanted, and you're ruining it."

"A smart woman once told me that everything is nothing if you're in pieces."

I'm fine.

"Don't lie to me." The words are a grated snarl that shreds the silence and attacks the sensitive spot below my ear.

My heart races. Skin flares.

"Get. Out."

"Is that what you really want?"

He moves impossibly close, crushing me in ways that make me feel held.

I don't want to be held.

I don't deserve to be held.

I ball my hands into fists. "Yes."

He doesn't move or breathe or speak, but the air around him screams—pleads with me in a way I don't want to understand.

Fury erupts, and I whirl, snarling.

But he's gone, leaving nothing but his lingering scent for me to choke on.

I look to the open balcony door, to the curtains billowing in the breeze, lit by a blade of moonlight piercing through ...

He's never going to stop.

I reach behind my arm and pinch an inch of flesh. Pinch harder than I ever have, tears welling in my eyes.

Perhaps he's my penance for the monster I am inside—a hollow love that churns and burns and destroys.
Just like me.

Chapter 38
Baze

"This one is well stocked," Zali calls from within the wreath of tall, black stones three times her height. Lanterns are strung around them that she's taken the time to light, creating a stark barrier that pushes back the gloomy press of evening.

"Good," I say, dragging two limp rabbits off Ale's back. "I'll get a fire going."

Tethered to a tree that's caught in the light spilling off the stones, Ale slurps at the bubbling brook while I scan the dense forest that's losing more light by the second, shadows spilling from its confines.

I shiver and edge between a gap in the stones, pausing, running my hand over the white marks slashed across the smooth face of the one to my left—a Vruk's failed attempt to break down the barrier and get to whoever was hiding within. I look to the trench dug into the soil surrounding the outer base, as though the beast tried to gore down enough to tip the massive monolith. But these stones are pierced so deep into the ground, it's as though they're rooted to the world's core.

Some even believe they were thrown down by the hands of a God.

I step within their stony clutch, lump the rabbits by the firepit, then kneel in the grass, using my dagger to till some soil before flicking a stare at Zali. She's bent over, plucking watercress from the brook that weaves through the space before cupping her hands full of water and splashing her face, dragging droplets through her hair.

I swallow, rip my stare away, and dig my fingers into the soil.

A full-body shiver ignites my skin ...

Fuck.

I almost groan, letting my eyes shut, drawing from the earth in greedy gulps, as though chugging back a bottle of rum.

A krah shrieks across the sky, snapping me out of my reverie, and I clear my throat, glancing again at Zali before sifting through the soil for spuds and pulling out a few the size of my fist. "You were right," I say, brushing the dirt off their skins. "It *is* well stocked."

Nothing beats a whelve when you're bone-weary from riding for days with a smart-witted, strong-willed woman bouncing up and down between your thighs because her horse got eaten by a Vruk.

All *that* considered, these piles of rock dispersed across the continent are the only thing I'll thank the fucking Gods for.

Shirt rolled to my elbows, I dip the spuds in the chilly current and rub them down, watching the object of my welling frustrations as I do. Hair falling in a strawberry ripple, she crouches before the bushes planted at the base of one of the stones, using her dagger to hack off some rosemary stalks with a fierceness that's too captivating.

She looks over, striking me with that bold stare, brow raised. "What ... do you not like rosemary?"

"On the contrary," I tell her, pushing to a stand and stalking toward the unlit firepit in the center of the space. "It's becoming my new favorite thing."

Her cheeks redden, and she quickly looks away.

I build the fire, then get to work filling the heavy cauldron with water while Zali digs through the metal chest bolted to the ground. She pulls out bowls, spoons and knives, then chops up the spuds while I skin the rabbits I caught earlier and keep the fire blazing.

We sit on stumps on opposite sides of the fire, silently watching the flames lick at the bottom of the blackened pot while the liquid bubbles away, filling the air with the hearty smell of rabbit stew. The last of the evening light drains away, scattering the sky with a litter of stars.

"It's got that *feel*, you know?"

I look up, catching her intense stare. "What do you mean?"

She drags her fur shawl tighter around her shoulders, the flames reflected in her unblinking eyes. "That something big is coming."

"I'm still stuck on the last big thing," I mutter, leaning forward to dig my spoon into the pot and give it a stir, drawing deep on the rich bouquet of sage and rosemary.

"Do you ..."

She pauses, and I raise my eyes to hers. "Do I what?"

"Have much memory of the time before?" The words thunk into my chest like stones, and she shakes her head. "I'm sorry, that was rude. You don't have to answer that."

I drop my stare back to the stew, stirring, lifting a small strip of meat and blowing on it. "Not as much as I would like," I say, pushing away images that have never rubbed out.

Women running, then thudding to the ground—shot with whistling arrows that ripped through their chests. Men howling for their mates and children, their hoarse cries cuffed as pronged shackles clamped around their necks and wrists.

I toss the meat back in the pot without testing it. "I was only five when my family was rounded up and checked over for any marks or strange scars ... the females slain and hacked to bits."

"Oh, Baze ..."

Another stir, and I scrape the spoon across the bottom to make sure nothing's getting the chance to burn. "I was torn from the cold clutches of my dead mother by the man who became my ... *captor,* for lack of a better word," I say with a careless half smile that's a lie in every way, shape, and form. "He became all I knew until Rhordyn came along."

A long silence slips by while I continue to stir the stew, though my appetite has gone. If anything, the thought of eating makes me want to heave.

"I never heard the full details ..."

"It's not something I ever talk about," I mutter, dropping my spoon in my empty bowl and lumping another log on the fire, making the flames dance.

"How long?"

The question is choked.

I glance up into Zali's russet eyes flecked with gold, her bottom lids heavy with unshed tears. "How long what?"

"Were you kept for?"

"Long enough that I forgot the feel of soil beneath my feet. The taste of fruit. He fed us with a single beam of sun and not much else. Liked us limp when he feasted."

She sucks a sharp breath.

I lean back, crossing my arms as I watch the flames whip at the base of the pot as though they're desperate to crack through its hard outer shell. "I hated Rhordyn for killing him," I admit, remembering the times I clawed at him like some broken animal, begging him to take away the pain.

Remembering the way I fought him and wished it was *he* who'd died. Or that he'd struck me out at the same time he'd struck him.

"Then Rhordyn put a sword in my hand and told me to break something else so I'd stop breaking myself. So my insides could have a chance to heal."

"Did you, though?" she whispers, her voice too soft. "Heal?"

I clear my throat, kicking a throbbing ember back amongst the pit from where it had been spat out onto the grass, thinking back to the spike of pleasure I would feel when my skin was punched through with the unrelenting pierce of those drugging canines ...

My captor. My torturer.

My *rapture*.

He was—in some fucked-up way—my family.

But he was also a monster.

I watched my friends wither beneath the crunch of his teeth.

Told myself he'd never do that to me, even though a part of me knew one day he would. One of his *friends* would. He'd lose control. Lose interest. I was nothing more than a pet who served a purpose until my blood was no longer bright enough for him to enjoy.

I pat my pocket, searching for my flask, then dash my hand through my hair when I realize it isn't there.

Did you, though? Heal?

I offer Zali a wry grin, brows raised. "Apparently not."

She gives me a smile that doesn't meet her eyes, and we fall into a stretch of silence, the sparks from the fire a crackling distraction to my staggered thoughts.

The clop of hooves stirs my nerves.

Zali swivels on her stump, staring out into the forest as my gaze flicks to our swords leaning against our packs on the other side of the fire. Too far away to reach without causing a scene.

"No need to startle," a deep, raspy voice calls through the darkness. "Just a friendly traveling merchant looking for a place to spend the night on this lonely forest trail."

The clops grow louder, and I see a bobbing light, its intensity growing until a white horse comes into view through the window between two stones. A man leaps off the side of the well-packed saddle dressed in a red merchant's robe, the thick trim around his hood storm-cloud gray.

Shulák.

My heart jumps a beat, my hand threading down the side of my boot.

To my small, concealable dagger.

"They're not all the same, Baze. You know that," Zali

whisper-hisses. "Let me do the talking. Do you understand? You're *mute*."

The man untacks his horse, lifting his saddlebags off its back before he tethers it to the tree beside Ale.

My hand tightens around my dagger, a savage fury popping through my veins.

"Do. You. Understand?"

My gaze whips to Zali, and I flash her a smile that's all teeth. "Clear as crystal."

Frowning, her eyes drop to my hand still pinching the hilt to my dagger.

I relax my hold, straighten my spine, and flick my hood up as I fold my arms and narrow my stare on the bubbling pot of stew.

The brutish man eases between two stones, walking with a stiffness that suggests he hasn't climbed off his mount all day, his robe swishing around him as he moves closer to the flames. His face is a little strained around the eyes, jaw covered in a thick, black beard. He flips his hood, and I wince at the sight of his bald head—at the mark on his forehead.

He laughs low, face beaming as he takes in our boiling meal. "That, my friends, smells delightful." He spreads his arms wide, looking between us both. "Do you mind sharing this whelve with a lonely merchant on a crisp night?"

Do you mind fucking bowing for the Eastern High Mistress?

Maybe he doesn't recognize her. Even so, I twist further around, look him up and down, then lift a brow at Zali. She seems to purposely avoid my stare.

"Of course," she chirps, offering him a small smile, furs still wrapped tightly around her shoulders.

The man looks at me and I give him a wink.

"He's mute," Zali offers, swifter than she strikes a blade.

"Ahh." He nods knowingly. "Hardly surprising with this world we live in. See some horrors on the road these days." He looks to Zali again, gesturing to the spot between me and her. "May I?"

At her nod, the man sits, warming his hands near the flames.

"Mind me asking where you're headed?" she asks, reaching to stir the stew.

"I'm just traveling from village to village, spreading the words of the stones and selling my wares." He rubs his hands together, then reaches into the folds of his cloak, revealing a leather pouch he digs through. "Saje?" he asks, brows raised as he stuffs a pipe full of the dried buds I haven't tasted in years. Part of a bygone era I stumbled through blindly on a cloud of lapsed judgment before replacing one vice with another.

"I have this spare pipe you can have for half price in exchange for sharing your stew? I haven't had meat in over a week," he says, tamping more of the saje into his pipe. "Not the best hunter, you see."

He extends it in my direction, and I waver, half tempted to accept before Zali butts in.

"He doesn't smoke," she says, hooking my stare with a narrowed one of her own, and I raise a single brow. "Gives him the shits. I'm the one who has to travel with him."

I bite down on a few choice words I'd *love* to throw at her.

"Fair enough," the merchant chuckles, rolling his eyes at me.

I return the gesture.

He gets to work lighting his pipe, puffing from it, blowing the excess toward the sky and dousing us all in the sweet, potent scent.

"You got anything else in that bag?" Zali asks.

I take the spoon off her and crouch before the pot, occupying my hands with filling our bowls.

"Like what?" I hear the eager lilt in his voice.

Zali prods a withered branch at the fire. "I don't know ... *candy?*"

The man draws a long puff from his pipe, then looks at Zali with a knowing glint in his eye. "That'll be the answer to your ... *sublime* complexion," he says, and I can tell by the tone of his voice that he's no longer picturing himself at the bottom of the food chain. An intruder in our camp.

Zali passes him a shy smile. "So?" she asks, tilting her head, voice hooked with an air of desperation.

"Hard to come by these days." Another puff, and the man reaches down, taking her serving of stew with both hands.

I still, stare flicking to Zali who stabs me with her own and the faintest shake of her head.

This *no talking* business is really pinching my fraught, sober nerves.

I bite my tongue so hard it bleeds, handing her my own bowl as I watch the merchant slurp at the broth, then stuff his mouth full of the rabbit I caught. "There was a surplus of it for a while there," he swallows, then fills his mouth again. "But *now* ..."

"Which is why I always ask," Zali purrs, then takes a delicate sip of her stew.

To him, she probably looks harmless.

Desperate.

Not at all like she could carve him into six chunks in a matter of seconds.

"Well," he says, slurping back the remainder of his meal in three deep gulps, wiping his beard with his arm. "You're in luck. However ..." He drops his bowl on the ground between his feet and groans, stretching.

"However?" Zali whines, her eyes twin wells of desperation.

"It's going to cost a lot more than a simple bowl of rabbit stew. Delicious as it was."

Zali sets her bowl down and digs beneath her furs, through her robe, pulling out a heavy pouch and tossing it at the man.

He snatches it from the air with a swift hand, loosening the tie, tipping the cascade of gold coins into his palm.

His eyes flare.

"Well," he breathes, placing his pipe on the ground and stuffing the coins in the sack, not even bothering to count them. He's probably holding a small fortune—enough to build a bunker large enough to protect an entire family and then some. "I'm at your whim."

He stands, stepping over the log and scurrying toward his saddlebags, looking far more agile than he did when he entered the camp.

I let my gaze fall into the pits of Zali's—hard and unblinking. The stare is ruthless, drenched in bloodlust, sending a spike through me that electrifies my fucked-up soul. "And did you harvest it yourself?" she asks, holding my stare.

"Most of it I got from Madame Strings," the man chimes as he rummages through his pack, and I hear the clink of jars banging against each other. "She's based in Parith most months, but she's the only truly reliable source these days. I do, however, have one small jar I harvested myself."

Fire flares through my veins.

Not the best hunter, you see.

What a fucking lie.

Zali nods the slightest amount, and I slide the ring from my finger, feeling my shell split apart.

She doesn't blink. Doesn't tear her gaze away from the ghastly sight that is *me*.

I pinch the hilt of my blade and stand, taking five silent steps toward the man, placing myself at his back.

He pushes up, spins, and only has a moment to take me in through his widening eyes before I slash my blade across his throat with a snarl. He wavers, mouth gaping as his life force bubbles from the deep gash preventing him from drawing breath. Then he crumbles in a convulsing heap at my feet, the three jars packed with tiny, crystal thorns scattering amongst the grass.

Looking down my nose, I watch the life drain from his eyes until he finally stills.

I feel Zali's hand settle on my shoulder. "Baze—"

Sniffing, I pluck up the jars and charge toward the brook. "Found you a replacement horse," I mutter, rinsing the blood off. "So long as it makes it through the night."

"Yes," Zali whispers, and I jolt when I realize she's crouched right beside me.

She grabs one of the jars and helps me clear away the blood before I relieve her of it and move to the fire.

Popping the cork on the first, I reveal the stash of crystal thorns that harbor their own light, radiating every color of the rainbow. I have to bite back my urge to vomit or scream or ... *something* as I scatter them through the flames, watching the fire flare with an array of pastel hues, whispering the ancient words of release.

I have no doubt in my mind that the souls packed into these tiny jars didn't die with full hearts—meaning I doubt any of them passed through Kvath and into Mala.

That thought ...

It's too heavy to bear.

CHAPTER 39

Rhordyn

A bell tolls, the sound skipping across the river like a stone.

The thatched awning of a riverside tackle shop shields me from the drizzle cutting through the morning murk as I watch the portcullis rise in slow, clunking increments, stirring the layer of fog that's settled on the water's surface. Through the yawning gap, I see the dark outline of a river barge with bulging sails, lanterns strung between them and around the edge of the ship.

The River Norse snakes all the way from beyond the Alps in the Deep North—a two-way trading route that services the entire continent. South-sailing barges drift with its gentle flow, and those traveling upstream require the hulls to be packed with oar-wielding men who power the boats against the water's sludgy current whenever the wind is down.

Touching every territory on its journey to the sea, the Norse finally pours into the ocean right here in Bahari's capital. It carves an open path through Cainon's thick, fortified, and well-lit wall that surrounds the city, cuts through the corner of the busy precinct, then spills into the bay. But rather than have an open freeway that allows ships to come and go as they please, that single cleft in the wall is barricaded with a metal portcullis regulated by heavily armed guards. It's lifted whenever a barge requires passage—iron teeth of control that can clamp down at the simple pull of a lever.

I sigh, using my dagger to clear the dirt from under my nails as I set my sights back on the huge whaleboat docked straight ahead of me across the wide, cobbled road. Its patched blue sails hang loose, baring all their bruises, suggesting the latest voyage was far from smooth.

That and the withered state of the crew, their steps wobbled on frail legs, finally dismissed after three hours of rolling barrels of oil down the pier and into the warehouse across the street. I frown at the memory of their open sores and rotting teeth, a sure sign they've been scraping the bottom of the barrel for months, perhaps surviving on rum, blubber, and whale meat.

A man steps off the whaleboat and stalks the pier, his loose pants held up by a length of rope, scroll in one hand and a stuffed sack slung over his shoulder. The ornamental cap indicates he's the captain.

Well, what's left of him.

He passes a huddle of sour-faced soldiers stationed at the pier's entrance, steps up to a leather tent that drips lanterns from all four corners—housing a wooden trestle table he sets his scroll atop—and waits.

The general sitting behind the desk continues to flip

through a ledger, his features long and sharp, burnished hair pulled back in a tidy bun, gold epaulets polished to a gleaming shine.

Rubbing at the wiry beard covering half his face, the captain says, "Somethin' wrong, General Grimsley?"

Grimsley stabs his finger at the ledger. "Captain Rowell. I see you last docked at this port over eight months ago."

Rowell frowns. "Yes. That's how long it took me to fill the hull ..."

Peering up through shrewd eyes, Grimsley says, "Forgive me, Captain, but I find that *very* hard to believe."

"It's the truth!" Rowell blurts, eyes wide as he waves his hand at his ship. "Yuh think I'd want to stay on that there shit heap any longer than necessary?"

Grimsley glances down the pier. "I will admit, your ship certainly looks like it's weathered more than usual this round."

"That's because it has. We were lucky to make it back alive." Rowell nods at the scroll. "Now if yuh don't mind, please look at that there record, tally the numbers against the stock we just stored in yuh warehouse over there, and bag me some coin so I can get home to me fam—"

"You know," Grimsley cuts in, "you're only allotted the lease of that ship on the provision of performance. Our city's survival relies on the oil you procure. We lose the flames that keep our wall lit up at night, we *all* die."

"I'm well aware, sir. And I would've sailed back much faster had the pickings not been so slim."

"You mean to tell me you hunted through the migration season and it still took you *eight months* to sail back with a full hull?"

"Correct," Rowell seethes, dropping his sack and planting his fist upon the table. He leans forward. "I lost three men out there. Good men with women and children I now have to visit, look right in the eye, and tell 'em their pa ain't coming home. Sooner or later yuh gonna have to bribe people to do this shit, and that's the fuckin' truth."

A shiver runs up my spine as I look between the men, the ten soldiers standing guard with sharp eyes and hands clutched around their spears.

"Well," Grimsley ponders, procuring a handkerchief from his breast pocket, using it to wipe Rowell's spittle off his face. "Not today. Today, I won't even be paying you for the oil—at least until I've seen your ledgers, spoken with some of your crew, and am certain you haven't docked in Rouste or Ocruth and delivered to them for a premium in the months you've been away. I trust you've kept the records up to date?"

I lift a brow.

We haven't purchased from whaling ships in years, and even then, it was only because our olive yield was down due to a particularly bad patch of weather. We paid a heavy premium—Cainon's demand in exchange for his expended resources since he owns the fucking ships—but I have no doubt that ended up padding the right pockets. The sailors were tipped handsomely and had no reason to skim the top. It was a *very* lucrative year for Bahari. Which begs the question ... why is the narrative suddenly being soured?

Perhaps they thinned the ocean too much and they're looking for someone else to point at.

"Of course I kept my records up to date," Rowell sneers, before spitting on the ledger spread across Grimsley's desk.

"Go find them yuhself. Block yuh nose on the way down. We ran into some weather and it smells like puke."

He picks up his sack and spins, storming past me on his way down the street, muttering curse words.

Interesting.

Grimsley clears his throat, cleaning the spit off his ledger with his handkerchief before tossing it in the bin.

Frowning, I flip my dagger into its sheath and pull my hood lower, noting the Ocruth barge has finally docked. Weary passengers are disembarking, pushing carts or carrying baskets on their backs with babies wrapped close to their chests and wide-eyed children clinging to their legs.

One of the soldiers drags a thick chain across the cobbled ground, rattling the silence. It's clipped high on another post, creating a barricade the men, women, and children are expected to line up behind.

A blow of wind stirs through them, dragging the sharp scent of fear straight past my nose.

My frown deepens, senses prickling.

A dark-haired man wearing the red cloak of a merchant is let past the chain, dragging his cart packed full of wares. Soldiers descend like vultures, swiftly scouring its contents. Clearing his throat, the merchant steps close to the table, casting nervous glances at a woman with two children still stuck behind the chain.

"Name?" Grimsley asks, quill poised.

"Ruslan, sir."

A horse and cart stacked with baited shellfish pots ambles between the tackle shop and the tent, momentarily breaking my view.

Grimsley's scratching at the page. "Why have you come to Parith?"

"I'm a traveling merchant, sir."

"Official paperwork?"

Ruslan hands over a scroll, which Grimsley unrolls, studying it, jotting something on the ledger. "You'll have to get a new one printed while you're here. This one's starting to fade."

"Yes, sir."

One of the small children dips beneath the chain, scoots past a swooping soldier, and latches onto Ruslan's leg.

Grimsley frowns, looking from the child to the woman behind the chain cradling the younger one close. "Do you also speak for these people?"

"Yes, sir," Ruslan says, nodding. "My family."

Grimsley waves them forward, and a soldier loosens the chain to let the woman and her young pass.

"Refugees?"

"From Ocruth. Our home was destroyed. We, ahh ..." Ruslan clears his throat, reaching down to run his fingers through his son's inky hair. "We barely made it down to the bunker in time," he chokes out.

His woman steps close, setting a reassuring hand on his shoulder.

Grimsley nods, jotting something down. "So you're seeking to relocate?"

"Yes, sir. We are."

"That's fine." He hands the paperwork back, then excuses Ruslan with a swift wave. "You may pass. Your family will catch a barge to one of the outer islands. Please follow Quill," he says, looking at the pale-faced woman as he gestures toward the sailor standing sentry at his back. "He'll take you to a temporary hold where you'll stay until the next barge sails later today."

My chest constricts.

He can't be serious.

"But *sir*," Ruslan blurts, grip tightening on his child, his other hand tangling with his woman's shirt in a possessive grip. "I have the paperwork—"

"For *yourself*. That does not cover your kin. I'm sorry, there is limited space in the city."

"B-but trade is best in the city! I need to sell our family heirlooms so we have enough coin to reestablish—"

"Then I suggest you do it fast," Grimsley states, giving Ruslan a tight smile. "Either that or forfeit your heirlooms and join your family on the next barge. Your choice. Make it quick, we have lots of people to process."

Ruslan's screaming son is pried from his leg.

"Let him go!" the woman howls, clawing at the boy while the younger child—a girl—clings to her chest, howling.

"That's not fair!" Ruslan cries, shoving the soldier and grasping the boy by his shoulders, holding him close. "Please be merciful. *Please.* We have nothing left. Without this, we'll all starve—"

A soldier grabs his arms and holds them behind his back.

"Ruslan, if you don't calm down," Grimsley seethes, "I'll tear up your papers."

A dark surge rears inside me, slashing at my skin. A desire to step out of the shadows and stalk across the wide road, punch my fist through Grimsley's chest, and feel his heart pulverize between my squeezing fingers. Or maybe I'd grip his ribs and use them to pry open his chest like a split book. Watch his lungs breathe their last breath.

I turn from the scene, seeking calm from the dimly lit innards of the tackle shop. The child's screams continue to belt across the otherwise silent morning, and I close my eyes. Squeeze them tight. Crack my knuckles and my neck. Picture my lungs packed with the smell of amber and wildflowers.

"Next!" Grimsley hollers.

I force myself to turn and unclench my fists as I watch a familiar woman with dark skin and white, dreaded hair that falls to her hips push her cart up to the desk, her red merchant's coat trailing through filthy puddles behind her.

There's a scar that travels from the corner of her mouth to her ear, her stark eyes so brown they almost look black.

Grimsley frowns at Cindra after looking over her papers, uncertainty staining his features. "Merchant? How come I haven't seen you before?"

"New to the trade, sir."

Grimsley looks at her paperwork again, holding it up to the lantern light.

I grit my teeth so hard they ache.

"Something wrong, sir?"

One of the soldiers searching her cart flips the pelt back over the mound of leather satchels, chewing on something as he steps forward. "Black maple leaves, sir. It's on the list."

Grimsley nods and waves Cindra through.

She wheels her cart past me, and I wait until she's halfway down the shop-lined street before I follow. Turning down a tight alley, we meet behind a stack of damp crates. "How many sailors on this one?"

"Seven," Cindra replies through clenched teeth, flipping the pelt back and snatching one of the leather satchels off the top. Unbuttoning it, she digs her fingers through the innards and sneers. "If they all make it past that *rat*. I wouldn't be surprised if half of them get sent back up the Norse on the next barge."

I don't tell her that based on the last two river shipments, that's *exactly* what's going to happen.

To sail these ships out of Bahari waters once we've secured them, we'll need a small swarm of able-bodied sailors baring deep Rouste or Ocruth roots with their feet on *this* side of that wall.

So far, we only have forty-three.

"I have this urge to storm back there and feed him my fist," she mutters, pulling a black leaf from the satchel and stuffing it in her mouth.

I want to do far worse than that.

"I noticed the travelers were all frightened the moment they stepped off the barge ..."

She nods, chewing. "We almost missed a stop last night after seeing a pack of Vruk edging along the riverbank."

My heart lurches. "Toward *Lorn?*"

Another nod. "*This* side of the border. Not your problem."

No, but if Cainon's attitude at the Conclave is anything to go by, I doubt he's going to bother the risk of pinching a nerve in the effort to protect them.

"They're traders, not warriors."

"And the village will surely be missed come his

yearly tithe." Cindra extends the open pouch toward me. "Want some? Blunts the edge."

Ignoring the offer, I turn and stare out the mouth of the alley.

In *her* direction.

I have everything I ever wanted, and you're ruining it.

I tighten my fists, knuckles popping.

I need to respect her wishes. Give her space. Drain some of the murderous energy crackling through my veins before she's forced to see that side of me ...

Fuck.

"Isn't it best to just let the Vruk inch their way here?" Cindra says past her mouthful, and I hear her spit. "Perhaps the Southern High Master's help would come easier once they weather the same wrath."

No.

"That's not how I do things." I reach into my pocket, pull out a loop of keys, and toss them at her. "Graves Inn. Shit end of town."

"Charming," she chimes, pocketing them.

"You can trust the innkeeper. See the crew make it to their lodgings. Make sure everyone's comfortable and heartily fed."

I dig my hand in my pocket again, pulling out the heavy weight of a silver token that I flip at her.

She's swift to snatch it, frowning. "Master?"

"There is a very disgruntled whaling crew. Captain Rowell's ship is berthed on the other side of the pier. If I don't return and our people keep getting pushed back, follow that lead. He could be a viable backup, and from the looks of that ship, they know how to sail in rough seas."

I spin, stalking down the alleyway.

"He wouldn't show your people the same respect!" Cindra belts at my back as I turn onto the main street, it's only occupant a rat that scurries over the cobbles, then disappears into a hole in the wall.

"I know," I murmur, charging toward the river.

Chapter 40
Orlaith

"You're not trying hard enough," Elder Creed says, his words stabbing down at me—lumped in a sodden, heaving pile on the floor amongst my puddle of spew.

The banana I ate for breakfast didn't taste so great coming back up.

"I do nothing *but* try," I bite out through clenched teeth, every muscle in my body burning as I push up onto my hands, strings of spit clinging to my cheek, my heavy braid dragging along the stone like a dead snake.

A set of waves drum against the walls with such violence, it sounds like the space is full of thunder.

I picture the next set bigger.

Angrier.

Picture it battering the bold, blue stone until it caves, releasing a torrent that drowns the place like a blood-filled lung.

"Then why are you making no progress?"

Arms trembling to hold my weight, I groan, the sound

cut short when my spine arches and I spill another burping splat.

I'll never eat bananas again.

"Tell me ..." He drifts closer, his hooded robe a gray blur in my peripheral. "Do *you* think you deserve this?"

"Deserve what? To be vomiting my guts all over your scribed floor?"

"To be the High Mistress. To be with this great man who has chosen *you* above all others."

I laugh, low and hollow, staring at the tiny words etched in the stone, illuminated by a beam of light pouring through a hole in the ceiling.

... twist and sow

Smother her while she sleeps or catch the lethal grace.

My stomach knots on a retch that rips my throat, leaving the taste of blood thick on my tongue.

"This is a waste of time," I grind out. "My worth shouldn't be defined by my ability to climb out of a stupid pool."

"Bowl," he corrects, and I snarl, another dry heave cramping my guts. "And whether you agree with it or not is of no consequence. This is the way things are done. May I suggest you pour less energy into complaining about one of our greatest traditions and more into conformity."

The words burn more than the slur of bile scalding the back of my throat.

Conformity.

I bunch my hands into fists, force my knees up under myself, and push to my feet—standing before Elder Creed on legs that can barely hold my weight. Behind him, the electric eels twist and turn, bumping against their glass cage.

His head tilts to the side, face a shadowed hollow I'm forced to sketch from my imagination. "Do you have something you'd like to say, Mistress?"

So many things.

Too many things.

The entrance doors open, and Cainon appears at the top of the stairs, arms folded, looking down on us.

I swallow the words. Pack them somewhere deep and dark.

"No," I mutter, turning toward The Bowl, easing my shoulder into a stretch as I prepare to leap back in again. "No, I don't."

I set the blade on the pad of my finger and give it a flick, feeling the sharp tip pierce my skin as it spins. A bulb of blood dribbles free ...

I close my eyes and picture feeding it into that crystal goblet.

Setting it in The Safe.

Listening to *him* scale the stairs. Open the tiny wicket door. Close it.

A full-body shiver scrapes across my skin, and I suck on the wound, open my eyes, look at the door to my suite ... mind dragging back to the way he pressed against me.

To his words—a cold grate against my ear—poised to strike that raw, vulnerable part of me I'm trying so hard to hide.

But there is no door between us anymore. He made that perfectly clear last night.

There's nothing for me to cower behind. To shield myself with.

Snarling, I fling the blade toward the door. At the same moment, it swings open, and Kolden and a woman I've never met before barely dodge the whistling weapon.

I gasp, heart hammering as it thuds into the lobby wall behind them.

Both sets of eyes sway from the wobbling dagger to me—cross-legged on the bed, hand cupping my mouth.

"I ... ahh ... apologies. That was *very* poor timing."

"I did knock, Mistress ... then got worried when you didn't answer."

I wince, looking at Kolden.

Didn't hear a thing.

"So sorry ... maybe a little louder next time?"

The woman smiles—a bright, confident embellishment to her exotic beauty.

Young with golden skin, her honey hair is pushed back over her shoulders, eyes a dark shade of purple with a burst of blue rimming the pupil. She's *stunning*, swathed in a blue silk dress with gold trim—modest, yet clinging to all her shapely curves.

She looks me up and down with a sweep of heavily lashed eyes. "I like you."

The woman steps back into the lobby, grips my blade, and yanks it free.

"Who are you?" I call after her.

She turns to Kolden and says, "Thanks. I'll take it from here," before closing the door on his startled face. "Happy to be alive," she chimes with a wink, gliding into the room and handing me the dagger. Hilt first.

I think I like her, too.

"Name's Gael." She sits beside me on the bed and grabs the end of my heavy, sodden braid still dripping down the front of my shirt from my early morning stab at The Bowl, removing the band and untangling the plait with deft fingers. "Mother received a sprite from the High Master instructing me to come to the palace and give you a tour of the city. My family owns a monopoly of trade ships that we use to import glass blocks from the outskirts of Arrin, so I know my way around." She stands and invites herself deeper into my suite, opening my dressing room door before disappearing into the bowels of it. "There's a carriage waiting out front. Oh! I like this dress!"

My brows almost jump off my face. "*There is?*"

"Mm-hmm."

I leap to my feet and sprint across the room, pulling the balcony doors wide and dashing outside, peering over the balustrade.

Sure enough, there's a gold-brushed carriage in the courtyard below, strung to a pair of white horses pawing puddles from last night's rain.

Nice to see Cainon stuck to our deal.

A burst of anticipation electrifies my veins, and my grip on the handrail tightens.

I might find Madame Strings today.

Gael emerges onto the balcony with a frilly gown draped over each arm. "Blue or blue? Personally, I like the blue."

Internally, I wince.

I've grown somewhat comfortable in this long, simple skirt with an equally simple shirt tucked into the waistband.

It's a far stretch from my preferred shirt and pants, but it's better than her dazzling, primped, and fluffed proposal.

"Neither. I'll just wear a cloak over what I'm wearing."

Her eyes nearly bug out of her head. "Absolutely not! I'm under strict instructions to pamper you. And that's exactly what I'll do."

"Instructions from ... Cainon?" I ask, trying to get a gauge on where her loyalties lie. How closely bound she is to the man who seems intent on *only* letting me see the city from the back of a carriage today.

She rolls her eyes. "Okay, I lied. I just want to dress you up. You have so many pretty dresses, and I've never had a sister. Humor me," she pleads, extending a garment in my direction.

I chew the inside of my mouth.

Unfortunately for me, stamping down her excitement is no means to weasel my way into ditching the carriage.

"Fine," I mutter, taking the dress.

She squeals and claps her hands as I stalk into my suite.

Glancing over my shoulder to see her looking out upon the city, I snatch my dagger off the bed and ease my vanity drawer open, pulling out a strip of material I tore off the end of my bedsheet this morning. Moving into the bathing chamber, I top up the water in my propagation jars stashed along the windowsill, then undress, strapping the blade to the outside of my upper thigh with the length of material. Another quiet *fuck you* to Rhordyn and his unwanted gift that I can't bring myself to toss away.

I step into the dress, pull it up, and fumble with the unfamiliar clutches down the back, twisting and turning to see in the mirror. After a few minutes of me muttering curses, Gael knocks on the door.

"Need help?"

I gladly accept, trying not to fidget as she pushes my hair to the side and buttons the many eyes and loops that line the length of my spine.

"So ... I heard the Ocruth High Master kept you locked in a tower, and that he feeds his people to the Vruk."

I choke on my breath. "You're—"

"Dazzling? Charismatic? Impeccably styled?"

"A straight shooter."

She shrugs. "You have to be to survive the tiers of our society."

A few more buttons, and the dress gets tighter, clinging to my curves in that way I hate.

"He offered me refuge," I finally say. "And as far as I'm aware, he does *not* feed his people to the Vruks. Though I could be wrong."

"So you lived there all these years but you barely know him?"

Something inside me arches up.

Is she trying to get information out of me? Perhaps she's been commissioned to report back to Cainon ...

I shake my head. "I barely saw him until I came of age. Then he began trying to shove me out the door. And here I am," I say, flashing her a hollow smile. "Successfully shoved."

She scrunches her nose—a look that suggests that's nowhere near as juicy as she thought it was going to be. "Well, it looks like you landed on your feet."

I drop my gaze, heavy with the knowledge that I'm

not on my feet at all—that I'm floating in an angry ocean, powerless to the push of the storm that won't stop lashing at me. That I drowned that day in Puddles, and every breath I've pulled since has failed to drag me back to the world of the living.

That every day I fail to pull myself out of The Bowl, my heart and soul decompose just a little bit more.

"Yes, I'm very lucky."

Fastening the final loop, she scoops my hair into her hand and drags a wide-tooth comb through the wet length.

Her eyes widen, fingertips brushing the back of my arm. "This looks really sore ..."

I slap my hand over the spot, catching her hardened stare in the mirror. "It's nothing."

"Did somebody do this to you, Orlaith?"

"No," I bite out, equal parts denial and an omission of the ugly truth.

I did it.

I hate the way pity stains her eyes when she looks at me.

She offers me a sad smile. "You don't trust me ..."

"I don't trust many people," I admit. "Certainly not people I just met."

She nods, glancing at my arm again. "I value the honesty. Especially in a world where lies are used as currency."

A token of useful information I pocket for later.

She seems to deliberate, chewing on her bottom lip before she closes my washroom door and leans against it, stare dropped to the floor. After a few deep breaths, she looks at me, that vivacious sparkle gone from her eyes.

Frowning, I turn, leaning against the vanity with my arms crossed over my chest.

"When I was sixteen, I met a boy. He worked at the docks, and from the moment our eyes met, we just ... fell into each other so effortlessly," she says, tucking a fallen curl behind her ear. "I snuck him into my room and gave myself to him—because I *wanted* to." A brief pause, and she swallows, dropping her stare to the ground again. "One of my guards found out, told Mother, and I never saw him again. Anywhere. Like he just disappeared off the face of the continent."

My heart plummets.

"Apparently, he wasn't *good enough*. Really, Mother had plans to couple me off with someone who would knot advantageous ties for the family line—someone who shared her chosen faith in the hopes that it would coax me into their religious fold—and my *discrepancies* ruined everything because of their rigid beliefs that women must remain chaste until they're coupled."

"Gael ..."

She shrugs. "Mother dragged me to the Elder to atone, and I was told that I must take twenty lashings to purify my body." She pulls her hair over her shoulder and turns.

My eyes widen at the tapered tips of risen scars scribbled across her back. I step forward, brushing my fingers across them, feeling their knobbed tracks. "That's—"

"Messed up. I know," she says, looking at me over her shoulder. "And to really top it all off, I was told to *never* voice my *impurities*. To anyone. Because if word got out, I would bring shame upon my family."

"I won't tell anyone," I assure her quickly.

"Neither will I," she says, turning, nodding at my arm and giving me a half smile. "Now that you hold my greatest secret in the palm of your hand, I can cover the bruise if you'd like?"

"You can?"

She nods, then starts opening and closing drawers. "There's sure to be a tinted cream amongst all these cosmetics ... Aha!" She holds up a small compact, then flips the lid and dabs its contents upon my skin with a sponge, blowing it dry before applying a second layer. "There," she says, leaning back to inspect her handiwork. "Can't see a thing."

"Thank you ..."

She smiles and turns her attention to my hair, pinning sections into a half-updo with gold clips, then spins me by my shoulders, head tilting to the side. "Some kohl, perhaps? You've got such beautiful eyes. I could really make them pop."

I shake my head and she sighs, coiling one of the strands left loose around my face with her pointer finger. "Well, you look beautiful without it."

Frowning, I glance down at myself—the bodice cinching my curves all the way to mid-thigh, where it spills out in a burst of silky ribbons.

"You're displeased ..."

I pluck up a tendril, letting it breeze back to the floor.

"It's just ... there's a reason I was hoping to go with something simpler."

"Oh?"

I nod, tugging at my bottom lip with my teeth.

"There's only so much of the city I can see from the back of a carriage. I was hoping to get a more ... *in-depth feel* for the city." I peek up at her from beneath my lashes, shrugging. "If you know what I mean."

Realization widens her eyes before a smooth smile brightens her face—dazzling and full of mischief. "I *knew* I liked you."

From my spot close to the sheer curtain covering the window, I watch tawny-haired children dash into the streets, leaping up and down and throwing flower petals as our carriage clatters along—an insatiable attention magnet that dredges up a fresh swell of onlookers with every turn we take.

Faces appear through the small gap in the curtain, eyes bright with expectation. I cringe at their attention, hugging the corner of my seat.

With two guards sitting behind the driver's box, two on the rear boot, and Kolden following behind us on horseback, we're *drowning* in guards.

"I'm nervous," I murmur, breathing deeply to loosen my tight lungs.

"Don't be." Gael peeks out the window. "I reckon we've been out long enough. We've circled past all the major social spots, so the geese will gaggle about seeing the carriage." She shifts seats, sliding a little latch at the front of the cab and dishing the driver a bunch of directions that make no sense to me.

"That worked?" I ask when she sits back down.

"I can be *very* persuasive," she tells me, waggling her brows. "This should buy us a few hours of freedom."

"So ... what are we going to do?"

She brushes a piece of long hair back over her shoulder—something I've noticed she does a lot. "What do you *want* to do?"

"Are there any markets today?"

"I don't think so, no." She frowns, tapping her finger to her lips. "No, just the night ones in the market square. There's a monthly one on the esplanade that runs during the day, but that's not until next week."

My heart drops in synchrony with my shoulders.

Damn.

"In that case, I have no idea ..."

"Well, what do you *want* to do? For you?"

"For *me?*"

"Yes. What does your *heart* want?"

To not care for a bit.

To let go.

I look at my hands for a long moment, up again. "Freedom," I whisper, the word my own horrific secret offered to her in place of her own.

She gives me a soft, knowing smile and nods. "Then I have *just* the place."

The horse that was trailing behind us canters forth, and Kolden hollers for the crowd to thin. The carriage begins to roll faster, bumping around so much I have to grip hold of the handrail.

Restless rebellion wrestles in my chest as we take turn after turn, moving into the shadow of the wall, then along the side of the river, allowing me a broad view of the rippled stretch of water. Of small piers that house clusters of rowboats and the odd larger ships with various shades of sail.

I look out the window, see a big, ornate gate being swung open—access to what appears to be an opulent community.

We trundle across polished cobblestones, past manicured gardens hosting large, bejeweled homes with windows mosaiced in slivers of bright color, their pitched roofs capped with gold shingles. The air turns salty as we finally slow, edging toward the sea sparkling in the distance, pulling up beside a large house bearing so many windows it's more glass than stone.

I look at Gael. "Your home?"

"Sure is. I told the driver we're going inside for a three-course lunch followed by a tour of my mother's renowned art collection," she says in a pompous voice that makes me laugh. "He ate it right up. This is the best part of town with a nonexistent crime rate, so they'll probably find a tree to nap under."

"You're a genius," I say, grabbing my bag as the door opens.

The footman concedes a step and offers me his gloved hand. "Mistress."

I step out in a gush of blue fabric that spills across the cobbles and tip my face to the sun, drinking in the scent of freedom.

Smiling, Gael takes my hand and leads me past our stoic entourage through a garden gate, into a courtyard framed with a variety of citrus trees that pinch the air with their zesty scent. Lifting a rock from a tailored garden bed, she plucks a key from the mulch and uses it to unlock the simple, blue door.

"Back entrance," she whispers, rolling her eyes. "Don't want the servants to see. They're such incorrigible gossips."

We step into a bright hallway, the floor paved in gray marble to match the stone walls. Not what I was expecting, considering the outside is the classic blue stone of most Bahari homes.

"I've lived here forever," Gael says, closing the door behind us, then walking ahead. "Papa died when I was six. Mother refuses to leave. This house hasn't changed a bit since then." She looks at me over her shoulder, the train of her silky dress dragging along the floor. "Guess you know how it feels. To lose someone, I mean."

The words hit like a physical blow to the chest, and something inside me withers.

I didn't lose anything that wasn't my own fault.

"I was a lot younger than you." I offer her a soft smile. "I don't remember much."

Lie ...

I remember it all.

The deadly wrath that boiled up until my spine curled back, grubbing cracks in my skin that felt like split seams.

I remember the screams and the silence that swiftly followed.

I remember looking around and wondering where my mommy was—that's when my heart got really scared.

I wish I could erase it all again, but I can't.

It's stuck with me. My penance for taking all those lives.

My *mother's*—

"Sometimes, I wish I could forget," Gael says, leading us through another door and down a curling set of stairs, the air growing colder the deeper we walk. "Make Mother forget, too. She spends so much time and resources trying to liberate his death that everything else pales in significance. In a way, I became an orphan that day, invisible as I am."

My heart flops at the thought of Gael growing up in this big house with everything to give and nobody willing to *take*.

"I'm so sorry, Gael ..."

"No, I'm sorry." She laughs, the sound hollow as she steps off the stairs and into another hall. "Poor little rich girl, complaining about her plush life. Stupid, I know."

She offers me a smile that doesn't reach her eyes, and ushers me through a doorway, turning the dial on a large lantern, shedding light on an impressively stocked wine cellar.

"Wow ..." Kicking off the ornamental shoes that were giving me blisters and making my feet sweat, I spin, scanning it all with wide-eyed wonder.

Baze would have a field day in here.

Reaching onto her tippy toes, Gael plucks a bottle from the top shelf, blowing some dust off the black and white label. "This looks expensive," she mutters, retrieving a corkscrew from behind a barrel and digging it into the stopper.

I drop my bag to the floor and crouch, pulling out my change of clothes.

She takes a long swig, wiping her lips with the back of her arm as she offers me the wine, hissing out a breath. "Yup," she croaks. "That's the good stuff."

"Have you done this before?" I ask, taking it from her.

She flashes me a bright smile. "I'm well versed in the art of running from my problems."

"Well, that's something I can toast to." I tip the bottle to my lips and draw deep, wincing from the way the sharp liquid pinches the back of my throat.

Gael gets to work on my dress, easing me out of the suffocating bodice in breath-giving increments as we share the wine back and forth until my back feels free and bare.

"I'll be back," she says, taking another swig before handing me the bottle and gathering her skirts. "Going to sneak to my room on the fourth floor and find something else to wear while you get changed."

Stepping out of the dress, I rip one of the long skirt panels free and use it to bind my breasts, then pull on the pair of brown leather pants and the blue shirt I bought at the market. Twisting my hair into a low knot, I pin it close to my nape.

I'm tugging my cap down over my head, my belly warm and fuzzy as Gael walks back in the room wearing a simple hooded cloak that's a rich shade of azure, her cascade of hair tucked away from view.

"Amazing," she gasps, taking me in through wide eyes as she closes the door behind herself, two black masks hanging from her other hand.

I tuck some loose strands of hair into my cap. "What is?"

"You look like a boy. A pretty one, but a boy nonetheless. Nobody will ever suspect."

A smile tips the corner of my mouth.

She tucks the masks in my bag, and I frown, passing her what's left of the wine. "What are they for?"

"You'll see," she says, throwing me a wink. "We're going

to the place I frequent when I want to be free. You'll love it, I promise."

I stuff my bag with the rest of my things while she polishes off the bottle, then fiddle with the latch of my cupla, trying to pry it open.

Gael pauses mid-draw, dropping the bottle from her lips. "I don't think you're meant to do that ..."

"I'm the only one with a lapis lazuli cupla. It could give me away."

She chews on her bottom lip. "I don't know ... are you sure?"

"It's fine." I battle the clasp, yanking it. "This isn't the first time I've taken it off. It just clips right back on again."

"What if—"

It comes away at once, a piece of the gold clasp clattering on the stone floor between us.

We look down at the lump of gold, and I break out in a cold sweat.

"Shit." I slip the cupla from my wrist and study the broken clasp dangling from it. "I thought these things weren't supposed to break."

"They're not," Gael whispers, and I look up into her wide, fearful eyes. "It's a bad omen if they do. Really, really bad."

"I'll fix it," I murmur, stuffing it in my bag. "He'll never know."

But even as the words tumble past my lips, the echo of hers weave their hands around my throat ...

Bad omen.

Chapter 41
Orlaith

We enter a tunnel, its entrance hidden behind an empty barrel in the cellar, the exit popping us out along the rocky shoreline beyond the community's gates. Following the waterfront, we come to the esplanade.

Gael leads us along the bustling streets, through the vibrant, colorful part of town, turning down side alleys that are increasingly quiet, until the lights appear dimmer, the buildings less towering. The deeper we delve, the rougher it becomes; the tighter the streets, the more solemn the atmosphere, and the more people's stares have begun to stick to the ground rather than ahead of themselves. Men smoke pipes under the shade of weather-worn awnings, women scrub their washing in wooden barrels right in the middle of the street, and kids wear clothes patched up with all different shades of blue, their laughter not as free and wild as the kids' who live closer to the ocean.

We pass into the shadow of the wall, so tall I have

to crane my neck to see the massive turrets dotted along the top that always ignite an hour before the sun goes down and blaze through the night. The mighty barrier that protects the city against the nest of Irilak that apparently dwells in the surrounding jungle.

I jog to catch up with Gael, so busy looking around I'd fallen behind. "Where are we going?"

"You'll see." She tugs her hood further around her face. "Most people who live in the shadow of the wall are strapped for coin. It's cramped and damp and riddled with mold, but it's rich with *secrets*."

A flutter hits my heart.

I like secrets.

I follow her around a sharp turn into a narrow alley. A web of strings crisscross overhead, laden with dripping clothes and bedsheets. I dodge the puddles, watching the fluttery train of Gael's cloak grow more sodden by the second. "And how did you learn about these secrets?"

She pauses, stepping closer to dig through my knapsack, then pulling out the masks and handing one to me. "I used to sneak out at night and explore the city. It's a different world when the sun's down. More *thrilling*."

I smile at the spike of rapture in her voice, feeling it infuse me with a bout of excitement that makes my heart race.

She sets her mask on her face—like coating the upper half in a lick of blue paint—and I follow suit. She leads me into a tighter alley that slopes into a shadowed staircase tunneled through the earth. "And then one night, just shy of my nineteenth birthday, I stumbled upon *this* place ..."

She raps her knuckles on the worn, blue door at the

bottom of the stairs: three rapid knocks, two slow, three rapid again.

I plant my hip against the wall and cross my arms. "You're not going to murder me, are you?"

She leans back, inspecting her nails. "After seeing you almost decapitate your guard and considering you have a blade strapped to your right thigh, I don't think I'll risk it."

Well then.

"Good eyes."

She shrugs. "In this city, it pays to be observant. Literally." She chuffs a humorless laugh. "I think it's the only important thing Mother ever taught me. A lesson that's saved my rebellious ass more than once. Parith can be merciless if you don't know it well enough."

"Actually, there's something I've been meaning to ask, seeing how familiar you are with the city …"

She lifts a brow.

"You don't know where I might find a woman named Madame Strings?"

She makes a face like she just smelled something sour. "I've seen her around. She creeps me out. What do you want from her?"

"I have questions. I heard she knows a lot of … *things*."

"That's true." A small pause, then, "Is that why you wanted to go to the markets?"

I nod, and understanding dawns in her eyes.

"I'm sorry I can't help …"

"Nothing to be sorry about," I tell her, and the door creaks open, spitting out a stout man with sharp eyes and a fuzzy beard that smothers half his gruff face, the other half covered by a mask much the same as ours.

They give each other curt nods before Gael grabs my hand and leads me through the doorway. Down a tight spiral of stairs, we shoot out into a long, damp cave that seems to go on forever—lit by strings of small, circular lanterns hanging from the roof. A low throbbing pumps through the ground, like a heart sits beneath the bare soles of my feet, the beat growing deeper.

Deeper.

The walls become clothed in vines, and I run my fingers over their velvet branches, feel the same dramatic beat thumping through. The rich, salty tang of sweat knocks me in the back of the throat, accompanied by the sweet, floral nectar I recently grew far too familiar with.

The rich bouquet of wanton *need*.

My head spins, the smell so intoxicating, it alleviates the weight of my body. Makes my breath speed up and my nipples pinch painfully beneath their crushing bind.

"What is this place?" I ask close to Gael's ear as we reach a curl in the cave, the stone softening with a coat of spongy moss my feet sink into.

She throws me a cunning smile over her shoulder. "A forest nymph lair." We step up to a thick fall of vines that bar the way. "Clutch thy pearls, High Mistress ..."

My heart rate accelerates as Gael pierces her hands between the natural curtain and cleaves an open path for us.

Sound explodes—the drumming thud hacking through me with such force I'm sure it rattles my bones.

I step forward, looking down from a mezzanine carved into the stone, out across a huge cavern strung with a web of lanterns that drape the space in a soft, golden glow.

A small waterfall at the far side pours into a pool, then

streams through the center of the space. Trees heavy with clusters of bold red fruit twist up from the mossy ground; a strange sight in an underground cavern. A statuesque trio of red-haired drummers draped in loose clothing sit on stools atop a large, flat stone that sets them higher than the gyrating crowd.

There must be over two hundred men and women—heavy lidded, most sparsely dressed, others wearing nothing but masks and the erotic confidence of their utter bareness as they move to the beat like a throbbing heart. The raw smell of sex is heavy in the air, making my skin tingle with a disarming warmth.

I swallow thickly, taking in the scene with damning intrigue.

"During their heat, women drink tonics that keep them barren," Gael yells over the pounding racket, unclipping the clasp of her cloak. "Then, they come here and fuck whoever—*whatever*—they want until the blaze dims."

My eyes widen. "*Whatever?*"

"I took a nymph once," she says dreamily. "They're very elusive, and often appear the same as everyone else, but I assure you, they're *not.*"

My cheeks heat, her implication striking a rebellious ember low in my belly. Or perhaps that's just the beat. The smells. The masks. The moss beneath my feet.

She shrugs off her cloak, revealing a strappy garment made from golden material that sculpts the curves of her body like strokes of paint, and I envy her for the ability to strip down and bare herself so beautifully.

Confidently.

"Some people come here to feel the beat and let loose

and just *enjoy* themselves ... and then there's those who simply want to screw," she purrs with a wink, ripping one of the plump, red fruits from the net of vines woven across the wall that seem to sprout from the stone, the colorful bangles caught around her wrist tinkling against each other.

"What sort of fruit is that?"

"Not the sort for you." Her tone is less playful now. "The forest nymphs grow these. They heat your blood and drug you with reckless desire."

The words thud through me like blazing arrows.

"The *last* thing you need right now. Women have been labeled witches and burned at the stake for breaking their seals in the lead up to their coupling ceremonies."

"*What?*"

A nod. "Less so recently, but ..." she shrugs, waving at my bag, "For some, the moment you accept a cupla, your body no longer belongs to you."

Heart in my throat, I stare at her, chewing her words from all angles.

She takes a deep bite of the fleshy fruit, red juice dribbling down her chin while Cainon's words ring loud in my ears ...

So, if I took you right here, right now, you'd bleed for me?

They made my blood crackle then.

They make it *sizzle* now.

Gael moves toward the stairs carved into the wall. "You coming?"

I draw a deep breath that does nothing to shift this suffocating lump that's sitting on my chest. "I'll be down soon."

She frowns. "I haven't scared you, have I? We can go if you'd like."

I shake my head. "It's fine. I want to stay. I just—I need a moment."

"Okay." She smiles, her eyes starting to twinkle over with a lusty haze as she takes another deep bite and speaks through her mouthful. "I'll be near the waterfall. There's usually a few familiar masked faces there I enjoy the company of," she says with a wink. "Just make your way down when you're ready. No pressure."

I watch her descend the stairs from the quiet mezzanine. Watch her embrace a masked woman baring a short pixie cut. They share a deep, tender kiss before Gael weaves their hands together and leads the woman into the charged beat, disappearing from my line of sight.

I step back and lower to the floor, spine planted against the vine-smothered wall.

The moment you accept a cupla, your body no longer belongs to you.

I gouge my fingers through the fluffy moss and into the cool soil beneath, pretending they're roots of a tree digging into the calming earth. But it barely takes the edge off this claustrophobic pressure I'm being crushed beneath by the echo of Gael's words.

I shouldn't be here.

If I got caught in a place like this by the wrong person, the consequences would be catastrophic. That much is clear. A thought that shouldn't spike my blood with a bolt of thrill that electrifies me from the inside out.

Women have been labeled witches and burned at the

stake for breaking their seals in the lead up to their coupling ceremonies.

I scoff, shaking my head, wondering how many of those women felt the same as me—like they'd sold their body, not their soul; like the white sheets they slept in felt like a cage they were doomed to wither between.

Promising yourself to another shouldn't mean you *lose yourself in the process.*

The cavern's vibrations thump through me as I feed the rich, botanical smells into my lungs, feeling my body erupt with thick, pulsing *life.*

A ball of laughter bursts up my throat.

I didn't leave my Safety Line to be forced into another box. To be owned by a man who doesn't even know me.

I told Cainon I'd be his perfect High Mistress, and I will. But I'm not *his* yet.

I'm still *mine.*

And right now ... I want to dance.

I shove up, looking down upon the dimly lit crowd lost in their own erotic splendor, their features half hidden by their masks. All I can see is a wash of bare, thudding movement and tangled limbs. I run my fingers along the edge of the soft material melding to my features.

Nobody's going to recognize me.

Another giddy surge strikes, and I whip off my cap, unpin my hair, and let it fall, heavy and free. I stuff the pin and cap in my bag, then tuck it behind a dense patch of vines before descending the stairs, bare feet padding across the mossy ground as I inject myself into the throng, heading in the direction of the waterfall.

Sweat-slicked bodies push and slide against me, glassy-eyed people feeding each other those plump, red fruits while they grope and grind and sway.

I'm nobody—*nothing*. Just a body in a swarm of carnal movement that has no rhyme or reason.

My steps begin to slow, and I stop pushing forward, charmed by the drum's rousing beat. Surrounded by the gorging pulse, my body sways, fueled by wild, reckless abandon that lightens my limbs and heats my blood.

My head tips back, hips and shoulders loosening, pelvis swaying, my hair a messy tangle as I shift like tiding water. But the band around my chest is too tight. Pinching me and constricting my arms. Controlling my breaths.

I'm sick of control.

I weave my hand beneath my shirt and rip at the tail end of the wrap flattening my curves, unraveling myself with fierce, frustrated fingers, breathing an intoxicating sigh of relief when the fabric falls at my feet. Hands threading through my loose hair, my heavy breasts bounce with the rhythmic pulse of my motions, throat aching as emotion wells up—and I let go.

For the first time in my life, I truly *let go.*

Free.

I lose all sense of time and self. There is only the beat. The moss cushioned between my toes. The rich smells heaping into my parched lungs.

When a hand slides around my front and makes my skin prickle, body lining up with my back, my movements come to a crashing halt.

"You're *magnificent*," an unfamiliar voice whispers against my ear—deep and rusty.

I look over my shoulder into pale blue eyes that hold a

lusty glint. See short, golden hair and a young, handsome half-face, his dimpled smile beguiling, accentuated by a scar that curves from the corner of his mouth and up beneath his mask.

"Thank you ..."

My heartbeat and the drums gallop along in synchrony ...

Boom.

Patter-patter.

Boom.

Patter-patter.

Boom.

"I didn't frighten you, did I?"

I lift my chin. "No, this is actually perfect."

I don't step away from him when he times his movements to match mine. When his strong arms weave around my front. Instead, I let myself enjoy the closeness of having a body surge to *my* beat for a change, with not a thought in my head but the next roll of my hips.

When his lips brush the side of my neck, I tip my head and give him better access, letting him lave at me like it means something.

Like *we* mean something.

I turn, take in his tall, broad physique, his face flushed with a roguish grin and eyes stained with cosmic lust.

A bloom of something beautifully selfish sparks low in my belly—an ember throbbing to life. And I don't want it to dim. I don't want to douse it in thoughts of what's right and wrong and what's *expected* of me. I don't want to think about what I've promised. Who I *owe* myself to.

I certainly don't want to think about the hideous

consequences of this rebellious thought I'm suddenly transfixed with.

My heart smashes a brand-new rhythm when I realize I want this. To take back the power I've lost over my body simply because two powerful men can't play nicely with each other.

For once in my life—for this tiny, selfish moment—I want to bleed for *myself*.

His eyes widen in shock as I grab his hand and pull him through the crowd, leading him past fruit-laden trees and mossy boulders, across the gurgling stream and into a shadowed nose of the cave, its low ceiling riddled with glowing stalactites.

Turning, I fist his shirt and pull him forward, taking his mouth in a desperate kiss that first makes him pause before his deep moan pours into me.

I rip at his shirt buttons, slide my hands beneath the fabric, palms skating over lean muscles as I shove the shirt off his shoulders.

"Slow down," he mumbles against my mouth.

I undo my own buttons with the same frantic voracity. "I don't want slow," I bite out, ripping it away, my bare skin licked by swirling humidity.

I just want to be free.

His hands cup my naked breasts. "Fucking hell."

I eat up his words with a kiss that swallows his resonating moan, taking him by the wrist and threading his hand down the flat of my stomach.

"My Gods," he grates, flicking the buttons on my waistband.

Weaving beneath my panties, his fingers delve through

me, coaxing that delicious throb as I grind against him, forcing them deeper.

Deeper ...

"I need more," I murmur, hands slamming back to tangle with the vines cushioning the walls. He pulls my pants and underwear down my legs. Pauses when his fingers brush over my blade.

"What's th—"

"Leave it," I gasp, and he plants a kiss against my leg, murmuring something about being full of surprises as my pants are tossed aside—more kisses peppered up the inside of my widening thighs.

I grip his hair and yank his head back seconds before his mouth can make contact with *that* part of me, because that feels too intimate.

Too personal.

I don't want him to taste me. I want him to *break* me.

He straightens, and our mouths collide again, his hands spearing down between us as he rips at his pants, his movements becoming frantic when he releases himself, his solid length pressed against my belly.

Fuck.

My heart gallops as he grabs my leg, takes its weight, and widens me—*parts* me—the blunt head of his manhood nudging at my tight, uncharted entrance.

Every muscle in my body locks, lungs seizing.

I look up, focus on the glowing stalactites littered across the ceiling, and remind myself to breathe.

Grabbing his ass, I urge him on ... then stifle a scream when he punches his hips forward and splits me open.

CHAPTER 42
Rhordyn

I run along the muddy bank, the river growing frailer with every sweeping turn it weaves between the trees. Peering through my hair hanging over my eyes, I spot the first sign I'm getting close: A tall, glass tree weeping toward the ground—a taste of the blast that punched down from the sky and all but eliminated the entire toxic race of Unseelie, freezing the Central Territory of Arrin in a vitreous eternity. Veins from the blast even crackled and stretched their jagged fingers into the outskirts of Bahari, Rouse, and Ocruth.

Everything it touched, it destroyed.

Arrin is now a time capsule that bears all its bruises for those brave enough to venture into the glassy graveyard, though not many dare. There is no vegetation. Nothing but clear dunes and a harsh wind that slowly sands the desolation into a fine, white powder that gets in your ears and eyes and mouth, making it hard to breathe.

But on the outskirts, miners carve out a living from the solid corpse of dunes, and transparent forests and jungles provide unshadowed refuge for people too afraid to rely on lantern light to keep them safe from the Irilak. Lorn is one such village caught on the fault line between dead and alive, glass and soil. It sits on the prominent point of the thinnest elbow of the River Norse, cradled by its tight curl that's tricky for larger ships to maneuver through.

I keep running until the lush, fertile jungle turns crystalline and cold despite the bold blades of sun striking the see-through canopy and the clusters of buildings, shrubs, and stones. Jagged glass veins stretch across the soil and up into the trees. Covering small cottages. Tempering horses—some with their heads bent, grazing on blades of grass caught in a lucent eternity they'll never grow out of.

I know I'm too late by the harsh reek upon the air. By the vaporous huddle of Irilak flitting excitedly, collecting in heavy pockets of shade that pour off thick patches of untarnished jungle.

I don't pay them any heed as I slow my pace and crouch behind a bush. Fist tight around my stolen spear, I watch a large Vruk grub the soil with its stubby nose just shy of the glassy fault line, cast in a large, timely shard of sun that fends off the Irilak nesting in the wing.

Talons punch free from its paw and it slashes, *slashes*—like a cat toying with its food. Wood rattles, muffled screams howling from beneath the ground ...

A bunker.

Before a glass barn that's splashed in blood, another Vruk is hunched over a messy lump of flesh, head to the side as it crunches through its meal.

Bones pop. Snap.

Splinter.

Someone screams in the distance, the sound swiftly stifled by a fetid roar that makes the hairs on my arms lift.

I crack my neck from side to side.

Three. At least.

Movement draws my eye to yellow liquid trickling down the side of a trunk not far from me, pinching the air with the distinct waft of urine. My gaze climbs up into the fragile canopy to a little boy with straw-colored hair and tear-stained cheeks, blue eyes locked on me, knobby knees barely keeping him wrapped around the branch he's clinging to.

A wobbled sound spills from his trembling lips, and I lift my finger to my mouth.

He nods, burying his face into his arm.

I inch onto the glass terrain and crouch in a blade of sun, set my spear down, then slide my dagger from its sheath—its wooden hilt cold in my clenched fist as I stake the weapon into the ground.

Drag it sideways.

A shrill scratching sound ratchets through the air, making my teeth grind.

The beast digging at the bunker whips its head in my direction, bits of the splintered trapdoor caught in its wide maw, those black eyes stabbing at me. Blowing puffs of steam from its flared nostrils, it tosses the wood aside and roars, charging, rattling the ground with its thundering approach that lures the attention of the other Vruk feasting by the barn.

I draw my sword and focus on the one closest, holding my ground until the moment I feel its pungent breath blow against my face—raising my arms and slamming the long weapon deep into the glass beneath my feet.

The sharp tip screeches through the layers.

I leap back, watching recognition flash across the animal's feral face.

It falters, paws slipping out from under it as it skates across the smooth surface, bared chest colliding with the lethal blade.

Curdled yelps squeal out of the beast as its body swallows the weapon, fur and flesh and bone giving way to its honed edge. Blood gushes from the fatal blow, every breath a labored howl until the creature falls limp, tongue lolling from its gaping maw.

There's a sharp popping sound, then another, and *another*.

I step back from my blade, watching a fracture weave through the glass—up the trunk of the tree the boy is hiding in.

The branch he's clinging to cracks, and he screams, his meager grip jostled.

He plummets, and I leap, snatching him with a swoop of my arm before he can strike the ground. I tuck him close to my chest and jump over the slain beast, slam my dagger into its sheath, and put my back to the two Vruk still thundering toward us, lifting the boy high and shoving him into another tree. "*Climb!*"

Sobbing, he clambers up, weaving his frail body between the brittle foliage once vibrant with life.

I stalk toward my spear—

Something plucks at that tender string in my chest—the

slightest twinge that makes my step falter, eyes whipping south. A wildness scratches at my skin.

I search the trees as though I'm searching for *her* face. Her eyes.

The ground continues to thunder beneath my feet, but I barely notice as that feeling flatlines like a snapped stem, leaving a hollow, senseless void I fill with murderous *rage*.

Roaring, I sweep my spear off the ground, spin, and crank my arm, looking at the howling creature galloping toward me. I swing my body forward and hurl the honed weapon into the air, impaling the Vruk straight through its wide-open maw.

Its legs crumble beneath its might, and it tips, colliding with the brittle trunk of a glass tree that shatters from the force, spilling across the ground with a violence that's deafening.

Gripping the hilt of my sword, I rip it free from the corpse wrapped around its length, pulling my dagger from its sheath with my other hand and flinging it through the air. It *whumps* deep into the eyeball of the third beast as I charge forward, boots crunching on the scattered shards. I wrap both hands around the hilt of my sword and cut it straight through the Vruk's meaty neck with such feral force, I cleave it from the body.

It thuds to the ground in a shower of pulsing blood.

Silence.

I stop, heaving breath into my parched lungs, shoulders loosening, tipping my head and looking up through crystal clear leaves to the blue sky above.

Breathe.

I thread my hand over my chest, right atop that warm pouch of *her*, and beg for something other than *silence*.

The silence is the worst.

Forcing my muscles back into action, I scan the bloody scene, gore dripping off my face, hands, and sword.

The Irilak nesting in the shade are practically vibrating, making sharp clicking sounds, growing bold and edging closer to the light, perhaps waiting for a cloud to blot out the sun so they can feast.

I look up at the little boy, his cheeks sapped of color.

"You okay? Anything hurt?"

He doesn't blink. Doesn't speak. Just looks at me like I'm worse than the monsters I just slaughtered.

"*Row! Faster! Faster!*"

The belted command has my head whipping around, looking through glass trees splattered with blood.

A small, north-bound barge strung with lanterns pushes out of the gloomy jungle, drifting into the sunlight spilling through the crystalline canopy as it edges toward the tight elbow that weaves around the village. The numerous oars poking through the ship's hull pull in erratic chaos.

A blur of movement catches my eye—a large, dark Vruk bursting toward the ship in long, powerful strides. "Shit," I mutter, watching it leap from the river's edge, ebony talons bared, trying to bridge the nine-foot gap. Two red-cloaked merchants scream as it thuds against the portside, making the barge tip to a symphony of muffled cries.

The beast scrambles, but the vessel begins to roll from the sheer weight of it clinging to the side, until it loses traction and falls—dunking beneath the water.

The barge bucks with a violent swing that sends the merchants sliding across the deck.

Seeing the Vruk pop up downstream in the midst of the gloomy, Irilak-infested jungle, I sprint toward the riverside.

"Throw out your anchor!" I bellow, using the back of my arm to wipe the gore from my face as I weave between glass cottages with pitched roofs. "These people need refuge!"

One of the merchants looks right at me from beneath the scoop of his hood. "*Row!*" he howls, knuckles blanching as he grips onto the rail and pulls himself up.

The barge begins to power forward, and I shake my head, stalking it along the riverbank. The second merchant pulls himself up by the tiller, steering the vessel, looking straight down the nose of it.

"Cowardly fucks." I sheathe my sword and concede a few steps before sprinting forward, bounding off the bank, and leaping through the air. I land on the deck with such force the boat bucks, bloody gore splashing off my boots and muddying the floorboards as a handful of shrill screams vibrate through them.

Frowning, I stare at the floor, attention sliding to the man with a tight grip on the tiller. I barely catch a glance of his wide eyes beneath the fall of his blood-red hood before he stumbles a step and leaps off the back, landing with a heavy splash.

I grunt, whirling, and stalk toward the man at the nose—now facing me.

Chanting.

"*Oh bright ones, please deliver me through the gates of Kvath—*"

A blow of wind flips his hood, revealing his smooth face

and bald head. My eyes widen at the sight of the upside-down v carved into his forehead.

Shulák.

"I can smell your fear," I growl as I draw close.

He continues to squeak words past his trembling lips.

"*Gods have mercy, for my heart is not at peace. Please take me in your warm embrace and ease me into the Mala, for I am but your loyal servant.*"

"Hate to break it to you," I mutter on a low laugh, "but nobody's listening. They don't give a fuck about you."

Or anyone else, for that matter.

He reaches into the fold of his cloak, pulling out a short blade that catches the light. I quicken my pace, hands bunching into fists, stopping when he whips it up and drags the sharp length across his throat, spilling ribbons of blood down his chest. Mouth gaping, his eyes roll back as a bloody breath gurgles from both the slit in his throat and his lips, before he crumbles in a heap on the deck.

His blood leeches down the floorboards, stretching toward me like crimson fingers.

I clear my throat, give him my back, and grab the anchor—a heavy, metal claw I toss off the side of the boat. It clatters against the sparkling riverbank, snagging between huge, crystal clear boulders.

Pulling with all my weight on the chain, I hiss out harsh breaths, shoulders bulging, the tendons in my arms pushing to the surface as I force the ship's nose toward the shore. We clunk against it, and I secure the chain.

Swiping hair slick with sweat off my face, I look over my shoulder to the trapdoor near the back of the boat.

My footsteps thud across the deck, stomping the Shulák's

bright red blood with every step. I reach down, grab the metal handle, and pull. The stench of shit and piss and fear fills my nostrils—a putrid blend that makes me want to dry heave.

Checking my surroundings, I buffer the lower half of my face with the fall of my cloak and ease down the tight stairs that lead beneath the deck, stepping into the lantern-lit hull.

Eyes widening.

Sitting upon benches that line the space—benches that usually house grown, sturdy men—are *kids*.

Eight rows of two. Each of them bald and wide-eyed.

Wearing gray robes.

Each of them with an upside-down v branded on their foreheads.

Electric fury crackles through my veins, nipping at the undersides of my skin as I take in the ropes bound around their hands, forcing their grip on the oars. As I note the fact they're sitting in their own shit, some of them with lumpy vomit poured down their fronts.

"Where are your parents?"

My voice booms through the dim, met with a silence that's deafening.

I take another step down, stopping just shy of the muck sloshing across the floor as a small voice croaks out words that skate across my skin.

My heart stops. Slams back into action again when a second voice joins the dry, monotone chant. Then a third, and a fourth, until the entire hull is reciting the damning, poisonous words ...

I take in the deep-rooted fear ingrained in their eyes, and realize it has nothing to do with the rope or the shit or the spew, but the tail end of a familiar prophecy they're belting at me.

"*The world will fall to shadow's hand. The world will fall to shadow's hand. The world will fall to shadow's hand—*"

"Fuck."

CHAPTER 43
Orlaith

The ceiling looks like a constellation, I realize, gaze dragging from one neon stalactite tip to another. Such a pretty blanket for such an ugly deed.

Maybe they're pointing at me, whispering between each other. Maybe they know what's in store for me next, and they're too afraid to say.

Perhaps Vanth was right. Perhaps I am a witch, after all.

The man's spent weight upon me feels significant. He's in me, through me. A male I don't even know. And though I feel free—*liberated* even—I also feel just a little bit rotten inside.

I didn't expect it to hurt so much. Didn't expect for there to be no 'blinding vortex of pleasure that shatters my soul' like I read about in *Gypsy and the Night King*. Like I felt that time Rhordyn touched me on the balcony of Stony Stem.

I didn't expect to feel so filthy afterward …

But it's done now.

He arches up, kissing me. I give him a little shove. He eases back, and a wince cuts between my teeth as he slips free and rolls to the side. "You're fucking amazing," he pants, dull lantern light outlining his silhouette spread across the moss.

"Thanks," I mutter, scrambling for my underwear, my hair a shameful mess I try to smooth with my other hand. "You were really good, too."

I clamber up, threading my feet into my panties, hating the feel of him still smeared between my thighs. I undo the makeshift sheath around my leg and shift it to my waist before easing my shirt on and swiftly securing the buttons, then dragging on my pants, battling with the fastening as he stands and steps before me—not even bothering to search for his own clothes.

"Can I see you again?" he asks, sweeping hair off my face, fingers tracing the outline of my mask, his touch too warm.

Too tender.

Eyes too blue and soft and needy.

"No. But thank you." His mouth turns down, and I offer him a small smile. "For not treating me like some precious, breakable thing."

I give him a chaste kiss on the cheek, then disappear into the messy crowd as fast as my feet can take me, something spiky blooming in my chest—a surge of crushing panic that's *sickening*. That makes the people around me feel too close. Too warm.

Makes my skin feel more foreign than ever.

I dash through the cluster of pulsing bodies, this vile

thing wrestling inside me—threatening to shatter my ribs if I don't give it space to *breathe.*

Feet churning, heart racing, I shove past tangled limbs, eyes on the ground until I stumble into an open space.

My desperate gaze scrapes the dimly lit surrounds, finding a dark, sheltered corner that's private and still. I fall back against the vines cushioning the wall and tuck myself into a ball. Allow myself one moment to mourn the loss of something I always hoped would be special.

Just one crumbling moment where I dig my face into my knees and wish this hurt between my legs belonged to someone else before I wipe my face, pick myself up off the floor, and search for Gael.

CHAPTER 44
Orlaith

I check around the waterfall, weaving through the writhing chaos of people slathered in sweat and sweet-smelling fruit juice, prying myself free from the claustrophobic press of it all when I can't find her anywhere.

What if something bad happened to her?

Panic flogs my heart, filling it with fiery fear.

Figuring the man guarding the door might have some ideas, I dart up to the mezzanine, snatch my knapsack, and redo my hair, covering the low bun with my cap. I sprint down the tunnel and up the stairs to find him leaning against the door.

"Thought you'd turn up eventually," he says, reaching for the handle. "She needed some fresh air. Requested that I ask you to meet her at the top of the stairs if you came this way."

Frowning, I dart past the moment he opens the door wide enough, and charge up the cobbled stairs, whipping off my mask and shoving it in my bag.

My heart skips a beat when I make it to the top and she's not there.

Sprinting, feet slapping through puddles that splash up my legs, I exit the alley. "Dammit," I mutter, scanning the busy crowd.

My frantic gaze settles on a figure leaning against a wall a few doors down. Though their face is hidden by the fall of their hood, I'd recognize the swathe of that expensive velvet cloak anywhere—stark against the surrounding squalor.

Relief bubbles up so fast I almost vomit.

I run, snaking between people and swirling clouds of sweet smoke blown from long pipes.

She flinches when I grab her arm, head whipping in my direction.

"*Oh,*" Gael gasps, hand shielding her heaving chest. "It's you."

My heart flips at the sight of her pale cheeks and wide eyes that scan the busy street, gaze darting behind me nervously. "What's wrong? Did something happen?"

She sniffs, wiping at a smudge of kohl beneath her eye as she tucks her mask into my bag. "I'm so sorry I left. I know that's such a shit thing to do. I just had to get out of there ..."

"Gael, what happened?"

She draws a shaky breath, nibbling at her lower lip. "I was having a really good time dancing, and I wandered off to pick some more fruit when a man ran into me and knocked off my mask. He was with two others, and one of them recognized me. They backed me against a wall; said something about their kid brother who was earning a wage working at the docks in Mother's hangar last year. That he started acting strange, then never came home one day."

I frown. "What does that have to do with you?"

"That's the thing, I have no idea." Another sniff. "None of it made any sense."

"Did you see their faces?"

"No. But they got a very clear look at mine. Meaning they now know I frequent the lair. A secret they can use against me or my family."

"Shit ..."

"Yeah, shit." She wipes at her nose again. "It completely destroyed my buzz. I threw fruit at them and ran."

My eyes widen. "You threw *fruit* at them?"

She nods, spilling a laugh that crinkles her eyes and makes a tear fall down her cheek, letting the sound taper as she wipes at her snuffly nose. "I'm sorry. I know I promised you fun ..."

Fun ...

Today's small dose of it might cost me my life. But I'd rather die by the sword of my own decisions than be stripped of the ability to make them.

"I think fun is overrated," I admit, planting my hip against the wall.

"Maybe I'm growing out of fun, too."

I tuck a fallen lock of hair behind her ear. "How about we find somewhere that's quiet and peaceful and just ..." I shrug, giving her a soft, lopsided smile, "*nothing.*"

Her eyes focus on me. "Nothing sounds really, really good."

"Yeah?"

She nods, eyes twinkling as she looks at my bag. "Do you have a lantern in there?"

"I have a few candles?"

"Then I know *just* the place."

The tall building wedged almost flush against the wall leaves only a frail pathway—so tight there's no room for us to walk side by side. Having left her shoes at the lair in her rush to leave, Gael's feet are bare like mine, the hem of her cloak so filthy and wet it looks more black than blue.

The path leads to a curved, cobbled bridge that arches over a deep drainway cradling a stream of gently moving water that spears through the city's guts and burrows beneath the wall. A bridge I expect Gael to lead me over, leaving me stunned when, instead, she sits on the edge of the drainway and leaps off, landing knee-deep in a splash of water.

She turns, flashing me a big smile. "Coming?"

I slip my bag off my shoulder and toss it to her before crouching on the edge, heart racing as I leap.

My feet skate across the slick of algae, whipping out from under me, and I squeal, falling on my ass with a sloppy splash to the tune of Gael's laughter.

Brow raised, water dripping off my face, I look up at her laughing so hard she's folded forward, hands stamped on her knees for support.

"Am I sitting in pee?"

"Best not think about it," she giggles, wiping the tears

from her cheeks before reaching her hand down to help me up. "Sorry, I should've warned you."

"It's fine," I say, glad to see her happy again, even if it is at my expense.

I brush off some green muck while she digs through my knapsack and pulls out two candles—handing one to me.

"We don't really *need* these, but I'm not a huge fan of the dark. Do you have matchsticks in here?"

I take the bag off her and fish around, emptying one into my hand from a small jar, then striking its head on the stone and lighting both candles. She waggles her brows and leads me beneath the bridge, toward the mouth of the drain that flows under the wall, a collection of blazing lanterns hanging at its entrance.

"We're going through *there?*" I ask, slime surging between my toes as I trace her steps, remembering Rhordyn's pinched warning.

Don't climb the wall that borders the city. It's dangerous.

To be fair, he said nothing about not going *under* it ...

"Sure are. We're going somewhere I used to go when I was young and needed space." The words echo as we move past the entrance, stooped over, feet sludging through the thickening muck.

The air is dense and stagnant, the curved stone edges pressing in on us from all angles as we creep through the drain, our blazing candles highlighting a myriad of cobwebs woven across the top. Something slithers against my foot, and I shiver, tamping the urge to scream, certain that things are crawling across my arms and head.

The hairs on the back of my neck lift.

Looking over my shoulder, I see nothing but the drain's hollow throat that lengthens with every sludgy step we take.

The air begins to thin until I no longer feel like I'm packing my lungs full of mold spores.

Gael slows to a stop, blowing out her candle. "Shit," she mutters, and I peer past her to the metal grate that blocks the exit. To the *padlock* hanging off it, glazed in firelight from the various lanterns bolted to the curved wall.

"Shit," I parrot, and Gael sighs, jiggles the lock, tugs it. She even gives it a little kick.

"This is stupid. It wasn't locked the last time I came here ..."

"Let me have a go."

She steps back, pressing herself flat against the edge of the drain so I can shuffle past.

I blow out my candle and stuff it in my bag, then pull out my hairpin, freeing my heavy tumble of hair. Digging the long, tapered tip into the lock's pinched mouth, I twist ... flick ... *flick*—

The padlock clunks open, and I flash Gael a victorious grin.

She laughs, shaking her head as I swing the grate wide and gesture for her to lead the way. "You're full of surprises. If your coupling falls through, I'm snatching you up and keeping you for myself."

Cheeks blazing, I redo my hair, then pluck a tentative trail over big, smoothed stones clothed in a layer of algae, squinting into blinding daylight as I peer at our surroundings.

We're on the edge of a small rise that fringes a large glen, cobbles spewing out the drain and down the shallow slope with the spill of water that feeds into the unruly jungle below. There's a river roaring somewhere in the distance, the hilly stretch of untailored grass sparsely dotted with trees beneath a powder blue sky that makes my heart soar.

I can't see the wall past the thick jungle clothing the hill behind us. "So we're—"

"Outside the city, yeah. Pretty cool, huh?"

I nod, bagging her candle before I trail her down the hill—toes digging into the soil, legs lost amongst the grass ...

My eyes sweep shut and I pause, listening to the wind weave between the foliage as I tip my head to let the sunlight sink into my pores like a warm cloth set upon my face.

The hearty, organic smell of nature *infuses* me, dissolving the heaviness in my chest. The echo of ache between my legs.

Out here, everything feels easier. Less serious. Like everything *in there* melts away.

"Come on."

I open my eyes, seeing Gael's big, bright smile.

She leads me over a rise, down into a gully poked with a sparse collection of trees drooping with big, vibrant bulbs of fruit, thick tufts of grass pillowing the ground.

Gael unbuckles her cloak and looks up into the foliage of a gnarly peach tree laden with fruit. "I'm not sure anyone else knows about this place." Grabbing hold of a low-hanging branch, she swings herself up, then pushes to her feet, looking like something out of a fairytale in her gold-brushed dress that blows in tendrils around her body. "Don't look up my skirt," she jests.

I laugh, whipping my hand up, snatching the peach she drops.

"Quick hands," she says as I sit cross-legged in the grass and set it on the ground, waiting for the next. Once we have a mound bigger than my head, Gael leaps down, landing in a flutter of sparkly gold fabric, sitting down on the other side of the pile.

"Now what?"

"Now," she grabs a peach, inspects its fuzzy skin from every angle, and bites into it, sending a squirt of pink juice dribbling down her chin. "We eat until our bellies ache. That's what papa and I used to do ..."

A heaviness settles between us as she chews, looking at the raw, exposed flesh—brow pinched, her golden curls dancing in the breeze like a restless aura.

It's on the tip of my tongue, to ask her how he died.

The thought grows wings in my chest that flutter about ...

She shoves a peach into my hand. "*Nothing,* yeah?"

I take a deep bite of the sweet, juicy flesh, swallowing the question down, and garnish her with a gentle smile ...

"Nothing."

Chapter 45
Kai

A soft beat tapping against my ribs pulls me to consciousness, radiating through my heart and my fucking soul.

'Zykanth …'

Silence.

That hollow, aching silence.

But I can *feel* him.

A deep, relieved sigh saws out as I open my eyes, looking down through the blushed water lapping at the mark on my chest—a fading stamp of pinched, red skin covering the remnants of the hurt.

I lift my hand and press at it, running my fingers over the puckered skin.

"She healed me …"

Where is she?

I scan the pool's harsh edge, seeing a pile of limp, blue crabs—some bigger than my hand, most smaller than my thumb nail. My stomach growls, stare stabbing up the ravine and the stream that feeds the pool, then along the edge of the sheer, crystal cliff where I spot her. Naked.

Her wild hair sweeps past the curve of her lower back as she reaches up, stretching her body, her hand lifting slower than the rising sun. She slaps it against the rock so fast I flinch, the corner of my mouth curling up when I see a tiny, squashed crab fall off the wall and into her palm.

She holds the thing up and inspects it from all angles before dropping it in her mouth and crunching down. Swallowing, her eyes widen, arm striking through a cleft in the cliff.

The swirl in my chest churns faster, *faster* ... while every other piece of me settles.

She whips her arm out, hand laden with a huge crab snipping at the air, and she slams it against the ground by her bare feet, her beautiful breasts bouncing with the motion. She bends down, picks up the limp crustacean, then cracks the thing in half—slurping at the meat inside.

A warmth swells inside my chest as I drink her in from afar. Every soft curve, every raw, wild edge, the deep dip I want to explore.

A familiar prickle rises on my chest, and I look down, seeing a silver scale swell to the surface.

'Zykanth ... I thought I lost you ...'

The surge of relief almost flays me, and my rusty laugh ripples across the water, spilling out in giddy torrents. Vicious whips her head around and stills, her face slathered in crab innards, a thick, severed leg hanging from her mouth as she looks straight at me.

My heart flips.

A shrill sound spills from her, and she spits the leg, drops the crab, then scrambles along the river's edge on a flurry of steps that tumble over each other. She reaches the pool and *jumps*, splashing my face and chest.

She disappears beneath the ruffled surface, then rises between my legs, her white hair slicked back from her face, cascading down her shoulders as she straddles me, paws at me, dragging her fingers across the scale Zykanth just gifted me from within.

She tilts forward and rubs her cheek across it ... like she's *treasuring* it.

My skin erupts with goosebumps.

Eyes glistening with unshed tears, she sets her hand upon the scale and nods. "*Mmmine*," she murmurs through plump lips, the smooth curl of her watery voice spiraling through me, drilling down into my gut ...

The urgent slither in my chest stills, and my throat swells as I cradle the wisp of her delicate voice in my heart like a jewel.

"Vicious—"

"*Mine*," she repeats with the same confidence she had when she smashed that crab against the ground, nodding more fiercely now.

I thread my hand around the side of her face and grip tight, stilling the motion, looking straight into her sunshine eyes. "*Yours.*"

She blinks, a tear rolling down her cheek.

I lean forward and drag my tongue up the track of it, over her silky skin, tasting the burst of her emotions. Savoring them like the treasures they are.

A soft sound shudders out of her, and I feel it in my chest, dragging my nose back down, pausing with my mouth a hair's breadth from hers. I swallow. Lick my lips. Feel the tremor of her breaths batter me as I cradle the side of her face, cherishing this moment—wishing I could set it in my trove and fawn over it for eternity.

"*Yours,*" I growl, then seal my lips against hers, taking her in a deep, crushing kiss. She moans into me, and I feed on her lush sounds, tilting her head for better access, delving, tasting her salty splendor.

My length hardens, throbbing, nudging at her spread entrance—bared and utterly exposed for me.

Pulling back, her eyes go wide like saucers, her full breasts rising with every sharp inhale, lips swollen, cheeks pink like the sky just before the sun crests over the ocean.

"You're an exquisite thing," I whisper.

She scrambles off, leaving me bereft, heaving, heart pounding—watching her clamber from the pool. "Where are you—"

She shoves the pile of dead crabs aside, then kneels on the edge and bends forward, planting her chest on the ground, face turned sideways, exposing her flush sex.

The view strikes me through the chest and takes my breath away.

Rocking forward, I wade through the water, stepping up onto a shelf in the pool and rising behind her. I plant my hand down the line of her spine and press it between her shoulder blades, her body quivering beneath my touch.

Her lashes flutter, and she releases a soft, pleading sound that snaps me.

"You want me to take you, Vicious?"

She nods, mewling, pushing her bum back so it brushes against my hard, heavy, aching cock.

Fuck.

Sliding my hands down her back, I spread them across the perfect globes of her ass and take my fill.

Her hips rock the slightest amount.

I trail them farther down, grasping handfuls of the fleshy crease between her ass and thighs, spreading her apart.

I crouch. Look at her flush opening.

More soft whimpers, and she skirts back another inch ...

With a hungry growl, I drag my tongue up her gaping entrance, moaning at her raw, salty tang when she backs onto my face. Forces me deeper between her crease.

I dig my tongue into her hungry core, gorging on the taste of her crude desire, cock twitching. Her whimpers turn to moans as I spear my tongue into her warmth, and her insides clamp around it.

Pulling back, I leave her smeared across my chin and grip my cock, dragging it up and down her pulsing core.

She arches her spine, presenting, panting soundlessly, then looks at me over her shoulder, mouth popped open and those golden eyes alight. I hold her blazing stare and sink forward one stretching inch at a time, staking my claim on her tight, velvet depths.

Her eyes roll into the back of her head as I ease myself to the hilt, then hold her hips, pausing ... mesmerized by the sweet rapture that pours across her features.

"*Mine.*"

Her voice almost breaks me, my hard length surging with a hot ache.

"*Yes,*" I grind out, pulling my hips back, then thrusting forward, drinking from her raw, erotic sounds that still that tap in my chest.

Again and again and *again* I drive into her in long, claiming strikes, voracious grunts trapped behind my clenched teeth.

I lower upon her back, shielding her with my body, easing my hand between her legs. I delve my fingers through her folds and caress her swollen nub, and her entire body shudders. Her hips roll, pushing into me, her ass and thighs absorbing my thrusts as my thick shaft slides in and out of her perfect trove.

"Who am I?" I rumble against her ear.

"*Mine!*"

I groan, a hot surge swelling through me, tightening my balls and making my hips dig deeper, *deeper* ...

She tilts her head, exposing the stretched slope of her delicate neck for me to nuzzle into, and her muscles clamp down in a pulsing flutter.

That beat inside my chest strengthens, growing into a fierce, ancient throb ...

'*Claim* ...' Zykanth growls, his voice wild and unleashed, swirling through my chest. '*Claim!*'

I whip my head forward with the strike of rapture, and Vicious breaks apart around me, milking me as I sink my teeth into her neck. Her flesh bursts, and the smooth, velvety taste of her lifeblood cracks what's left of my composure.

I spill into her, planting my seed so deep inside her body I picture it taking root, entwining us until the end of time.

My own savage, unbuffered burst of sun and sea ...

Mine.

CHAPTER 46

Orlaith

Hands cushioning my head, body stretched across the ground, I'm lulled by the fronds of grass painting secrets on my cheeks. By the warm, dappled sunlight that drips upon my face, breeze rustling through the peach tree arched overhead, jostling leaves and making the branches creak.

My belly is heavy, hands and lips and chin sticky with peach juice, eyes shielded by the rim of my cap as I dream of a life where I could stay out here forever. Disappear and let everything else just ... *fall away*.

An aching niggle between my legs pulls my mind from the clouds, a thread of dread stitching through my chest with thoughts of what I did today. That rebellious, beautiful, *hideous* thing.

It was right. I know it was.

I owed it to myself—to ease some of that suffocating pressure and give myself some room to breathe.

Even so, the aftermath threatens to swallow me down a cleft in the soil.

I stuff the thought aside as Gael groans beside me, and I sense her stretching out her limbs, peeling my eyes open in time to see her sit up.

I tip my hat, heart sinking. "Time to go?"

Golden coils of hair blow across her face as she twists, squinting at the sun that ignites the blue bursts around her pupils. "We have another hour before the light starts to fade and the Irilak get brave enough to creep close, but I think we should probably go soon. By the time we get back to my house, the guards will be getting antsy. I'm going to wash my hands in the brook just over the hill. Be right back." She pushes to her feet and slowly wanders up the rise, dropping out of view.

I let my eyes sweep shut again, toes stretching, mind drifting, chasing some sounds and dismissing others. Feeling a cold, incorporeal pressure scribble across the pads of my feet, my eyes snap open, heart flipping a beat as I edge onto my elbows, looking down the spine of the gully and into the thick tuft of jungle that plugs the far end.

It doesn't take me long to see them shading the deeper pockets of shadow in messy clusters that float and sway and pulse and flutter.

The corner of my mouth turns up.

Irilak.

Too many to count—big and small, tall and round. Some have their bleached faces exposed, beady eyes pinned on me. Others watch from beneath their vapor veil, peeking out from behind tree trunks and steel-blue shrubs.

"I'm going to have to catch some mice ..."

A muffled scream comes to me on a shove of wind that hits the side of my face. My head whips to the right, stare lashing in the direction she went. "Gael?"

Seconds drip by as I push into a seated position, ears straining, dissecting every sound ...

Another muffled scream—sharper this time.

A spear of icy panic impales me.

I'm on my feet, legs churning, hand weaving up beneath my shirt and gripping the hilt of my blade, ripping it free before I even have time to think. I rise over the hill, looking out across the clearing caught in the curl of a rushing brook, dominated by a large tree that shades three men I don't recognize.

They're wiry, dressed in patchwork clothes, faces knotted with rabid rage that spits from their twisted lips as they kick at a gagged and bound figure on the ground, swathed in a shimmer of gold.

Gael.

Crouching beside her, one of the men tries to maneuver a sack over her head, and she kicks and bucks, her muffled screams battering the air.

I plunge into that cold, dead place deep inside that drops my heart in an icy lake, sprinting across the clearing like an arrow shot to kill. Lips peeling back, a snarl rips free, my hat flying off my head as I spear toward the man who has a fistful of Gael's dress, catapulting through the air—landing a kick to the back of his head that drops him like a bag of bricks.

I hit the ground hard and roll through the grass, hair unraveling, stabbing my blade into the soil and grinding to a crouching halt. I flick my head up, seeing him twist into a groaning knot of muscle and sinew.

The other two run at me, belting brutal words.

Gael tips to the side, her wild, frightened eyes pleading with me as she jerks at her bound wrists, moaning muffled words through the blue material stuffed between her teeth.

I rip my blade from the soil and charge to the tune of crackling thunder.

Dropping low, I slide between the men and dodge their flailing hands, slashing my blade through the back of an ankle. Reaching Gael, I saw through the bonds wrapped around her ankles, then slice my blade through the rope binding her wrists, a muffled squeal dragging my attention to her wide, wild eyes.

The hairs on the back of my neck lift.

I kick my foot out and whip it around, swiping the legs out from beneath the man who was just about to swing at me, clambering atop him when he falls. Knees straddling his chest, rage tunnels my vision and scrunches my fist into stone.

I crack at his face, feeling his nose crunch beneath the brutal force. I swing again and again and *again*—knuckles splitting as I release my wrath on his skull.

He stops trying to shield his face. Goes limp between my legs.

Still, my knuckles collide with his cheek, his mouth, his temple—blood splashing up at my face with every crushing collision.

"*Orlaith!*"

Gael's distant voice niggles at me, and I look up through

the veil of my bloodlust, fist halting mid-swing. Lungs halting mid-draw.

She's standing atop the hill, dress torn, kohl blurred across her bruised cheek, knees so skinned they're bleeding down her shins.

Something hard and cold clouts my temple.

I drop.

Drift.

My body lightens ... loosens ... my limbs shifted for me. Lifted. My head flops forward, something tight binding my wrists, my chest, leaning me back against something hard and rough.

A boom of thunder rattles the ground and electrifies the air, cutting a gasp through my lips.

Someone fists my hair, ripping the weight of my head off my shoulder, settling a cool sharpness upon my bared throat.

My eyes pop open, a deep throb pecking at my temple as I take in a pair of pale blue orbs and a face slashed with wrath.

I'm certain it's my own dagger poised at my throat.

A surging pressure bloats my brain, and I feel a warmth leak from my nose, dripping off the tip of my chin. My vision splits, feet threatening to slip out from under me, but there's something bound around my chest, keeping my back against the tree.

Rope.

A slow, lazy blink, and my gaze drags past the male hissing his rancid breath at me to the man on the ground with a gory face.

Unmoving.

Another is crouched over him, hand wrapped around the back of his bloody ankle.

My focus shifts, sharpening on Gael—on her knees at the tip of the rise, hands gripping her face as she screams.

My mouth falls open, a single word rasping free. "R-run ..."

I'm backhanded so hard my head whips to the side, teeth rattling, eyes rolling back.

I barely feel a thing, my flesh and muscles nothing more than a numb tomb that houses whipping, scolding lashes of caustic *fire* grubbing at the underside of my skin. Blood whooshes through my veins, the hissing drum morphing into a slither of noxious voices that chant a deadly tune ...

Kill.

Kill.

Kill.

Another gush of blood pours from my nose. I taste it on my tongue as a fork of lightning scribbles through the clouds rolling across the sky, blotting out the light.

"What's this?"

The words somehow manage to dig past the hissing chant, and my gaze rolls to the male before me lifting the black jewel strung around my neck. His eyes ignite as he beholds it like he's wielding all his dreams come true in the palm of his hand.

Kill.

Kill.

Kill.

"Would you look at that," he spits past a grill of yellow teeth. "Think I'll have that, you little bitch."

I groan.

He tightens his fist around the gem and *pulls*.

I hear the chain snap; feel the heavy weight of it slip free from around my neck. The voices stop, that pressure abates, as though whatever it is inside me just sat up and listened.

My shell peels down, and the man stumbles back a step. He gasps, my startling reflection bouncing off his wide eyes—shimmering back at me.

Murderer.

My skin begins to tear in agonizing increments, cracking me open one searing split at a time. A flock of sizzling death untangles from that cleft inside my chest, and my mouth falls open, muscles immobilized by the blazing trails shredding me apart as I scream the howls of a hundred tortured souls rattling the chains of their mortality.

He only has a few more seconds to take in my shattered beauty before all the ugly pours out.

Chapter 47

Orlaith

The grass is tickly and sweet smelling.

I push my curls from my eyes and pick another flower—this one tall with tiny, pink petals that make me smile.

I add it to my pile, squeezing my fingers around the stems.

My brother giggles, and I look up to where he and Mommy are snuggling under the shade of a sad-looking tree, making shapes with their hands.

Love hearts. Diamonds. Birdies.

I pick another flower, blowing away the bee that tries to land on it.

If I pick lots and lots, maybe my brother will make me something pretty with them.

"Momma ..."

"Yeah, my boy?"

"What happens when we die?"

I look up, watching them through the gaps in the grass.

Mommy's hand-bird stops flying, but only for a little bit.

"Well, it's said that your heart must be full to pass through Kvath—the God of Death—on your journey to Mala. The afterworld. But once you're there, your soul will soar on an eternal wind through a world where the colors never fade and the smells are always sweet. Where the sea is always warm and clear and kind, and the sand sparkles just like your beautiful eyes," she says, leaning forward to kiss his nose.

Those are my favorite sort of kisses. One day, when I have my words, I'm going to tell her that.

"Oh ..."

Gripping my blooms, I crawl through the grass that tickles my cheeks and lips.

Mommy smiles when I reach them and pass my flowers off one by one, putting them on my brother's tummy until I have only one left. My favorite.

It's smaller than the rest, white like the stars; shaped like them, too.

My brother knots his fingers together and makes the shape of a dog.

A *monster*.

"Nom, nom, nom," he says, making the beast snap its jaws around my pretty little bloom, swallowing it whole.

He ... he *ate* it ...

My bottom lip wobbles, the backs of my eyes stinging as I look down at my empty hands.

"Oh, Serren, I'm only playing. It's okay," he says, giggling, untwisting his fingers. He holds out his hand, my perfect flower sitting in his palm. "See?"

It's okay.

I smile, leaning my head against his leg as he tucks it

behind my ear. "Want me to make you a pretty crown just like the one I made you yesterday?"

I nod really fast, and Mommy smiles big.

"You're her favorite person, you know."

"She's mine, too. And you, of course! And Papa!"

Mommy laughs, nuzzling his cheek. "I know, sunshine. I know."

He makes a hole in one of the long stems and threads another through it, his face all serious looking. The chain gets longer and longer with every color of the rainbow while Mommy brushes her fingers through my hair in the way that always makes me want to close my eyes.

I pick the next flower up, handing it to him.

He smiles at me, but his eyes go all serious again really fast.

Maybe he's sad that we're running out of flowers?

"And if it's not?" he asks, punching a hole through its stem with his fingernail.

"If it's not what, baby?"

"If your heart's not full when you die. What then? Do you just ... stop?"

Mommy's hand stops moving for a long time.

I pass him another flower.

Another.

Another.

"Then we go back to the earth that brought us forward. We become flowers and rocks and water and trees and—"

His hands stop, eyes wide and worried looking. "But I don't *want* to be flowers, Mommy! I want to stay here with you and Ser and Papa. I don't want to be alone ..."

He sounds so scared.

I don't like it. It makes my eyes sting.

Mommy pulls his face close, brushing his shiny freckles with her thumb. "You won't be, baby. Your big, beautiful heart is safe. I promise."

"But what if it's *not*?"

Her sad smile makes my heart hurt.

She kisses both his eyes, her lips sparkly from his tears. "Then I'll come with you, and we'll be flowers together."

A wet drip to my cheek rips me back to the now.

I'm not even sure where I was …

Somewhere. A soft, happy place that felt too real, with people that no longer exist.

Serren.

He called me Serren.

The name strikes something in me, a hurt flaring to life that's so raw, I feel like my chest is being split open one snapped rib at a time.

He called me his favorite person.

I whimper, open my eyes, expect to see a canopy of lush leaves and plump, dangling peaches—instead confronted by the spindly, charred fingers of a burning tree, popping and sparking as flames gobble it up.

A harsh smell hits the back of my throat, making me gag—the raw, sulfurous reek of burning hair and flesh spawning from the pit of my darkest nightmares.

Still asleep. Must be.

"Wake up …" I rasp, squeezing my eyes shut, hands pressed flat against my temples while I choke on this emptiness inside, like my chest could cave at any moment.

Like someone just rummaged through my body and hauled out everything but my thumping heart.

A blow of wind sprinkles me with icy rain, making goosebumps jump all over my skin that feels too bare ...

My eyes fly open.

I look down at my naked body sprawled across the ground, dusted in ash. See the charred remnants of my clothing and bits of rope scattered around me.

Reality plunges a stake through my chest, a sob bursting up my grated throat ...

I'm not dreaming.

This is real.

My gaze drifts past my feet, catching on a severed leg, its flesh a blistered mess of bubbled, oozing welts that stagger my heart to a standstill.

Memory shards bore into my brain. A different place, similar scene. Same smell. Same eerie silence void of life—a moment of still before chaos erupted, the beasts no doubt drawn to the reek of burning death.

Past and present meld and drift and reach down my throat, gripping my heart in a crushing fist.

What have I done?

Get away. I have to get away.

I roll to the side, almost colliding with an arm, flesh melted from the clawed finger bones that are reaching for me. My entire body locks, a scream bubbling up my throat, cut off as a fierce cracking sound ratchets through the eerie silence. I roll my gaze back to the tree. See its torso tilting—squashing the space between us in a fiery frenzy. I tumble sideways, the singed arm crunching beneath me, leaving a warm, wet smear across my cheek and chest.

Nausea spills through me, and I gag, rolling, *rolling* ...

The ground shudders, sparks burst, and I cover my face, tucked in a protective ball that doesn't save me from the rank smell sticking to me, making my guts twist into an aching knot.

Silence blankets the world. Not even the birds are singing.

Perhaps I killed them, too.

Gael—

Eyes popping open, I look up into heavy gray storm clouds threatening to bear down, dusting me in a cool sprinkle.

What if she didn't leave?

I scramble up, a sharp breath cutting through me as I scan the singed glen. A gust of chill tills up ashen flurries that do nothing to soften the harsh landscape clothed in thick smoke and dashed through the middle by the felled, smoldering tree.

It's hard to picture anything ever growing here again.

Bouts of smog clog my lungs, and I cough and splutter and heave, batting the air, clambering between the scattered bits of dead while churning ash with every frantic step.

"*Gael!*"

Another violent cough hacks out of me as I spin, stumbling, my gaze landing on a lithe torso—face down, head still intact, the skin bubbled and blistered beyond recognition.

I fall to my knees.

Please no.

Please ...

I crawl forward, little whimpers breaking past my chattering teeth.

Reaching forward with trembling hands, I roll the body. Layers of flesh slide away, sticking to my palms like the thick skin that forms atop cooling custard. Bile spikes up my throat as I catch sight of a small patch of hair that somehow managed to survive the singe.

A too-dark shade of blonde.

I twist and fold forward, belly cramping, a rush of half-digested peaches burning a trail up my throat before pouring from my lips in a lumpy splatter.

Not her.

I hack out a cough, insides curdling ...

Not her.

She made it out in time. I have to believe she did.

I crawl between the charred lumps of flesh and bone, sieving through the ash, searching for my necklace—skinning my knees and the palms of my hands. My fingers brush against something hard, long, sharp ...

I dig my blackened blade from the muck, the sharp burnished black, the opaline hilt now stained with an inky sheen that makes the detailed blooms etched into it look like tiny, macabre roses.

Sitting on my heels, hair heavy around my shoulders, I let the dagger lie loosely across the palms of my limp hands.

Another blow of air stirs the ashy ruin, sprinkling me with a burst of rain, the drips dragging clear paths through the filth to expose my pearly skin beneath.

Untarnished.

No cracks. No scars or burns or blisters. Nothing to pay homage to the fact that I just tore people to bloody shreds.

The necklace was the only thing keeping everyone safe from this slithering *thing* inside me. This vile, deadly, noxious thing that does not discriminate.

This thing that took my mommy.

A sob erupts from my lips as I close my eyes and think of my dream. Think of the beautiful woman that cuddled us close and ran her fingers through my hair ...

A wild, frantic panic makes my heart gallop and my thoughts spin—spiraling someplace dark and final.

Without my necklace ...

I peer down my nose at the blackened blade. Back to my heaving chest. A shudder rakes through me, mind drilling into that shadowy place that's weighted down with a final full stop.

Without my necklace, nobody's safe.

My hand tightens around the hilt—

A blow of air batters me as a crackle of lightning splits apart the sky, making me flinch. My gaze flicks to something that catches on the flash of light amongst a stir of ash: my necklace, coiled on the ground not too far away.

My curse and my salvation.

A strange feeling floods me that's not quite relief.

I would have done it. Would have taken myself out rather than risk another lethal detonation.

The realization hits so hard I struggle to breathe, blinking, a single tear dripping down my cheek.

I scramble forward—scramble from those thoughts left somewhere in the ash behind me as I snatch up the gem and conch and inspect the broken latch with trembling fingers coated in charred flesh.

I notice it all at once, stomach knotting, another gag

making me dry retch. Head swiveling in the direction of the stream, I leap up and sprint toward the water, dressed in nothing but the fried remnants of my actions.

Dropping the blade and necklace on the bank, I stumble in on legs that have forgotten how to work, and the water swallows me in a cool gulp; a purifying rinse that cradles me and wipes me clean in none of the important ways.

Murderer.

"*Shut up!*"

I drop below the surface, just short of the rushing current. Sitting on the rocky bottom, I press my palms into my eyes and *scream*—bubbles exploding from my twisted lips on their race to freedom.

If only Rhordyn knew what I was capable of, perhaps he would have put a stop to me years ago. Way back when he first rescued me from the Vruks.

I remember my nightmare. Remember the way his blade pierced through my heart ...

Perhaps that's exactly what he'll eventually do.

Lungs jerking for breath, I shove to the surface, drawing a deep, shameful gulp of life-giving air. Hair slicked down my back, I pry a rock from the riverbank and use it to scrub myself raw.

Stare catching on my rippled reflection, my attention narrows on the black vines scribbled across my right shoulder, their tapered tips weaving over my collarbone.

I swear that's spread.

My hand whips up, fingers running over the jagged, black branch now partially protruding from my skin like a gnarly scar—icy dread washing through my chest when I feel a round bulge poking off a particularly risen bit.

I let go of the rock, chin dropping as I look at the mark, fingers prodding at the burgeoning lump flaring with a scathing itch. I scratch at it, and a thin layer of skin collects beneath my nails, exposing a black bud no bigger than a blueberry.

My heart does a nosedive.

Teeth gritted, I lift it up off the branch that seems to be woven beneath my skin ...

Delicate black sepals curl back, revealing a cluster of crystal petals huddled together in a shimmering swirl.

A tiny, crystal bloom.

Shock and confusion wrestle inside me, but one overriding emotion overpowers them both.

Revulsion.

Off. *I need it off.*

Face twisted, I pull at the tender bud, ripping an aching moan from deep inside my gut, feeling like the flower's roots are woven around my clavicle—like the only way to get it off is to snip through its stubby stem.

Nausea slathers the internal walls of my chest.

I give it another aching tug, tears welling, and my mouth falls open in a silent scream.

It's stuck.

Panic claws up my throat, sharpening my breaths. I cup water over my shoulder to soothe the throbbing hurt, then watch in horror as it frees those petals free from their twisted bind, coaxing them to bloom ...

I need it off.

Teeth gritted, I pinch it again—

A low, rumbling sound makes the hairs on the back of my neck stand on end.

Slowly, I look over my shoulder.

My blood turns to ice, every muscle locking at the sight of a mammoth beast prowling through the smoky residue of my desolation, enormous paws stomping deep prints in the ash, its head tucked between wide, bulky shoulders as it sniffs the ground with heaping whuffs.

Vruk.

It's twice the size of the ones etched into the folds of my brain—ink black, bulging muscles shifting with each roving step. Its sharp ears are pinned back, fur slick and smooth aside from its thick, regal mane.

Run, that voice inside me screams.

But I can't move ... think ... *breathe.* My feet are cast in stone, tethered to the silty riverbed.

A fallen branch crunches beneath the weight of its mighty paw as the beast sniffs at the fried remnants of a leg, and its low, thunder-borne growl ripples across the water's surface.

Across my pebbled skin.

Maw renting open, it takes the limb between its piercing fangs, drops low onto its haunches, and feasts—twisting its head to the side, masticating the remains to a savage rhythm of crunching, popping, grinding sounds.

My stomach twists, a small breath puffing free as I look to the spot I entered the water. To where I left my necklace and blade sitting on the edge of the bank.

My heart smashes against my ribs so hard I fear they might crack.

I edge my foot forward an inch, then another, then set it down, keeping my stare trained on the beast. Its ears twitch while it chews, using its mighty paws to reposition the leg for its next pulverizing bite.

I know how to be silent—I do. But right now my heart is *screaming;* pumping in fast, urgent beats.

Too loud.

Its thick, pink tongue threads out and laps around its chops before it pushes up off the ground, its inky underbelly stamped in ash as it prowls toward another heap of flesh.

The torso I flipped.

My fingers reach for my chain and blade, gripping them both, pulling them back along the grass—stare caught on the scenting beast.

Its head whips in my direction, black eyes hitting me with such bold, primal force that I can almost *feel* those fierce, gore-covered teeth splitting through my flesh, releasing a burst of blood.

It snarls, the sound sawing through the space between us like a serrated blade.

Run!

I kick my feet out from beneath me and fall back into the water, letting the swift current snatch me under.

Chapter 48
Orlaith

My breathing is choppy as I creep up the hill, sodden hair slick against my ribs and dripping down the backs of my bare legs. Crouching low, I edge over the rise, seeing the small orchard—blessedly unaffected by my blazing force of destruction.

I inch down the grassy slope, gaze nipping at the rise on the opposite side where twists of smoke lick at the darkening sky, the smell of ash and burnt flesh clogging my lungs.

The distant sound of popping, crunching bones hammers nails into my kneecaps, threatening to make me stumble.

It's still there.

Still *feasting*.

Irilak are smudged into shadows of the jungle, tucked within its safe confines, seeming tentative to flit forward and feed despite the heavy clouds blotting the light.

Surely they'll come forth soon. Suckle the Vruk into a dehydrated lump of flesh and bone.

I hope.

Watched from the jungle's gloomy guts by countless pairs of eyes that scrape across my naked skin, I move forward, heart in my throat and stomach in knots. I sneak beneath the tree Gael and I ate peaches beneath and wrap myself in her cloak, stuff my blade into my bag, then edge back up the rise one stolen step at a time, stealing glances over my shoulder.

Just a little farther.

Grass tickles my shins as I quicken my pace and dash toward the drain that stabs beneath the city wall, just picking a path over big, slippery stones when the hairs on the back of my neck lift.

A full-body chill rips across my skin.

I swallow. Look over my shoulder to see the Vruk skulking over the knoll beyond the orchard in long, robust strides, nose dug into the grass, whuffing at the soil.

Fear knifes into me.

Another prowling step, and it lets out a low rumble that rakes up my spine, then slowly lifts its head, maw smeared in the gore of the men I just slayed.

A web of lightning forks across the sky as our eyes clash, ricocheting off its catastrophic stare.

My foot slips on a patch of slimy muck.

I fall hard, cracking my knees on the stones to the tune of a slashing growl that cuts straight through me. Hands slamming down, my necklace falls from my grasp, lost in the filthy water.

The ground begins to tremble, like a thundering heart is hacking at the soil beneath me, and I look up to see the beast lunging across the glen in great, barreling strides.

Coming straight for me.

Digging between the stones in clawed, frantic motions, I snatch harrowing glances of the approaching beast—bounding closer ...

Closer ...

My fingers tangle with my chain, and a relieved breath fills me with the power to clamber up and scramble over the unrelenting chaos of the slippery stones, toward the drain's illuminated mouth that looks too small for that beast to fit through.

Please be too small.

A blow of hot air attacks me from behind. Tingles explode from the soles of my feet, lashing up my legs and spine, and I release a strangled gasp as I duck my head and dive past the opening, water splashing up my shins with every frantic step.

The ground beneath me stills, and a sharp sound splits the air, like the metal grate is screaming. There's a distant thud, and the lantern light chasing me through the drain is dimmed in smashing increments until it snips out entirely.

A deep, foreboding rumble blasts through the shaft, infusing my skin and sanding my bones.

It's *everywhere*—all around me. *Through* me. Breaking down the very fiber of my being.

My legs threaten to crumble, palm slamming against the curved stone edge, and I dare to look back into the pall of darkness ...

Gruff whuffing sounds saw down the space, and my heartbeat scatters.

"Oh my—"

It's trying to shove its face down the drain.

Another low snarl frays my composure, and it pulls back,

weaves its paw through the hole, and swipes at the empty air—as though it's trying to *reach* for me. My stomach drops, and I dash toward that distant promise of light in sloppy steps that feel too slow.

Too slow.

Cobwebs stretch across my face as I near the end, and I choke back a squeal, batting at them with desperate swipes, until I burst past the spill of lantern light and out the other end—shrouded in a sense of safety.

A fall of rain caresses my upturned face, the stormy evening bathing the silent city in a bleak blanket. I scour my surroundings, looking past the bridge that saddles the deep ditch I'm standing in, up the edges of lofty buildings crammed close together. Up the city's wall—its blazing turrets spilling a shield of light that doesn't make it into the city's dark gullies.

I turn, looking down the drain, heaving breath into my starved lungs. If I listen hard enough, I can hear the beast breathing from the other end. Can still feel the blazing trail of its perusal carve across my face like it's hunting every freckle sprinkled across my nose and cheeks.

A blow of relief batters out of me.

I scramble up the side of the ditch and burst down the desolate alley. Lowering myself behind a barrel, I spin, spine to the wall so I can see through the thin sliver between barrel and stone. Despite knowing the beast won't emerge, I keep my stare on that drain as I blindly dig through my knapsack, fingers grazing against my snips. I pull them out and thread my finger through one hole, thumb through the other, trying to stop my teeth from chattering.

I drop my gaze and coax the cloak away from my tender

shoulder, revealing the black vine and the tiny crystal bloom that's now baring a full nest of delicate petals—soft to the touch when I brush my thumb across them.

Face twisting into a knot of disgust, I pinch it between my fingers, tilt it to the side to expose its sable stem, and open the snip's pincers against the stalk.

I draw a breath, holding it in my lungs as I pinch the handles together.

My mouth falls open, a scream threatening to burst forth when the blades slide off the stem, scouring deep gouges on either side.

Pain explodes across my shoulder, the muscle and bone and flesh a mess of mangled nerves, making tears pool in my eyes. The fierce throb radiates across my clavicle, lashes up the side of my neck, and bores into my eardrum.

My stomach churns.

Harder—I have to cut harder.

I hiss through gritted teeth, tilting the tender bloom again, hand shaking, settling the snips against the stem ...

Lightning scribbles across the sky, and I squeeze the callous blades together.

A clipping sound plucks at the air as I sever the stalk, struck with a blinding bolt of pain.

I smack the back of my head against the wall and slap my hand over my mouth to smother a scream, snips clattering across the stone as the hurt knots my limbs and fires my blood. I writhe, thrashing through broken whimpers, churning my legs like it'll alleviate the devastating throb bruising my bones.

It's gone.

I got it off.

A relieved sob breaks free, and I tip my head, letting the drizzle wash away the tears tracking down my face until I mine the courage to look at my shoulder again.

I slowly turn my head.

The severed nub leaks a black substance down my front, swiftly attacked by the rain, diluting it into inky swirls that get lost in the fold of fabric. I poke at the swollen skin surrounding the hurt, then drop my trembling chin to my heaving chest, gaze sliding sideways. To the golden snips lying on the stone with their sharp mouth wide open.

To the tiny crystal bloom nesting between two cobbles.

My pain seems to sprout more roots at the sight, as well as a seed of melancholy I try to ignore.

The rain grows into a drumming symphony while I shore up the courage to reach for it. I swallow thickly, pluck it from the stone, and cup it in the palm of my unsteady hand.

My lungs are mortar, throat tight as I study the crystal bloom.

Delicate. Beautiful.

Hideous.

I touch the silky sepals, rolling one down, pressing hard before pulling my finger back. It unravels, crimped from the folded bruises I just forced upon it. Tearing it free from the stem, I rub it between my fingers until it begins to break apart, familiarizing myself with this strange thing that somehow sprouted from me.

My attention narrows on the shimmering petals ...

I press my finger against them, sucking a tight breath when I find they're no longer flimsy like a rose. They don't yield like the sepal did. Instead, they crinkle, then crack—little slivers of their brittle edges breaking off like shards of glass, blunting the hardened bloom that must have begun to calcify the moment I snipped it off.

Like it ... *died.*

A surge of nausea clogs my throat, and I stuff the bloom in my bag. Not wanting to look at it. Think about it. *Feel* it.

Tittering laughter and hurried footsteps stop my heart, my stare flying down the alley to the right. A boy and a girl dash from the rain, running straight at me.

"Shit."

I bag the snips, flip my hood, snatch my necklace close to my chest, and tuck myself into a ball pressed against the barrel—easing the edges of my cloak over my bare legs, feet, and arms.

Please don't see me.

Their steps draw closer, the sound of my rapid heartbeats surging in my ears, battling with the distant memory of a conversation I had with Kai. Back when we were going through *Te Bruk o' Avalanste*, looking at the illustration of an Aeshlian climbing from the volcanic basin ...

"*What happened to them?*"

"*That's a very long, very sad story. One I wouldn't taint your pretty ears with.*"

"*But you tell me everything ...*"

"*Not that, Orlaith. Never that.*"

My mind fires with possibilities that blister my insides.

What if these people see me—will they look at me like I'm an abomination?

Will they worship me? Hunt me?

Bind me to a stake and burn me?

They draw close, stalling.

Fear wells up inside me, and I huddle deeper into my hood.

A coin clatters to the stone by my bunched legs, and then they continue sprinting down the alley, dashing from the rain on hurried steps. My breath pours free, relief blossoming through my chest so fast I feel like I'm going to be sick.

I peel back the edge of my hood and look at the small, silver coin in the puddle before me ...

That was too close.

Hands trembling, I thread my necklace around my neck and try to knot the ends together, but they don't hold.

My skin doesn't peel back up again.

"No, no, no ..."

I fumble, knot, re-knot, then pinch the clasp together. My false skin takes me in a claustrophobic gulp that's never felt so good, and a relieved sob bursts free as I tip my face to the sky.

I need to get out of here.

I rap the door with torn and bloody knuckles, eating the spike of pain like the penance it is.

Forehead pressed to the grain, I breathe deep, stare cast on the Bulbs and Botany mat scuffed with mud as the thick fall of rain continues to pelt my back.

If this isn't Gun and his partner's store, I don't know what I'll do.

I have nowhere else to go.

Another crack of lightning, another blow of wind, and the sign hanging above me squeaks as it rocks with the rhythm of the crackling storm.

My pinch on the chain tightens, arm aching with the effort to hold the short lengths together, the dress I managed to climb into on my own only half done up at the back and drenched through beneath the fall of the equally sodden cloak.

Another knock—louder this time. More desperate.

Please be them.

Please be home.

Heavy footsteps thunk on the other side, and my chin wobbles. I feel the vibrations of a lock sliding sideways before the door is pulled open, almost taking me with it.

I straighten and lift my head, squinting into a pair of russet eyes from beneath the shield of my soaking hood—years etched in the fine lines pinching the corners of the man's narrowed stare. A fine blue garb hangs loosely off his shoulders that are broad, despite his slight form, his face long and sharp, hand gripping a lantern that's casting warm light across his tawny, freckle-dusted skin.

Behind him, an array of plants hang in planters, nest on wall shelves, and are eloquently piled atop a table in the center of the room.

No sign of Gun.

Panic pounds my chest in deep, crushing blows …

Perhaps this was a bad idea—perhaps I should have tried some of the other plant stores I passed on the way.

The man looks past me, left and right, rusty brows pulling together. "Are you lost?"

Maybe.

Swallowing, I use my free hand to push back my hood. I'm not sure what he sees in my eyes, but all the color saps from his cheeks, making his freckles stand out in stark comparison. He turns, his voice bellowing through the room. "*Gunthar!*"

Relief compresses my lungs. Almost buckles me.

There's the sound of a door swinging; heavy footsteps thumping. Gun steps into the spill of lantern light, pinching the gold buttons into place on his dark blue tunic, eyes widening as he casts his gaze across my face. My hands. My bare and bloody feet.

"Orlaith …"

I'm not sure why, but the sound of my name on his sturdy, familiar voice makes my eyes sting.

He grips me by the arm and pulls me out of the cold.

Chapter 49
Orlaith

I stare blankly at a fading family portrait in the middle of the powder blue wall, framed by the aged branches of a tree that creeps from a terra-cotta pot perched in the corner of the room—the branches stuck to the walls reminding me of the mark that weaves across my shoulder.

Of the bloom I snipped.

Killed.

Of the men I *also* killed.

I flinch from the thought, absorbing another stab of sting as Gun dabs at my knuckles with a damp piece of cotton.

Their house is all old-world elegance, filled with houseplants I couldn't bring myself to appreciate while I was led through the shop, up two sets of stairs, and down a hall into this room. It's immaculately kept, smelling like freshly baked oat cookies I can't imagine Gun making.

I study the framed rendition of him—much younger. Looking more like Zane and less like the Captain I know. There's also a girl, perhaps younger than him, tucked between who I suppose are their parents, her hair twisted into a golden coif.

I stare at her, mesmerized by her petite features, and the regal way she holds herself. At her big, lilac eyes—a little too large for her face—and her lips, thin yet shapely.

There's another dab to my knuckles, and I feel Gun's gaze flick across my face.

"That hurt?"

"A little."

I hear the words rasped in my voice, but barely feel them leave my lips. As though all my feelings, all my emotions, *everything* just ... slipped away.

He gives a small grunt, then, "There's something in there. Try not to scream while I dig it out."

I think he's jesting, but I can't find it in myself to smile or even peel my eyes from the painting.

I'm still dressed in my gown and cloak, refusing to part with them for fear of exposing that vile mark on my shoulder. A thick, fluffy towel is draped over me to soak up some of the wet—the extra weight making the tender nub on my clavicle throb.

There's a light knock on the door, and Captain mumbles a curt "come in" while digging through my flesh with a pair of tweezers.

The man who answered when I first arrived breezes in with a steaming mug in one hand and a clay bowl in the other that he sets on the rug beside Gun.

"Did you send the sprite?"

Sprite?

"You think so little of my attention span that you think I'd lose sight of my task only moments after you dished it?"

Gun stills, glaring over his shoulder at the man who swiftly throws him a wink. "*Captain.*"

Another grunt, and Gun gets back to digging between my knuckles while the other man offers me a steaming mug of something that smells like vanilla-and-cinnamon cocoa.

My hand tightens around my broken chain.

"I'm Enry." He offers a warm smile that reaches his eyes. "It's nice to formally meet you."

"Same to you," I say, pulling my injured hand from Gun to take the mug, setting it down on a small table beside the overstuffed upholstered chair I'm seated in. "Thank you."

He moves toward the couch on the opposite side of the room where he sets a laden basket on his knees, busying his hands peeling garlic bulbs.

"You ... sent a sprite?" My voice croaks with the question, heart heavy with the thought that it might have gone to Cainon.

That he could already be on his way here.

"To my sister," Gun rumbles, and I breathe a sigh of relief, even as he pries a sharp splinter of wood from where it was lodged in the dip between my knuckles. He drops it into the bowl of water, rinsing his cotton before dabbing at my wounds again. "Hopefully, she'll soon be over with a change of clothes."

I nod, lifting my stare back to the family portrait.

Family.

Something inside me twists.

"What happened, Orlaith?"

Long moments drip by while he continues to dab. I don't let my stare drift from the painting. Don't even blink.

What happened ...

Her.

Them.

Me.

I want to scream it. But I want to hide it more.

From him. From myself.

I don't want to think about Gael—about what they would have done to her had they succeeded in whatever it was they set out to do. I don't want to think about the thrill I got from breaking that man's face beneath my fist. I don't want to think about the way my skin mosaicked as that fiery rage busted free—sawing.

Slaughtering.

I certainly don't want to think about that brief moment right before, when whatever it is that lives inside me sat up and stilled—*listened*—as though it were asking for permission. As though I could have possibly prevented it had I only known how to say no.

Or perhaps it's something else ...

Perhaps I said yes.

That—

I don't want to think about that.

I realize Gun's hands have stilled. "Is there anything you need me to do? Anyone you need me to take care of?"

I blink, letting my gaze drop.

He's sitting on the backs of his heels, elbows on his knees and brow pinched tight. The fierce look in his bright blue eyes settles something within, like I've been drifting down that river for the past few hours and have only now stopped. Like that child deep inside—the one who gifted her brother flowers to be made into a crown—senses the anchor he's offering me.

My bottom lip wobbles, a lump forming in my throat. "My necklace is broken."

He nods. "I can fix that."

He reaches out a hand armored with thick calluses, the lines of his palm telling a story of hard labor.

Another shaky breath.

I swallow, release the necklace. Watch it fall into his awaiting hand with a dense thud.

My mask peels down, freeing me from its soul-crushing embrace, and I watch all the color bleed from his face. Watch his eyes widen so much I can almost see more white than blue.

The basket that was atop Enry's lap clatters to the ground, garlic bulbs scattering across the faded rug, and Gun stumbles back, gripping hold of a short, wooden stool. Eyes locked on me, he sits upon it as Enry leaps to his feet and dashes the curtains closed on the massive windows lining one wall, blocking out the bold glow of the lanky street lanterns looming over the world outside.

He spins and stares at me through glazed eyes.

"Aeshlian," Gun whispers, as though the word is a stolen secret.

I blink, sending a tear down my cheek. "I, um ... I think so ..."

His eyes soften, despite the hard set of his jaw, knuckles clenched around the chain he lifts between us—my pendant and conch both swinging back and forth. "How long have you been wearing this, Orlaith?"

How long have I been hidden?

"For as long as I can remember," I whisper, voice cracking at the end.

He mutters something that might be a curse word, spoken in a language I don't understand. "Enry?"

"I'm right here, Gunthar."

"Not a word to anyone, you hear?"

Enry pats his chest, face aghast. "Do you not know me at all?"

"I know you *too* well." Gun studies the broken clasp on my chain. "Your mouth is somehow my least and most favorite thing about you."

"*That's* ..." Enry wobbles his head from side to side, deliberating, "actually rather charming."

I bunch my hands into fists, making the raw wounds smart. "I don't understand," I blurt. "Why the secrets? Why do I have to hide?"

Gun shares a side-eyed look with Enry, who says, "You were never told?"

"I've been told *nothing*. That's why I've been hunting for Madame Strings. I heard she knows a lot of things and I ... I just ..."

"You don't hunt for her," Gun growls, the color bleeding from his face. "You don't even *breathe* her name, do you understand?"

My heart stills, like he's lumped something heavy on it.

I'm just not sure what it is yet.

"Shit." He looks to the floor, up again with a stare that plunges through me. "Orlaith, Madame Strings is a member of a cult religion that hangs off every chiseled word of the prophet Maars. A small band of the truly hardcore worshipers have spent *years* hunting your people in the name of the stones, believing they're doing the Gods's work."

An itch flares across my shoulder, making me want to scratch the tender wound that's throbbing with newfound life. "Shulák?"

He nods.

"What ... what are they doing with us?"

"They believe your kind will hail the world's end," he mutters gruffly. "An end that'll never come ... if you're all extinguished."

The blood drains from my face as the realization of what he's saying dawns on me, every sharp word a withering strike.

"They *kill* us?"

He nods. "You show yourself to the wrong person, and yes, you'll be put down. Hacked in—"

"*Gunthar!*" Enry pads the air with his hands. "Stop! You're scaring the poor thing."

Thing ...

"She needs to hear!" Gun bellows, and there's a fury in his voice that rips right through me.

He looks at me again, and I want to clap my hands over my ears. Want to crawl under a table and hide from the blows.

"Show yourself to the wrong person," he repeats, slower this time, "and you'll be hacked into pieces." All the breath rushes out of me. "Sold on the black market—"

"*Stop!*" I scream, and he does, holding my stare for a few stretched moments before hanging his head.

A heavy silence fills the room.

Gun clears his throat, looking up from beneath his bushy brows. "I'm sorry, Orlaith ... but I need you to know."

I nod, swallowing the ache rising up my throat, the bile threatening to spill.

I've been looking for answers, now I'm desperate to shove them back in the tomb. To leap back in time and keep the questions raging in my chest, gnawing at their bars.

It hurt much less than *this*.

"There's some sick, twisted people out there, Orlaith. You don't trust anyone, do you understand? *Nobody*. Not even your promised."

The words toll in my ears like a warning bell …

"Tell me you understand."

"I understand," I rasp, and his shoulders loosen.

"This"—he shakes the necklace at me, held in the clutches of his clenched fist—"I'll fix this." Then he's up, moving toward a desk in the corner, setting a wiry pair of spectacles on his face as he gathers some bits and begins tinkering away beneath the golden glow of a candelabra.

Show yourself to the wrong person, and you'll be hacked into pieces. Sold on the black market.

That's the reason Baze was hiding. The reason I haven't seen more of my people around.

They're either scared to show themselves …

Or they're dead.

My gaze drops to a nick in my thigh, almost the exact spot as the wound Kai healed with his tongue—directly above the heart-shaped birthmark that's strangely absent without my mask.

I watch the opaline substance dribble from the hurt, captivated by the liquid shimmering with light of its own, leaving a soft rainbow smear that paints over the red.

That pretty shade of pink I loved so much when I dripped

my blood into the water I gifted Rhordyn ... it seems even *that* was a lie.

Enry crouches before me.

I blink, and his gaze chases a rogue tear rolling down my cheek.

"May I?" With my nod, his hand drifts up, catching the bead. The pad of his thumb comes away glistening, and he stirs it through the water blushed from my wounds. After using the cotton cloth to dab at the cut on my leg, he drops that in the bowl of water and stands. "Be right back."

A chill hits when he swings the door open, and I wait, listening to the shrill metallic taps of Gun fixing my necklace.

When Enry returns, he's carrying some waxy material, some string, and a small terra-cotta pot the size of a mug, filled to the brim with soil. He kneels, scooping his hand into the blushed water, dribbling some atop the soil before wrapping it into a well-contained package he offers me.

Frowning, I take it, seeing a soft smile touch his lips. "You are light, my love. Light and life and all that is good." He sets his hands around mine, his touch warm and grounding, palms smooth. "*That* is what you cling to."

I nod, even though the words feel like another skin that doesn't fit right.

Gun casts me in his big shadow, necklace in hand. "May I?"

"Let me just ..." I clear my throat and reach for my knapsack, easing the package into it, "put this away."

I look down at my hands as Gun pushes my hair to the side and threads the chain around my neck, clipping it in place.

My mask suctions to my polished skin, painting me in the lie.

I watch the pearlescent shine drain from my hair, the heavy locks tinting gold. Watch the blood oozing from the hurt in my leg begin to bleed red, blotting the evidence with my cloak.

I look up to see them watching on, Gun rubbing at his stubble while Enry shakes his head, one hand on his hip, the other cupping his mouth.

A distant knock splits the silence, and I look to the door, white-knuckling my towel—feeling just as bare as I did the moment I climbed from that brook, despite the wet layers of clothing and my reconstructed mask.

Gun frowns, speaking to Enry in hushed tones. "Relieve Della of the parcel and send her on her way."

"That's going to go down like a bag of horse manure." Enry snorts. "Do you even know your sister?" He shakes a hand, muttering as he clicks the door shut behind himself.

Gun rubs at the stubble on his jaw again and lets out a deep sigh. "Gonna grab some ointment for your knuckles," he says, moving toward a cupboard at the back of the room. "I'm sure Enry stashed something in there one time."

The door shoves open so fast it cracks against the back wall, and Zane spills in like a ray of sunshine and mischief, making my heart lurch into my throat.

"How did you get here so fast?"

"Back window," Zane boasts, dashing toward me as I tuck my hair behind my ear and try to smooth it down so I don't look as frightening as I feel.

Shaking his head, Gun pulls the cupboard open, disappearing inside it with a lantern. Zane stands before me, pushing the flop of hair from his worried eyes. His gaze bounces across my split knuckles, down to the bowl of bloody water now stained with a hint of shimmer.

I open my mouth to speak. To ask him how he is; tell him I missed him; that I've got something special at the palace I can't wait to gift him—

"What's happened?" he blurts before I have the chance, wearing a look that makes him appear so much older than he is. A look that reminds me of my brother—of the way he tucked me against the wall beneath the table after holding me close and saying he'd look after me.

Always.

"It's ..." The word comes out choked. "It's nothing for you to worry about. I promise."

"Are you in trouble?" He pulls something from his pocket and holds it out. "Do you need my—"

My heart shatters, tears welling at the sight of the token in his hand. "No, you keep that for yourself." A smile skims my lips as I reach forward and fold his fingers over the piece of gold. "I'm fine, Zane. Cross my heart."

His eyes go all stern and stubborn, jaw set, hand still outstretched. "Don't lie to me. I'm not a kid, you know!"

Oh, Zane ...

Gun shuts the cupboard door and spins, carrying a tin tub, and I squeeze Zane's hand, urging him to put his token away with a pleading look.

Finally, he does—stepping back, allowing Gun to get to work smearing an ointment on my knuckles under his intense scrutiny.

"No, I will not just hand you the clothes, you daft oaf!"

A female's voice, shrill and stern, accompanies a chorus of thundering steps.

Cap stills, stare stabbed at the doorway. "Dammit. Should've gone myself." He sighs, popping the lid back on the tub as the woman continues her piercing scald from somewhere down the hall.

"A female turns up bruised and bloody and, I'm sorry, the last person she's going to want to talk to is my rough and tumble brother!"

"I assure you, Della, we have everything under contr—"

"*Codswallop.*" The woman bursts through the door in a flutter of blue silk sodden from hem to knee—an explosion of fiery energy that fills the room.

The woman from the portrait.

Though she's older now, she still holds the same lithe beauty.

She takes one look at me and halts, dropping a soft package to the floor at her feet, every ounce of determination slipping from her elegant face.

I still beneath the power of her slack-faced stare, blood icing in my veins. Perhaps the necklace isn't properly fixed? Perhaps she's seeing through the cracks to the real me shining through?

Her gaze drops, landing on my bare thigh, on the cut that's yet to be bandaged.

Hand flying to her mouth, she releases an anguished sob.

"Della?" There's a sharp edge of concern in Gun's tone as he steps toward his sister, and then she's on her knees, hands cupping her crumbling face, rattling off words in a different language—one word rolling into another. Gun kneels before her, holding her by the wrists.

Shaking his head.

She babbles, sobs, points ... Zane's eyes widen as he watches his mother break apart on the floor.

Cap looks at me over his shoulder, then shakes his head, hard and fierce. "Sheil de nah pa. Gahs ke, Viola! *Sheil de nah pa* ..."

Della snarls, shoves him back, and pushes to a stand. She snatches a lantern and dashes to the cupboard, pulling containers off the shelves she starts to dig through.

Enry studies me from the door—*really* studies me—as though he's seeing me for the first time.

I frown. "Is everything okay?"

Silence.

Della emerges from the cupboard with a book clutched against her chest, hands trembling as she walks to me, kneels at my feet, and splits it open, pointing at the first page.

The painting.

Della's there—a perfect depiction of her much younger self, cradling a small child no older than one with big, lilac eyes and a mop of curly hair the color of straw, her chubby face struck with a smile that lights her up. She's wearing a blue tunic trimmed in gold, her otherwise bare legs capped in little bootees with a lace frill.

"I don't understand," I admit, and she points to the child's leg. To the birthmark—a love heart.

Same color.

Same spot.

My birthmark ...

My heart lurches, breath hollows.

Her warm, soft hand comes up to cup my cheek.

"Viola ..." It's whispered. The word such a gentle thing passed to me in a shaken voice.

"*Viola,*" she repeats, and I let my eyes lift, landing in the wide, hopeful, lilac pools of hers.

"Her daughter—" Gun starts, voice cracking. He clears his throat as my focus shifts past Della to his troubled stare. "My niece. She, ahh, contracted the Blight as an infant. Della was only eighteen at the time." A long beat, then, "We buried her in the backyard with her grandparents."

My throat tightens, stare sliding back to Della. "I'm so sorry for your loss ..."

She shoves the painting in my face, shaking it so much I flinch. "*Viola!*"

Realization knifes into me, and my heart drops, splits, *shatters ...*

She thinks I'm her daughter.

I'm not. I have a mommy. A family.

Had.

Though I can't deny the resemblance between myself and her daughter, I'm something very different beneath this skin she thinks she knows.

I can't look at the painting. Can't look in her eyes and tell her this is nothing more than a tragic coincidence. That her little girl's not here, not coming back, because I know the burn of that hopeful flame, even when you know it's useless.

Sometimes, it's the only thing that keeps you warm.

"I'm so sorry, I have to go ..."

Her sobs attack me as I slip my towel off my shoulders and stand, easing past. I grab my knapsack, give a slack-faced Zane a kiss on the head, and make for the door. Barrel down the stairs on feet that won't move fast enough.

It's only once I'm outside, backed into a large cleft between the big rocks the fishermen use as seats, that I stare across the angry ocean, press the back of my hand to my mouth, and break.

Chapter 50
Orlaith

The storm rolls offshore, its bulbous clouds pulsing with a fierce, electrical heartbeat while it continues to rumble like a restless beast that nests beyond the palace. Another wave crashes, dusting my face in salty spray as I stare at the bridge—long and lit and daunting. Picture it crumbling beneath my feet the moment I climb back up the rocks and step onto it.

I just want to sleep, but despite being able to see my balcony from here, my bed seems so far away.

So foreign and unreachable.

I'm a different person now than I was this morning. I left that room a maiden, naïve, and packed full of questions.

I left that room *Orlaith*.

Now, I'm *Serren*—plucked, snipped, so achingly aware of my fragile existence and painted in another layer of murder.

I'm struggling to bridge the gap. To force myself to

power on with the knowledge of my slain species sitting heavily on my shoulders. To picture myself sleeping in those pure white sheets without feeling compelled to bunch them up and feed them to the fireplace.

I'm living in a shell that doesn't fit right anymore. Perhaps it never did.

This plush life feels so exorbitant compared to the bigger, uglier picture.

The distant clop of hooves snaps me out of my reverie. I clamber up the craggy face, peeking over a rock to see a gold-brushed carriage pulled by two horses clatter down the otherwise desolate esplanade.

The carriage.

Kolden follows on another horse, posture strong and sturdy. His long sheet of tawny hair stuck to the back of his equally sodden garb as he looks around, pinched gaze sweeping in my direction.

I duck, heart leaping into my throat.

I won't get another chance like this. Either I sit here staring at the sea, feeling sorry for myself, avoiding all my problems until they metastasize or I shove it all deep, pick myself up, chase that carriage down, and try to convince Kolden not to snitch on me.

Perhaps they saw Gael.

Perhaps they know if she's okay.

The thought has me leaping up just as they turn down the bridge, and I chase them on silent steps—dashing from one slab of shadow to the next. The carriage spills onto the palace grounds, and I wait until the soldier manning the bridge has his attention dug into a pine-leaf pouch, pipe caught between his teeth, before I peel free from the darkness and flit forward on feet that barely hit the ground.

Pausing behind a bush while I gather my breath, I watch the carriage settle close to the gates. Watch Kolden steer his horse onto the patch of grass below my balcony, a frown staining this face.

My gut cramps, guilt crouching heavily on my chest.

He looks pissed.

Stealing a nervous glance up the tall walls, I lift my chin and step beside him as he heaves his leg over the back of his horse and drops out of the saddle.

He spins, jolting, hand slamming against his chest. "Fu—"

"Hi."

He blows out a breath, gaze sweeping the grounds, before shielding me with his horse, looking straight at me. "Permission to speak frankly?" he bites out, and I wince.

"Yes ..."

"*What the fuck?*"

"I deserve that," I admit, tucking sodden hair off my face.

His gaze snags on my split knuckles, eyes widening.

I whisk my hand behind my back and pretend he didn't see. "Have you heard from Gael?"

He watches me for a long moment, unblinking, stare tracking over the throbbing spot on my temple. "Orlaith—"

"Have you?" I insist, desperation riding my tone.

"Yes, I have."

A pit of emotion swells in my throat that's hard to swallow past, my hand stabbing back to steady myself against the wall. It takes every ounce of self-control not to crumble into a ball of relief.

She's alive ... She's okay ...
I didn't kill her.

"A maid came out with a scroll bearing Gael's family seal." He digs through his pocket, pulls out the scroll, and waves it at me. "Said you'd decided to walk back to the palace because you needed some *air*. Is that what happened? Did you need air?"

I nod, too scared to blink for fear of sending tears dashing down my cheeks. "Yes, that's exactly what happened. I'm sorry to have worried you."

"Not only did you *worry* me," he growls in hushed tones, pointing toward the carriage, "but these men were under strict instructions not to let you roam the city on your own. You put us *all* at risk! Forgive me ..." He clears his throat, jaw clenched as he regains himself. "I'm done being frank."

"Well, I'm back now, so ..." *Cainon doesn't even need to know.*

Kolden sighs, closing his eyes and pinching the bridge of his nose—a look that reminds me of Baze and makes my throat ache. "Fine. You go upstairs before the High Master gets back and sees you like that," he says, flicking a hand at me. "I'll talk to the other men."

I offer him a small smile. "Thank you, Kolden."

"Just promise not to throw another knife at me," he mutters, jerking his chin toward the palace's front gate.

"Orlaith!"

Cainon's voice booms through the foyer, slamming me to a halt with my fingers stretched toward the railing of the grand staircase that leads to my suite.

I draw a deep breath that does nothing to quell the frantic beat of my heart, then turn to see him striding across the polished floor toward me. He's a vision of wind and rain—cheeks flushed, his dark blue top soaked through and clinging to the tailored slabs of his muscled physique.

My gaze drops to his gray pants, a similar shade to that of which the Shulák wear ...

My heart flips.

He has connections to the faith, that much is clear from his reliance on Elder Creed. But how deep do those veins dig?

Does he condone the slaughter of my people?

I swallow the bile burning a trail up my throat.

Brow buckled, his stare carves over me as he rolls his sleeves. "Did you just get back?" I catch sight of his lapis lazuli cupla caught around his strong, sun-brushed wrist, and my heart leaps into my throat, my own wrist burning with an emptiness I stab behind my back.

Shit.

"Yes, we ahh ... we got caught in the storm."

He pauses, frown deepening as he assesses me from a few strides away, and then he's charging forward, snatching my wrist from behind my back, holding it between us.

He steps so close our bodies are flush.

Our breaths mingle—sharp and harsh, a crackle of tension snapping at my wet skin. "Where's your cupla?" he whispers against my ear, the words too quiet to have such a grating effect.

Why didn't I think to ask Gun to fix it?

"In my bag," I rasp. "The latch broke ..."

Seconds slip by to the beat of my hammering heart while I stare at the buttons on his shirt. At my grazed knuckles bunched between us.

He pulls back, looking down into me, and rather than the expected wrath I was shoring myself up to weather, there's concern swirling in his eyes. "You should have come directly back the moment it did. Anything could have happened to you. This is your protection," he urges, squeezing my bare wrist. "Your *safety net*."

I suck a bolt of air through parted lips ...

Safety net.

I don't want one of those. Not anymore. I haven't since I stepped a toe across my Safety Line at Castle Noir. Not even with the newfound knowledge that the *me* beneath this skin is being hunted every second of the day and night.

Perhaps that's been our problem from the start. Perhaps he wanted the naïve, scared, moldable girl he found barefoot and broken at Rhordyn's castle, thinking he could bend her weaknesses into his own strengths.

But the new me doesn't bend.

I *snap*.

"It's okay, though," he says, brushing his knuckles against my jaw and flashing me a smile. "Nothing I can't fix."

Keeping a tight grip on my wrist, he leads me out across the concourse and through a small door on the other side. A coil of stairs drills us down into the bowels of the palace—an area I've yet to explore, though I know where we're going the moment the distant *ting* of metal on metal hits me like sharp nails to my tired, unfortified brain.

I'm smacked with a smoky, metallic scent I've smelled

before—on the southern border of Vateshram Forest, and only ever when the wind blew a stiff northern breeze.

He's taking me to the smithy.

Those sounds keep pecking, *pecking* ... until we come to a massive room that's carved into the cliff face. Flaming kilns line the walls, workbenches packing the space, each occupied by hunched-over men dripping sweat down their temples, banging away at their various projects, most of them swords from what I can see at first glance.

The open wall at the far end, windowing an empty wooden pier glazed in moonlight, exposes the space to the elements, though it does nothing to alleviate the dense humidity.

"Get out!" Cainon bellows, and the shrill racket is sponged in an instant, followed by a symphony of clattering tools that makes me wince.

Boots scuff against stone as the men leave, their heads down and gazes cast on the sooty floor. Cainon seems to pick a workbench at random, drops my wrist, and reaches out his hand.

I dig through my bag, throat clenching at the sight of the tiny, blunted crystal bloom tumbling around in the bottom. Retrieving my cupla and the piece of gold that broke off, I hand them over.

He studies them, eyes cast down. "How did it break?"

"I knocked it against something," I lie, and his eyes flick up, down again.

"Our gold is very soft because it's such high quality. I'll replace the latch with an iron one."

"Iron?"

"A type of metal. Not so commonly used anymore, but it's hardy."

He gets to work, melting, tipping, pinching things with long pliers, then dipping them in a bucket of water that boils instantly. Then he's banging—making sharp *tinking* sounds with every determined strike, concentration knotting his brow.

I pull a deep breath and blow it out, teeth gritted as I force myself to maintain my composure, picturing myself cross-legged in a grassy glen with soil between my fingers.

My gaze wanders across the bench, landing on a vicious-looking chisel with a bulbous wooden handle, the flat metal length honed to a squared tip.

That looks handy ...

Cainon turns to the forge behind him, the glow of the flames licking at his bronze, sweat-dappled skin, and I blindly reach for the tool, pluck it up, and tuck it in my bag.

He turns, eyes narrowed on a small, dull piece of metal pinched between a pair of blackened pliers. More sharp taps with a small hammer, and then he holds up my cupla, looking at it from all angles. "Much better," he murmurs, gesturing for me to reach my hand across the wooden table dusted with shards of metal and marred with messy black divots.

He threads it onto my wrist and clips the dull gray latch into place. "I know they're uncomfortable sometimes, but they're not supposed to be unclipped," he says, looking up at me with a knowing glint in his eyes. "It weakens the latch."

I stare at him, heart pounding so hard I can hear it.

Does he know I've been taking it off?

"Perhaps it was loose?" he asks, a single brow raised. "Did the latch ever unclip on its own?"

"Yes," I blurt, locking onto the offering like the lifeline it is. "That happened a couple of times. Very frustrating."

I meet his gaze, daring him to challenge the lie.

He nods and plants his fists on the table, broad shoulders bulging, flashing me a friendly smile. "How about we use a little solder? That way you never have to worry about it coming off again. Ever."

The words hit like stones to my chest, planting seeds of wild panic that root around my ribs.

No.

I don't want this.

The voice screams at me, over and over again as I twist the conversation, look at it from all angles, and realize there's no way for me to free myself from the crushing jaws of this verbal trap.

His brows lift. "Orlaith?"

"Yes," I whisper, then clear my throat. "That's a good idea."

"Right. Then let's get it sorted," he says with a satisfied smile.

He turns and plunges a thin metal rod into the flames, letting it sit for a long moment while my heart beats me up from the inside. When he pulls it out, its pointed tip glows with a fiery pulse, much like my needle after I'd fire the tip in my candle flame.

He threads a tiny piece of silver wire against the pinched mouth of the iron latch, then brings the blazing prong close.

I swallow words trying to bludgeon my throat, desperate

to jerk away—to escape the radiating heat and my tethered fate.

The scalding metal *chews* the fragile skin on the inside of my wrist—the smell of burnt flesh smacking me in the senses, gouging through my conscience, dashing visions across my mind.

Burnt bodies.

Blistered skin that slid away. Stuck to my palms.

I clench my teeth, watching through a sheen of unshed tears as he touches the flaming tip against the wire, and it turns to liquid, seeping into the latch's nooks and crannies. Cainon tips a cup of water over the permanent seal, and it sizzles much like the blood in my veins and the hurt on my wrist.

He just burned me ...

Soldered my cupla in place ...

Turned it into a shackle ...

What's more, I practically *asked* him to.

I swallow, pulling my arm close to cradle it, fingers trembling, a fireball burning on the tip of my tongue.

"That should prevent any further breaks. You're happy, yes?"

Similar words are soldered through the folds of my brain from the night he first slipped this cupla around my wrist ...

This is what you wanted, yes?

No.

This is not what I want. Who I am.

I can't live with a bitten tongue and unsaid words in my chest.

A little part of my soul slips further away with every

deep throb on my wrist—the part that thought I could secure these ships without burning myself to the ground.

"Petal?"

I look up, give him a small smile, and nod.

"Good," he murmurs, easing around the table. He takes my hand, brings my knuckles to his lips, and plants a gentle kiss on the wounds there. "What happened to these?"

"I caved a man's face in for hurting someone I care about," I say, holding his unflinching stare.

He laughs, low and throaty, brushing his lips across them again. "Seriously, though. Did you fall?"

You have no idea.

"Just a little trip. Grazed them on a wall. By the way, I enjoyed seeing your city today."

His eyes light up. "You did?"

I nod. "Though I did overhear someone mention a Vruk was roaming not far from your city wall …"

"What?" His head kicks back, a flash of fear in his eyes. "Did you tell anyone?"

Who have I got to tell?

I shake my head.

He swallows, nodding slowly, then pushes between me and the table. Leaning against it, he weaves his arm around my back, pulling me closer, and straddles me with his outstretched legs. "Rest assured, you're *safe* here. Nothing can get through that wall, and even if it did, I could crumble the bridge in seconds."

A wave of nausea makes the insides of my cheeks tingle, but I keep my face smooth. Pretend I'm the girl he met in Castle Noir as I look up at him with worry-filled eyes. "Really?"

He tucks a loose tendril behind my still-damp hair, making me want to flinch away.

"Flick of a lever ..."

No ...

He grazes his lips across my knuckles again, holding my gaze. "I've been quietly building up the outer islands. Our future is certain, no matter how far the Vruk infestation spreads."

My heart dives, mind churning, the world seeming to fall out from under me ...

No wonder he wants to keep his fleet to himself. His backup plan *relies* on it, but at a steep cost.

Everyone else on the continent.

Again, I think of those ships—of the flames that tore them to shreds.

A single word powers through my mind, spoken in his blunt voice while his people sizzled and screamed ...

Sacrifices.

Chapter 51
Orlaith

Izel retrieves my tray from the late-night meal Cainon insisted upon and leaves without noticing me tucked beneath a table in the corner of the room—knees bent, chisel in my hand, empty knapsack slung over my shoulder.

The door clicks shut.

I look at the pristine, perfectly made bed. At the starched white sheets, crisp and clean and so unlike my blackened conscience. I close my eyes and hear the crunching sound that severed arm made when I rolled over it. Feel the wet flesh smearing across me like a warm paste.

My skin erupts with a violent shiver that rattles my organs, and I smack my head against the wall.

No.

Swallowing thickly, I weave my fingers beneath my cloak and scratch at the itch flaring across my tender shoulder, choking on the stab of pain.

The memory.

Refusing to look at the huge, golden urn in the corner

of the room that now houses the crystal bloom so I don't have to see it every time I open my drawer, I keep my head tipped back against the stone, watching the ever-bloating moon through the glass balcony doors ...

The gravity of everything that happened today punches me in the gut.

I'm not going to bleed for him. But with the sting attacking the blistering skin on my tender wrist in deep, painful throbs, I refuse to feel guilty.

He once told me it's in our nature to fall in love with the shackle that binds us, but I am no regular person. I signed up for this political pairing for a fleet I'm yet to receive. To save lives.

Make a difference.

Instead, I'm spending my days trying to clamber out of a basin, reaching for empty promises like a string puppet. Destroying myself.

Destroying others.

It's become blatantly obvious Cainon has very little interest in parting with his ships—helping the people I grew up watching through the peephole in the throne room. A theory backed by the fact that he keeps dangling them just out of reach.

Chances are, his word doesn't stand for shit, and I just gave him a perfect reason to whip them further away. Or burn me at the stake.

I promised the ships. I promised myself. But there's no guarantee I'm going to crawl out of that bowl, and even if I do, no guarantee I'm going to be around after the coupling ceremony to ensure the fleet comes to fruition.

It's time to take matters into my own hands.

I sit until the moon has lifted from my frame of view. Until I'm certain it's late enough that most servants have gone to bed. Ripping my stare from the sky, I bag the chisel, crawl out from beneath the table, and push to a stand, wincing as the heavy material of Gael's cloak abrades the tender, throbbing area on my right shoulder.

The spot where I snipped the bloom.

I unclip the cloak, ease it off, and drape it across my vanity. With a mix of dread and revulsion swirling in my gut, I raise my gaze to the mirror.

Nothing.

I pull a tight breath. Finger the patch of scratched skin; all that is left to pay homage to the disgusting pain I'm wearing beneath my mask—like it doesn't exist at all. Like there are no black vines creeping across my shoulder. No strange bulges or seeping, headless stems.

Meeting my own vacant stare, I turn from the mirror and exit the suite dressed in the ornate, strapless gown I don't have the energy to peel myself from, loosely tied at the back and barely keeping me contained. I move through the lobby and rip the door open, coming face to face with a yawning Kolden leaning against the wall, bathed in sleepy, golden light from the chandeliers.

Shit.

He shoves off and blinks at me, rubbing his eyes.

I walk straight past.

"*Orlaith!*" The word is a whispered hiss wrapped in desperation, casting my feet in stone.

Slowly, I turn—just enough to look at him down the line of my shoulder. "I'm not leaving the palace grounds, so you won't get in trouble ..."

"I'm not worried about *that*," he growls, stealing a look past me and stomping forward. Jaw clenched, he takes me in—from the tip of my bare toes peeking out from the bottom of my dress, to my cupla, and finally my eyes.

He swallows. "Avoid the third floor. He's in a meeting there."

I blink, working through my brief wave of shock before I give him a brisk nod and spin, making for one of the back stairwells I became acquainted with while I was hunting for the library.

Threading my hand into my bag, I wrap it tight around the chisel, feeling the sharp edges pucker my skin.

I have a tunnel to dig.

Tucked between the wall and a thick, heavy tapestry, I stab at the stone with fierce, shattering force, cracking off shards of blue that collect on the floor. I sweep them into my knapsack, which I then lump onto my shoulder, lugging it all the way back up the stairs to my suite.

Kolden lifts a brow when he sees me approaching. "What the hell have you got in there?"

"Part of a wall," I mutter, and the other brow bumps up as he opens the lobby door, shutting it behind me.

He can't get all *frank* on me if I tell him the truth.

I dig my raw, blistered fingers around the side of my dressing room mirror and ease it open, hit by the stagnant wash of lukewarm air. I don't bother with the lantern sitting on the top of the stairs, instead easing down Old Hattie's tunnel by sense alone.

Pushing out into the damp jungle, I'm painted in the

prickly perusals of the Irilak nesting in the shadows—so stark on this bright, moonlit night, creating a maze of lit paths woven across the ground.

I dig my hand into the stone shards, gripping a fistful and sprinkling it through the underbrush, the mindless motion keeping the ugly thoughts at bay until I've emptied my knapsack. Realizing I'm halfway down the path toward the tree Old Hattie showed me, I keep on.

Easing from the jungle's patchy protection, I step out into the rinse of moonlight pouring down from the clear night sky sprinkled with stars. I reach into my bag and pull out the chisel, holding it tight as I climb the tree, folding up on the lower branch with my back against the trunk. Knees caught close to my chest, I watch the jellyfish dance—all those bright little souls drifting through the waves. So beautiful and free.

It makes my heart ache.

I look to the sky instead; to the moon and the stars and the nothing in between.

In the moon, I see a clock that won't stop ticking.

In the stars, I see my brother's eyes.

In the black between it all, I see the inky death that poured from my skin, the charred bodies I left strewn across the ashy stamp of desolation, the Vruk that prowled through, crunching back the evidence.

I see the black vine woven through my shoulder and the little crystal bloom I severed.

Killed.

I stuff my skirt into my mouth and *scream*—releasing it all in one horrific howl that still leaves me splitting at the seams. I do it again, and again, and *again* until I'm breathless and heaving.

Releasing the material, my face crumbles, and a fierce, silent sob breaks free, cramping my insides and making me think I'll never breathe again. I squeeze the chisel. Squeeze it so hard a sharp, merciless pain cuts through my palm …

Cool hands slide beneath my knees and around my back, and I don't flinch—like part of my shredded soul knew he'd be here, even though he shouldn't be.

He should be with *his* people. Helping *his* people. Not getting muddied in problems that are *mine* to fix.

I'm lifted from the tree, pulled close to his chest by his flexing might, my limbs tucked amongst his devastating embrace as he sits beside the trunk. Catching my trembling hands, he pries my fingers from the chisel, one by one, whipping it away when I finally relent.

He takes my hands, bunches them up, and presses them close to his heart—thudding along so much faster than I remember. "Breathe," he growls, nuzzling the word into my neck, nose dragging up as he draws deep and plants the next word against the shell of my ear. "*Now.*"

My lungs knock into action, drawing a heaving breath that's all *him*. A safety shell for me to fall apart within that I certainly don't deserve.

He shouldn't be here.

My sobs become rough, tangible things—ugly and twisted and hoarse. But he holds me as I empty myself, his hands wrapping me tighter with every sob until we're bound so tight there's only space for my lungs to inflate. He turns to mortar around me, the stirring wind melding our scents into an intoxicating elixir that tames my rioting soul.

My cries lose strength, all my energy bleeding free; those bloody, gory visions dissolving from my fraught mind until there's nothing left—just this coil of sizzling death tucked deep inside my chest.

Still, he holds me as though he's afraid that by letting go, I'll shatter again.

I didn't deserve to be put back together in the first place. Not after everything I've done.

I wish you'd let me die that day.

The burden of those words sits heavy in my heart, reaching up my throat with clawed hands that threaten to rip my mouth wide so they can spill.

A violent noise rattles up his throat—raw and primal. Then he's pushing to his feet, moving toward the moonlit path with a ground-covering gait.

"Where are you taking me?"

"*Home.*"

My breath flees.

If he takes me ...

War.

More death.

No ships.

Home ...

I allow myself to sip on the pour of relief I feel from that one, tiny word, tipping my head to nuzzle deep into his chest—thinking of honey buns and planting days and my roses in full bloom.

I hate that it fills me. That it makes me want to knot back up and cry again and pour all my weaknesses against him.

Drawing another great gulp of his winter-borne scent,

I rally my strength and shove, twisting out of his hold, thudding to the ground in a crash of limbs that knocks the air from my lungs. Breathless, I roll across the grass and scramble back.

He stalks me like the fall of night determined to gobble up the day.

I push to my feet, and he stops one long pace away. I can see his chest is heaving. Can garner it in the way he's feeding his scent straight from his lungs into the tight space separating us in deep, drugging puffs.

"You need to understand," he growls, fist tightening around the handle of my bloody chisel. "Just standing by and watching you *suffer* goes against my basic instinct. But I'm trying, Milaje. I'm fucking trying."

I laugh, cold and low, wiping my face with the back of my arm. "Once upon a time, those words would have sustained me, you know. *Before.*"

I swear the world stills. Like even the stars stop their lazy spin.

"Before what?"

There's an imbalance in his voice, tipped off its scale, scratchy and charged.

Murderous.

"Before you decided to care."

"*I've always cared.*"

His words burrow between my ribs with piercing force, but I shake my head, fists clenched. Look him straight in the eye while I deliver my cut with every drop of conviction I can muster. "Well, I don't."

He bares his teeth in a silent snarl and looks away, back again. "Funny. I'd almost believe you're telling the truth."

"I am," I say on a hollow laugh, stepping forward until we're pressed close and I'm looking up into onyx eyes—cold, ancient, and winking with the hint of silver sparks. "You'd think losing my entire family was the worst thing to happen to me, but it's not. It's *you*," I whisper, my words laced with poison.

He doesn't move. Doesn't flinch or breathe or blink. Just watches me with that crushing stare.

"You're a monster, Rhordyn."

I see a flash of hurt in his otherwise stoic gaze, gone the next second. It takes me a moment to realize I'm talking about myself, but I don't stop—too caught up in the rush of my outburst to stem the flow.

Too desperate to see him crumble beneath the weight of my words.

"Well ..." he rumbles, his voice gravel against my skin, "nice of you to catch up."

"Oh, I've been here a while," I say, and he pushes forward; a hard wall at my front, so close that I can feel the thunderous beat of his heart. "If I could take it all back, I would. I'd prefer being torn to shreds over the nineteen years I spent living in your shadow."

He seems to swell, upper lip peeling back as a violent rumble attacks me from somewhere deep inside his chest.

He cracks his neck from side to side, and then his hand journeys around my waist, as though he's trying to return to the moment we had when I was small and broken in his arms. But I'm not broken anymore.

I'm dead.

I lunge, ripping away. "Don't touch me. Don't look at

me. Don't even *breathe* in my direction. I hate you, do you hear me? With every fiber of my being. I. Hate. You."

His hand bunches into a fist, the static between us *buzzing*.

"I hear you, Milaje." Still holding my stare, he offers me the chisel slathered in my blood—enough to satisfy more than a year's worth of offerings. "Loud and clear."

I let him drop the handle into my hand, and it feels much heavier than it did. Then he's before me, crushing the space between us, pouring himself all over me as he plants a kiss upon my forehead.

He pulls away and spins, charging down the moonlit path, his cloak a fierce flutter trailing every brutish step.

I stumble back, lungs deflating, as though my spine just snapped.

Caught by the tree trunk, I drop, grating my spine down the bark, gulping at air that feels utterly empty now that he's gone.

Chapter 52

Rhordyn

My fingers ache with the crush of my hands, strangling nothing, swinging at my side with each stoning step. I whip one back, then punch my fist through a tree trunk, shredding the skin on my knuckles.

The ancient thing splinters, groaning, then tips like a felled giant, quaking the ground as it assaults the jungle floor and rips a luminous hole in the shadows.

I fall to my knees, heaving breath, trying to keep my itching skin from splitting. I tilt my head, looking through the gapped canopy, studying the smattering of stars like a hunter stalks its prey.

They want me to bend.

To break.

Well, I want them to blink out until there's nothing up there but a sea of suffocating blackness.

"I won't do it," I say on a low, maniacal laugh. "I'd sooner watch the world burn."

No response.

They'll regret their silence soon enough, taken from someone who knows. Regret is a poison I'm forced to drink daily, but not for the right reasons. Not because I hid Orlaith from herself—I could never regret that. And if she knew why, her anger would sputter into understanding, but then I'd lose her in a heartbeat.

Forever.

I know her too well to tempt her with the truth. To admit that we're a disaster in slow motion. Existing on a fault line destined to split.

No ...

What I regret is letting her believe she doesn't hold my cold, crippled heart in the palm of her hand. Because she does.

She always will.

Chapter 53

Orlaith

I thread between the pedestrians walking the esplanade, my cap pulled down low enough to cover my eyes.

The shadowed dents beneath them.

I frown, thinking of how I slept all day, only to wake feeling more tired than I was when I crawled into bed at dawn.

My thoughts turn to Kolden's absence; my disappointment at finding a stand-in guard when I peeked out the door, putting a stop to any midnight tunnel digging without drawing suspicion. But with one plan thwarted, I'd quickly made another: to sneak out once my evening meal had been cleared away. A meal I rarely indulge in due to my lack of desire to be poisoned to death.

With feet planted on the Bulbs and Botany welcome mat, I retrieve a big, soft parcel from my knapsack. Zane's cloak—wrapped in a piece of sparkly gold material taken from the underskirt of one of my gowns I'll probably never wear, complete with a curtain-string bow and a note tucked into one of the breast pockets:

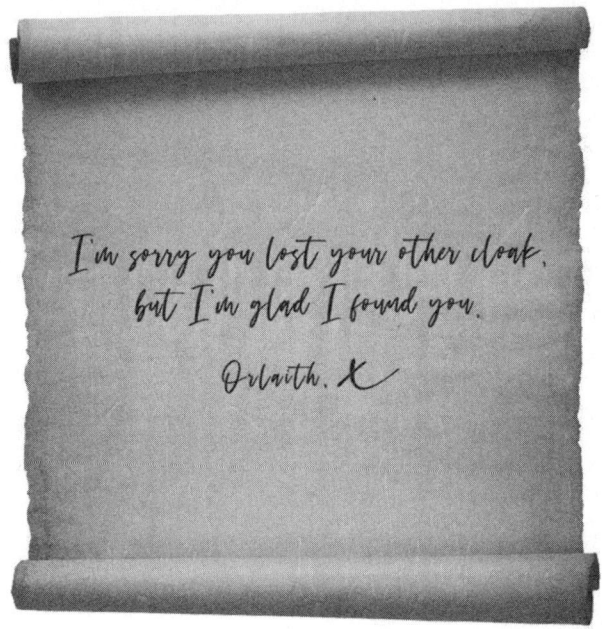

I'm sorry you lost your other cloak, but I'm glad I found you.

Orlaith. X

I rap my knuckles against the door, then dart down the esplanade that weaves around the shore, shops and people growing more sparse the closer I get to Gael's shorefront community.

The street ends at a pair of ornate gates, a stern-looking security guard standing sentinel in the light from the lantern hanging at the entrance.

Whistling a tune, I nod in his direction, push my hands into my pockets, and turn to walk the perimeter, scoping the seemingly insurmountable wall beneath the curve of my hat. The well-lit path veers to the right, and I see a tree that's woven up the side of the wall like a parasite.

That'll do.

Glancing over my shoulder to check I'm alone, I swing myself up, teeth gritted when the rough bark bites into my blistered fingertips. Pulling myself onto the ledge, I drink in a blow of sea breeze, then crouch amongst the foliage to peer down at the ornamental houses and quiet streets. Such a contrast to the bustle of town.

Some of the houses are brightly lit from within—a sure sign that people are home for the evening, and I realize with a twinge of trepidation that I could easily be seen.

Clusters of trees hug the wall's interior, branches sweeping the top, offering me some protection from the flickering lantern lights dotted at regular intervals. I scurry toward the first, pausing amongst the leaves, heart hammering as I hug a branch and spot the familiar glass and stone façade of Gael's home not too far ahead.

I take a deep breath and peel from my cover, slinking into a shadow between lanterns, then another, and another. Looking down onto their manicured backyard, I see a bloom-speckled lattice bolted to the wall, excitement zapping through my veins in hot bursts.

Almost there.

With a final scan of the quiet streets, I dart into the lantern light, drop to my knees, and clamber down the lattice, leaping onto a thick, spongy bed of well-tailored grass, its blunt tips shoving between my toes as I dash behind a bush.

I scan the vast windows of the opulent home. Remember Gael telling me her room is on the top floor—four stories up.

I see with relief that it's the only one brightly lit.

"Must be hers," I whisper, tiptoeing closer.

I just need to see with my own eyes that she's okay, then I can pull this thorn of dread from my heart.

Taking a moment to scan the neighborhood, I ease my knapsack over my head so it's secure against my back, then grip hold of the drainpipe, ignoring the deep throb pecking at my clavicle as I haul myself up, scaling it like a ladder. I lift onto her window ledge and inch toward the opening plagued by the gray, gauzy curtain frolicking at its entrance.

Peeling it back, I peek inside.

The riot of colorful clutter warms my heart, and I immediately know it's Gael's room.

I smile at the array of vibrant scarves draped over her four-poster bed, the blown glass sculptures in all colors of the rainbow decorating every flat surface, and the assortment of rugs spread across the floor—none woven with less than three bright colors. Various bits of art hang on the walls, mostly abstract or nature scenes that remind me of the tiny orchard we visited.

The place she once shared with her papa.

My gaze is lured to a large piece hanging above her writing desk, so unlike the other pictures.

This one is a painting of *people*.

Of Gael—aureate curls a cropped swirl around her face while she beams one of her intoxicating smiles—held in the arms of a man dressed in a gray robe.

I drag a shuddering breath, gaze transfixed on the man's hairless head. On the upside-down v etched into the spot between his eyes.

Memories flash, loud and boisterous, gouging their claws into the gnarly scars on my heart ...

A big man walks toward me and the boy. His head is shiny, and there's one of those wood-cutting things hanging from his hand. I think it's called an axe.

Why is there red stuff dripping from it?

"No ..." I whimper, the word barely audible past the clog in my throat as that memory continues to hack and hack and *hack* ...

"Get out of the way, kid. Mercy is not preserved for those who stand against the stones."

The boy runs forward with the sharp thing held above his head. His scream stands out the most ... until Mommy makes a louder sound at the same time the axe is swung.

He stops.

I push to my feet, try to follow ...

Watch him fall.

Watch the light leave his eyes.

I can't think. Can't breathe. Can't stop staring at his big, bright smile—much the same as Gael's.

A man who loved his daughter. Who climbed fruit trees with her and gave her all of her *best* memories ...

Then took my brother from me.

I stumble back a step, my foot sliding off the edge of the windowsill, hand whipping out to snatch hold of the drainpipe before gravity can land her deadly blow. I slam against the wall, a pained sound slipping free.

"Hello?"

Gael ...

There's a small sniffle, then, "Is someone there?"

Her voice comes at me from inside the room, shoving me into action.

Teetering somewhere on the precipice of losing myself

entirely, I scurry down the pipe, body and mind trapped beneath a shroud of numb oblivion.

I barely feel the pain in my raw fingertips as I climb up the lattice. Barely notice where I'm placing my hurried footsteps as I negotiate the wall; barely feel the shock that ratchets through my legs when I leap off the tree from halfway down, landing in a crouch on the esplanade below.

I dash through the streets, pausing on the outskirts of the busy market square where I lean against a wall amongst a swirl of people, the chaos and smells nothing but a haze on the fringe of my new reality.

There was a kinship with Gael—like our threads ran unnaturally deep for the short amount of time we'd known each other. The sort of bond I'd imagine sisters would have.

Now I know why.

We're sisters in death—both victims of the same tragic end that changed our lives forever. Took from us the people we loved most.

Her papa took my brother from me. I took her papa from her. In a way, I took her mother, too.

Took her naïvety. Her childhood.

How will I ever be able to look her in the eye again?

The world is spinning—churning around me in a blur of black and light. Face tipped to the drizzling sky, my hands wobble around like tentacles.

"I'm a jellyfish riding the ocean!" I giggle, moving my hips and my arms and twirling on the ball of my foot. "I'm freeee ..."

I stamp my heel down, and I think my body stops, but my mind keeps going round and round and *round*.

"Wow," I mutter, dropping.

Dropping ...

My knees crack against the stone, and a bubble of laughter pops from between my numb lips that still taste like cinnamon and cloves and rich, merry things.

I smack my tongue against them ...

So many merry things.

"Damn, I taste good."

Clambering to my feet, I battle gravity as it tries to tip me to the side again. I don't want to be down, I want to be *up*. I want to be high above the sky, dancing with the stars ...

I swirl again, around and around and around, before slamming my foot to the ground and peering down the tight alleyway to the bright blur of babbling merriment churning beneath the twinkly mail tree.

I need more wine.

It takes me a flurry of unsteady steps before I realize I left my bag atop the wooden crate I was drinking by, including my coins. Probably my dignity, too.

My shoulder knocks into something hard, and the entire alleyway rocks to the side.

"What the *fuck,* boy!"

My arm is snatched, and I'm spun so fast I giggle, catching a glimpse of a tall, scruffy male. I somehow manage to dodge the meaty fist that comes barreling toward my face with a swift arch of my spine. Impressive, considering my current circumstances.

The man snarls, sparking me full of reckless *thrill*.

I twist my body and rip away, then dance back, hopping from foot to foot, weightless like a mail sprite as I size him up.

I whistle low.

He's big. *Huge* even—dressed like a sailor, arms tree trunks and his weather-worn face twisted with fiery wrath as he sneers at me.

But right now ... I'm bigger.

I'm a fucking *giant*.

"Come on then, big guy. Let's see what you've got." I gesture for him to take another swing, but as he begins winding his arm back, my stomach lurches—*violently*.

"*Wait!*"

To my surprise, he does.

The back of my hand slaps against my mouth as my insides rebel against the jug of mulled wine that's threatening to spill all over the ground between us.

I hold up a finger. "Two seconds, just ... let me work through this."

Breathing deep, I wrestle the cramping surge, swallow the excess saliva pooling beneath my tongue, and stand. "Apologies. That was inconve—"

Gravity knocks my knees out from under me, pulling me sideways, and I stumble, crashing against the merciless cobbles, letting them take my grueling weight as I lump myself back, feeling my hair spill around me.

Actually, this is probably better. I'm much less wobbly down here. And I weigh less.

My hat is no longer on my head, allowing me to look up at the sky from the ground. Rain sprinkles my face, and I open my mouth to catch some on my tongue.

Footsteps thud close, and my gaze rolls down to the meaty sailorman now standing between my wide-open legs, loosening the ties on his trousers with frenzied hands.

His pupils are dilated with a sick sort of excitement that makes me want to vomit again.

"Poke that thing at me, and you'll lose it."

My slurred words don't stop him from ripping at his seam, nor do they swipe the leer from his face.

Strong hands thread around the sides of his head, whipping it with a sickening *crack* that ratchets through me. His limp body is tossed aside like it's made of air, exposing a broad man sheathed in the shadow of his cloak—a too-familiar sword poking over his shoulder.

I groan, rubbing my eyes, and breathe a sigh of relief when I see that he's gone.

Must have been imagining things.

That's nice.

I roll, shove onto my hands and knees, looking sideways at the sailorman passed out on the ground with his head tipped at an impossible angle.

"That looks uncomfortable. You're going to wake with a real crick in your neck." I stagger to my feet, looking down on him. "That's what you get, you big dickhead."

I stumble toward the busy market square, realize I once again forgot my coins, and spin on my heel. The world keeps turning, and I topple backward, caught by unyielding arms that sweep me off my feet. Not in the romantic way I've read about in my romance books, but like a dead body—arms hanging and head tipped back so I'm looking at the world upside down.

I groan, strain my neck forward, and glance up at a

scruffy black beard that looks so soft from this angle. "Ugh." I let my head fall back again. "*You.*"

"Yes, Milaje." Rhordyn begins walking, the world bumping by with each thump of his steps. "Me."

The word hits like it's spoken from between gritted teeth.

"You know what I don't appreciate? *Your*—"

"Tone," he finishes, and I frown, wondering how long I can manage this angle before I vomit mulled wine up my own nose.

"And your arms. I'm a graceful jellyfish, and you're fishing me out of the sea."

"Yes," he mutters. "Very graceful."

Aw, a compliment. Perhaps I should repay the favor.

Straining my neck, I lift my head again, gulping down the view of his profile. "You're a *very* pretty man. Even with all this hair on your face. Actually ..." I bat my hand up, only slapping him in the jaw a little in my effort to brush my fingers through the softness there. "*Especially* with this hair on your face."

I stop just short of telling him I've pictured how it would feel between my thighs.

More than once.

Barely dropping his chin, he looks down at me, slicing me with his silver stare, and I feel that look in my chest.

Ugh. Feelings.

I don't want those right now.

I let my head flop back, arm tumbling to the side as I sigh. "Why are you here, Rhordy?"

"My indifference is just as lethal as my affection," he murmurs, the smoky words drifting from my grasp the moment they ignite.

"Lethal for who?"

The world continues to thump past.

"*You.*"

"You're not making any sense," I slur, hearing his lucid response moments before I slip into a thick sludge of sleep ...

"Good."

CHAPTER 54
Rhordyn

Shoulder leaned against the windowsill, I push the filthy curtain aside and look out upon the moonlit night, scouring the cobbled street three stories below my room that smells like a brewery.

A man wobbles past, pausing in the middle of the road to flop his cock out and take a piss, whistling a tune to the sky, belting out the chorus in slurred, broken notes. He walks straight through his own puddle to continue on his way, weaving a crooked path through the cramped neighborhood.

Cindra strides into view, dressed in her fake merchant's robe that drags along the ground behind her, white dreaded hair hanging down her back. She glances up at my window and gives me a curt nod, face tight. Three men follow, each pulling a cart piled high and covered with furs.

Three—not the eight the last mail sprite suggested would be coming on that barge.

"Fuck," I mutter, peeling the curtain further back so I can check down the street for stragglers.

All I can see is the empty road that weaves deeper into the city.

"*Please no ...*"

My pulse goes wild, and I whip my head around, looking at *her* tucked amongst my crumpled sheets—hair a tangled mess spilled across the pillow, her tortured expression lit by a single lantern hanging off the wooden headboard.

She thrashes her head, hands reaching for nothing as a shrill cry splits her lips. "D-Don't take him. *Please—*"

I charge across the room in two strides and drop onto the bed. Leaning against the headboard, I stretch my arm over the back of it. Face crumbling, she blindly pads at my chest, another whimper ripping free as she grabs my shirt, using the fisted grip to pull herself close—clawing at me like she's hanging off the edge of a cliff. Like I'm the only thing stopping her from plunging.

Leg threading over mine, she fits herself to me, and slowly—so fucking slowly—I let my arm settle upon her back.

"I ... I can't do this again." Her murmured words attack my chest. "Please—I can't. Take me instead ..."

My blood roars, crackling through my veins.

Take me instead ...

I draw my chest full, hold it, force the wild surge back down, cracking my neck.

I uncurl her fist from where it's clenching my shirt like she thinks I'll ever leave, prying the material from her iron grip.

Another whimper. "No—*no, no, no ...*"

The hurt curdling her sound tills imbalance in my chest.

Stare stabbed at the room's only exit not far from the foot of my bed, I bring her tight, trembling fist up to my mouth and nuzzle my nose against it, easing it loose as I draw on the rich, spicy scent of amber sweetened with a floral pinch. "Once upon a time, there was a boy who had everything," I rumble, then kiss the tip of her thumb. "Until someone he cared about found an unbreakable love that broke her."

Broke everything.

I swallow and clear my throat before kissing the tip of Orlaith's pointer finger as another whimper splits apart her trembling lips.

"The boy learned that love destroys."

She nuzzles deeper into my chest, her tremble melting away when I drag my nose up the length of her middle finger.

Kiss the tip.

"That boy became a man with nothing left to lose," I murmur, planting a kiss on the tips of her two smallest fingers. "Until he did."

Her sobs lose strength, as if part of her is listening.

I think back to *that* day—when I replaced Baze in the training room to knock some sense into her. I remember her cutting through my shirt with her blade. The look in her eyes when she thought she'd wounded me, like it mattered to her.

Something more than just protective instinct sparked inside me. A flame I wanted to immediately douse.

I hate you.

Oh, precious. You don't even know the meaning of the word.

I look down at her face tipped to the side, her warm breath skating over my thin shirt. "He did what he knew best." Brushing the hair back from her cheek, I watch her lashes flutter. "He destroyed."

Destroyed it before it could destroy her.

But ...

"It didn't change her fate like he'd hoped," I dredge out, dragging my thumb across her lower lip. "Didn't *save* her. And though she was tied to him inexplicably, he lost her in all the important ways."

I thread my fingers through her hair, tip her head the slightest amount. Pretend she's looking up at me with those heartbreak eyes I want to piece back together again.

"But that didn't stop him."

It would *never* stop him.

"Because he was hers—forever—even though he knew his love was lethal."

He was hers.

Chapter 55
Kai

A harsh *tap-tap-tap-tap-tap-tap-tap* against my ribs rouses me, and I groan, rolling over, nuzzling into mounded furs that smell like the raw musk of our lovemaking. 'Go back to sleep, Zyke.'

'Wake. Mate gone. Zykanth trapped in little man chest.'

My eyes pop open, and I scan our nest ...

Empty.

Shit.

'Why didn't you wake me earlier?' I blurt, heart lurching, scales prickling to the surface of my chest, spreading across my shoulders, down my arms. 'And get back in, or you'll rip apart her home and destroy her treasures. She won't like your scales so much then.'

'*You have weak skin. Need strong scales. Protect soft little mate who thinks big strong.*'

'Calm down,' I groan, leaping up while Zykanth churns inside me.

'*Go. Find. Move fast little feet.*'

Growling, I dash toward the wooden door and drag it open. "Vicious!" I yell, wrapping a piece of cloth around my middle, stepping onto the platform that juts out from her little crystal cottage nesting in the sky—almost at the tip of one of the iridescent spires that make up the island.

Looking right, I scan the wiggly path that carves all the way to the crumbled-stone shore glistening in the morning light, then out across the stretch of silky water bathed in a spill of pink.

I hope she didn't go down there without me. Perhaps she's done it before, but now that she's *ours* ...

The thought of her putting even a toe in those waters has my chest filling with a deluge of bone-crushing fear.

If the creature who haunts this island were to snatch her up, I'd hunt her down. Rip the seas to shreds to get her back.

'*Find, find, find,*' Zykanth chants, and I step forward, looking over the edge, feet tingling as I peer down to the jagged ravine far below ...

Perhaps she went to bathe in the red pool and hunt for crabs?

Our little mate does love crabs.

Keeping as close to the wall as I can, I skirt left around the path that hugs the spire and stop—though Zykanth keeps slamming against my ribs like a whip. The trail carves along the saw-tooth ravine, then up and over a smaller, stubby mound of crystal, at the top of which I spot *her* standing with a cloaked figure.

Both their heads are bent as Vicious rifles through a basket, dressed in nothing but that oversized shirt dancing around her long, golden legs.

'*Run little feet! Eat strange man. One crunch, gone.*'

A sharp frill rips through my skin, all the way down the line of my spine as my jaw pops, widening to accommodate Zykanth's ferocious maw.

'Get down,' I snarl, muscles bulging as I battle his might.

Ignoring me, he hisses through my bared teeth, scales pushing up over my neck and jaw and legs.

Vicious and the man look my way, and a small child scurries up from beyond the rise, peeking out from behind the folds of the stranger's brown cloak.

Zykanth stills his swift ascent, fangs and frills sinking within as my heart lurches to a stop. '*Little sparkly one ...*'

The child has a bouncy crop of iridescent curls, tapered ears tipped in a delicate line of thorns, eyes buffered crystals that catch on the pink sky bearing down on us ...

Aeshlian.

CHAPTER 56
Orlaith

I swim through the inky layers of a suffocating bog, clawing at something ... *nothing*. Saliva pools beneath my tongue, and I groan, swallowing the urge to vomit as a deep thud attacks my temples. Rubbing my eyes, I draw my lungs full of the thick musk that drops a boulder of recognition on my chest.

The air in this room ... it's all *him*.

"Oh, no ..."

I drag my hands down my face and look around, wincing as the cloying weight of my poor decisions makes my stomach flip.

Definitely not my room.

My gaze slides around the space, over the rough stone walls to the flimsy curtain covering a low window. The room feels small, much of it taken up by the large bed I'm lying in. There's a desk to my right littered with stacks of paper, chunks of blue rocks, sharpened sticks of charcoal. A sketched map covers the wall behind the desk, bits of parchment piecing it together.

I lean forward, moaning at the pounding in my head as I peer at the map, trying to make it out. Quickly realizing it's a map of the city, islands mottling the sea of otherwise empty space beyond Parith, all connected by the intertwining vines of what appears to be the tunnel system Rhordyn was telling me about.

The same tunnel system I'm currently trying to hack a hole into beneath the palace.

Big areas are missing, marked by blank sheets of paper or large, black crosses in areas that perhaps mean the tunnels have been barred off.

I look at the spare sheets of parchment, the sharpened sticks of coal ...

I need to jot this down for myself.

Leaping up, I'm struck with a brain-bruising thud that resonates from the tip of my spine. Teeth clenching, I waver, eyes watering as I groan through chalky lips, slamming my hand against the headboard for support.

I'll *never* drink mulled wine again. I feel like shit scraped off the pavement, then stomped down a drain.

My desperate gaze falls on a mug set atop the wooden stool used as a bedside table, and I scramble for it, drawing a deep gulp of the contents. My entire body shudders at the taste—like a wash of chilled evening rain spiced with flower petals and a dash of sunshine.

I pull the mug from my lips and look at the clear liquid swirling inside.

"Wow ... That's the most delicious water I've ever tasted."

Cradling the cup in my trembling hands, I sip at it, savoring each drop that flows across my tongue and drains down into me, soothing my belly from the inside. Easing the tender drum in my head. I set the empty mug on the stool, yearning for more.

The creaking strain of rusted hinges has me spinning, attention whipping to the shadowed figure filling the doorframe. My heart labors as I take him in—cloaked, hooded, yet I can still feel the chilled path of his focus carving across my face, tracing the slope of my lips ... my neck ...

My skin prickles, nipples pinch. This room feels so much smaller now that I'm dwarfed by his hulking presence. Now that he's taking up the main exit with his broad shoulders.

Tipping his hood, I'm exposed to the full brunt of his savage beauty. To his eyes—a catastrophic mix of hunger and hell.

Scruff covers the bottom half of his face, and the vaguest memory of my hand slapping against it while I contemplated the feel of it between my thighs flashes on the backs of my eyes.

A deep, unsatiated throb has me swallowing thickly.

Kicking forward another step, he closes the door, the clunk of the lock sliding into place reverberating through my skin, flesh, and bones. He sets an orange on his desk and unbuckles his cloak, watching me as he drapes it across the back of the low chair that swivels and rocks with the weight of it.

My gaze travels down, up again, attention snagging on his loose pants hung low on his hips and his shirt clinging to every brutish pane of his body like a second skin.

Another deep throb almost buckles my knees ...

"This is your room?" I rasp, like I didn't already know—*desperate* to fill the silence. Anything to distract myself from the vision before me. From his piercing stare, as though there's nothing in this world aside from the two of us and this room.

This bed.

This empty, yearning space between us.

"Yes, Milaje."

I nod, allowing myself a moment more to enjoy this delicious peace before I let reality sink in and shred it apart. He must feel the moment I recompose those shields because his own stare hardens, arms crossing over his bulky chest as he widens his stance, quirking his brow as if to say *there it is*.

I lift my chin and smooth my crumpled shirt in an attempt at composure ... the hazy memory of wandering the streets, drunk and scrappy and seconds away from spewing all over the cobbled ground a mortifying slap.

But here we are.

"What's the time?" I ask.

"Late in the day."

My heart drops.

Shit.

"Why didn't you take me back to the palace?"

His stare savagely maims me. "You expected me to scale that palace wall with you passed out in my arms, snoring and smelling like a brewery?"

I internally cringe.

Very, very poor life decision.

"You could've just done the *normal* thing and dropped me at the gate. Asked someone to carry me back to my room."

His eyes flash, as though lit with a silver spark.

Silence. The soul-destroying sort that makes me want to squirm.

"Just so we're clear, Milaje, I will *never* ask someone else to carry you."

My hands bunch into fists, and I look away, stabbing my stare at the closed curtain and the dull haze of light filtering through.

"And where did you sleep?" I bite out, looking at him again, trying to ignore the burning blush that cups my cheeks.

"There," he says, jerking his chin at the bed to where the sheets are still stamped with the rumpled evidence of my body's departure.

"But I woke up there ..."

"Yes," he rumbles, kicking off his boots, setting himself in the captain's chair—elbows on his knees after he plucks up the round of fruit and digs his nails into the rind. "You rolled over to my side the moment I got up."

That heat flares, boiling my cheeks, an embarrassed flash of anger tightening my knuckles until they're aching from the strain.

Comatose Orlaith is fucking senseless.

"*I told you not to—*"

"Breathe in your direction," he mumbles, carving off a large shard of peel, spritzing the air with its zesty freshness. "I know. I had my face pointed the other way the entire night. Promise."

He segments the fruit, then puts it on a dented tin plate before he stands, dissolving the space between us with a few powerful strides.

I'm forced to tip my head to hold his stare.

"Eat," he rumbles, shoving the plate in my face. "It will alleviate your migraine."

"How do you know I've got a migraine?"

He gives me a deadpan look. "Because even if I didn't watch you chug two jugs of mulled wine on a no-doubt empty stomach, I've been through this with Baze. I know the signs."

"Ever thought of finding a hobby?" I grit out through clenched teeth.

"I have one. And right now she's a bratty little pain in my ass who won't take her medicine." He drops the plate on the bed beside me, making the segments jump as he grabs my empty cup and spins.

I'm tempted to pick up a piece and lob it at the back of his head.

Tamping my violent, knee-jerk urge, I watch him disappear through a side door that likely leads to a washroom, gauging by the sound of gushing water that swiftly follows.

I stare at the fruit with narrowed eyes, hating the way my stomach growls like some ravenous, teeth-gnashing beast.

It probably tastes like fucking sunshine.

My mouth tingles in anticipation, and I cave, sitting as I pluck up a segment—letting it glaze across my lips. I poke my tongue out the slightest amount, intending on a sample, except an explosion of zesty sweetness sends my taste buds into a rioting spasm.

A little moan slips out when I bite into the flesh, relishing the bursts of sweetness as I chew, sighing between mouthfuls, the sticky juice dripping off my fingers and my chin.

Rhordyn returns with a cloth in one hand and my freshly filled mug in the other, just as I'm polishing off the final piece. He sits both on the side table and makes for the desk, and my stare tracks him every step of the way while I use the damp cloth to wipe my hands and chin.

"So it's not okay for Cainon to serve me up, but it's okay for you?"

"Cainon meant it as an insult," he mutters, dropping back into the chair with a weighty thud. Swiping a piece of charcoal, he begins scratching against some parchment. "My intentions are the opposite. Now, try and get a few more hours of sleep."

My hands still. "You're kidding."

He looks at me from beneath the shelf of his lowered brows. "Do I look like I'm kidding?"

My mouth opens, closes, opens again, words finally bursting forth. "My *promised* is probably searching for me ..."

"Exactly." He plucks the piece of parchment and blows, studying it from a sideways angle before setting it back on the table. "He won't notice me stealing one of his ships to scout the surrounding islands."

I laugh, then pause, momentarily paralyzed by my own stupidity.

"You slimy son of a bitch." Pelting my washcloth in his direction, I shove to a stand, my wild, golden locks heavy around my shoulders like a layer of armor. "You used me."

He leans back in his chair, planting his chin on his fist and looking at me with a cutthroat intensity. "Ocruth forces are slowly sifting into the city, ready to sail the promised ships. I'm on the back foot until I locate them."

I gobble the information like a spiked sweet, wondering why he'd willingly hand me such a valuable secret. Cainon would have a field day with that piece of knowledge. Would see it as evidence that Rhordyn's trying to infiltrate his territory and steal it for himself.

Precisely why he cannot find out.

I snatch another swift look at the map behind him, branding it to the backs of my eyes. "Well, you still threw me under the carriage," I say, rooting through the blue sheets in search of my hat and hairpin.

"You're the one who fell into my arms. Literally."

My stare whips at him, then to my bag lumped in the corner on the ground at his back. "Tip for next time," I snip, charging forth and snatching it up, rooting around for my hat. Pegged with disappointment when I realize it's not there—pocketing my pin. "Let me fall, then leave me on the fucking pavement. I don't need your help." I spin on my heel, then stalk toward the exit, shoving the lock aside.

Swinging the door wide, I barrel along the sparsely lit hall, then down a tight flight of creaky wooden stairs. It's only once I near the bottom that the bustle of gruff chatter hits me. Then the rich smell of hearty, well-seasoned stew and baked bread—as though my senses needed time to recalibrate after drowning in the wash of Rhordyn's dense, primal scent.

I peek around the corner to see a host of men gathered around tall tables dotted throughout the space, digging bread into deep bowls and sipping ale from frothy mugs. There's a bar that lines one side of the room, a stern-looking barrel of a man standing behind it, polishing a glass.

My heart falls as I look to the exit—all the way on the other side of the room.

Crap.

I charge back up the stairs, storm into Rhordyn's room, and close the door behind me—spine planted against the cold, wooden planes.

"Back so soon?" he drawls.

"I can't be seen exiting here. Especially not looking like this. Or"—I pull my collar to my nose and draw a whiff, but my scent is lost beneath the thick, heady layers of *him*—"*smelling* like this."

"Then climb out the window, Milaje."

My gaze flicks to him bent over his drawing, his hand moving in short, artistic sweeps. "You're kidding."

He rocks back in his chair, peeling the curtain and glancing out the window.

He grunts. "Looks fine to me. I've seen you scale worse—in worse conditions."

I charge over, snatching the curtain and pulling it wide, poking my head out the half-open window and dousing myself in fierce, shafting rays of afternoon sun. Sweat prickles my brow from the wash of humidity, made worse when I peer down and realize the walkway three stories below appears to be a popular thoroughfare.

A man walking his dog, women with baskets packed with fresh produce milling around, children zigzagging through the crowd, laughing. A cluster of guards charge past, faces pinched and spears caught in their white-knuckled fists as they scour the face of every person they cross paths with.

"Shit," I mutter, ducking inside so fast I almost vomit. I flick the curtain closed, put my back to the window, and strum my fingers against the sill, watching Rhordyn work—every line, every shaded smudge drawn with such conviction, I doubt he ever makes a mistake.

I look at the map. Back to Rhordyn. "So ... what are you doing?"

Can I interest you in making a miniature version for me to take back to the palace for when I break through the wall?

"Calah used to store his fleet at one of the islands. I've only ever traveled there using the underground tunnel system I was telling you about," he says, not looking up. "I have no idea how to get there otherwise."

"Who's Calah?"

"Cainon's father." He draws another stroke, blowing off the excess.

"Why don't you just send a sprite?"

"I've sent two," he mumbles. "Neither of them have returned. Seems cruel to send a third." Another long line, then, "I just need to discern a direction so I'm not forced to waste precious days sailing waters I'm unfamiliar with."

A nervous seed roots in my chest, delving between the fractures of my heart ...

He's talking like he's planning to *steal* them before the ceremony has even had a chance to take place. But if he swipes them from under Cainon's nose, war will spark.

With Bahari.

If the ships are secured by *me* ... Rhordyn will be utterly blameless, and I don't care about the kickback I'll receive.

Not anymore.

"Just don't do anything rash. Cainon and I will be coupled by the full moon," I say, trying to hide the trepidation in my voice—stare still traveling the lines of the map, etching them deeper into my mind. "Then I'll get you all the ships you need. Free of charge."

Free of war.

It takes me a second to realize it's silent.

Too silent.

He turns, and I drop my stare, landing in the pits of two black eyes.

"Free of charge?"

There's menace in his tone, and I swallow, edging away from the windowsill, taking sharp steps backward as he rises from his seat—a tower of seething brawn.

"Free ... of *charge?*" He growls, louder now, and there's a shake to the words, like they're battling their confines.

The back of my knees collide with the bed, and I tip, landing with an *oomph* upon the mattress as he stalks across the room. He looms over me, and I swear he's bigger than normal, his muscles so pumped full of rage that I can feel it ricocheting against my skin.

He steps between my opened thighs, pins his hands either side of my head, and lowers himself slower than a setting moon—teeth bared, breath a cold assault against my fervid skin.

I hate that his mere closeness makes me throb again. That I picture him tearing at my buttons, ripping my pants down, widening my thighs. Picture him settling between them and shoving deep—stretching me.

Claiming me.

Destroying me from the inside.

My spine curls, breaths sharpen.

His lips skim the shell of my ear, casting a shiver down

the side of my neck that pinches my nipples into painful peaks. "You think so little of yourself ..."

I gasp as the words carve beneath my skin, dragging their delicate undertow across my blackened heart, making it ache from the assault.

Stop digging, I want to scream.

"What I think of myself is none of your business."

"*Wrong,*" he growls—not giving my words time to breathe before he smothers them in his own. "Your pain calls to me. You can tuck it down deep and cover it up all you want, but I can still see it clear as day."

"You can't see *shit.*"

He digs his face into the crook of my neck, inhaling, nuzzling my head to the side and making my skin tighten with delicious anticipation. He could pop it in a heartbeat. Burst my flesh and bleed my carotid.

What would I do if he did? Fight him?

Maybe.

Or maybe I'd wrap my arms around his neck and *pull*— keeping him locked on until he'd drained every drop.

"I can see your self-hatred," he whispers, the word a violent patter against my ear. Every bone in my body locks, the backs of my eyes stinging so much I'm afraid to blink for fear of what it will send dashing down my cheeks. "You didn't just roll into my spot when I left the bed, Orlaith." His crumbled words gallop across my skin. "You clung to me all night like I was the only thing tethering you to the world."

"Stop—"

"*Never,*" he snarls, stamping more crushing pressure along my body. Letting me eat up his weight and bathing me in his masculine scent. "I'll *never* stop hunting this pulse." He presses a kiss against my neck that burns like an icy brand.

He wouldn't be saying that if he knew what I was capable of.

What I've done.

I want to scrape the admittance into his skin with the blunt of my nails.

He rolls his hips, drawing a sharp gasp from my lips when his solid shaft grinds against the softest part of me, assuaging that restless ache.

"Show me ..."

His words come to me through the fog of rapture as I raise my hips to meet another roll of his, making his cock—barely sheathed by his soft pants—charge at my opening with every breaching intention.

I moan, absorbing the drum of delicious heat, widening my legs so his next thrust assaults every flushed and swollen part of my aching core. My hands dig down the carved brawn of his back, beneath the band of his pants, where they settle on his flexing ass as he stabs his hips forward again.

And *again*.

That throb incinerates me from the inside out, and I whimper, wanting to delve my hand between us and rip my pants right off.

"Milaje, I said *show me*—"

I tip my head to give him full access to my throat, my body devouring another blunt thrust.

"Sh-show you what?"

I want him to fuck me. To use me and wreck me.

I want to do the same to him.

He cups the side of my face, hips stilling as he catches my stare.

Holds it hostage.

"Your *damage*."

I still. Even my heart gutters to a halt.

He doesn't want my body. He wants my fucking *soul*.

No.

I shove his chest. "*Get off me.*"

He does—instantly—pulling back so fast I gasp from the shock of his sudden absence. Then he's charging into the washroom like an angry shadow, leaving me in the wake of his emotional warfare.

The sound of falling water reaches me through the open door, followed by a thick fog of steam that's all *him*. A narcotic dose of primal desire that stirs me up in filthy ways I should be ashamed of. I squeeze my eyes shut, tunneling down on that well of self-hatred, pinching the back of my arm so hard my eyes blaze with a fresh promise of tears.

No. He does not get to pick me apart and analyze my insides. To look at me like he wants to thread me back together.

He does not get to be my fucking *hero*.

Pushing off the bed, I unbutton my shirt, then yank it off, unbinding my achy breasts that fall heavy and free. I remove my pants and underwear, digging through my bag for my blade and gripping it tight. My hair is a weight against my bare back, brushing the curve of my ass as I sway toward that doorway, swallowing the remaining scraps of trepidation and dropping myself into that cold, dead place that feels nothing.

The room is larger than I thought it would be, the

chiseled rock dominated by a wall of falling water spilling from a slit in the top crease between roof and wall. But it all pales in significance to *him*.

Naked. Glorious. Brutally statuesque.

A beast in his prime.

His strong hands are planted against the wall, accentuating those broad, powerful shoulders, head dropped as he lets the water batter the back of it. My gaze travels from his spread fingers, over the trail of veins bulging in his forearms, down the line of his spine, devouring his ass and muscled thighs. The sight blazes my insides, kicking my blood into a rushing torrent, and that deep, empty throb takes on a violent life of its own.

He's all dark, masculine beauty licked in a silver scrawl. My own damnation carved into a roughly hewn sculpture of agonizing temptation.

There's not a single part of me that doesn't appreciate the sight.

Not a single part of me that doesn't want to destroy him, anyway.

"You want to see my damage?" I purr, and his head lifts, twisting so he can see me over the swell of his right shoulder.

Through the rope of his sodden locks, that flash of startling silver hits me, blackening.

Widening.

His chilled stare carves down me in a way that almost flays my vicious intentions, so I don't give him more than a second to take me in before I'm at his back with my blade notched between his shoulders. I grasp his thick, silken shaft in my other hand ... the one cuffed in Cainon's cupla.

He's heavy.

Huge.

His chest inflates, and a dense growl rips up his throat while I wrestle my shock.

Having all this man in the palm of my hand, I'm struck with a wash of primal, erotic *power* that dissolves the trepidation of my inexperience ...

Grip firm and movements smooth, I pump, exploring his length. He balks, muscles tensing, as though he's battling instincts screaming at him to take control as I drag my fingers over the head of his cock, squeezing. It jerks in my grasp, swelling, becoming rock solid.

His right arm lashes back, and he takes a large, claiming grip of my ass cheek, exposing my core to the warm kiss of humidity. His head falls to rest on top of mine, and a deep, throaty rumble fills the room, punching into that ache between my legs and making my insides clamp down on nothing.

I arch my spine, giving him better access to my flushed and throbbing core as his curled fingers graze against me, zapping me with a strike of pleasure I want to drown in.

Teeth gritted, forehead pressed against his back, I work him faster, harder, my grip traversing over the velvet shaft of thickening veins and his hardening head.

I can feel his pleasure in the tense of his muscles. The jerk of his cock. The low, abrasive grunts every time my hand skirts over his most sensitive parts.

His grip becomes more desperate, dragging me so close my bare breasts ache from the crushing impact, my hand shaking with the effort to avoid impaling him through the back.

He spins.

I gasp.

Somehow managing to maintain my grip on him, I'm shoved through the pour of water and slammed against the wall so hard my breath knocks free. His hand comes up to grip my jaw, the other pinning my weapon-wielding hand to the stone beside my head.

The sharp, intoxicating scent of his blood fills the room, curling up into me on tendrils of steam.

"*I cut you—*"

"I don't give a fuck," he growls, bucking his hips against me, warm water splashing over us as he works his cock through my clenched grip.

I look down, watching the thick, pink head—glistening, swollen, and angry-looking—pushing up through the curled grip of my fingers and presenting itself between my breasts.

A low, throaty moan spikes another wave of heat between my legs, echoing in the hollow behind the fall of water.

It takes me a moment to realize the sound came from me.

His muscles lock, hips jerking, *jerking* ... head digging into my neck. I feel his teeth clamp against the thumping, yearning, thin layer of skin—

His hand spears down, fingers brushing up the inside of my thigh, reaching so close to that hot, swollen nub that's aching for friction. I tilt my hips away from his touch, knowing that the slightest brush will send me tumbling into him in more ways than one—working my hand faster, *tighter* ...

A dense, primal sound rattles in his chest, threatening to rip it to shreds from the inside out, his entire body locking around me like a shield as warm, milky ropes spurt all over my heaving breasts and dribble over my fingers still clenched around his manhood.

Gasping for breath, I gulp down the potent scent of his pleasure as those teeth pull back, replaced with the cool press of his lips—so soft.

A *too* soft strike to the soul.

His kisses sow a tender trail up the line of my throat to my ear, along my jaw, his grip loosening on my weapon-wielding hand as he rumbles—like a deep purr. Rough fingers graze my breasts, painting me in himself, smearing it across the firm peaks of my nipples, making them tingle with a delicious spike of rapture while I try to soothe my ragged breaths.

He's trembling, water pouring down the savage planes of his beautiful body as I look up at him from below my lashes, delving into the swirling pools of his unguarded eyes. Impossible to appreciate when my reflection is all I can see.

That well of self-hatred bubbles.

His thumb skims my lower lip, water dripping from his hair and beard, stare dipping to my mouth. Curled over me like some great beast, he drops his head, chilled lips grazing mine—

I jerk from his grip and shove to the side, walking backward as he spins—heaving, his heavy cock impossibly hard between his thighs and pointing straight at me.

I have a moment to take him in; stripped of his walls, muscles bulging as that knot of tension that's always held us together is stretched to its limits. Or perhaps it just makes it more difficult to untangle.

I lift my chin.

"*Milaje—*"

"Consider my debt repaid for the time you pity fucked me with your fingers. This won't happen again."

I snatch a towel off the rail and spin on my heel, breaking from his sawtooth stare and stalking from the room, wiping myself clean of the mess he made across my chest. It's only once I'm free of the thick, intoxicating aroma of our actions does realization sink in.

I just taunted the beast.

Snagging my bag and clothes, I dig my feet into my underwear, then my pants. I don't bother wrapping my breasts before swiftly pulling my shirt on and fumbling with the buttons.

Shouldering my bag, I flip my sodden hair out from under my shirt and storm toward the window, hand planted against the pane to shove it open when Rhordyn's fingers wrap around the handle. He pulls it forward, slamming it closed.

The windowpane rattles in synchrony with my thundering heart.

"*Let me out,*" I snarl, refusing to turn. Knowing that if I do, part of me might shatter. "I need to get back to my promised."

"You're showing him more respect than he deserves," he booms, his energy a violent static battering my back. "His *love* is driven by agenda and greed. He's not good enough for you. Far from it."

"You don't get to tell me who I will and will not love," I snap, and the air chills so fast my breath turns milky white.

He steps closer, his wet, naked body aligning with my back. Stilling my breath and my heart and grinding all my thoughts to a crashing halt. "No. And I won't. But I will tell you this," he growls, digging his face into my neck and almost buckling my knees. "I'm getting those ships before the full fucking moon, and then you can decide if you still want to be with that man."

No.

I whip around, heart in my throat, head tipped as I look up at him poured over me like a shield. "You're going to go to war with him? Over *me?*"

He doesn't blink or flinch. "I'd strike the fucking *world* down for you."

All breath escapes me.

"Rhordyn, no ..."

"I told you I won't let you fall, and I've drawn that line in the stone," he growls, warfare waging across his savage expression.

My entire chest aches, as if he just busted his hand through it and drew that very line with one of my cracked ribs.

"You're going to leave Parith without the ships. You're going to leave the sailors and your pretty drawing over there," I say, stabbing my finger at his map with fierce determination, "and you're going to *go.*"

He laughs, but it's all teeth. "Not happening, Milaje. Not in a million years."

Desperation reaches down my throat and grips my heart. Cracks it open. Fishes around until it pulls out a token of my own to offer him with bloodied hands.

I harden my stare, looking him dead in the eye. "You know what I've learned?"

He frowns.

"My ... my *kind,*" I snarl, gesturing to the jewel hanging

around my neck, "have been hunted. *Slaughtered.* Apparently, simply showing my unmasked face in public is practically a death sentence." I shrug, holding his catatonic stare. "Guess my tutor missed that little part of my history lesson."

There's an agonizing pause, and his gaze nips at my necklace, like he's already anticipating the blow I'm about to land. "If you don't leave," I say, voice dropped low as I thread my hand up to the heavy jewel and grip it tight. "I'll walk down the busy esplanade and rip this off my neck."

His eyes flare with a flash of realization, like he can see the truth in my own.

I've got nothing to lose except myself.

A deep, bone-chilling silence takes root between us, his eyes dipping so dark I picture something very different staring back at me ...

Something ferocious and spilling bloodlust.

"Do you believe me?"

"Yes, Milaje. I do."

I ignore the crack in his voice, lifting my chin, his black eyes boring into me. "Then step back."

A vicious rumbling spawns in his chest, but he abides, hands falling at his sides. I turn, shove the window open, and climb through—catching sight of him as I spin.

His onyx eyes impale me.

Struggling to maintain my grip on the stone, I drop from his line of sight, but it doesn't stem this sickening feeling deep inside my chest ...

I may have choked a war with Bahari, but at what cost?

CHAPTER 57
Orlaith

Clouds fold over the crisp blue sky, smudging it, dumping a heavy sheet of rain that drenches me through but does nothing to rinse the feel of *him* from my body.

My soul.

I'd strike the fucking world down for you.

I shake my head and snarl, stalking across the wet cobbles in long, determined strides.

Too much. Too late.

I've dealt with Rhordyn, but only half my job is done.

I've been out all night. All day.

Cainon's not stupid.

I need to own my wrongs. Make them right. Tell him I've finally put the beast to bed—sealed him in a tomb he cannot rise from.

I don't bother hiding from the rain like everyone else clustered in pockets of dry beneath thick trees and wide awnings, their gazes nipping at my skin. Seeing a flock of guards ahead, searching every female they cross, I stop in the middle of a street.

Rolling my sleeves, I put my cupla on bold display, and stare at the ground while water hammers the back of my head ...

And I wait.

The harsh wind whips at us as I'm led across the bridge, gaze climbing the different levels of the palace until it lands on my balcony.

On Cainon—standing at the balustrade with his hands planted on the railing, looking straight at me. Watching his four heavily armed guards escort me back to the palace clothed in the filthy garb of shame that clings to my skin more than the rain.

My heart plummets like a rock, bare feet hitting the stones in synchrony with my human barricade, and I swallow the nausea rising up my throat.

I'm escorted through the palace gates, the front door, across the pristine floor, and up the sweeping staircase, shoulders shoved back as we enter my suite.

The guards release me into the lobby, then fall back.

I clear my throat, drag the door open, and step through wearing a mask of confidence, stopping once I catch sight of Cainon—dressed in gray pants and a dark blue shirt rolled to the elbows. Still standing in the same spot overlooking the bridge, despite being doused in heavy pelts of rain while bolts of lightning crackle across the bulbous clouds. The curtains have taken on a life of their own, whipping like flags yielding to the gusts of wind baying into my room.

Cainon's back swells with a full breath, the veins in his arms pushing to the surface of his sun-kissed skin slathered in rain. His grip on the railing tightens, whitening his knuckles.

Another crackle of lightning lifts the hairs on my arms and the back of my neck.

"Nice of you to return," he snips, and there's a warning in his low, abrasive tone that grates across my skin.

"Cainon, I—"

"Did you fuck him?" He spins, catching me off guard with a stare that flays. "Did you split your legs and let him take what you *promised* me?"

There's no disappointment in his eyes, but something much worse. A look I've seen before—years ago—hollow of humanity.

The look of a man set on a path that can only end in death.

"No," I whisper. "I didn't—*haven't* done that with him."

"Then *what?*" he blasts, head canted, lips curled back as he spits his fiery rage. "What could you have possibly been doing with that barbaric beast of a man that left you looking like a sodden street rat and smelling like his whore?"

The words lock their jaw around my throat and clamp down.

Hard.

Another gust of wind and rain batters the side of the palace, plowing through the open doors and dusting my face in spray. He stalks forward, and for some reason I picture an axe hanging from his hand, dripping blood all over the floor.

My feet move of their own accord, carrying me backward through the suite until my spine hits the wall beside my bed, breath punching from my lungs as he advances. "We're not officially coupled," I rasp, feeling smaller by the second. Like I'm sifting through the ages, body crimping down to a much younger version of myself.

A weaker, more vulnerable version.

"You wear my cupla." His hands slam against the wall either side of my head, and I flinch, his thick, muscled thigh notching between my legs and pressing against *that* part of me. "You're *mine!*" he roars, stamping his forehead against mine, the blow of his words smacking my face and my fucking pride.

Eyes squeezed shut, teeth bared, he sucks in a deep breath, and I realize I'm holding mine. That I'm preparing for the worst. Perhaps he's going to call those guards back in and drag me to the stake to be flamed before his people? A fitting end, all things considered.

He shoves back and spins, spitting a snarl.

My lungs labor over their freedom as he drags a hand down his face, his muscles seeming to swell.

"Fuck, I'm sorry," he says. "I'm letting my anger feed on my fear, and I'm taking it out on you."

Fear?

A frown sweeps over me. "Is ... everything alright?"

"No."

The word is lumped on my chest like it's made of stone.

He turns, and his sea-swirl eyes have softened, his

face composed into regal refinement, all traces of anger combed away. "No, Orlaith. It's not." He reaches out a hand. "I need you to come with me."

"Why?"

"Because, petal. You need to know the truth."

Chapter 58

Orlaith

Cainon is all agile grace as he lands atop the rocks on the other side of the chasm of churning water, spinning, looking back at me with expectant eyes. I'm already flying through the burst of misty sea spray, landing beside him in a crouch.

Because, petal. You need to know the truth.

The words spear through my mind as I straighten, brushing sand from my hands. "Now where?"

The storm rumbles in the distance, and he looks me over, then grabs my hand, leading me across sharp, slick stone and barnacle clusters he seems to think I'm incapable of traversing on my own. I let him believe it. Let him guide me around the craggy edge of a small, sheltered cove with a weathered longboat chained to the shore above the waterline, twin oars jutting out from its hollow. We're not far past it when Cainon turns toward the cliff face, and it's not until he's stepping into the tunnel bored through a cleft in the stone that I even notice its presence—hidden in plain sight.

My curiosity sprouts wings and flutters about.

Stairs lead us deep into the ground, and I choose my footfalls delicately to avoid the slippery waterweeds cast across the stone. The farther we go, the less light there is, and the thicker the smell of salt and stagnant water. We turn a sharp corner, plunging into a sheath of darkness, and Cainon shifts my hand to the swell of his shoulder. "Grab the other one, too."

I oblige, allowing him to lead me deeper, *deeper* ... my chest growing tighter with every step. That voice inside me a gagged scream trying to tell me to stop.

To run.

"How much further have we got to go?"

"Not far," he mutters, and a glimpse of light swells ahead—a trickle and then a wash of it as the stairwell balloons into a mammoth cavern, a giant cleft running the span of the ceiling. A shard of sun illuminates the puddle of gently sloshing water lining the bottom, like it's breathing with life of its own.

I frown, letting my hands fall off Cainon's shoulders, gaze scraping the walls—damp and dappled with large clusters of barnacles and tendrils of weed suctioned to the stone. "This looks like a tidal death trap."

My words echo.

"It is." Cainon scales the edge of the wall in smooth, agile motions, grabbing a torch from a high, rocky shelf. "The only access is at low tide," he grits out, smashing a black stone against the wall so hard sparks burst and ignite the swirl of oily cloth wrapped around the torch's tip. "There used to be other ways in, but they were closed off years ago."

He leaps, dropping like a rock, his flame roaring from the rush of wind as he lands directly before me—half his face cast in the flickering, golden light, making his eyes look like shadowed dents.

My foot slides back, but he snatches my hand, tugging me toward the far end of the cavern with long, determined strides that are hard to keep up with, forcing me to jog just to prevent my feet from slipping out from under me.

We reach the wall and another stairwell dug into the stone, the entrance just above the water line. I steal a peek behind before I'm dragged into the dark again—down the seemingly endless steps that eventually bottom out, shooting upward after a small, flattened walkway.

As we climb, the wet, algae-covered stairs are replaced by dry stone that's powdered with dust, and a different smell tickles the back of my throat, thickening with every step into the unknown. An aged scent hard to choke down. Something that makes me want to lift the front of my shirt and breathe through the material to dull the hit of it.

Death.

Old, long-forgotten death.

That voice inside screams for me to flee.

The tunnel begins to splay, and I stop, yanking on Cainon's grip. His head whips around, and I feel the blaze of his narrowed stare, his body a dark silhouette plugging the light from the room ahead.

I'm not sure I *want* this truth.

"Cainon, I—"

Snarling, he yanks me forward, and I stumble up the final step, losing my feet and propelling across the roughly hewn floor. He catches me before I faceplant, curling a powerful arm around my heaving chest and whipping me back against his hard body.

He's behind me—*around* me—forcing me to look down a wide tunnel sparsely lit from beams of powdery daylight shooting through holes in the low roof. The air is thick and stagnant, despite the unnatural chill that abrades my skin as I take in the cells lining either side of the walkway.

So many.

Too many.

The one on my left is unlocked, the swung door providing a glimpse into the tiny space and its meager contents: columns of pale, stubbed candles; a filthy, dented mattress; and the twisted knot of a blanket dusted with silky cobwebs.

Cainon grips my chin, ripping my stare to the cell on the right, and a gasp cuts into my lungs like a blade.

There's a person ... a *woman* huddled on the ground by the bars, her weathered fingers wrapped around the rusted shafts of metal as though she slipped away clinging to the hope of a freedom that never came.

My knees buckle, and Cainon's grip around me tightens.

The shrunken remains remind me of the mice I used to throw across my Safety Line to Shay ...

"Wh-what is this place?" I whisper, voice cracking. Only the small, curious part of me wants to know. Every other bit is screaming to turn and dash down those stairs. To run faster than I ever have and never look back.

"An old, abandoned Unseelie burrow. Raided by Irilak."

The words pour my lungs full of mortar.

Unseelie.

I remember the illustration in *Te Bruk o' Avalanste*—the way that male looked out at me from the page through eyes that made me feel small and fragile.

Hunted.

Those *monsters* almost tore our world to shreds. There's not a single part of me that wants to see what they were capable of doing to these captives.

"I need to go."

I shouldn't have come.

Cainon's lips brush my ear, blasting my skin with a burst of goosebumps. "No. Not until you've seen it all." I'm pushed forward, his firm grip on my chin lashing my head sideways, forcing me to look at the cell on my left.

There's a child on the bed, perhaps a boy, curled up, held together by moth-eaten clothes and dehydrated skin that's sucked close to his frail remains. And his hands ... they're covering his face like a shield.

If I can't see you, you can't see me.

A sharp sound carves up my throat. He's small.

Too small.

"This is the black smudge in our history books that most struggle to look at," Cainon drawls. "Mostly the ones who have something to hide."

He releases his hold on me, and I thud to the ground, knees cracking against the stone as he rounds on the bars.

I can't breathe. Can't move or think or blink, moored in place by an anchor lanced through my heart.

"The world was once driven by more than just the desire to govern more land. It was a ruthless, brutal age of greed and bloodlust, where those with power ruled and those without were the corpses the High Masters and Mistresses built their thrones upon."

Cainon drops into my line of sight, snapping my view of the child.

I flinch, looking up into his emphatic stare with a mouthful of words and a severed tongue.

"The Unseelie fed off the life force of others, Orlaith. Men. Women. *Children*," he bites out, dashing his hand toward the cell. "It bolstered them. Gave some of them yield over the elements. Filled others with unparalleled strength."

"*Stop*—"

"Until The Great Purge that set most things in order, their *one* mortal weakness was a Vruk talon through the heart," he says, brow pinched as he watches a tear slip down my cheek. "Not even the Irilak would touch them."

Is that why the Irilak don't eat me?

Am I part Unseelie?

"For thousands of years," he continues, "they were unstoppable—plagued with an unquenchable thirst to tear the world to bloody shreds in their bid to be the best."

He collects my tears with the pad of his thumb, slipping it between his lips, and I wonder if I taste scorched.

"Come," he rasps, wrapping his hand around my wrist and pulling me up, dragging me past cell after cell after cell.

Too many.

His steps thud with conviction. Mine do the opposite, stumbling along the floor in his wake.

I force myself to look into every cell. Force myself to see what I know will be branded upon my soul for the rest of eternity. Because whoever lorded over this burrow ...

They favored children.

"Some grew an appetite for the sweet nectar of young blood," Cainon mumbles, perhaps sensing the crevice of my thoughts.

More tears bud, stinging the backs of my eyes.

"And then the Unseelie discovered *Aeshlian* blood." The words rip my stare forward. "So potent and packed full of light," he continues, "that it brought forth a swell of power more catastrophic than anyone could have ever imagined."

He stops before a small, circular arena scattered with moth-eaten pillows and blankets. A shaft of light pierces its center, illuminating a woman.

No clothes to maintain her dignity, even in death.

The line of fine thorns decorating her tapered ear glimmer in the stretch of sun like diamonds, casting the space in a confetti of color and light that does nothing to brighten the scene.

My thoughts shudder to a stop, knees give way, and I'm left hanging off the mast of Cainon's arm like a spent sail, an itch flaring across the skin on my right shoulder.

The woman is held in place by a pronged, metal cuff that bites into the chewed flesh of her neck. A vision of Baze's throat cuts into me—the gnarly twist of scars that looked as though the skin had shredded, then healed. Shredded, then healed.

I drag a shuddered breath, picturing *him* in that heap on the ground.

Broken.

Lonely.

Naked.

Dead.

"They were hunted," Cainon continues. "Kept as prized

possessions. Fed their daily dose of daylight to keep their blood from blackening."

My heart shatters into a million broken, bloody pieces.

You don't know what it's like out there, Orlaith ...

The words attack me over and over, and a small sound bubbles forth—blunt and hollow. My hand whips up, cupping my mouth, preventing it from morphing into the scream threatening to punch out of my chest.

I squeeze my eyes shut, tears slipping down my cheeks. "Why are you showing me this?"

I hear Cainon shift and open my eyes to see him crouched before me. I catch his icy stare as he grips me by the shoulders, shifting us both, blocking my sight of the corpse in a small act of mercy. "Because some believe not all the full-blooded Unseelie were wiped out in The Great Purge. That some survived." His gaze narrows, eyes becoming hard flints. "Hiding in plain sight. Perhaps even in seats of *power*."

I flinch from his daggered words, their fierce implication carving a jagged path to my soul.

"You think Rhordyn's Unseelie." My voice is a whisper, yet it thunders in my ears, battling with the sound of my blood—a pounding torrent through my veins.

The small stretch of silence that follows tells me everything I need to know.

"In all the years I've known him," he says, voice dropping an octave, "your *High Master* hasn't aged a day. If anything, he's gotten bigger over the last two decades. *Stronger*."

Like a shadowed ghost from my past, I see *him* through my two-year-old eyes that night so many years ago. His face illuminated by the lick of writhing flames. His eyes wide as he looked upon me, perhaps seeing me for the open wound I was.

Am.

Above all, I see the eternal truth ...

A man in his prime, just as he is today.

Flinching, I dash the vision away.

I don't want to see.

Cainon's grip on my shoulders tightens. "They can't stem their desire to own and control and dominate, Orlaith. This ... *unrest* could just be the tip of the iceberg. What if *he's* the one thriving off all those missing children?"

My thoughts tumble to The Tangle. To the child I found bunched on the ground, eyes puffed from the rise of her tears ...

She was frightened when I found her. Frightened when I returned her to the doors she seemed reluctant to slip between.

Cainon pinches my chin, tips it, forcing me to look up into his condemning stare. "A full-blooded Unseelie needs blood to survive. Daily."

I feel something inside my chest split. Feel a coldness flood through me.

No ...

"You lived with him for years. Did you ever witness him drinking blood? Did he ever drink from *you?*"

"What? No!" I shake my head, burying memories of my blood dripping into that crystal goblet. Of Rhordyn's teeth hovering over my thumping carotid. "*Never.*"

I'm going to be sick.

Cainon's brow pleats. "Are you certain? Think hard, Orlaith. This is important. A possible matter of life or death for many, *many* people."

I rip my chin from his grip, upper lip peeling back. "I'm positive, Cainon. I'd remember something like that."

I'm not lying. I'm simply not telling the full, unguarded truth. I've never *seen* him consume my blood.

Not once.

There has to be another explanation.

I scream it internally, over and over. I know Rhordyn's a monster. That he's capable of cruel, unmerciful things. But I refuse to believe he's ... *this*.

Please don't be this.

"Well, did he ever eat with you? A proper meal?"

Another surge of nausea, and that split in my chest deepens to the point where I want to curl around the pain and nurse it. My gaze shifts past Cainon to a corpse lumped on a mattress tucked in the corner of a cell.

My lids flutter, yearning to sweep shut and close me off.

Is that why he never shared a meal with us? Does regular food simply not ... not *satisfy* him?

"No," I'm forced to admit, then recall the time I pressured him to eat that piece of bread at the ball. "I mean *once*, yes ..." I hate the desperate spike of relief that soothes my fraying veins. "He was always too busy," I'm quick to tack on, stare swaying to Cainon.

He frowns. "Too *busy*," he repeats, shoving the words back down my throat and making me choke on the pathetic lump of them. There's disappointment in his eyes—cold and blatant. "You're smarter than that, petal."

My cheeks flare, and I want to slam my hands against his chest so hard he stumbles from the assault. Most of all, I just want him to stop speaking.

I don't want to see.

"In my eyes, he's guilty until proven innocent," he mutters, lifting his chin and looking down his nose at me. "He's circling, Orlaith, and I'm scared for my people. They've been through too much already." He trails his finger down my face, my shoulder, the heaving tilt of my breast. "I want this connection with Ocruth. I want a future with you and the safety of an alliance secured with our coupling. But he's marked you."

I shrink away from his touch. "*Marked* me?"

"Yes," he says, nose screwed and lips peeled back. "You fucking *reek* of him. Short of giving you his own cupla, he's contested my claim. And it doesn't look good for you. You're either his whore or his mole or he bent you over and fucked you against your will. Which one is it?"

"*None of them,*" I growl.

I don't want to show him the map of my bruises. There are too many, inside and out. And the *smell* he's condemning me for? It's just another blackened patch of self-hatred he wouldn't understand.

"If he took you by force, I could decla—"

"*He didn't.*" The words rip out of me, and I watch Cainon's eyes glaze over like hardened shields.

A beat passes.

Another.

The space between us seems to swell.

"Well. If Rhordyn's Unseelie," he finally bites out, "there's only so much I can do to save you. And only so much I'm willing to do to save *him* from getting slain by what's quite possibly his one and only weakness: the Vruk."

There's a ruthlessness to his words, and again, I recall the writhing flames chewing his ships and the men screaming inside them ...

Sacrifices.

His hand rises, the tips of his fingers sweeping a lock of hair behind my ear, gaze tracing the motion. "I want to help your people. I want to help *you,*" he whispers, gripping my cheek so tight it hurts, gutting me with a look that holds more weight than my fraying composure. "But you can't help someone who doesn't want to be saved."

I hold his solid stare. "And the ships?"

The words wobble free, as though my hands are clasped around my throat and I'm gasping for breath, my knotting stomach trying to reject the poison he just spoon-fed me.

"You said you could handle Rhordyn." His eyes narrow. "You failed."

My heart plunges onto a rib.

He drops his hand, leaving a smudge of his wrath that bites.

"So long as *he's* still sniffing around, there will be no coupling." He pauses, gaze scoring my face. "No ships."

My nostrils flare as I drag in air thick with death.

No ...

"I can't risk it. Not when I have a city of people to protect." His voice is a soft placation I barely hear over the frantic thump of my heartbeat pounding in my ears. "And you should be very careful. I can't bear the thought of your light blinking out simply because you've underestimated him."

He touches my cheek with his fingers, head tilted, then lets them drop. I almost crumble, watching him stalk back the way we came.

Panic roots through my chest, the tapered tips of this poisonous tree strangling my ribs and heart and my fucking conscience. A thousand lives caught within its cage, condemned, chanting ...

You failed.
You failed
You failed.

"That's it?" I choke out. All this death and hurt and suffering, it was all for nothing?

I fixed nothing?

He stops and turns sidelong to look at me. "No, petal," he says, offering a kind smile. "You have a home here while you work things out."

While I work things out.

He doesn't get it. There's nothing to work out. There's no way back—the only way forward being a solid stone wall I have to punch my way through with wounded fists and a fractured heart.

There's not one single part of me that wants to see what's on the other side.

The monster you know is safer than the monster you don't.

Cainon gives me a once-over, a deep sigh sawing out of him as he offers an outstretched hand and a pitying look that burns. "The tide's rising. Too much longer and we'll be trapped down here until it drops again."

I look at his hand, whipping my gaze away in the next beat and staking my stare on the female chained to the cold stone floor. Then across to the shaft of light that's clearing the dust of denial that had settled into the grooves of my mind.

My thoughts tumble to the room in the heart of Castle Noir—the one where Rhordyn and Zali held the Conclave.

I suck a small, unguarded breath ...

The table.

The hole in the middle.

The shaft of light piercing down from the roof to who knows where.

The hollow, melancholy vibe that swept over me the moment I set foot in that room, leaving me feeling bereft, as though I'd just cracked the seal on someone's resting place.

What's been below that hole—that *table*—this entire time? A corpse? Or maybe there's a living, breathing person chained to the floor, counting down the moments until someone comes and rips into their throat.

Not just *any* someone ...

Him.

Slowly and then entirely too fast, I unravel the threads of my life, examining every fraying piece like the venomous snakes they are.

My muscles tighten. Fists clench.

He didn't tell me about the Gods or the Unseelie or their wicked, twisted ways.

He knew I'd ask questions and work out what he was. Knew that he'd lose his *pet*.

Instead, I was tucked in a tower, nurtured and clothed, spoon-fed my daily dose of sun. For whatever reason, I was the lucky one—perhaps because I was an idol of survival to inject hope into his people and stem the discord for a few more years.

What about the rest?

If Cainon's theory proves true ... I only gave Rhordyn

a single drop of blood a day. Nothing more. Certainly not enough to survive off.

Again, my thoughts rip to Baze—to his twisted, ravaged flesh.

Anger flares, a pulsing ember born of nineteen years of unquenched curiosity, because suddenly all those locked doors and secrets make too much fucking sense.

I don't want to look. Don't want to see.

My upper lip peels back ...

But I'm going to, anyway.

I shove to a stand and stalk toward that shaft of light, kneeling before the female Aeshlian as I dig through my pocket for my hairpin.

"Orlaith, what"—I plunge the pointed tip into the mouth of the lock, twisting, flicking—"what are you doing?"

There's a dull clunk when the lock opens.

"Freeing them," I mutter, opening the jaws of the cuff and releasing the woman in the only way I can, draping one of the moth-eaten blankets over her bare body. Gifting her a scrap of modesty.

"There's no point. They're already dead."

Stalking forward, I stop by the gate of the first cell and get to work on the lock, swallowing the lump in my throat, fingers itching to reach behind my arm and *pinch*.

I don't deserve tears.

I don't deserve *anything*.

I failed.

I can't right the wrongs of my past, but I can right something else, and in doing so, I can fix this fucking mess.

Rhordyn stripped my mask, shattered my self-perception,

forced me to look through the blackened cracks of my beautiful, broken self and face the monster I am inside.

It's only fair I repay the favor.

Chapter 59

Orlaith

I once sat at a vanity while Rhordyn disassembled my self-perception. Perhaps that's why I'm drawn to this one while I ruminate on the flaming pit of anger whipping at my insides, trying to tone it down to a dull simmer.

An impossible task.

There's ire in my eyes. Fire in my veins. Hurt in my heart.

A hot meal comes, chills, goes. Someone enters to fluff my pillows and pull down the covers on the bed I don't shift into. I'm offered tea—I don't answer.

Too scared of what will spew forth from my flower-pressed lips should I open them.

They leave it anyway, scurrying off, pinching the air with the sharp tang of fear. I watch the whorl of steam disappear, and the remaining light in my room drains, dropping me into a black pall.

Still, I stare at the mirror I can no longer see, hand cast palm-up upon the vanity, hairbrush hung loosely in my limp fingers. The other is curled around the pot cradled in my lap—the one Enry gave me, stuffed with soil that was fed my blood and tears that has now sprouted a bouquet of wildflowers that boast every color of the rainbow. Flowers that somehow managed to germinate, sprout, then *bloom* in just two days.

The seconds tick by, a slow, steady drip ...

Tick ... Tick ... Tick ...

The gulls make their morning calls, and a rosy shaft of sun cuts through my room and caresses my sallow skin.

I release a shaken breath, letting my gaze trace over the darkened dents below my eyes ... down to my necklace ...

I would have lied to you forever if I thought I could get away with it.

My fist tightens around the hairbrush, hand whipping back and hurling it at the mirror, the collision akin to lightning smacking down from a black-smudged sky. Glass shatters—some bits popping off the surface and flying back at me while the rest remain stuck to the stone.

I look into my fragmented reflection that finally mirrors how I feel inside.

Gaze dropping, I pluck a shard from the scattering and flip it in my palm, studying its many sharp angles ...

He taught me to bleed so beautifully.

I wonder ... will he bleed for me?

The crisp morning air bites into my lungs as I make for the city beneath a grapefruit sky, the shard of glass loosely caught in the clutch of my hand. A layer of fog swirls off the cobblestones, still wet from the deluge that raged through the night. The streets are empty apart from a smattering of women swishing the contents of chamber pots down drains and a few men sitting on doorsteps, puffing on pipes or sipping from steaming mugs.

I pass beneath the spindly reach of the mail tree—catching curious peeps from some of the sprites hanging upside down from gnarled twigs—then head into the thin alleyway Gael led me through what feels like a lifetime ago ...

I tighten my grip on the shard, relishing its bite. The sharp edges slice into the flesh of my palm, and a slippery warmth wets my skin, dripping in rhythm with my steps.

I toss the shard in a dumpster, painting the side with a splash of red, and continue.

Drip, step.

Drip, step.

Drip, step.

The back of my neck prickles, and my heart toils.

He's there. A monster who caught a whiff of his prey. Because that's what I am, I realize ...

Prey.

I lead him into the sordid shadow of the wall, down the tight alleyway that runs along the base of it, and past the wooden barrel that I sat beside as I snipped my crystal bloom. I reach the edge of the drain and drop onto my bum, then leap into the soggy muck that splashes up my calves when I land. Turning to the drain, I take a deep breath and step past the cluster of lanterns illuminating the entrance.

With every step I take down the tunnel, *his* footsteps splash behind me—loud and hulking. As though he's purposely making his presence known. Like I could ever miss a beat.

I'm tuned into him. Innately.

I always thought there was something special about the fact that I feel the scrape of his stare across my skin. Or that his scent has such a physical effect on my ability to function. That he could see into me, through me, exposing the very core of my being to his intoxicating self.

Now I wonder if it was just my body's built-in awareness screaming at me that there's a predator in my midst. If my sick addiction to pain confused me into thinking it was something *more*.

I have, after all, always been a sucker for punishment.

There's a new grate at the end of the tunnel, lit by the halo of blazing lanterns. Also replaced.

I can feel Rhordyn crushing the space behind me like death come to steal my last breath. Can feel his silent questions hammering into me like nails through my vertebrae as I pull my hairpin free and dig it into the lock.

Twisting.

Flicking.

It clunks open, and I shove the grate wide, leaving a smear of blood across the bars. I pocket the pin and step out across the large, slippery stones glistening in the morning light that does nothing to ease the wild thoughts thrashing inside me.

The long grass tickles my sodden calves as I walk down the hill with a set jaw and a firestorm in my heart. The small orchard Gael and I ate beneath comes into view, and I feel *them* watching me from the shadowed pools hugging the jungle ahead—so deep and dark in contrast to the places where the sunlight hits.

Irilak.

Lured by their attentive stares, I pass the peach tree in

long, determined strides, drawn to that hard line between life and a swift, dehydrating death that separates me from the truth.

The nest of Irilak converge like a dark, flickering storm of vapor—so many of them it's hard to pull the individuals apart. A divot in the swarm forms before me as my foot slides into the shadows.

A large, chilled hand clamps down on my arm.

My head whips around, and I look into Rhordyn's pewter eyes. "*Let go of me.*"

He snarls, hand snapping down at his side.

I rip my stare forward and step deeper into the gloom, paving a path through the Irilak like splitting water.

The silence is deafening.

There are no birds tittering their morning tune, no bees bouncing from bloom to bloom, no wind rustling through the trees. Nothing but my footsteps crunching across the underbrush, announcing my every step that's not followed by *him*.

"Orlaith, that's far enough."

"No," I bite out through clenched teeth.

Not even close.

I keep walking, putting distance between us until I'm fully immersed in shadow and the noose of predatory stares. Finally I stop, my heart a hammer in my too-tight chest as I spin.

Still.

He's standing in the spill of morning light—a pillar of robust beauty caught on the edge of uncertainty, his features shadowed by something I can't interpret. Dressed in black leather pants and a shirt that hugs his chiseled physique, I can see every breath barrel into his broad chest.

He's breathing faster than me ...

I think he's nervous, too.

"The Irilak feed off anything with a heartbeat. Anything but ... *me*," the rasp of my voice echoes through the hungry hollow between us—a chasm gored by the secrets he kept, "and the Unseelie."

The still between us grows more fragile than the mirror I shattered.

He doesn't move, doesn't speak, but there's a question in his shadowed eyes. Unlike him, I'm not going to make him wait nineteen fucking years for the answer he craves.

I reach behind my neck, and he severs the space between us with a bone-rattling growl. The Irilak flinch in tandem, like an undulating wave.

I undo the clasp, releasing the necklace.

Releasing the face of my felled species.

The jewel thunks heavily into my palm, and my skin peels down, loosening me from its crushing squeeze, leaving me bare in the ways that matter. A fragile rose exposed to his violent, snipping stare as I toss the necklace into the empty space between us, and it lands with a thud amongst the underbrush.

A beat passes. Another.

I lift my chin. Look down my nose at him.

Challenge him.

He drops his head, and his chest inflates as a savage rumble rattles free—reminiscent of the sounds the ground makes when an earthquake strikes.

The storm in my stomach churns.

Cracking his neck from side to side, he crunches his fists, upper lip twitching. Slowly, he lifts his head, looking at me through thick shreds of hair, the swirl of his silver eyes turning matte black.

A violent energy radiates off him, rippling the air between us and electrifying my skin, making it pebble.

His foot lifts, and my heart stops, then starts again in a frenzied array of beats that chase each other for traction.

He sets his boot down over the line.

No.

Another step, and there's a swirl of scurrying darkness as the Irilak drift back ...

Please no.

All the silver bleeds from his hair to match his ebony gaze that fades into the skin around his eyes, and his tattoos ignite with flickering, slashing bolts of light, like there's an electric storm caught within their scrawled confines.

His features harden.

Sharpen.

The tapered tips of his ears peak out from thick, inky locks, and his muscles swell, chest broadens, his face carving into something transcendent—a brutal beauty that feels lethal to look upon, like he's borne from the dark space between the stars that bears no life. A hollow, never-ending blackness.

An eternal fall I just slipped into.

The Irilak shy away from his presence, shrinking like shadows squashed by the rising sun.

My feet refuse to shift, but my heart gallops against my ribs as though it's desperate to escape his barbed energy.

Still seizing me with his grave stare, he plucks my

necklace from the ground, dangling it from his fingers, striding forward.

A hunter closing in on his snared prey.

The awareness inside me has its hand wrapped around my spine, trying to jerk me backward. Screaming for me to *run*. Fighting the urge, I stand exposed, naked and raw, shame and guilt my only veil as he towers over me.

There's something just behind his eyes that makes me feel dominated. Like one prolonged stare could have me tilting my neck, pleading for him to clamp onto my flesh, burst my skin, and drink from me in greedy gulps.

He pushes my hair back with a sweep of his hand, and I gasp at the purity of his frosted touch ...

"You really are a monster," I rasp, like I just swallowed a thorny seed that's stuck in my throat.

Choking me.

He rakes my face with his glacial gaze, settling on the thorned tips of my ears. "*Your* monster," he whispers, and I draw a staggered breath.

Hold it.

Leaning close, his icy exhale pours over me, fingers threading through my hair, tugging me close, fitting me against him so perfectly—as though we're bound together by something greater than ourselves. "*Just* yours."

A tear escapes, and I let it track its course.

He pulls back, looking down on me, his gaze gentle and brutal as he slips the chain around my neck, slowly, his touch a wintry caress on my fervid skin. I hear the clasp close, but barely feel my mask peel up as I watch my light blink out in the reflection of his sable stare.

"Are you afraid?" he asks, and I catch a glimpse of sharpened canines.

"Should I be?"

"Yes." He brushes my hair off my shoulder with a look that pilfers my soul. "I'm far worse than anything you're imagining."

He shackles my wrist with his hand and drags me deeper into the jungle like a weed freshly torn from soil, still crumbling from its exposed roots.

My heart labors. "What are you doing?"

"Something I should've done a long time ago."

"*Which is?*"

"Letting you see the worst of me," he growls, a roughness to his voice that sends a gush of icy dread pulsing through my veins. That stabs the shards of that broken mirror through my fleshy heart.

I know the worst of it. I've seen it with my own eyes.

I want to scream it at him, those shards digging deeper, *deeper* ... splintering through the organ. Threatening to drag me under the dirt before I have the chance to do the *right thing.*

The thing that betrays my heart and him in the worst possible way, but saves those who don't have the power to save themselves. Those who are flowers to be crushed beneath his booted feet.

Rhordyn lugs me down the slope of a frail path hacked along the edge of a steep ravine. A river barges through the gorge with ferocious force, charging toward a waterfall roaring ahead—an angry swirl of misty spray.

A broken sound splits from my trembling lips as I gather my emotions in the crush of my palm, rip them from my ribs and my heart and my lungs like the weeds they are, their bloody roots coiling up. I stuff them into that cold, dead place deep inside, then trap them there with a crystal shell for them to wither beneath.

I draw a long, unburdened breath, feeling my chest loosen.

My shoulders straighten.

I'm dragged toward that juncture between channeled rage and pouring destruction. Can feel the waterfall's thundering violence in the pit of my chest, churning with baleful ferocity, alight with the shrill, tortured screams of a slaughtered species ...

I look down into the frothy fall, unable to see the bottom past the storm of angry mist battering my face, dousing me in my *own* need to spill.

For my people.

For *Baze*.

My corrosive anger, my crippling hurt, my world-rocking devastation of what Rhordyn really is—what he's done—it all boils into a thick venom pulsing through my veins.

A thousand slaughtered souls seem to chant my name ...

Serren.

Serren.

Serren.

"*I have something to say!*"

He stops so abruptly I almost slam into his back, my hand coming up to buffer the collision—fingers splayed over the solid panes of his muscled physique.

Such a beautiful monster.

I drop my hand at the same time he drops his grip on my

wrist, and a waiting silence ensues while I stand, staring at the spot between his shoulder blades.

A pit of tension clogs my throat, blocking my words.

I swallow it back, gritting my teeth against the bloom of tears stinging the backs of my eyes. "A confession." The word comes out damaged, and I clear my throat, tip my head to stall the spill of tears, and stare at the pale blue sky through gaps in the canopy. "You and I ... we've done horrible things."

His breath quickens, his shoulders rising and falling with its pace.

"I think that's why I can't let you go," I admit, chin trembling. "Because we've both been forged by the lives we took."

The sawing labor of his breath slams to a halt, like he's suddenly cast in stone.

I blink, those tears finally falling down my face. "I killed my mother ..."

The words are whispered.

Choked.

Barely there.

An ashy confession that wraps me in a shroud of melancholy, spoken to my beautiful, broken ghost.

A single bite of my damage he craved.

One final blow for him to absorb.

"Orlaith ..."

I sense him shift, slip my hand behind my back, and wrap my sweaty palm around the thick handle that feels so cold and final.

"My name is Serren," I whisper, and he spins.

There's a sorrow caught in his eyes as they begin their

gentle fade from black to the familiar, safe silver. Fissures crackle through my crystal shell as his chest inflates with the ammunition for words he doesn't get a chance to speak before I rip my hand up and drive it forward.

I feel the tip of the brutal weapon pierce the hard meat of his chest to the tune of his hollow grunt. Feel it drive through muscle and sinew to the round of his heart, where it splits the organ keeping his life afloat.

Eyes wide, his stabbing stare *bleeds* me ...

And then it drops, landing on the weapon protruding from his chest. To my hand, still wrapped around the hilt, painted in the life force spilling out of him as something inside me withers so fast the world rocks beneath my feet.

My bloody hand falls heavily at my side.

His lashes sweep up, and he looks at me, silver gaze fading, his lips shaping silent words I try and fail to read.

More fissures crackle through that shell, releasing spores of emotion that clog my throat.

I can't breathe. Can't think or blink. Can't peel myself from the sense that I just plunged the talon through *both* our chests.

We fall to our knees as one, and a line of blood dribbles from the corner of his mouth as his hand cups my face in a silent goodbye that burns.

He smears a tear across my cheek with his thumb. "Don't ... c-cry," he rasps, and his chest jerks with the inability to draw breath. There's a sadness in his eyes that screams a thousand words of sorrow he can no longer draw the air to speak.

Words chant through my memory, attacking me with their softness ...

It's said that your heart must be full to pass through Kvath—the God of Death—on your journey through to Mala.

A sob bursts free.

The thought of him drifting into that endless nothing that haunts my nightmares flays my chest with a slice of panic, tilling a truth I pass him on a hand still slick with the blood I drew. "I told you you're the worst thing that ever happened to me," I choke out, and his face buckles like I just twisted the talon, the blunt end of a grunt punching through. "I lied—"

He tips forward, pressing his lips against my forehead—a kiss that burns in a way that makes me gasp.

Warm. Not cold.

Warm ...

My cheek, too, is cradled by a warm grip, and I cup my hand against his, sealing it there, heart shattering into a thousand bloody pieces.

I broke him ...

I did this ...

I can't take it back ...

"And I don't hate you at all," I sob, eyes squeezed shut. "I just love you so much it hurts. Both of us."

His hand grows heavy, and I struggle to keep it pressed against my cheek.

Nuzzle into it.

Don't leave me.

"You're the happily ever after I don't deserve." I whisper, then feel his body waver.

His kiss falls away.

I open my eyes in time to see the light bleed from his,

and gravity eases him backward. He tumbles off the edge of the cliff, and I snatch at the air, an agonized scream ripping up my swollen throat.

Arms reaching, he plunges through the pillow of mist that does nothing to soften his fall ...

Gone.

Epilogue
Baze

Darkness presses in on me like ink, the chill of the winter night blowing out in puffs of white from between my chattering teeth, nipping at my candle flame and making it flicker. Making the three lanky shadows watching me from just beyond that line between dark and light look so much bigger.

One of them reaches out a hand—a stretch of bony fingers that click against each other as it paws at the edge, making the same scary rattling sound that came before the flames flickered out in the other cells.

One by one the candles died, cries snatched in suckled slurps that broke my heart into a million pieces.

I release a brittle sob as a wave of fear consumes me ...

What if my Lord doesn't return?

I shake my head, pushing the thought away.

Of course he'll come back ...

Another blow of breath, another flicker, the sound of my

teeth cracking against each other smothered by the rattling chorus of the other Irilak joining in.

I focus on that flame, make myself smaller, my sharp, bony arms wrapped around my empty body.

The food ran out days ago. The first four candles burned too fast.

Why would my Lord leave us like this? Does he not *care* about us anymore?

Does he not need me like I need him?

This foreign hurt feels worse than the shackles with their bladed metal teeth that he sometimes clamps around our necks. Feels worse than the times he bites so deep I'm certain he's going to take a chunk of me with him when he lets go.

The shrinking knob of wax left on my remaining candle will burn off before the night is through. Before light shines down from the sky-holes and dashes away the monsters edging closer with every flickering sway of tiny light.

A whimper battles past my chattering teeth ...

I don't want to die this way.

My lower belly aches with the urge to burst, and I glance at my brimming chamber bowl in the corner of my cell.

If I shuffle toward it, my flame might blow out.

I release the aching burst, a tear dragging down my cheek as a warm puddle swells beneath me. My teeth clank together so hard I nip my tongue. Taste blood.

I'm not ready to go yet.

I don't want to go.

My Lord might still come back.

Footsteps echo down the tunnel ...

I pull a staggered breath, gaze flicking to the murky outline of my barred door, to the black of the tunnel beyond.

Has he come for me?

The Irilak waver, shriek, then flit through the bars of my door, disappearing into the darkness.

"M-My Lord?" I call, heart heavy in my throat, skin tingling with hope. My voice echoes off the walls, dashed by the weight of the approaching steps.

Thud ...

Thud ...

Thud ...

No—too heavy. The gait too long. My Lord usually *hurries* to me. As desperate for me as I am for his attention.

A broad, cloaked shadow stops at the bars of my cell, looking in, and I can feel that gaze rake across my quivering form. My torn and soiled clothes.

Across the bite marks on my neck and arm that have scabbed over in my Lord's absence.

I sniff at the air, catching the hint of a strong, male scent.

The man shoves something into the lock, twisting, and the clunking sound of my door unlocking beats against my ribs like a booted kick. I tuck myself into a tighter ball as he pulls the door open, filling the opening in a way it's never been filled before.

Panic explodes in my chest.

There's a clicking sound, and a lantern hanging from his clenched fist flares to life.

"No ..." I plead, the backs of my eyes stinging as he stalks forward and crouches before me. He sets the lantern on the ground between us and pushes back his hood.

I stare at him, eyes wide.

His face looks like sculpted stone—carved from the Gods my Lord speaks about. His hair is black like the tunnel with lighter bits threaded through, but he doesn't look old. He looks big, strong, and scary.

He's frowning, his silver eyes scraping across my face.

"Wh-who are you?" My voice wobbles free, scratchy and raw.

He grips my chin, his hand much warmer than the ground or the air or the blood in my veins that is maybe a little bit black. My Lord doesn't like our blood black. He throws us away when it turns. That's why my Lord needs to come back and give me time in the sunbeam.

The man turns my face, inspecting it, then lets out a low rumble that rattles my bones.

"Wh-where's my Lord?" I squeak, eyes darting behind him. "*My Lord?*"

"Gone," he booms, the word so heavy and deep it swallows my scream and bounces off the walls.

Slices through me.

No ...

No, no, no ...

My aching heart feels like it splits ten ways, the fractures spreading through to my very soul as my breaths come hard and sharp.

I rip my chin out of his grip as my upper lip peeks back. "*What did you do to him?*"

The words hiss out of me, jagged and raw and broken.

Condemning.

His silence is answer enough, and my insides flare with wild, tangled emotions.

"You killed my Lord ... my Lord. No, *no, no, no ...*"

I twist my body into a tighter knot, clawing at my arms and back. Lowering my chin, I stare at him through a mess of matted hair. "*You killed my Lord!*"

He claps his hands on either side of my face, and I gasp. "You need to bury that weakness the same way I buried *him*," he growls, the words a coarse grate against my skin and soul. "Cover that up. Shield it and move on or you're better off dying down here with the rest of them."

My face crumbles as he releases it.

He unclips his black cloak, dragging it off his shoulders, setting it in a pile beside me before sliding the lantern closer. "I'm leaving," he rumbles, his deep voice filling my cell as he pushes to a stand, looking down on me still huddled in my pool of piss. "I have food in my saddlebags and a change of clothes. Come if you want, or don't, but life doesn't have to hurt like this."

He turns and walks out, leaving the door *open*—his footsteps retreating.

All I can do is stare at that wide-open door.

His steps begin to fade, and I look through the dim lantern light to the cell on the opposite side of the tunnel. To the girl curled in a shrunken knot who lost her flame last night.

Omara.

I miss her soft words and smiles.

But now her face is twisted, her mouth caught in the shape it made when she screamed seconds before her light went out—the sound still sharp in my ears.

I swallow. Look at the cloak. Reach out and pick it up, rubbing the material between my trembling fingers—so much thicker and softer than anything I've ever been given before.

There are no holes. No frayed ends. It smells clean and safe.

Standing on wobbly legs, I swing it over my shoulders and huddle in the warmth still caught within the fibers as the Irilak creep closer, padding at the shell of my lantern light, making that rattling sound.

I stare at the space between my cell and the tunnel beyond.

A memory creeps in of a family, smiles, laughter. And then that other memory of it all ending.

A memory that hurts as much as the ones made in here.

But maybe that man's right ... Perhaps life doesn't *have* to hurt.

I snatch the lantern's wiry handle and stand at the doorway, his fading footsteps nothing more than a whisper of something hopeful.

Dragging a shuddering breath, I step into the tunnel.

Epilogue
Orlaith

I look at my bloodied hands like *they're* the enemy—not the man I just staked through.

That voice inside me sits in stunned silence while my heart wages a war against itself. A beat that's a distant echo felt through the layers I've stuffed between me and my caged emotions.

I don't want to feel.

Don't want to look at this brutal, bloody scene without the numbing veil, because I know I'll hurt in ways that'll threaten to split me down the middle.

Perhaps I'm halfway there.

Tipping my head, I look to the sky, draw a shuddered breath, and crack that crystal shell I'd built inside myself, freeing the swarm of hurt and hate and love and guilt and spine-crushing sorrow.

My mouth falls open, and I suck a hollow gulp as the feelings culminate with the force of a thousand thorny vines slithering for release.

They coil around my ribs, crunch them into shards, sowing the seeds of more vines that germinate from the marrow they spill. They puncture my lungs then snare my helpless heart so tight the organ withers and rots, proliferating, mounting themselves on the walls of my chest until there's nowhere else for them to grow.

Spearing up my throat on a slashing rise to freedom, they leave a trail of snapped thorns wedged in their wake. And then they're sitting coiled on my tongue with a weight too heavy to bear, forcing my lips further apart as they spew their anger, hate, and hurt to the sky with a sound that shreds my throat.

Gravity pours upon my chest with such violent force I doubt I'll ever be able to stand again ...

What have I done?

Look out for the next book in the Crystal Bloom series
TO FLAME A WILD FLOWER

Thank You

Thank you for reading To Snap a Silver Stem!
I hope you've enjoyed the journey so far.

As a lot of you know, this story first came to me
in a dream, and it hasn't let me go since. I'd planned the
entire series before I wrote a single word—
it just *spoke* to me.

The *Characters*.
The *World*.
The *Relationships*.

Though we're just getting started, it felt so good to
expand that Safety Line and give you more of the world
to chew on in this book. I know I said this after
To Bleed a Crystal Bloom, but there really is
still SO much story left to tell.

I know this one hurt at times. I'm sorry.

Orlaith has so, so much healing to do, but that
needs to be done from the inside out, and she needs to
crack those layers back before she
can get there.
But she will. Get there.

When she blooms, it's going to be *beautiful*.
Again, thank you for reading!

—SARAH

Acknowledgments

I wouldn't have been able to publish this book without the help of my incredible team and the unending support of my family.

My babies—thank you for being so patient while Mummy wrote her book. Thank you for the endless supply of jokes and loves and hugs.

The Editor & The Quill—Chinah, thank you for everything you poured into this story. Thank you for your friendship, your mastery, your attention to detail. Thank you for digging so deep and for the late nights and early mornings. You go above and beyond, and I'm so lucky to have you in my life.

Mum—thank you for putting your life on hold to be there for me throughout the months leading up to this release. I'm not sure I would have made it through this without you. Thank you for all the heartbeats you poured into helping me polish this story, and for loving it as much as I do. Thank you for giving me the strength to go on when I was running on fumes. For plucking me out of the ashes more than once, dusting me off, blowing fire back into me, and telling me to keep going.

Philippa—thank you for moving in during that final month when I was at my weakest. For making sure our family was still functional even though I essentially stopped existing. Thank you for caring for the kids and feeding me and for making sure I had a clear run to make it to the end. I don't have enough words to say how thankful I am.

Angelique—thank you for the hours you put into reading my draft. For your sage insight, and for being a such a strong presence throughout the process.

Brittani—thank you for your friendship, your laughs, your listening ear, your attention to detail. Thank you for being there for me right up until the (very stressful) end. For boosting me when I was at my lowest, and for your beautiful insight all the way through. Love you so much.

Raven—thank you for the endless hours in the sprint room, for always being there to tell me to keep going, and for being my voice of reason. Thank you for your friendship and for the endless deep belly laughs that always pick me up. Love you to the moon and back.

Josh—my love. Thank you for supporting me, for loving me, and for always believing in me. Thank you for being two whole parents in the last few months leading up to my release. You're amazing, and I'm so lucky to be doing life with you.

A.T. Cover Designs—Aubrey, thank you for the stunning covers. For pouring so much heart and soul into every single one of my graphics, and for bringing this story to life visually. You are incredibly talented, and I'm constantly blown away by everything you do!

And of course, thank you to my incredible readers—the Bloomers—who spur me on every single day. I see the hours you put into your artwork, theories, and loving the book, and it breathes life into me. I can't wait to bring you more words!

Sarah. Xo

About the Author

Sarah A. Parker is the *New York Times* bestselling author of *When the Moon Hatched*. Born in New Zealand, Sarah now lives on the Gold Coast with her husband and three young children. Sarah has been writing since she was small, but has only recently begun sharing her stories with the world. She can be found on all the major social media platforms if you want to keep up to date with her releases.